TREE OF BONES

BONES

BOOK TWO: A FAMILIAR'S TALE

Verna McKinnon

WolfSinger Publications 🐺 Brackettville, Texas

DEDICATION

I dedicate my novels to my loving husband, Rick Hipps,
who always supported my writing and believed in me.

CHAPTER ONE

Runa huddled in her cloak against the night's chill, her sleepless vigil broken by glimpses of a wily fox or a shy deer rushing past in the gloom. Beams of moonlight filtered through twisted ghost-pale birch trees and the wind touched leaves whispered a night song. She craved sleep, but sinister dreams plagued her the last few nights, snatching precious slumber away. The crackling fire dimmed. Runa ignited the flames with a spark of magic. Warmth restored, she sighed and returned to her empty bedroll a few feet away. Mellypip had been sleeping there only moments ago.

Concerned, Runa called through the bonding, *Melly, where are you?*

I'm over here, Runa! Mellypip replied, poking his head up from behind the food packs.

What are you doing? Runa asked.

Searching for yummy treats! The furry wampu scratched his enormous round ears, and then resumed his hunt for a snack.

Don't wander off like that, she scolded.

But we're surrounded by mighty sorcerers and warriors, Mellypip protested, sniffing a bruised apple. *The apples are pulpy. Not magnificent at all!* He discarded it to hunt for more succulent goodies.

Our mighty band is asleep, except for those guarding Koll, Runa reminded him.

Mellypip chose a slice of round flat bread from the food sacks. He offered her some bread, but Runa shook her head.

"I'm not hungry, but thanks," she whispered.

"You're not sleeping again?" Mellypip asked, joining her and nestling next to her for warmth. "Need sleep to make magnificent magic."

"How come you're awake so early?" Runa asked.

"Hard to sleep when my sorceress is troubled."

"I'm not troubled," Runa insisted. "It's just that my dreams are filled with weird images."

"You cannot fib to your familiar. Perhaps it was something you ate," Mellypip suggested. "Our food stores are dull. We don't even have cookies or drobba." Mellypip sighed and looked at his bland piece of bread. "I miss drobba. And jam. Bread is boring without jam. Do they make drobba jam? That would be magnificent!" Mellypip nodded, his furry cheeks puffed out as he chewed. "We're dream bonded. That's what Belwyn calls it. I see your dreams. They're strange, but all I remember is fragments. Then I wake up so hungry! I thought if I had some nibbles, I would get drowsy again."

Runa opened her silver locket and gazed at the tiny portraits of her mother and grandmother. Mellypip waddled over to her and rested his head on her arm. The firelight cast amber shadows on the tiny pictures of Runa's mother and grandmother. "They were so pretty. You look a lot like them too, Runa, well except for the lack of pointy ears. Yllia and Rualla! They had magnificent names too!"

"Magnificent is quite a big word you're fond of lately," Runa observed with suspicion, scratching Melly's head. "What is going on?"

"Belwyn gives me a new word every day for my vocabulary lessons. Yesterday it was 'magnificent.' I haven't received a new one yet, so I am making good use of it now. I never escape the schoolroom, even in the wilderness."

Caliste stirred and stretched. "Runa, why are you up so early?"

"I'm sorry I woke you," Runa apologized. "Go back to sleep."

Caliste draped her blanket around her shoulders and sat down next to Runa by the fire. "You didn't, really. The rocky ground is a misery. At least we're out of that damned desert. I'm still brushing sand out of my hair." Runa's locket glowed in the light of the campfire. Caliste's eyes misted when she looked at the pictures, her voice wistful with memory. "I remember when they had those portraits painted as a special gift for Cathal's birthday. They wanted to include me, but I thought it would be nice for Cathal to have a special portrait of just them."

"Which birthday was it?" Runa asked with a grin.

"He never confessed. You know, I was about your age when Cathal and Belwyn told Rualla and me of their adventures during the Bloodstone Age. Cathal was scarcely older than you are now," Caliste whispered. "Cathal and Yllia had some very exciting adventures. Belwyn is especially good at relating their tales into thrilling stories."

"We haven't had much time for stories since my birthday," Runa said.

Caliste brushed back a wisp of Runa's short hair, and smiled, "We've been quite busy, haven't we, sweetheart?"

Runa grinned. "Battling evil mages and scary wraiths is very time consuming."

"Don't forget Opaline turning the slimy mage Gorvanus into a troll," Mellypip added.

"I wish I could have seen it," Caliste said, grinning.

"It's a marvelous tale," Mellypip agreed with a vigorous nod. "I'll write it all down when I can spell better. I wish we were home. The journey is taking so long because we have to—" Mellypip paused, looked around then whispered, "keep the nasty one chained up."

Runa cuddled Mellypip in her arms. "I know it's terrible having Koll here."

"We'll be rid of him soon," Caliste assured him. "That's why we came to Thill."

Runa glanced over her shoulder at the sleeping figures of Iona and Panthara. "I still can't accept Panthara is my half-sister. Yet, I cannot deny we share the same blood though my father."

Runa leaned against Caliste's shoulder. She gently stroked Runa's short hair. "I know it's hard. I suspect Panthara received little love growing up, judging by what we witnessed of her mad mother. Koll certainly wasn't a good influence. To her credit, Panthara chose to stop the ritual."

"At least Iona and Amun will look after her," Runa said. "And her familiar, Azmadu, is still devoted to her."

"That bond will never break," Caliste affirmed.

On silent wings, Belwyn landed next to the fire; irate, golden eyes chastised Runa. "Humans must sleep, else they go mad, you know."

"So do sarcastic owls," Runa replied. "Can't you rest either?"

"No—well, at least I'm supposed to be nocturnal," Belwyn replied. "Also, dragging Koll across the continent is making me twitchy."

"Koll makes everyone twitch," Runa agreed.

Runa looked at the end of the camp where Koll sat cross-legged in the constrictive iron-barred cage. Hands and feet bound with chains to prevent his escape through mortal means and a collar of sorcerer bane locked around his neck to prohibit magical escape. She sensed Koll's stare as he sat stony-eyed.

Belwyn looked at him suspiciously. "Koll hasn't spoken since we captured him. He just sits there and stares like the village idiot, except I know how dangerous his mind is. He refuses food and drink yet hasn't had the courtesy to die from it. His slimy familiar, Xabral, is still free. It all reeks, I say. Just a question of time before Koll attempts something vile. I feel it in my bones."

Sanura, Caliste's bronze-colored cat, lifted her head. "It's not even sunrise, please keep it down to a purr," she groused.

"Sorry, my sweet," Caliste apologized.

"Why did Grandfather choose to take Koll to Thill? I thought we were supposed to deliver Koll to Tarsicius?" Runa asked.

Belwyn shook his head. "Thill is closer for one, plus we have old friends there. We lived here for a long time. It's too dangerous with Koll in tow to risk the long journey across the bloody continent. Koll has too many dark allies who would attempt to free him. There's strife in the Ivory Kingdoms now that Levandius is in exile. I also detest the way Tarsicius treated poor Opaline after she risked everything to save his pompous life. The Emperor can go rot! Many nations have a bounty on Koll, but Thill has a strong and legitimate claim. The evil bugger slaughtered thousands in Thill with dark magic during the Sorcerer War. Time to pay with his bloody wicked head, I say!"

Runa clutched the locket in her hand. "Koll's soul is black with the murder. My father, mother, grandmother, and even Striker, my mother's familiar, are dead because of Koll. If Striker had not rescued me, I would be dead too. The seed of our all my family's misery is Koll!"

A grey and white owl flew down by Runa's feet. The owl shimmered into Cathal, his flinty grey eyes stern. "Young lady, why aren't you asleep?"

"Sorry Grandpa. What about you? Where did you go?"

"With Koll in our midst, sleeping is a dangerous luxury. We have guests coming to relieve that torment," Cathal assured her. "King Caladynn of Thill is meeting us here. I met him down the road. Caladynn is bringing an escort of soldiers to welcome us—and take *him* into custody."

"Can't wait to unload the annoying dark mage?" Belwyn asked.

"You know me so well, Belwyn," Cathal replied.

"They can take Koll with my blessings," Belwyn said. "I'm sick of babysitting the evil one."

"Perhaps we wake everyone up, so we can properly greet them," Cathal suggested.

"Quite a magnificent occasion," Mellypip agreed.

Cathal raised an eyebrow. "Vocabulary exercises again, Belwyn?"

Belwyn chuckled. "Sorry. I must confer to Furball the sin of repetition."

Cathal grimaced. "Pick another word, Belwyn. He's used *magnificent* hundreds of times since yesterday. Even Dabiro's belching was magnificent!"

Belwyn chuckled. "Well, the old badger is pretty vocal."

"I heard that, you musty old feather duster!" Dabiro grunted as he waddled by.

"Your manners aren't exactly resplendent, you mangy flea-ridden rodent!" Belwyn retorted.

Dabiro responded with a thunderous belch, and then resumed waddling to the shallow stream.

"Well isn't that bloody charming!" Belwyn called after him.

News of the king coming roused the camp. Broda and Talwyn brewed fresh coffee. Runa longed for cream and sugar, but drank down the strong, bitter coffee to combat her fatigue. Mellypip clung to Runa's shoulder to avoid getting trampled in the early morning hubbub as they crowded around Broda and Talwyn for the precious coffee. Runa grabbed a bucket in one hand and Mellypip in the other to walk to the stream to fetch water.

"Fair morning, Runa," Ryen said when she joined him at the water's edge. "Girl, you look tired."

"Morning, Ryen. I think everyone's spent," Runa commented and filled a bucket with fresh water. Mellypip jumped down and drank his fill.

"Runa! Runa!" Rono the gryphon cried out happily, bobbing back and forth.

"I have fresh water for you. Hungry?" Runa asked, smiling.

The gentle black gryphon had been adopted by everyone. Runa was glad the perytons helped look after the gryphon, who though loving, was often confused.

"After breakfast, then we fly?" Rono asked with bright and eager eyes.

"Maybe later," Runa said with a laugh, rubbing his head. After feeding him, they went back to the group, Mellypip following with a drippy muzzle and soaked paws.

Everyone was rushing to prepare for King Caladynn's arrival, except Jiana. She and her tiger hare, Jasper, refused to wake up and remained snuggled in her sleeping bag until they smelled Hinkleburr toasting bread.

Only Panthara was silent. Azmadu, her crill lizard familiar, whimpered for her to play with him. She was a placid statue as Iona combed out her beautiful black hair.

Overwhelmed by a surge of pity, Runa was tempted to go to Panthara; but the pain was still too tender yet. Runa turned away.

Then Jadon walked by with Darkleaf, his peryton. "Morning, Runa," he said with a grin.

Runa smiled but lost the capacity to speak in his presence.

"Perhaps you need some vocabulary lessons,' Mellypip suggested after Jadon had walked by.

Sirah and her white wolf familiar, Arial, were warming themselves by the fire. Opaline yawned as she joined them and leaned against her mother for support.

"Good morning, sleepyhead!" Sirah said with a laugh, putting her arm around Opaline.

"If it's morning, where's the sun?" Opaline moaned, rubbing her eyes. "And it's so damn cold. I almost miss the desert, except for the sunburn."

Myrsalian joined them, his elf owl, Felisia, perched on his shoulder, both looking tired.

"Morning." Sirah nodded. "You two didn't sleep well either?"

"No," Felisia replied, sharp and cranky.

"I don't think anyone has lately," Myrsalian replied.

Broda and Talwyn passed out cups of coffee to everyone. Opaline accepted hers and sipped it, eyes half-closed. Liat and Dabiro took their turn to watch Koll, relieving Darcus for some much-needed rest. Ulan handed Darcus a tin cup of black coffee, which he downed in one gulp. Only Riva and his sloth familiar, Buzzy, were calm, floating in the air for their morning meditation.

Runa accepted another cup and drank it, hoping it would revive her. Dawn's light brightened the sky, and the fresh feel of morning felt good on her skin.

The thunder of iron-shod hooves beating the earth proclaimed the coming of the Thill King. Everyone's attention was on the fifty green cloaked warriors riding into their camp. The horse's flared nostrils issued steamy breath as they stomped the earth in triumph and circled them. These warhorses were immense, indeed giants among the equine clans.

"I've never seen horses so big!" Mellypip gulped.

"The Thills are famous for their warhorses," Runa whispered back. "Now I know why. Pictures in books do them no justice."

The massive warhorses were larger than the sleek steeds of Tarsicius' stables in the west. Thill horses had powerful, thick bodies; silky hair fringed the large hooves; long manes and tails trailed almost to the ground. The horses pawed the earth with giant hooves and shook their heavy manes with pride.

The King of Thill urged his mount forward and dismounted. Dressed in the royal red leather armor, tall and broad; his girth was more muscle than fat. He removed his polished golden helmet to reveal a vital middle-aged man; long earthy brown hair streamed down his back and his short beard was flecked with gray. He was the essence of potent manhood. He needed no crown. Each powerful stride proclaimed his kingship.

Cathal bowed. "Welcome, King Caladynn."

Caladynn marched toward Cathal with open arms. "Cathal, you old mage, I've missed you! Welcome to Thill."

"A magnificent king," Mellypip commented.

"Find a new word, Melly," Runa suggested in a pained voice.

"But I like magnificent!" Mellypip protested.

"Get over it," Belwyn snapped.

CHAPTER TWO

The black wolf twitched in his sleep, disturbed by whispers prodding him to wake. He resisted the urgings, seeking to stay in dream's soft shadows. In dreams he was not hungry, but bloated with fresh, red meat. His ribs did not protrude but were covered with sleek muscle. He took up the hunt in his dream state, running through open fields after a massive elk.

Grimm was happy.

Grimm had never known happiness in his waking life, only the stark loneliness of being a wolf without a pack or mate to cling to in his desolation.

The whispers turned into shouts.

"Wake up, Grimm!"

Groaning, Grimm awakened to see a shimmering black wolf standing before him, tongue lolling out of his mouth, amber eyes glowing in the dim light of dawn.

"Oh, Midnight, it's you again," Grimm said with a sigh.

"Yes, it's me, Midnight, your sire," the ghost wolf chided. "It's about time you woke up."

Grimm uncurled from his makeshift den in the shallow hole beneath an old oak. "You interrupted a hunt dream, Father!" Grimm shook damp leaves and grass from his fur.

"Were you the victor?" he asked with interest.

"I had not gotten that far," Grimm replied, impatient. "You saw fit to wake me, remember?" Grimm sniffed the morning air for real prey. Hunger demanded tribute.

The ghost wolf, Midnight, smelled not of earth and blood, but of stranger, more ethereal essences Grimm could not decipher.

"What was your prey in the dream?" Midnight asked.

"Elk," Grimm answered.

"A grand feast," Midnight approved.

Grimm glowered at his father. "My belly is empty. I must hunt."

"We must hunt the future first," Midnight said.

"I need food!" Grimm growled. "You are past hunger."

"I have my memories. The rush in my blood when I tracked my prey. Power surging through my muscles. The thunder of my heart and the burning of my lungs as I chased down the beast. The tang of fresh meat, skin, and bone devoured in hunger." Midnight looked at his son, "I wish I had lived to teach you the hunt. I'm sorry the pack drove you and your mother out when my rival killed me. I can only help you in other ways now. Follow me."

Midnight sprinted through the wooded landscape, darting between twisted hawthorns and majestic oaks, a specter of death in the host of vibrant life.

Grimm followed with reluctant obedience. Birds chorused in lofty trees; their presence hidden by thick leaves. His keen vision captured glimpses of squirrels and wampus jumping high above, scavenging for sweet, meaty nuts and plump berries.

Grimm followed his spirit father, for he had no one else. His paws pads were damp with chilled dew, the earth not yet been warmed by the sun. A rancid smell spiced the air. Grimm stopped running and crouched low. He flattened his ears with revulsion when he saw a stout, lumbering troll stagger above him on the hill. Trolls hated sunlight. It shaded dull, red eyes against the cruel beams of the sun with its shaggy arms.

Midnight's ghost shape sat next to Grimm. "Take care. Though the creature is stupid, it's very strong. It has only vague memories of what it once was."

"Filthy creatures,' Grimm growled. "Trolls are neither magical nor animals, but monsters of the lowest caste."

"An aberrant quirk of evil," Midnight agreed. "Dragon fodder. Unfortunately, there are no dragons around to feed on this feculent carrion with a heartbeat."

The troll's fetid odor diminished Grimm's appetite. "Only dragons can eat trolls. They are poisonous to all others. Why bring me here? If it was to spoil my appetite, you succeeded."

Midnight howled with amusement. "The troll is part of your destiny."

"How can this *thing* be part of my destiny?"

The troll began to screech and growl, and spin about in circles. Something frightened it. Perhaps the monster could sense Grimm— or his spirit father?

"What's next?" Grimm asked. "A family of ogres? A nest of goblins?"

"The troll will help you find your path in this world, Grimm."

"Maybe the long winter alone after my mother died of the

shaking sickness left me rabid?" Grimm pondered aloud. "Maybe you are not here at all. Maybe you are a curse of the bleak life in which I am an outcaste."

"I named you well, Grimm Darkrunner," Midnight said. "You're so morose; it is amazing you carry a piece of my spirit even though we look the same, except you have your mother's eyes, silver as the moons. You must follow the troll, Grimm!"

"I won't go!" Grimm retorted.

Midnight loomed over Grimm, and his voice became ominous. "Obey me! Follow the troll. Keep your distance. It hates the sun, so your travels will be by moonlight."

Grimm scratched at the earth with frustration. His paw pads were damp with dew. "It smells putrid."

"Of course it does! It's a troll! But what else do you sense? Concentrate, Grimm!"

The young wolf obeyed, and shut his silver eyes, sniffing, exploring. Another scent mingled with the troll's. It was neither foul nor evil, but pure and light. It stirred Grimm's soul.

"You sense it now?" Midnight asked.

"Yes," Grimm cried with rare joy. "It is like a beam of sunlight. Pure. Mystical. The troll's unsavory essence hid it until now. What is it?"

Midnight barked with pleasure. "Magic! What you perceive is the signature of the sorcerer who made the spell."

Grunting above, the troll uprooted bushes and grabbed large branches to hide from the light.

Curious, Grimm looked at Midnight. "Signature? I do not understand what that is."

"I forgot you don't know how to read yet," Midnight grumbled. "Let's call it marking our territory. The troll was once human."

"That troll was a two-leg?" Grimm shook his head in amazement. "A powerful spell indeed to change how the gods made us."

Midnight agreed. "The troll was evil in its human form. It was also a sorcerer. It's still evil, though its magical powers are lost, as are most of its human memories. It killed for lust and greed and squandered its magical gifts."

"Is this the sorcery you have told me about?" Grimm asked. "It is pure and sweet. There is no mark of darkness or evil from the hand of this sorceress."

"How do you know it was a woman's magic?" Midnight asked.

"I just know," Grimm said.

"Very good, my son. You will hone more of your magic, Grimm. That is why I am here to teach you."

"To be a familiar? To live with the two-legs? Never."

"You have no pack, Grimm. You are a familiar, like I was. To find a mage and bond is your only hope."

"If they are so wonderful, why did you leave that life?" Grimm challenged.

"Because death took my mage during the Sorcerer War, over fifteen winters ago. I returned to the wild in grief. Despite terrible sorrow and loss, I found my beloved mate." Midnight's eyes dimmed with sadness. "Wolves mate for life, Grimm. She waits for me on the Otherside, as does my sorcerer. I cannot return to them until you are safe in this world. So stop whining and obey me!"

"I don't whine," Grimm protested.

Midnight's voice softened as he huddled next to Grimm. There was no physical touch, as Midnight was not corporeal, but Grimm sensed warmth and love. "You're my only cub. Nothing can ever sever our bond of spirit and blood. Trust me."

Grimm hung his head. "I'm sorry, Father."

In the distance, the troll's shrill cries broke its uneasy slumber.

"What torments the monster?" Grimm asked.

"It has few memories of its human past, but a new force pulls the troll. Given it a new desire to cling to."

"What desire?" Grimm asked.

"To serve the dark queen who sings in his dreams."

"I don't understand," Grimm replied.

"You will soon," Midnight replied with a low growl. His iridescent form glowed, and then faded into a single ray of light and vanished.

"I hate it when you're cryptic!" Grimm cried.

Frustrated, Grimm sat down on the moist, cool earth and howled at the sky.

CHAPTER THREE

The Thill king really likes hugging people, Mellypip commented through the bonding as Runa moved behind the others. *Why are we hiding, Runa?*

I'm hoping we'll go unnoticed. Remember my last encounter with royalty? Tarsicius didn't like Ashur's daughter. Who knows what this king thinks!

Mellypip sensed this king was different. *King Caladynn is nothing like the nasty old Emperor. He smiles a lot, though it is difficult to tell because his face is so furry.*

Cathal and King Caladynn embraced with genuine affection. An attachment of soldiers departed from the delegation and circled Koll's cage with pointy spears.

Caladynn received Myrsalian and Sirah, hugging them with boisterous enthusiasm. "My heart is glad both of you are safe and sound. My Queen, Sorcha, has been worried sick for weeks."

Sirah guided Opaline toward the King. "Your Majesty, I would like to present my daughter, Opaline. She will be staying with me now, and with your kind permission, make Thill her home." Opaline curtsied before Caladynn gracefully, head bowed.

"Rise, Princess Opaline," Caladynn commanded formally though he was grinning.

"I'm no longer a princess, but merely plain Opaline now. My noble father has exiled me, Your Majesty."

"You will always be a Princess." He kissed Opaline on each cheek, "Thill is your home now. Welcome."

"Thank you," Opaline whispered with sincere gratitude.

Ambassador Hinkleburr Crowyn and his aids made their way in haste to the King and bowed. Hinkleburr bowed deeply. "Hail King Caladynn! I'm Hinkleburr Crowyn, and these are my aids, Broda and Talwyn." The two young men bowed in unison and resumed their attentive stance behind Hinkleburr, who whispered to the king. "Do you know if Sovereign Arawn is very vexed with me?"

"He's actually quite pleased," Caladynn replied. "In fact, Sovereign Arawn and Queen Dagmar even sent you a purse for your recent expenses. Our Ironian Ambassador, Thorgid, will advise you on the rest. In the meantime, you and your aids shall be my guests at the palace. I do know you're excused from going back to Tiamet."

"Thank the gods," Broda and Talwyn whispered together.

Hinkleburr bowed again and stepped back, looking quite relieved.

Caladynn shook hands with Ilyrrans, but Darcus intrigued him. "You're the first human among the Ilyrran Raven Wing for a thousand years. If Emperor Tarsicius had more men like you, he would truly rule the continent."

"There are none like Darcus," Cathal affirmed sincerely.

"The Ilyrrans saw your worth," Caladynn nodded in approval. "I commend them for seizing your sword arm, Darcus; else I might have claimed you for myself."

Caladynn's expression darkened when he glanced to Koll. "You have the gratitude of a nation for delivering Koll to me."

"I relinquish Koll to your justice," Cathal said solemnly.

"Yes, please take him," Belwyn added.

"I'm pleased you came here instead of the Ivory Kingdoms. It'll gall Tarsicius too," Caladynn said with a laugh. "We'll feast together at my palace when you have properly rested. Now, I will personally escort you into the city."

Cathal summoned Runa with an impatient wave of his hand. "Come over here, dear. It's alright, no need to be timid. He won't bite."

Runa obeyed, keeping her head downcast as she walked toward them. She stopped before King Caladynn and knelt as Opaline had done.

Amused, Caladynn lifted Runa back on her feet. "No ceremony! Don't be afraid, my girl. Let me see you!"

Runa looked up at the king. His gentle manner evaporated her fears. She could not help but smile.

"My gods, your eyes are pure Ilyrran!" Caladynn exclaimed. "Beautiful as my emeralds!"

See, this king is nice, Mellypip added, *I told you so.*

Caladynn took her small hands into his large ones. "The last time I saw Runa, she was just a baby! Why, she is nearly a woman now!"

"Oh no," Belwyn tittered, "Not quite that old."

"Hush, Belwyn!" Runa laughed.

"You must burst with pride each day!" Caladynn boomed. "She is so tiny, like a bird! Don't you feed her?"

"She eats quite wholesomely," Cathal assured him.

"Like a ravenous dragon in heat," Belwyn added.

"Belwyn stop!" Runa protested.

"Your eyes are just like your mother's," Caladynn said softly.

"You knew my mother?" Runa asked eagerly.

"Yes, of course. Rualla was a beauty, just like you. Rualla and Yllia often made the men at my court salivate with desire. They could not help it, for the gods blessed them with beauty and wit." Caladynn's attention then focused on Mellypip, clinging to Runa, peeking over her shoulder shyly at the great king. "Is this plump wampu your familiar?"

"Yes, his name is Mellypip. He's just a baby."

"I am not!" Mellypip protested.

"Of course you're not a baby, Mellypip! You are a brave wampu," Caladynn exclaimed, "A pride of hungry lions couldn't match your ferocity should your sorceress be threatened."

"I am quite fierce," Mellypip answered with pride.

The King is a great judge of character, Mellypip commented.

He is quite friendly. Tarsicius terrified me. Grandpa likes him. It's a good sign. Even Belwyn likes him. Belwyn doesn't like just anyone, you know.

Belwyn can be a poopy head, but he is often right about character, Mellypip agreed.

Caladynn eyed Cathal's head quizzically. "Tell me, why is your hair so gray now? I thought mages aged more slowly!"

"Here we go again," Belwyn quipped.

"It's going to be a long ride," Cathal moaned.

~ * ~

"Look at those pillars!" Mellypip cried. "They're enormous!"

Thanks for not using the "M" word," Runa said with a smile, "but even I must admit the pillars are 'magnificent.'"

"Belwyn said the word 'magnificent' needed to die a quick death or he'd peck me on the head next time I used it. He's threatened to peck me a lot lately."

"He's just tired, Melly," Runa replied. "We're all beginning to snap like dried twigs."

The two burnished stone pillars before the city gates were two hundred feet high. The top of each pillar carved into the stylized shapes of a horse's head. The stone columns were solid and resolute like an old oak with deep roots and scarred by old battles.

Memories shadowed Cathal's face. "The last time I saw these

walls they were burning. I'm glad these pillars survived the Sorcerer War. They're an ancient symbol of hope for the Thill people."

"I also got my feathers scorched the last time we were here," Belwyn grumbled. "Stupid humans should never play with fire."

When the gates opened wide enough for their small delegation, they followed King Caladynn into the city. Runa noticed many onlookers gathering. They began to cheer and toss flowers at them!

"We're getting a lot of attention," Opaline remarked to Runa, waving at the growing crowd with a practiced wave.

"Perhaps we are famous now!" Mellypip noted.

"Dust off your shiny armor, Furball, and enjoy it" Belwyn sniffed, holding his beak high. "It's not every day an alliance of Sorcerers, Dwarves, Ilyrran Rangers, and King Caladynn go riding together just for fun. Remember, Cathal was the Archon for many years. Add the capture of Koll the Sorcerer and that makes us victorious heroes. We're as shiny as a new coin for the moment. It fades fast, so enjoy it."

The crowds cheered and welcomed the new arrivals by tossing sweet blossoms as they rode past—until the people recognized Koll the Sorcerer. They pelted Koll's cage with rotted vegetables, rock, and sticks as his cage rolled by the crowd.

Unlike Tiamet, Aybarr was rich in color. Buildings lined broad streets, painted with rich colors, blues, smoky grays, deep reds, but often artistic scenes covered the walls. Trees and flowers were planted everywhere, adding a rich green to the atmosphere. Tiamet was like bleached stone in the unforgiving sun, even though many painted the buildings there; it still had a harsh feel. Mellypip sniffed the air, which had hints of spices, sweat, animals, and wood smoke. In the distance, a tall structure loomed over the whole city.

"What's that great building in the distance?" Mellypip asked.

"The Cathedral of Rhone and Araema," Sirah replied.

"It's a lovely city," Runa commented. "Unlike Tiamet, there are no slaves. I think that is wonderful!"

"Slavery is illegal here," Sirah remarked with pride. "The Thill nation was one of the first to abolish slavery. The Ivory Kingdoms still make a great profit from slaves and war. I was a slave once."

"I know," Runa whispered. "Opaline told me. How brutal for you."

"It was," Sirah replied. "I was sold to Tarsicius as his bound concubine when I was fifteen after he saw me dance in Rygon's temple. For a time my life changed. I was still a slave, but I had the love of a king."

"He never freed you!" Runa exclaimed.

"It never occurred to him," Sirah answered sadly, "even though I was the mother of his twin children. When my magic manifested, Tarsicius' fears ripped away any joy we had."

"Opaline's so lucky to have you for a mother," Runa said sincerely. "I don't know how she stayed away for so long. Tarsicius was lucky to have Opaline's devotion, but he rejected her, despite the fact she saved his life."

"Tarsicius is a deficient emperor, who makes poor choices," Arial, Sirah's wolf familiar, remarked as she ran alongside. "Runa, the gryphon is wandering again."

Rono's excitement overwhelmed him, and he followed a streamer of colorful ribbons. Runa steered the gryphon back along the road to keep him from exploring each new sight. "Thill has two capitols. Aybarr is the southern capitol and Karujat is the northern capitol. Have you ever been to Karujat, Sirah?

"Yes, often," Sirah smiled. "It's quite cold there because it snows most of the year. Karujat is quite beautiful. There are tall forests of conifers, snow-capped mountains, and lakes as large as oceans transformed to glittering ice so brilliant they can blind you with its brightness."

"It sounds magical," Runa said.

The procession stopped when they reached the gates to the royal palace. In the distance beyond the wall, Caladynn's palace of bluish stone rose in beauty. By now, hundreds had gathered in the streets, their voices loud with cheers for the visitors or cursed insults for Koll.

Caladynn raised his hand and the people fell silent to listen. "I now take custody of the criminal, Koll the Sorcerer. Koll will stand trial for his crimes. He will know Thill justice!"

A rush of cheers filled the air, and after a brief interlude, Caladynn raised his hand, and they hushed like obedient children. "We owe our thanks to my devoted friend, Cathal the Sorcerer, and all of his friends, for bringing this foul monster to our rightful justice," he said. "They are heroes."

Another series of cheers thundered around them. The sorcerers and their familiars all looked a little proud, even Belwyn was showing off, spreading his wings and looking regal.

Mellypip tugged on Runa's sleeve. "Is Belwyn showing off?"

"I think he is, just a little," Runa said with a giggle.

Koll's cage, under heavy guard, creaked over the road on its large wheels toward his prison. Soldiers kept their hands poised on the hilt of their weapons, ready to draw blood if Koll even blinked the wrong way.

"What now?" Mellypip asked, relieved to be rid of their wicked prisoner.

Cathal smiled broadly. "The Sorcerer House!"

~ * ~

The Sorcerer House of Aybarr was three stories high, much like the one in Tiamet. The yard had lots of rich trees to climb and lush grass to snuggle in. It was intoxicating to his nose, and Mellypip itched to ascend the big, gnarled oak tree in the front yard.

"Looks like a great place to play, just like our tree tower back home, but with borders!" Mellypip commented happily.

Rono's large eyes followed him, "May I play too?" he begged.

Runa dismounted the gryphon and patted him on the neck, "Of course you can, after we have groomed you down. You must be tired and hungry too."

"No, Rono not tired at all, but hungry, yes. I want to play with fuzzy Melly."

"I'll take care of Rono," Jadon offered, taking Rono's reins. "Melly will play with you later after you've eaten and rested."

"We go fly now?" Rono eagerly asked, dancing back and forth.

"Perhaps later this afternoon, just for fun," Jadon assured the black gryphon as he firmly took his reins. Darkleaf, Jadon's peryton, walked alongside, nudging the gryphon when its attention wandered.

"Come along," Opaline cried excitedly, tugging Runa by the hand. "I want you to meet my brother, Taran!"

A young man rushed out the door. His long pale blond hair was tied back with a leather cord, and he had the same blue-grey eyes as Opaline. He hugged Opaline with fierce emotion.

Opaline wiped away tears. "Runa, this is my little brother, Taran! This is Runa, my best friend."

Taran hugged his sister again. "We're twins. How can you be older?"

"I was born first. I am a full five minutes wiser than you," Opaline replied with smug humor.

Taran was as handsome as his sister was beautiful. Their coloring and features similar. Opaline had a round face and softer features, where Taran had a narrower face and high cheekbones like his mother, Sirah.

Taran hugged Runa and scratched Mellypip. "I'm glad Opaline is home at last. I'm glad you're finally away from that harsh palace, Opaline. It's about time you came to your senses and came home to us."

"Thank the gods! I was beginning to wonder if I should scry for them," an older, rotund man with close-cropped brown hair shouted. He was wearing garish robes of purple and yellow silk and a large porcupine was waddling at his heels. The chubby man embraced Sirah and Myrsalian with great gusto, and then lifted a stunned Opaline in the air like she was a feather.

Breathless, Opaline laughed. "This is Eberr. He often brought me messages from my mother and brother. His familiar is Pointessa. She's very sweet. Pointessa, this is Runa, and Mellypip, Runa's familiar."

"Hello Runa and Mellypip," Pointessa said sweetly. "Don't worry, children. My quills are reserved for enemies."

"Hello Pointessa!" Rosepetal chirped as Ulan walked by with her cupped in his hand.

"Hey Pointy Butt." Dabiro burped as he shambled up to her. "Poke anyone's eye out lately?"

"Dabiro, you're such a crude pelt," Pointessa remarked.

"I am a badger, madam," Dabiro replied. "I am also the bravest pelt you will ever meet."

"Really? Hug me!" Pointessa dared him, her spiny back rising with irritation.

Dabiro grunted and squared off nose to nose with Pointessa. "Your wimpy needles aren't such a threat, but I bet your fat bottom is dangerous."

"Oh no! Not again. Dabiro stop!" Arial growled in her throat, backing away as Pointessa's quills bristled high on her back.

"Should we take cover?" Mellypip whispered to Runa. "Or run?"

"Dabiro, I suggest you apologize," Runa begged in a tight voice, scooping Mellypip protectively into her arms.

"Go on chubby," Dabiro grunted at Pointessa. "I dare you."

"She dared!" Mellypip yelped, covering his eyes.

CHAPTER FOUR

Xabral despised flying.

The devastating vacuum of icy air between Xabral and solid earth made him dizzy. He was a noble scorpion snake, fashioned by the gods to glide across the desert sands, not fly above them on an idiot gryphon guided by a nervous Rashurkeen warrior. Xabral tightened his coils around the warrior as they flew higher. The man sweated fear. Xabral enjoyed that.

Koll still lived. For once he was grateful for the enemy's foolish sense of morality, so prone to mercy and mistakes. It gave Xabral time to plan.

They finally landed in Kra'zum, Capital of Urgonclaw, before Rygon's Temple at midday. Mitigated by their descent to terra firma, Xabral permitted the assassin to lift him off his shoulders and lay him on the dusty ground, as one would lay precious flowers upon a grave. Xabral felt the man's effort as he lifted his bulk, being over nine feet long and quite solid. The man's dread was palpable and amusing, since this man was a death dealer. Even the nervous twitches of the gryphon amused the scorpion snake. Gryphons! Were they a bad joke from the gods? Why imbue a race of creatures with magic that did not even have the sense to come out of the rain.

"You may leave me now," Xabral ordered.

The Rashurkeen, face swaddled in black and red cloth, merely inclined his head, mounted his frightened gryphon, and flew away — very fast.

Xabral tasted the air with his tongue and enjoyed the vivid and familiar sights. The streets were ripe with priests and soldiers, hawking street vendors, nobles in bright silks, whores begging for coin, strutting half-naked with kohl-painted eyes and red lips, and slaves in drab garments, trudging along with downcast eyes.

Rygon's Temple in Kra'zum also represented the Hallowed Dark Trinity. The temple towered over the city like a watchful shadow, a sacred symbol of the city. Ancient in design, it was fashioned after the old steppe pyramids from over a thousand years ago and consecrated in blood; it had stood resolute since the glorious era of the bloodstone, when Obsydia ruled over mortals. The exterior walls decorated with rich paintings—smoky shadows, ancient battles and sacred symbols, were a work of rare beauty. Scores of black-robed temple guards lined the entrance, their scimitars gleaming in the sunlight.

Within these sacred halls, the rituals of sacrifice were performed by its priest-kings for centuries, whose tradition of war and blood sacrifice was a virtue. Constructed of dusky stone, the temple spiraled to the heavens, but no homage was paid to the Light, only the Dark Eternals reigned here.

A black-robed priest, his long hair tied back with crimson leather cords, walked down the steps to greet him. He was shadowed by a dozen temple acolytes, distinguished by their shaven heads stained with red ocher and simple grey robes, billowing in the hot wind.

The priest bowed. "Welcome, Xabral, familiar to the chosen one, Koll. Zhelon is expecting you."

"Good. Take me to your master now," Xabral commanded.

The priest clapped his hands and the acolytes rushed to do his bidding. They returned with a velvet litter. Xabral slithered onto the soft cushions and welcomed the comfort. The priest guided them into the temple as they carried Xabral aloft.

Zhelon's suite of rooms was near the top of this celestial haven. The temple vibrated with hymns sung by the acolytes to Rygon, the God of War. Incense burned, its smoke creating a comforting atmosphere as Xabral was carried in his splendid litter. Xabral was eager to see Zhelon, for he had a new bargaining rune from his own discovery in the caves of Mowad—a treasure that would make Zhelon Thor salivate with desire.

They reached the double doors to Zhelon's private suite, the long corridor secured by a dozen temple guards carrying lethal spears. The priest opened the great doors, and they entered the private throne chamber.

Zhelon reclined in a chair, reading a scroll. His bracers of burnished gold and the beaten gold collar glittered in the sunlight streaming into his reception chamber. His black silk robes, woven from the best spider silk, shimmered softly.

The priest prostrated himself on the floor, awaiting permission to exist.

Zhelon, appearing bored by their intrusion, rolled up his scroll and laid it on a golden table. "Speak."

"I have brought Xabral to you as commanded, Holy Majesty."

"I see that," Zhelon replied. "The rest of you may return to your duties."

"I obey, Holy Priest-King." The priest bowed and backed out of the chamber, his acolytes following his example.

Xabral slithered off the litter, black and red scales glittering against the glow of the brazier fires in the sumptuous room. His stinger pointed up, Xabral slithered toward Zhelon, and greeted him with the customary salute. "Hail Zhelon, Priest-King of Urgonclaw."

"I've been expecting you, Xabral. Come with me," Zhelon invited, guiding Xabral to his personal suite, an honor offered to few.

They relaxed on a luxurious velvet couch. Zhelon's chamber was opulent as was his right. Silk and velvet cushions covered exquisite chairs and couches, tapestries of delicate weave covered the walls, tables crafted from fine ebony and teak gleamed, and giant bronze braziers made by the finest artisans burned bright with flame.

"Were you implicated in the assassination attempt against Tarsicius?" Xabral inquired.

"I was not directly implicated. Gambling on Levandius was a mistake. The added interference of Princess Opaline and her friends was unexpected. It changed all of our plans."

Xabral agreed. "Opaline was an unseen flaw we could not have anticipated. Who knew she had such deviousness within her? The clever wench secretly possessed sorcery! I almost respect her for it, if I did not want to pierce her heart with my stinger. Still, our goals are united."

"What goal is that, snake? Everything Koll promised has come to nothing. I am still bound to submit to Tarsicius as my conqueror."

"There are more important things to consider."

"Like what? What have you done lately, except hide under a rock while your sorcerer was captured by his greatest enemy."

Xabral's ego was raw from hiding like a frightened rat after the catastrophe in Mowad. Reduced to cowering in the shadows like a sniveling wampu vexed him! Mellypip, an impotent, fluffy, and useless creature had opposed Xabral and won! The shame would forever haunt Xabral. He vowed revenge. Mellypip and his sorceress, Runa, would pay one day for their violations! Xabral often imagined eating the wampu while his pathetic sorceress was forced to watch! Then he would sting Runa and slowly strangle her with his coils. It was a shallow balm, but one Xabral devised to soothe his loss of Koll.

"Too much has changed, snake. We failed to assassinate Tarsicius.

Gorvanus was transformed into a troll by the fugitive princess. Levandius was exiled; and is now a refugee living at my expense! He only survives because there's a chance to use him as a puppet in the future should Tarsicius perish. He has no heirs. They are all banished or proclaimed dead. More importantly, Koll is a prisoner in Thill."

"Koll lives because he is chosen."

Zhelon's tone became threatening. "Yes, you keep saying that, snake. But how long can one be chosen before they fulfill their destiny?"

"The secrets of the gods are not for me to speculate. The Dark Trinity chose him. Now Koll languishes in a Thill prison awaiting death. I have traveled long and endured much to reach you, Zhelon. Only you can help Koll now."

"How? I've no diplomatic relations with Thill. Caladynn despises our people and our faith." Zhelon leaned against the pillows. His delicate beauty of long flaxen hair and pale blue eyes gave a false impression of softness; he relished violence and cruelty. "Thill law demands a trial and trials take time, even for the guilty, but I fail to see how I can help him."

Slave women carried in chilled fruit and fragrant tea on golden trays. The handmaidens who served Zhelon's personal needs were chosen for their beauty and youth. The only physical imperfections permitted were the slave brands on their thighs, in the image of Rygon's sacred scythe.

Xabral perceived the women's fear of him. He shook his stinger at one, who jumped and dropped a goblet, but the thick carpet cushioned the glass. The young slave scooped it up with quick fingers, but Zhelon noticed her clumsiness.

"Come here, whore," Zhelon summoned in a smooth tone.

The girl swiftly obeyed. She dropped to her knees at his feet and pressed her forehead to the floor, her lush black hair spread around her like a cloak. Zhelon grabbed her by the hair and pulled her up. She winced but did not cry out. "Better to die, than have such a life," Zhelon remarked. "How do you respect such a lowly creature?"

"Forgive me, Holy Majesty," she wept.

"Clumsy idiot," Zhelon snapped with menace. "As a woman, you're less than nothing in my world. As my temple slave, you're lower than the dung beetle crawling in the filth. You should be grateful, slut! Your duties as my body slave are gentle and clean. Surely it is better than scrubbing away the stains of sacrifice or scouring in the laundry. If you are not worthy to serve me as my slave, perhaps you would better serve me as a sacrifice." Zhelon waited a moment, relishing her terror and tears, and then let her go. She crumbled to the floor, trembling with fear. "I will show mercy, slave. This once, you are spared the blade. Now go. All of you!"

"You handled that well," Xabral commended after the slaves fled. "Slaves need to be reminded of their low caste. My stinger frightened the slave girl. Forgive me."

"It's your nature." Zhelon shrugged. "Death is your purpose."

"Death will be my sorcerer's fate unless I can free him."

Zhelon took a fresh red pear from the fruit dish and bit into it with slow relish. "You know I've always honored Koll as a brother and fellow priest."

"Koll is a devoted black soul, a true apostle of the bloodstone way, Zhelon. Do not abandon him now! We cannot allow the infidels to execute him!"

"Koll should die as penance for failing me," Zhelon replied.

"Rygon is testing your faith, Zhelon. Koll came to this temple when he was just seven years old and offered himself to the Dark Trinity—Rygon, Obsydia, and their dark father, Ahridum. Koll proclaimed Obsydia came to him in a dream and demanded he come to the temple. When he offered his heart on the sacrificial altar, his sorcery manifested."

Zhelon glanced at Xabral with hooded eyes. "I know the legend well. Over three hundred years ago, when Koll was offered as a sacrifice in this very temple."

Xabral nodded with passionate fervor. "It happened on the Feast of Obsydia's Birth. An orphan boy with black hair and eyes ran to the priest willingly, saying destiny brought him. Koll was laid upon the stone slab, still steaming with the blood of the last sacrifice. As he awaited death, another vision came to Koll. Obsydia did not demand his heart's blood, but his life in service as her liberator! When the blade of obsidian glass was raised, Koll's first sorcerous spark shattered the knife. Then a crimson glow fell upon the wild-eyed Koll, who stood upon the altar in defiance cloaked in the blood light of the dark gods! People fell to their knees, calling him a prophet. The Priest-King embraced Koll, whose sorcery had just been born to serve the shadows, not the light. He decreed Koll was chosen to free Obsydia and restore Ahridum's Darkness in the world. Faith is the core of religion, Zhelon, but on that day your temple received proof of that faith! Do not abandon us now."

"Three hundred years is a long time to make promises," Zhelon replied with an arched tone.

"Eternals are forever," Xabral replied. "We're mere mortals of flesh, molded by the fate of an indifferent universe. I can offer you more proof. There is a new scroll."

Zhelon rose, his robes sweeping the floor, "There is always a scroll."

"This one is different. It's what we have sought for centuries. I found it in the rubble in Mowad. It tells exactly where Obsydia's temple palace is buried."

"Can it be true? Koll has promised me such things for a long time," Zhelon replied. "We made the mistake of thinking resurrecting Ashur would reveal those secrets. We were wrong. When the demon possessed Ashur's body, his soul and memories went to the Otherside, leaving only the demon consciousness that controlled the body. Mowad was a failure. I lost an old friend in Azrul. He was my mentor and guided me to glory. Be glad I do not cut off your head, Xabral, as payment for my loss."

"That failure led me to the path of the scroll. After the wraiths ripped through the cavern in Mowad, I took refuge in the tunnels. When they took Koll captive, he was unconscious; else they would never have captured him. At first, I thought his soul was taken by the wraith demons; but he lived! Koll was exposed to the angry Wraith Guardians! They are of Eternal forging—yet they spared Koll their deathly touch! Cathal bound Koll with sorcerer bane and locked his body in chains! Yes, I cowered in the cave tunnels until they left. I intended to follow them and free him somehow. The quakes the wraiths caused unearthed a rare treasure, a box of ebonite. I discovered it when I crawled through the rubble in the tunnels. It reeked of mystical promise! I opened it and found a bloodstone scroll from a survivor of the final battle who witnessed the mystical fall of Obsydia's temple palace."

Zhelon shook his head, bored. "A tale well known. For centuries dark pilgrims haunted the region to find her lost temple! They failed and died in their quests."

"The box contained a map, a very detailed map, to Obsydia's lost temple palace where she was defeated by the scions of light. I possess it now!"

"Where is this treasure, worm?" Zhelon inquired.

Xabral could sense Zhelon's heart beating with excitement and knew he had won. "Hidden, until my sorcerer is free."

Zhelon Thor's expression was deadly. "Are you blackmailing me?"

"No, I am protecting my interests and Koll's. My sorcerer is the chosen one. You know this. Koll has devoted himself to finding Obsydia's lost tomb! Now we have a genuine path to the dark goddess."

"Koll failed me too many times."

Xabral lowered his head in regret. "Yes, my Koll failed. But he has served the Dark Trinity for centuries. The resurrection of Ashur was a failure. It's a mistake we will never make again."

"No, you will not," Zhelon replied.

"You know Koll can find *Her!* Help me free him. Summon one of Koll's former apprentices, perhaps Dagon and his familiar, Gethen, to assist me. They have a talent for diabolistic magic. We will need only a small force of assassins. I know what to do. I have a plan."

"If I assist with Koll's escape, you will owe me one obligation—find Obsydia's temple. If you do not, you will both offer your unworthy hearts on the sacrificial altar in payment," Zhelon demanded.

"A fair bargain," Xabral said, shaking his stinger.

~ * ~

Gabriel waited in the moonlight, impatient. He took a swig from his canteen, welcoming the taste of warm beer on his dry tongue. At last, a small cloaked figure rushed toward him. She reached him, breathless and shivering. He suspected her shivering was not from the brisk night air, but fear.

"Are you alright? What happened?" Gabriel whispered.

"It's Zhelon Thor. I was clumsy and dropped a goblet. He threatened me with sacrifice and called me names. The usual dark promises."

"You can't do this anymore. It's too risky."

"But I have news, Gabriel. You were right. That scorpion snake is here."

"Xabral? Where?"

"He was with Zhelon himself."

"Like I asked—where? I need a new belt and Xabral's skin will do fine. I'm happy to cut down Zhelon too. He's a monster."

"There are more important things to think about. Zhelon will help Xabral rescue Koll, because he claims to have a map to Obsydia's lost temple palace. You must warn your friends of this."

"I will," Gabriel replied and took her by the arm.

"I cannot leave. I'm a slave. They will hunt me and then I will be sacrificed."

"Slavery is the product of evil men. You're coming with me. You have risked too much. You're not safe here. No one is in this hell."

"Where will I go? How can I escape?"

"I have friends in the north who help people who've escaped from slavery start new lives. I will take you to them. Then I must go warn my friends their troubles are a little more complicated."

Gabriel whistled and a sleek horse and clouded leopard stepped into view.

"That's a leopard!" she gasped.

"My name is Namir," the leopard replied. "I'm a clouded leopard to be precise about my clan. Gabriel, should you be riding a horse? You've had a lot to drink."

The girl gasped. "You're a sorcerer!"

"Of course," Gabriel grinned. "Why else would my traveling companion be a chastising leopard. He's my trusty familiar." Gabriel mounted the horse and pulled her up to sit in front of him.

The girl's eyes were eager but bright with fear in the strong moonlight. "What about my fellow slave maidens? They serve Zhelon Thor and may be blamed for my escape." She turned and gestured, drawing three terrified young women out of the bushes.

"Will you help them too?" she asked directly, though her face was pinched with fear.

"I can manage," Gabriel grinned. "In fact, the more the merrier." He waved his hand, and a shimmering cloud enveloped the women. When it vanished, all the slave girls had been transformed into priests complete with black robes, shaven heads, and red tattoos. One girl shrieked, though it had a male signature, when she saw her reflection in the pool.

"Fear not," he assured them. "It's only a surface illusion. You are all still beautiful. They'll just see a group of priests riding off the temple grounds. When they look at Namir, they'll even see a mangy old hound. Let's go the stables and see who I can beat up for some more horses."

"I resent that," Namir grumbled. "Despite our disguise, I would suggest you add a dusting of silence to our retreat from this miserable temple. It's getting dark, so once we're outside the gates and in the city streets we can bolt before they notice anything. The sooner the better. I despise this foul place."

Gabriel took another long drink from his canteen. "See, Namir always looks out for my better interests. Follow me, ladies. We ride to freedom."

They silently followed Gabriel to freedom in the shadow of the dark temple. The leopard walked with them, watching the path for danger, his eyes glowing the night.

CHAPTER FIVE

Tired and hungry, Runa and Opaline wandered into the kitchen, lured by delicious aromas. Mellypip followed, rather glum after the short and terrible battle of Pointessa and Dabiro. It left him lachrymose. That was Belwyn's new word for him today. He wondered how many times he could use it.

Eberr stirred a large iron pot on the stove, its contents rich with spices.

"Something very savory is cooking," Opaline commented.

The yummy smell even perked Mellypip's mood again.

"What smells so heavenly?" Runa asked. "I'm starving."

Eberr tasted a spoonful with a satisfied smile. "Barley and vegetable stew, my dears. Do help yourself to the honey buns and hot tea on the table."

They sat around the table, happily eating honey buns. Sirah walked in and fetched a jar of ointment from the cupboard. "How's the stew coming?"

"I haven't burnt it yet," Eberr replied.

"How's Dabiro?" Runa asked, grabbing another honey bun from the platter and sharing it with Mellypip.

"He'll recover. Dabiro always does. Liat managed to pull all the quills out of his bottom," Sirah told her. "My ointment helps take the sting out. Dabiro retreated to the backyard to sulk over a jar of honey."

"Do they always fight like that?" Mellypip asked, apprehensive.

"Pointessa and Dabiro frequently banter, though not always with such painful consequences. They're old friends, actually."

Opaline tore off small bites of her honey bun. "I didn't realize porcupines could actually shoot their quills, especially with such deadly accuracy."

Sirah laughed and took over the stirring from Eberr, adding a dash of seasoning. "They don't. It's a familiar thing. Pointessa's true power is levitation. Mellypip really loves those pastries!"

Mellypip rolled onto his back, purring as he gobbled the roll, cheeks puffed out.

"That explains his chubbiness," Arial, the snowy wolf said.

Jiana joined them in the kitchen. Her tawny hair was tangled, her leather tunic and pants were ripped and stained. She grabbed two rolls and gave one to Jasper, her tiger hare. "These buns are great! I could eat a dozen."

"We can make more," Sirah offered, watching Jiana stuff a whole roll into her mouth.

"I think the wampu has competition," Arial remarked dryly.

Jiana wiped her hands on her tunic. "Thanks. I'm going to bed early. I'm exhausted."

Jasper protested, hopping in front of her. "Bath. Now!"

"Why?" Jiana asked, scratching her armpit.

"Because you stink," Jasper replied."

"Alright, fussy. I'll take a damn bath," Jiana complained. The sorceress went downstairs, griping about demanding bunnies.

Taran and Caliste walked in, drawn by the platter of rolls and fresh tea.

"I'm actually desperate for bath," Runa said, eating another roll.

"Me too," Opaline yawned. "And a real bed to sleep in."

"I'll show you to your rooms first," Taran offered.

They passed Belwyn in the hall. "Did you give Furball sugar?" Belwyn inquired, seeing the wampu squirming in Runa's arms. "He'll be climbing the walls for hours."

"I'm lost in a lachrymose state," Mellypip told the owl.

Belwyn sighed and shook his beak. "Right now, you are the opposite of lachrymose."

"There are some impressive trees in the backyard," Cathal commented, collapsing onto the sofa. "Let him run it off."

Mellypip's long bushy tail swished in anticipation. "I can play?"

Belwyn tempted him in a tantalizing voice. "Yes! There's a large cottonwood tree, a hawthorn, plus if memory serves, apple and cherry trees."

"Our backyard does need a wampu to appreciate it," Sirah added. "Plus, along with the stables and a small pond, there is a large vegetable garden you can help defend. It has long needed a wampu to look after it properly."

"Go play, but stay in the backyard," Runa whispered in his ear. "Don't poke the badger."

Mellypip leapt down, brushed the pastry crumbs off his muzzle, and bounded out the back door.

"Don't worry, I'll watch him," Belwyn promised. "I think the old gang and I will take a sojourn to the backyard for a spell while the humans wash." He swiveled his head around to Cathal. "Have I mentioned what a high maintenance species you are?"

"All my life," Cathal sighed in a weary voice.

~ * ~

Runa and Opaline placed their meager belongings in their new room. It was cozy, with two beds, polished oaken chests at the end of each bed, a table and chairs, a few light crystals to brighten the room after the sun set; a large window offered ample sunlight with creamy damask curtains pulled back with matching rope ties. A blue cotton quilt covered Runa's bed and Opaline's had a pink quilt with a rose pattern.

Runa fell onto her bed with abandon and kicked off her shoes. "This is bliss."

Opaline got up and looked out the window. "Don't get too comfy. We need to get to the baths."

"How's Mellypip?" Runa asked.

"Running up and down a tree—repeatedly. Goodness, but he's fast! I wish I had a familiar. Can you believe Taran's had a familiar for almost six months? He's a marmalade tabby named MacTabbish!"

"Sounds adorable," Runa remarked sleepily. "Where was he when we met Taran?"

"Sleeping. Taran says he's a very slothful kitten. Taran wrote me about how quickly they bonded and how they practice magic together, when it's not nap time that is."

Runa looked at her friend. "Are you jealous?"

"Terribly." Opaline pouted. "I so want a familiar! I'm so far behind. You already have a familiar and a staff!"

"You just need to control your sorcery. Remember, you hid the fact you were a sorceress from your father."

"Speaking of magic, did you see the way Jadon looked at you?" Opaline asked.

Runa blushed and looked away. "Not really. I've been far too busy."

"Liar. Would you rather skip the bath, Runa? You look rather beaten."

"Thank you."

"I'm sorry," Opaline said with a laugh. "The dark circles beneath your eyes speak volumes. A young lady must watch such things."

Sirah entered, carrying fresh clothes and towels. "Until we go shopping, we will have to make do. My trousers and tunics will fit you well enough, Opaline, but Runa is much shorter, so I hemmed a couple pair of trousers for you."

"Thank you, Sirah." Runa happily took bundle, which smelled faintly of lavender. "It will be heavenly to have fresh clothes again. Mine are a little ripe." Runa turned to Opaline. "I could weep when I think of all those exquisite gowns you left behind."

Opaline shook her head. "I'm done with being a princess. Though I will admit, I looked quite fetching in a tiara. I look forward to a simple life where I can finally study magic openly and wear comfortable clothes."

Runa grinned and rolled over on her side. "You don't miss it, just a little?"

Opaline smiled. "Well, I miss the pampering. What girl wouldn't? I never truly had a home with my father. I thought I could erase his fears about magic, and he would want his family back. Was that wrong?"

"Of course it wasn't," Runa said, taking her hand.

"You did what you could for your father," Sirah said.

"Mother is right. I have a new life. I'm Opaline the Sorceress now, not Princess Opaline." She looked at Sirah. "Mother, may I have a familiar?"

"Not until you've studied magic more thoroughly," Sirah replied with firm resolve. "You must learn control and focus. Now, magic or not we have only three bathtubs in the basement, so hurry!"

They each grabbed towels, a change of clothes, and rushed down the stairs. Opaline abruptly stopped at the bottom of the stairs.

Runa smashed into her. "I almost knocked you over."

"Look at what he's doing!" Opaline hissed.

"What?" Runa whispered, confused.

Taran was helping Panthara into the Sorcerer House. Taran looked at the fallen queen with a gentle expression, holding her hand as he guided her into the living room. Iona followed, carrying a satchel, her familiar Amun on her shoulder. Azmadu, Panthara's familiar, padded in after them, looking disgruntled, his eyepatch askew.

"So this is Panthara," Taran remarked, brushing a strand of black hair from her deep blue eyes.

Iona took Panthara's hand and led her toward the stairs. "We can manage from here, Taran, but thank you."

Verna McKinnon

"*My* sorceress," Azmadu growled as he waddled passed Taran. Taran stepped back and grinned. "Of course she is."

"Come along Azmadu," Amun, the white raven commanded. The crill lizard followed them up the stairs.

Runa wondered if any thoughts lived inside Panthara now. Had the touch of the wraith dissolved all will and heart from her? What was left of her soul? Could Runa ever call her sister?

Opaline had other thoughts, not quite so philosophical, that morphed into sharp words.

"What do you think you're doing?" Opaline demanded when Iona was out of earshot. "Don't you realize who that was?"

Taran looked confused. "I was only helping Iona. What's your problem?"

"You were helping Panthara! That's my problem. She's the enemy!" Opaline snapped. "In case you have forgotten, Panthara was behind this whole conspiracy! She was trained by Koll the Sorcerer, the most evil man in the world! She nearly got us all killed!"

"Panthara appears to have been a victim of Koll as well," Taran countered. "She was trying to bring her father back. That was not evil —it was just misguided. Perhaps you need a lesson in compassion!"

"Maybe you require a lesson in common sense," Opaline replied sharply.

"Come dear," Sirah interrupted, taking Opaline's hand. "You can yell at your brother later."

"But Mother!" Opaline protested.

"Later, Opaline," Sirah insisted, her expression brooking no refusal.

In the bath chamber, they were both too happy to be immersed in steamy water to argue about it anymore. They were separated by heavy curtains, which gave a nice feeling of privacy. Runa relaxed in the large copper tub of hot water and lathered with jasmine-scented soap. She washed her hair, relishing the feel of being clean again. She rinsed her hair clean of suds and was enjoying her soak when sleep claimed her.

She was running through a cursed forest. The trees and forest loam had been sapped of all life, and the parched remnants of grass and foliage crumbled beneath Runa's small feet. Then a red mist blanketed the forest floor, and the gray sky was void of sunlight. Dark sorcery reeked.

Mellypip chased after her, telling her to stop, but Runa had to keep going! A cry summoned her, so strong now, so painful! The mist cleared and Runa faced

~ 32 ~

a vision so terrible, she fell to her knees to weep before a tree of bones with black leaves.

Runa opened her eyes in terror, her nightmare broken, and drowning! Mellypip was in the bath with her, his voice shouting in her head, *"Wake up, Runa!"*

Hands pulled her up to life-giving air. Runa coughed and sputtered water. Opaline and Jiana were there, wet and worried. Poor Mellypip perched on the rim of the tub, fur soaked and wild-eyed.

Opaline pulled Runa out of the tub. "You almost drowned! I couldn't wake you! What happened?"

"Is she alright?" Jiana asked.

"I'm sorry. I think I fell asleep!" Runa managed to say in a choked voice.

"Well, don't do that!" Opaline snapped; wet hair plastered to her bare back. She quickly threw on a robe and gave Runa a towel.

"I'll go get Cathal," Jiana said, Jasper hopping at her heels.

"Melly, are you okay?" Runa asked.

"I'm drippy," the wampu said sniffing. "And you scared me!"

"Mellypip suddenly ran down here, crying out you were drowning and leapt into the bath! I jumped out to check on you. You were under the water. You almost drowned!"

"You have already said that!" Runa said.

"You just aged me ten years," Opaline accused.

"We're mages. Ten years is nothing," Runa replied.

"To you!" Opaline protested, laughing now from relief.

"I'm sorry. Oh, Melly," Runa cried, picking him up and wrapping his shivering body in a thick towel.

"Bad dreams," Mellypip replied in a petulant voice. "Bad sorceress, you scared me!"

"How did you know she was drowning?" Opaline asked Mellypip, helping to dry him off.

"I don't know. I was playing in the yard. I made Dabiro mad, and he chased me up a tree. He's a very cranky badger, but I was faster. I was dangling from a bough and suddenly saw strange creepy things in my head, like a dream, except I was awake. I sensed you were drowning. I ran inside. You were under the water and not moving. I called for Opaline and then I jumped in."

"You were very brave, Melly," Opaline cried hugging the dripping wampu.

The voices of Cathal and Belwyn were outside the curtains.

"Runa! Are you alright?" Cathal's frightened voice boomed.

"Yes, I'm fine," Runa called out.

"That's not what we heard," Belwyn accused.

"She fell asleep in the tub and nearly drowned!" Mellypip barked. "And she had another dream! A nasty dream with bones and stuff!"

On the other side of the curtain, Cathal's voice was startled. "Jiana, thanks for coming to get me, but you should really cover up before you catch cold."

Opaline stifled a giggle. "I think she forgot to put on a robe when she marched upstairs to tell Cathal what happened," she whispered. "She was still naked, except for the dagger she keeps with her at all times." Opaline wrapped Runa in a soft cotton robe. "Come on. Let's go upstairs. Go straight to bed as soon as you get something to eat."

"You may no longer be a princess, but you're still quite bossy," Runa remarked.

"A family trait," Opaline replied lightly as she drew back the curtains.

Cathal, face ashen, was waiting on the other side of the curtain. Belwyn's golden stare spoke volumes. Behind him everyone in the Sorcerer House lined up with matching anxious expressions and staves in hand. Runa was very embarrassed for causing such a scene.

"Opaline is right," Cathal said. "Everyone can stand down." He looked at Runa. "We are going to talk about those dreams, young lady," he whispered in her ear. "Do you think I haven't noticed your trouble sleeping?"

Cathal immediately put Runa to bed and coddled her like a five-year-old. Opaline fussed over her, bringing her supper of savory stew and fresh bread with golden butter. Mellypip snuggled protectively on the pillow next to Runa, fretful, since the terror of the bath incident had not quite faded. Belwyn perched on the bed post, like a feathered gargoyle.

Cathal handed Runa a cup of warm milk sweetened with honey and nutmeg after her meal. Obedient, she sipped it. "Mellypip must be dream bonded to you, even when you are awake. This is unusual. What happened in your dream that frightened you so, Runa?"

Runa bit her lip and lowered her eyes. "A tree of bones, with black leaves. It's been happening since we crossed into Thill. There is more, but I can never remember all of it."

Cathal frowned and touched her cheek. "My poor dear, that's a very frightening image."

"Runa should rest now," Sirah said. "There has been far too much excitement for one day."

Opaline fetched a towel. "Her hair is still damp. She'll catch cold." She vigorously rubbed Runa's head. "You have such lovely hair, Runa. It's a shame you cut it all off. I wish it was like it was before, so long and—"

Magic sparked the air and Opaline's face paled. She dropped the towel and jumped away. "Oh no, I didn't mean it! I'm sorry! I'm so sorry!"

"Uh-oh, I smell sorcery," Mellypip murmured, sniffing the air.

Runa's hands flew up to feel her head as her hair began growing rapidly past her shoulders.

Frantic, Opaline paced in circles. "Oh, no! I'm so sorry, Runa! MOTHER! CATHAL! Do something!"

Cathal and Sirah could only look on with stunned faces.

"Runa, your hair is sprouting everywhere!" Mellypip cried.

Runa's hair trailed the floor, and beyond. It was growing out the door!

"This is a jolly mess," Cathal groaned with amazement.

Belwyn was stoic. "I think this beats the time Runa turned our tree tower pink."

"It's a good thing Opaline is your friend," Mellypip commented. "Just think of what she could do to you if she didn't like you."

"My head hurts." Runa moaned and raked the hair back out of her eyes.

Mellypip patted her head tenderly with his paw. "Poor hairy sorceress."

~ * ~

Koll endured his captivity with mute disdain. Confined in a large iron cage in a dungeon deep below ground and guarded by soldiers, chains confined his body and sorcerer bane around his neck bound his sorcery. Trial and execution awaited him.

Koll survived far more dangerous things in this life. *She* would not let him perish. A chill brushed his body. He glanced down to the dusty floor and one word formed in shimmering black letters before it vanished.

Rescue

Koll laughed.

CHAPTER SIX

Belwyn's exasperation peaked as everyone huddled helplessly in the hallway on the third floor in front of the attic door. "Must I always resolve the ills of the world? Does anyone ever consider how that affects *me*? Am I forever doomed to be the weary leader?"

"Give it a rest, Belwyn," Runa said dryly.

Belwyn dug his talons into the wooded rail by the stairs. "Well, no one is helping me, and I've traveled from one end of the continent to the other, battled evil assassins, and suffered dark magic; I've dodged wraith guardians, minded a chatty wampu kit, and tolerated a sulky badger. Why must I deal with Opaline because she can't keep her magic to herself?"

"Muzzle it, Belwyn," Sanura snapped. "Can't you see this is a crisis?"

"Opaline will come out eventually," Belwyn advised in a cool tone. "She's in an attic. Humans require food and water. She'll be out of there before dinnertime judging by her hearty appetite."

Opaline shouted through the door. "I heard that, Belwyn."

Arial joined the group. "What's going on?"

Belwyn sighed heavily. "Madness looms over the Sorcerer House of Aybarr; and I am its victim."

"I would appreciate a more specific answer," Arial replied.

"Opaline locked herself in the attic," Runa said.

Arial shook her muzzle, her snowy ears flattened. "I thought we resolved that last night after Sirah spoke with her?"

Runa threw up in hands. "Apparently Opaline never left the attic last night after she fled there. I don't remember much, honestly. After they undid the spell and trimmed my hair, I think Grandpa put some sleeping herbs in my warm milk."

"Did you sleep?" Belwyn asked.

"Yes, a little," Runa nodded. "I still had strange dreams, but they were very distant. Even Mellypip slept better." Runa glanced around. "Where's Mellypip?"

"Watching Sirah bake cookies," Belwyn answered.

Sanura rubbed her face against the door jam. "That should keep him occupied. Runa's hair did grow for yards and yards, but they reversed the spell. There's baskets of it downstairs. Opaline's botched sorcery was a boon for Melly. He snuggled in a basket of Runa's hair and purred for hours. I joined him. Most pleasurable."

"After the whole bloody incident, Opaline fled to the attic, but I thought her mother talked her out of there last night," Belwyn said. "What happened?"

"Sirah talked to her," Arial replied. "She left the decision up to Opaline."

"Never leave anything up to a teenager," Belwyn remarked. "I fail to see the trouble anyway. All Runa suffered was a bout of dizziness and a headache, but was, on the whole, unhurt. Just open the door magically. That's what we do, folks—magic. I can do it if you're lacking the skill or courage."

"Don't you dare!" Runa protested. "She's terribly upset. Her sorcery might spiral out of control again. We don't want to push her over the edge."

"True," Belwyn agreed. "She could blow up the house or transform the whole lot of us into stinky trolls."

Runa glared at Belwyn. "Don't mention trolls. You know she's been sensitive about her magic since the troll incident. She's just a little irrational right now."

"Are females ever rational?" Belwyn inquired.

The hostile stares of the females gathered in the hallway, both familiar and human, stilled Belwyn's beak into uncomfortable silence.

Rosepetal the hedgehog sniffed. "The male clan is no help, as usual," she said.

Arial was more pragmatic. "You're foolish to speak so when outnumbered by the female clan. An owl of your many seasons should use better judgment."

"Well, I'm tired, so excuse my lack of sage wisdom," Belwyn grumbled.

Runa rapped on the attic door again. "Opaline? Please come out! You can't stay in the attic forever. It's musty and smelly."

"Go away!" Opaline cried.

"The attic is crawling with spiders! You hate spiders, Opaline," Runa added with emphasis. "You told me you had nightmares about them as a girl. I had to check your sleeping blankets each night, remember?"

"Stop taunting me with spiders!" Opaline sobbed. "I'm a danger to everyone around me. Just leave my meals at the door. Forget about me. Have a good life. Pray for me at temple."

"My hair stopped growing and Caliste cut it off at my waist. My hair's long and pretty again, thanks to you. Come out and see."

"I almost killed you!" Opaline sobbed.

"Of course you didn't kill me!" Runa shouted, kicking at the door. "You don't die from long hair! Opaline! I swear I'm going to blast the door open! I mean it! Stand back!"

"Well?" Belwyn asked, after a space of silence.

"What!" Runa sighed.

"Next time, be prepared to follow through with your threat. She didn't believe your bluff. And I thought we didn't want to blast the door open," Belwyn said pointedly.

"Just keep talking to her gently," Arial advised.

Runa's face brightened and she whispered through the door. "Your mother baked cookies this morning, Opaline. Your favorite! Drobba chip cookies!"

"I'm not Mellypip," Opaline replied. "Promises of sweets will not seduce me to your will."

Runa pressed close to the door and whispered. "Well, your mother's cookies could put a spell on anyone. Those rich, chewy cookies smell like sweet heaven! Plus, there's fresh, cold, frothy milk in a large pitcher, just waiting for you to dip a newly baked cookie into!"

Opaline whimpered. "Now you're just being cruel!"

"I'm going downstairs. Opaline must decide to come out on her own," Belwyn cautioned. "If no one will force the door, then there is nothing I can do."

Belwyn flew toward the kitchen but was almost struck by the swinging door that led into the kitchen. He frantically flapped his wings backward as a wild-eyed Mellypip, a drobba chip cookie clenched in his mouth, dashed from the kitchen like a mad beetle, with Jasper in hot pursuit, babbling about cookie thieves. Belwyn landed on a dining room wooden chair, and grumbled, "Insolent wampu kit! Clumsy tiger-hare! You almost crushed my beak! And don't think you can avoid your morning lessons, Furball!"

Buzzy the sloth dozed in a potted tree by the window, oblivious to the chaos.

"How's your morning been, Buzzy?" Belwyn asked.

The sloth opened one eye. "I am at peace—because I am staying out of their way."

"Bully for you," Belwyn replied.

"Is there any tea left?" Belwyn asked with meager hope when Sirah came out of the kitchen.

"A fresh pot is on the table," Sirah replied. "Has Opaline come out of the attic yet?"

"No," Belwyn said with a sigh. "Opaline's imprisoned herself like a princess from a bad fairy tale."

"I'll take care of it," Sirah promised. "I thought a night of sleeping with dusty boxes and mice might force her out.

"You really should meditate, Belwyn," Buzzy suggested.

"When I have time, I'll give that a whirl," Belwyn replied.

Belwyn tried to enjoy his tea, but the constant churn of banging and cursing disrupted his respite. He looked around. Dabiro and Pointessa argued in the backyard. Jasper returned to the kitchen and chattered about nonsense, his tiger-striped ears twitching as he munched a cookie. Mellypip had vanished somewhere, but he was too weary to hunt for the little wampu. A burning smell caught his attention and he took flight.

Belwyn flew out of the kitchen, glanced at the tranquil sloth. "Doesn't anything ever rattle you?" he hooted.

Belwyn flew toward the burning smell. In the crystal room, Myrsalian was whacking the calling crystal with his staff. Felisia, his tiny elf owl, fluttered around him on frantic wings, begging him to be calm. Overuse had wreaked havoc on the enormous crystal and it spurted sizzling noises and colors flickered rapidly. A burnt smell permeated the room.

"Now what's happening?" Belwyn asked.

"Chaos, Belwyn," Myrsalian groaned. "Everyone's sending messages at once! The crystal's magic is congested. I fear the damn thing is about the shatter. Between the capture of Koll and everyone rejoicing Cathal is back, it is total mayhem. There are multiple requests for Cathal to take up the title of Archon again. Where is Cathal this morning anyway?"

"Cathal and Caliste received a summons from the King. They'll be back before lunch." He turned to Felisia. "Have you had a cookie yet, Felisia?"

"Who has time!" the tiny owl hooted.

The crystal, set into a sturdy iron stand, was about four feet high and as wide. It flashed a myriad of colors and sparked with hot threat. Myrsalian whacked it with his staff.

"Yes, do strike the magically infused crystal with your big wooden stick, Myrsalian! That will surely fix things!" Felisia scolded. "When it explodes, I'll remind you of this wisdom when we meet in the Otherworld."

"Got a better suggestion?" Myrsalian snapped.

"I can give you one right now!" Felisia retorted.

The crystal sputtered ominously, followed by loud popping sounds. Bursts of color flared. Apprehensive, they stopped their conversation. A surge of power and a colorful blast of blue and orange forced them all back. Then the crystal flared one last time and died, leaving a hollowed, dull crystal. Faint wisps of smoke and a burnt odor were all that remained.

"I can't believe it died," Myrsalian gasped. He approached it warily and examined the dead crystal.

"Don't touch it," Felisia warned.

"I know what I'm doing," Myrsalian grumbled. He gingerly touched it and snatched back his hand. "Ouch!"

"Told you," Felisia tittered.

"I think I'll leave you two alone to ponder this mess," Belwyn sighed.

Belwyn retreated to the second floor of the house to nap in peace, perching in a dark corner. Just after closing his eyes, an explosion erupted. Smoke drifted from Taran's laboratory. He flew to his room, just as everyone else rushed in, to find Taran floating in the air, waving away purple smoke. MacTabbish, his tubby orange cat familiar, was sleeping on the windowsill. The cat slowly lifted his head and blinked, and seeing Taran still in one piece, went back to sleep.

"You can't keep blowing things up, Taran," Sirah reprimanded in a stern voice, entering with a plate of cookies. "Your experiments are too destructive and heart-stopping for your mother."

"Sorry, Mother," Taran apologized. "I thought my formulas were accurate. I'll clean it up! I promise! Oh, those smell great. Can I have a cookie?"

"After you've restored things, you may have one of my cookies," Sirah insisted.

Runa rushed into the room, waving the smoke away. "What happened? It's chaos in here."

"A failed experiment in magic and science," Taran said with a shrug. "I really must check my notes, if they haven't burned to ash that is."

Runa took a cookie that Sirah offered. "Please Taran, before you destroy us with science, help me coax Opaline out of the attic? She won't listen to me."

"Is she still hiding up there?" Taran laughed.

"It's not funny," Runa replied darkly. "She's quite traumatized about last night, much like this room."

"Science is a messy and demanding discipline. Mix it with magic, and it's even more unpredictable. We could get Dabiro to ram the door open?" Taran suggested. "He loves ramming things. I've watched him charge that big tree out back over and over, just for fun. His skull is rigid and tough as iron." Taran searched the chaos of his table with broken tubes, cracked crystals, smoking parchment, and finally lifted a thin chain with a delicate silver ball. "Or we could give Opaline this? Inside the ball there's a tiny stone."

"Is that stone sorcerer bane?" Runa asked. "She used a ring of sorcerer bane in Tiamet to conceal her magic!"

Taran handed her the necklace. "This should make sure there are no more magical accidents until she's learned to control her sorcery. I made it pretty too. I've been doing a lot of experiments with sorcerer bane, so I had plenty lying around."

"Brilliant!" Runa declared and hugged him.

Sirah kissed Taran on the cheek. "You're a good boy when you're not blowing up the house. She can wear it when not practicing her magic."

"Plus no accidental transformations into trolls or growing miles of hair," Belwyn added. "And possible peace for me. Let's see if we can rescue the princess from the dismal tower."

"Now clean up the mess and air out the room," Sirah ordered with a smile. "It reeks."

Mellypip bounced into the room, eyes bright with curiosity. "What went boom?"

"My sparkling personality," Belwyn retorted.

"Are you cranky, Belwyn?" Mellypip asked. "Maybe you should take a nap."

Belwyn was about to snap, but Mellypip looked at him with such innocent eyes. "Why don't you go play, Furball."

"Really? No studies?" Mellypip asked, swishing his tail.

"Just stay in the yard and steer clear of Dabiro. That badger tends to hold a grudge."

Mellypip scampered away with joy.

They returned to the attic door. Runa told Opaline about what Taran made for her and laid the necklace on the floor and stepped away. The door clicked open, and a delicate white hand appeared and seized the necklace. She closed the door. In a moment, a pale and shaky Opaline emerged, wearing the sorcerer bane amulet. Her eyes were swollen and red from crying.

Sirah hugged her and gave her a cookie as she consoled her overwrought daughter. "Dear Opaline, your magic will become manageable soon. I promise. So stop fretting. Now let's go downstairs."

"Yes, Mother," Opaline said, nibbling the cookie and looking embarrassed.

"Now, how would you girls like an outing?" Sirah invited. "The cloth merchant has new bolts of silk, velvet and cotton, and some readymade dresses and pieces too! We have a special invitation for dinner with the King and Queen, so we must look our best."

Hope returned to Opaline's eyes. "New clothes!" She ate her cookie with gusto.

"Caliste is coming too!" Sirah said. "Jiana is not interested, so I will just have to pick out something for her."

"Perhaps Cathal would like to come?" Opaline suggested.

"Grandpa hates shopping for clothes. He does need some new garments," Runa said. "I'll pick out a couple things for him."

"Just make sure the clothes are simple and choose somber colors," Belwyn advised.

Runa kissed Belwyn on the beak. "Right...lots of pink."

"Young lady, you are vexing me," Belwyn warned.

~ * ~

Disgusted, Xabral turned away from the bowl of obsidian glass. He had witnessed too much revolting purity for one day. Finally, after a few moments of recovery, he returned to scrying, and more images inside the Sorcerer House formed.

He finally located Panthara in the pool of water. She was under the care of Iona. Panthara was pale and unmoving, a mere shell of her former self. That irritating crill lizard, Azmadu, was curled on Panthara's lap. She will be unable to resist should Koll want to claim her. Xabral resented Panthara. She brought trouble to Koll, but his sorcerer wanted her.

Xabral slithered across the room and nosed into the chest where some of Koll's more powerful crystals and scrolls were kept. He found an unassuming smoky crystal cylinder four inches long. It simmered with dark magic long kept contained. It was a key element in Xabral's plan. There was another relic he needed. Ah, there it was! A simple casket of ebonite set with rubies. What lay within was deadly, a powerful mystical weapon that could defeat light magic and that required the darkest bloodstone magic. It was one of Koll's favorite relics. Using it once would drain its ancient power, but it was necessary.

A priest entered the chamber and bowed. "Lord Xabral, Dagon and Gethen have arrived with the Rashurkeen warriors to escort you to Thill."

"Good," Xabral replied. "We have much work to do."

CHAPTER SEVEN

Grimm Darkrunner hated the troll.

The black wolf pursued the abhorrent creature every night. The troll sprinted across the wilderness toward its mysterious objective, as though pulled by a sinister force. Grimm kept tempo with the swift monster with the speed of his inborn familiar magic, a trait he did not even know he possessed.

A normal wolf has incredible endurance and can run at speeds exceeding five miles per hour and keep that pace for hours without a break. A wolf can leap a distance of more than sixteen feet in a single bound. Grimm's special magical power exceeded this feat. His unique familiar gift, that grows with maturity, had finally evolved. He followed the troll, who ran with supernatural speed. Grimm covered a vast distance in a short span of days. The landscape evolved from thick, green forests, to sparse wilderness, and now to arid steppes surrounded by grey snow-capped mountains.

Exhausted and hungry after hard nights of running, Grimm would hunt for food, and then collapse into a heavy sleep until sunfall when the monster stirred again. The troll's rank odor disturbed him, even from a distance. The troll disturbed Grimm. When it had been human, it was surely evil. It also disturbed Grimm that he sensed other creatures running with them; not substantial animals of fur or feathers, but those spawned of shadows.

"The sun rises," Midnight cautioned, "it's time to rest."

Grimm glanced at his spirit father running alongside him. "Good. I am weary."

The troll stopped running as the sun dispelled night. It hunted in the dim twilight before sunrise. Grimm trailed him, but cringed when the howls of the animal it slaughtered pierced the air. The wolf was never cruel when he hunted food, and always made the death quick. The troll killed a wild steppe horse. Grimm did not touch the sparse remains of the animal, fouled by the monster's touch. He declined to hunt now; his hunger ruined by the troll. After its feeding frenzy, the troll burrowed into a hole beneath an outcrop of rock.

Grimm sat on his haunches and welcomed the rising sun's

warmth. The light dispelled the gnawing fears he endured at night. He looked at his father. "What is the name of this land I must go to?"

"Skarros, the Wasteland," Midnight answered.

"Why must you send me to such a terrible place?" Grimm asked. "You told me wicked things had happened there long ago. It's a cursed land."

"Your destiny is there. People do not live there. Not for centuries. Since you do not like two-legs, you should be glad."

"You're mocking me," Grimm said with a sniff. "If two-legs no longer live there, it must be a barren land. How can I survive?"

"Desert rats, snakes, insects, and lizards still haunt the land. You will manage, my son. Now, we are in the northern territory of what humans call Ithuli."

"Thank you for the geography lesson, but what is in this Wasteland of Skarros?"

"Danger, but that's not why I am sending you there. You have a duty to perform, and when it's done, your destiny will be revealed."

"I'm weary of this destiny," Grimm replied.

"All creatures have a destiny. Now sleep, for soon the night will come."

Grimm curled into a ball and slept. Midnight remained to watch over Grimm, a shimmering specter in the wilderness. In the protection of his father's spirit, no phantoms crouching in the dark threatened them.

~ * ~

"Why is Opaline's eye turning purple?" Mellypip asked Belwyn, perched together on the back of a chair in the kitchen.

"Because I'm cursed with clumsiness," Opaline replied dryly.

"I would suggest sluggish reflexes," Belwyn observed.

Runa scowled at Belwyn and applied a cold compress to Opaline's bruised eye. "I'm sorry, so terribly sorry!"

Darcus leaned against the kitchen table. "Just keep ice on it, Princess. Duck faster next time."

Sirah chipped chunks of ice on the cutting board in the large kitchen. She wrapped the ice chips in a damp cloth and a shimmer of magic made the bundle glow. "There, now the ice won't melt for hours. Keep it on for only a few moments at a time, dear. I don't want your face to freeze."

"Thanks, Mother." Opaline smiled with wan resignation as she placed the ice bag over her puffy eye. "I must look hideous."

"Your beauty will recover, Princess," Darcus grinned. "Your form is improving."

"Not fast enough. My ambition to become a warrior is thwarted by my mediocre skill with a simple stick. Oh no! Dinner with the royal family! My eye will be deformed!" She glanced at Runa with suspicion. "You're a vicious fighter for such a tiny girl. This is the second black eye I've suffered since meeting you, Runa."

Arial ran into the kitchen. "That badger cannot be trusted! I knew it!"

"Now what did Dabiro do?" Belwyn moaned.

"Five jars of raspberry jam and two loaves of bread were missing from the pantry," Arial replied. "Eberr told me this morning when he was taking inventory before going to the market. We knew someone thieved them."

"How do you know it's Dabiro?" Opaline asked.

Liat carried in Dabiro, muzzle stained with red jam, groaning with pain. Pointessa followed them in. Liat carefully laid Dabiro on a blanket in the corner. "I'm sorry, Sirah," Liat said with dismay. "I found him in the bushes with the empty jars."

Belwyn hopped over to Dabiro. "You know, you remind me of someone much smaller, but equally fuzzy."

"Don't torment a dying badger, Belwyn." Dabiro moaned and belched with volcanic force.

Pointessa curled up next to the badger, sighing patiently. "Don't worry. If he gets worse, I will send for a healer experienced in treating gluttonous badgers."

"She mocks me in death!" Dabiro groaned.

Sirah looked down at Dabiro. "I will brew some mint and chamomile tea to help ease your distress but raid my pantry again and you'll never taste my homemade jam again."

"That is a grim fate," Mellypip agreed. Her jam is marvelous.

Eberr rushed in, carrying bags of supplies. "Excuse me folks, but I must hurry," the sorcerer huffed as he dropped the groceries on the large table. "Poor Caliste has been on guard duty watching Koll and I must relieve her."

"Thank you for doing the shopping," Sirah smiled. "I'll save you some dinner."

Eberr looked down at Dabiro and sighed. "I see we found our

jam thief, but I think his gluttony has doled out its own punishment. Stay with him, Pointessa. I think he needs watching."

"Take care when you watch the evil one," Pointessa warned as Eberr rushed out the back door.

Sirah took a large bowl and began gathering potatoes from the vegetable bin to peel. "I have dinner to prepare for a lot of people. Please clear my kitchen unless you plan to help, except for Dabiro and his guardians. Moving him may bring more dreadful consequences."

"He'll throw up?" Mellypip asked.

"Like a gushing volcano," Liat added dryly, stroking the groaning badger's head.

"Let's go, warrior princess," Runa laughed, pulling her friend to her feet. "You should lie down. I'll help Sirah with dinner."

Darcus quickly moved away toward the door. "I think I'll leave before things get too exciting. I'll be in the stables."

"Can I come, Darcus?" Mellypip asked. "I want to play with Rono."

"Yes, little one," Darcus nodded.

Mellypip bounced outside after Darcus and followed him to the stables. The vegetable garden was so tempting, but Mellypip decided not to raid the neatly planted rows of goodies. It would upset Sirah. The perytons roamed in the yard, grazing, and enjoying the afternoon sunshine.

He liked the perytons and would miss them when they returned home. A sudden pluck of emotion froze Mellypip in his tracks. Darcus would be going with them to his new home in Ilyrra. He would miss Darcus so much!

Mellypip nosed a walnut bush near the stables until he found his hidden treasure, wrapped in leaves. He picked it up in his mouth and raced to the stables.

The gryphon's vibrant brown eyes lit up with joy when Mellypip arrived. "Darcus groomed me. I'm pretty now," Rono exclaimed, turning his head to show off his fluffy glory. He blinked, long feathered lashes curling above his dark brown eyes.

Mellypip jumped to the top of the gate to greet him and took the leaf-wrapped object from his mouth and opened it. "I saved you an oatmeal cookie from this morning." He gave it to Rono, who munched it happily. "Jasper chased me for it—again. Every day is a cookie chase with that darned hare. This time I evaded him."

"Thanks, Melly. It was yummy. You're my best friend."

"You're mine too," Mellypip replied with genuine warmth. "Want to play ranger mage?"

Rono eagerly nodded his head. "Oh, yes please! Do we fight goblins or trolls today?"

"Goblins," Mellypip decided.

Darcus led the gryphon out of his stable. "You two be sure not to trample the gardens. Be careful now and don't get dirty."

Mellypip leapt to Rono's back, his black feathered body warm and cozy. Mellypip grabbed an old towel hanging on a peg, flung it over his back, and knotted it around his neck.

"This should make a dashing cloak. Prepare to attack the goblins!" Mellypip commanded.

The gryphon bolted out of the stables, pretending to be quite fierce. Eager to fly, Rono spread his wings and flew in wide circles above the Sorcerer House, Mellypip squealing with delight as he clung to him. They landed in the backyard and ran around the yard in circles fighting the make-believe goblins until they got bored with mock battles and decided to join the perytons in an apple feast.

Later, Mellypip relaxed on Rono's back, recounting their victories when he noticed Jadon sitting in the shade of the old hawthorn tree. Curious, Mellypip climbed up to Rono's head, and tried to see what he was doing. "What are you doing, Jadon?" he asked.

Jadon held up a tiny piece of wood and grinned. "I'm carving a present for Runa," Jadon whispered. "But you must keep it a secret." The piece of wood was a very fine ring, crafted from polished wood. At the heart of the ring was a beautiful carved rose.

Mellypip gasped with wonder. "It's pretty as any fancy ring carved from gold or silver."

Jason grinned. "Thank you. Among my people, when two people like each other, they exchange token gifts."

Mellypip frowned. "That's not a wedding ring, is it?"

Jadon looked stunned for a moment—then he laughed. "No. Not a wedding ring. Let's call it a ring of friendship."

"That's good, because Cathal might turn you into a toad if it was."

"Good to know," Jadon said with a laugh. "Do you think Runa will like it?

"Of course! It's so pretty," Mellypip said. "She likes you, but she gets tongue-tied around you for some reason. Perhaps it is a strange human thing."

"I have a surprise for you too. Jadon reached into his bag and pulled out a little staff made from dark heart oak. "I was going to give this to you at the same time, but I think you need this to fight the goblins."

The little staff was sized just right for him! The staff's top was the image of Runa! Jadon's artistry captured her beauty; even her crown of hair was shaped with such deft skill it looked real! "Did you use magic to carve this? It's amazing!" Mellypip enthused.

"Just my hands," Jadon replied with a gentle smile.

Mellypip accepted the wooden treasure with joy. "Thank you. Now I am truly a mighty ranger mage!"

He showed off his gift to Rono, who gave the staff an approving lick. With pride, Mellypip wielded his staff in triumph and puffed out his little chest until the sound of excited human voices in the street interrupted Mellypip's imaginary quest. The perytons stopped grazing and lifted their heads with curiosity. Rosepetal sniffed the air. Sanura prowled with curiosity. Jasper's ears twitched. Even the wolf Arial ventured outside, curious about the ruckus.

"Let's see what is happening! I smell danger!" Mellypip murmured to Rono.

A great thundering roar filled the air and Mellypip was reconsidering the danger element.

"I don't like things that roar," Rono grumbled.

"Me neither," Mellypip agreed. "We should approach with caution."

They ventured to the front yard and in the street, crowds of people gathered near the Sorcerer House, buzzing with curious excitement.

A deep voice boomed inside the crowd, "Make way! Make way good people! Don't crowd the bear!"

The crowd parted for the man, who marched toward the Sorcerer House. He must be a wizard, for a grizzly bear strode at his side, growling loudly. The Dwarven wizard had ginger hair and a beard woven into elaborate braids that hung to his waist. He wore a flowing blue coat embroidered with runic symbols over a long tunic and red trousers. He was tall, at least four and a half feet tall, and carried a staff, the head of it carved with the fierce visage of a bear.

The wizard rapped his staff at the front gate. "Cathal! Where are you? I didn't come this far south for my health!" The massive grizzly at his side thundered!

Everyone from the Sorcerer House gathered on the front lawn to greet the new arrivals, except for Dabiro, who was still recovering in the kitchen from the *jam incident*.

"Hello, Raghnall. That's quite an entrance," Belwyn commented as he flew overhead. "I see Baldur is still a ham."

"Belwyn, you old feather duster!" Raghnall beckoned and Belwyn alighted on his arm, clacking his beak with genuine pleasure as he stroked his feathers, "You look well, you wily old owl. Where's Cathal? I've got a rune to pick with him."

"I'm above you!" a grey and white owl cried, swooping to the earth. Upon landing, the owl shimmered into Cathal. "Welcome, Raghnall! What brings you to Thill?"

"My mother-in-law came to visit, so I came here for sanctuary."

"I'm so sorry," Cathal said with a laugh.

"So am I." Raghnall sighed. "Word is buzzing on every enchanted crystal and magic mirror in the world that Koll has finally been captured. Do you think I'm going to sit on my butt in Ironia when all the excitement is here? Anyway, I'm here as an official delegate from King Arawn and Queen Dagmar!" Raghnall looked around. "Where's little Runa?"

"Right here," Runa shouted as she ran toward him.

The wizard's eyes softened, and Runa hugged him and kissed his cheek. "It's good to see you, Raghnall! Is Greta here?"

"Her mother came to visit," Raghnall whispered with a tragic shiver.

Runa winced. "Oh, I'm so sorry."

"Don't I get a hug, Runa?" Baldur asked, rubbing against her shoulder.

Runa ruffled his massive head affectionately. "Hi there, Baldur!"

Mellypip watched warily. Apparently, this Raghnall knew most of the sorcerers, except Opaline. He kissed all the ladies' hands in greeting, except for Jiana. She refused to let him kiss her hand, and Raghnall feigned heartbreak, earning a hard-won smile from Jiana.

Cathal was introducing Taran when he asked, "Taran where's MacTabbish?"

"Sleeping. Maybe the bear could go wake him up," Taran suggested with a grin.

"Oh, that'll go over well," Arial said, tongue lolling in amusement. "Do you think we should?"

Mellypip hid from Belwyn's keen eyes behind Rono's feathered leg. "That bear is massive! I need a bigger staff."

"Oh, you haven't met Mellypip!" Runa looked around. "Melly, come meet Raghnall and Baldur."

"He's hiding behind the gryphon's leg," Belwyn remarked.

"I thought you were going to explore the danger?" Rono whispered.

Mellypip clutched his staff. "Hush. I'm doing it from a safe distance."

"Rono, tell Mellypip it's safe to meet the bear," Belwyn hooted.

Mellypip approached cautiously. The bear was staring at him!

"That's a beautiful staff!" Runa exclaimed with awe when she picked up Mellypip. "Is that my face? Who did this?"

Mellypip puffed with pride. "Jadon made it special just for me!"

"We must thank him," Runa said. She glanced around for Jadon, and blushed when she saw him. Jadon nodded her way, and she turned even pinker than Opaline's new gown. She always lost the capacity for speech around him. Maybe she was under a spell?

Runa held him up to introduce him. "Raghnall, Baldur, this is Mellypip, my familiar."

"He's an adorable little fellow, I see," Raghnall commented, scratching his chin.

Suddenly, Baldur's brown eyes misted, and his massive paws flew up to his muzzle. "He's so cute! You're so lucky, Belwyn! I never got to train such an adorable familiar!"

Without warning, Baldur snatched Mellypip from Runa's hands. Baldur rolled on the ground with Mellypip, giving him big, wet kisses. Mellypip squealed with terror and tried to beat Baldur off with his little staff. Even the crowd of onlookers gasped at first when Baldur grabbed Mellypip. Now they laughed and clapped, realizing he was just playing.

Cathal and Runa looked on, worried, but Raghnall chuckled, "That Baldur! He just loves children."

"Belwyn! Help me! I can't breathe," Mellypip wheezed as Baldur hugged him close. His screams were frantic, and his little paws waved about. Rono's feathers ruffled with concern.

Belwyn hopped over and poked Baldur with his beak, "Alright, that's enough. I think your chew toy has had enough. And you're upsetting the gryphon."

Baldur cradled Mellypip in his massive paws. Soaked and matted from kisses, Mellypip pushed the bear's face to a safe distance. "I am not a chew toy! I'm a familiar!" His remaining words were muffled by a big, sloppy kiss.

Baldur held the wampu before him. "I will call you little brother, Mellypip." He licked the wampu's head with affection.

Belwyn finally succumbed to a fit of laughter and was rolling on the ground.

Mellypip glowered at the owl. "Don't pee your feathers trying to help me, Belwyn."

~ * ~

Two black ravens hid in the trees until the lights inside the Sorcerer House were extinguished. Patient, they waited. The cover of night and sorcery concealed them from enemy eyes. They winged to the back door and landed on the stone steps. One of the ravens shapeshifted into a sorcerer, robed in black. Careful not to disturb any wards that might warn the inhabitants, he took two stones from a pouch and whispered words of magic. The stones shimmered and transformed into two eyes of ethereal black mist. They hovered in the air, and then with magical speed, they vanished within.

Dagon's familiar, Gethen the raven, nodded approval. "The spell worked. Xabral will be pleased."

"Pray it works without discovery, else his anger will sting us both," Dagon replied as he shifted back into a raven.

"Koll's anger would sting more," Gethen warned.

They flew away into the night.

CHAPTER EIGHT

Mellypip enjoyed King Caladynn's lush garden, bouncing on Runa's shoulder, eager to climb the trees and smell all the blossoms. He managed to nibble on a few choice buds in passing. People in fancy clothes milled about or sat at the small tables arranged on the green.

"It's silly for people to dress up just to play in the garden," Mellypip commented.

"Nature is wasted on nobles," Runa agreed. "Smell those flowers! I feel like kicking off my shoes and running barefoot. The grass looks so soft."

"Don't you dare!" Opaline threatened, walking arm in arm with Runa.

"Then take off that silly veil," Runa replied.

"No. Outdoors this veil will conceal my deformed eye with minimal explanation. A lady's complexion must be shielded you know."

"Your eye is not deformed," Runa insisted and looked around. "Where are Grandpa and Belwyn? For the matter, where's everyone? It's a special reception for the mages and rangers."

"I think they're late because of Koll's trial," Opaline whispered. "I overheard Cathal talk to my mother about it yesterday."

"What did you hear?" Runa asked eagerly.

"Only whispers, until Belwyn banished me. After that they concealed their conversation with magic. Goodness, but that owl's stare can be downright menacing."

Anything to do with Koll made Mellypip's fur bristle. The dark sorcerer was a palpable wet blanket of doom.

Several young noblemen, casually garbed in trousers and loose linen shirts, tossed a ball around the open courtyard a few yards away. Opaline froze mid step, yanking Runa back with her. "Look at him! Isn't he glorious?"

Runa shrugged. "I just see men tossing around a ball like eight-year-olds."

Opaline pointed with fervent emphasis. "No, over there! See that handsome man with wavy black hair and the physique of a young god. How swift he is! Look, he's caught the ball again!"

"Thrilling," Runa replied dryly.

Roughhousing, they battled over the ball until it flew out of their control and struck Opaline in the head. It knocked her solidly to the ground. Opaline desperately held the sheer petal pink veil to her face, though she was sprawled on the grass.

"Are you alright?" Runa cried, dropping to her knees. Mellypip jumped to the ground.

"Did anyone see my face?" Opaline muttered.

Runa sat back on her heels, crossing her arms. "Really? You're struck by a hard leather ball and that's your concern?"

"Is this why Belwyn says she's vain?" Mellypip asked.

Melly! We talked about oversharing.

Don't yell at me. Belwyn said it first.

The handsome young god rushed toward Opaline, his comrades followed, grave and contrite.

Opaline panicked as he approached. "He can't see me like this! Do something!"

"I could whack him with my staff," Runa replied with a deadpan voice. "Or we could just be polite and say hello."

Cathal and Belwyn arrived just when Opaline was struck. Cathal ran over to them, Belwyn winging above.

"Goodness, are you alright, dear?" Cathal asked.

The young man stopped before them and smiled. "Cathal, is that you?"

"Prince Ulric, you've grown up!" Cathal said. "I think you need to work on your aim. It can be lethal to onlookers."

"Prince," Opaline whispered in despair.

"What's wrong *now*?" Runa muttered under her breath.

"I can't be involved with a prince. I'm an outcast!"

"You're such hard work," Runa groaned.

Cathal lifted Opaline's head. "Can you stand? Let me check your eyes. Take off the veil."

"That's not necessary," Opaline insisted, clutching the veil.

"I think she's broken," Mellypip quipped.

"Her common sense is," Belwyn said.

Cathal pulled Opaline to her feet. "Prince Ulric, let me introduce my granddaughter, Runa, and her familiar, Mellypip. Her mysterious companion is Opaline."

Prince Ulric bowed deeply. "Your bravery is known to me,

Princess Opaline. Forgive my assault. Should I summon a physician?"

Opaline curtsied, holding the veil in place against the breeze. "You're too kind. I am well, truly. Just embarrassed."

Ulric boldly lifted her veil despite Opaline's protests. "Beauty such as yours should not be concealed. That's an impressive black eye. How did you acquire it?"

"Staff practice," Runa interceded. "Opaline is quite the warrior in her spare time. I can barely keep up with her."

"I'm impressed," Ulric laughed. "I enjoy athletics, as you have tragically experienced."

"Opaline is quite ferocious," Mellypip added with fervor. "Ask her about the troll."

Opaline shot Mellypip a withering look.

Ulric's companions, sensing they had lost their teammate, grinned and quietly departed with the offending ball.

"You must tell me of your exploits, Opaline," Ulric insisted, kissing her hand.

Speechless, Opaline could only nod as Ulric led her away. She glanced back at Runa with a look full of such giddiness, Runa stifled a laugh.

Runa scooped Mellypip into her arms. "Grandpa, what about the trial? And where is everyone? I thought they'd be here by now."

"Later," Cathal whispered. "I must confer with Caladynn first. I'll explain about the others later."

Cathal walked away with Belwyn perched on his arm, leaving Runa confused.

Something is going on, Mellypip communicated.

"Hail good friends!" Hinkleburr cried with joy, running up to them. "I have marvelous tidings! Thorgid just informed me I'm going to Thema as the new Ambassador!" I am beyond joy!"

"He is indeed," Broda intoned calmly.

"His joy is limitless," Talwyn added with equal seriousness.

"You boys will love it there!" Hinkleburr burst, hugging his stalwart twin aides. "Thema is a tropical haven with beautiful palm trees. A land ruled by queens for a thousand years."

Hinkleburr joined Ambassador Thorgid and his daughter Helga at the table. Runa noticed Hinkleburr was very attentive to Helga. He even acted a bit flustered.

Melly see; Hinkleburr cannot take his eyes off the comely Helga.

I think love has another victim, Mellypip agreed.

Love is striking a lot of folk lately, Runa remarked, looking at Opaline and Ulric. *I wonder where Jadon is. He said he'd be here.*

The green cloaked young man stepped behind up her, silent as an owl's wings. Mellypip flicked his tail with joy. *"Look behind you."*

Runa spun around. Jadon had an impish smile on his face.

"Don't you ever make a sound when you walk?" Runa snapped. "And you shouldn't sneak up on people. You should stomp—or hum a cheery tune."

"Rangers are stealthy," Mellypip stated. "It's their job."

"Humming would destroy my stealth. I'm sorry I frightened you."

"You didn't frighten me," Runa insisted, looking down at the grass.

"Startled? Surprised perhaps? Should we play Melly's word game? How can I make it up to you?"

"Drobba is a good start," Mellypip suggested.

They laughed and the mutual humor calmed Runa's shyness in front of Jadon.

Jadon reached into his vest pocket. Mellypip swished his tail, eager to see Runa's face when she saw the ring.

"I know you had a birthday a short time ago," Jadon stammered.

"It was ever so much fun. You should have been there. We had cake and giant ravens attacked us."

Jadon laughed. "Because I wasn't there, I thought I would give you—"

The pomp of the royal family arriving cut short their discussion. Cathal suddenly pulled Runa away. Mellypip inwardly cursed. He poked his head over Runa's shoulder. "Follow us!" he called to Jadon.

King Caladynn and Queen Sorcha took their places beneath the canopy. They wore matching slim gold crowns set with emeralds. The stunning queen's black hair was swept into a simple bun and her vivid blue eyes sparkled with intelligence. "Cathal, you're a welcome sight!" Queen Sorcha exclaimed, kissing Cathal on each cheek. "Heavens! Could this lovely young lady actually be baby Runa? And this must be your adorable familiar." Sorcha rubbed Mellypip's ears, much to his delight.

A young woman behind the queen carried a squirming two-year-old child who tugged on her velvet hat.

"This rambunctious boy is our youngest prince, Turas." Sorcha took her young son and held him on her hip. "His patient nurse is

Lady Margaret. I see Ulric has met Opaline," she smiled, noticing the two sitting together.

"Fuzzy!" Turas cried, reaching for Mellypip.

Sorcha held back his eager little hands. "Turas, you must not pull on his tail or ears." She handed the boy back to Margaret. "Best to take him back to the nursery, dear. Turas is near his nap time. I'll send a platter of delicacies to you."

After Lady Margaret left with Turas, a richly dressed couple joined the King and Queen. The man was younger, thick-set with a short beard, but unlike the king, a dour expression. A somber woman clung to his arm. Her beauty was flawless but lacked warmth, despite hazel eyes and porcelain skin.

"Cathal, you remember my brother, Prince Morydonn, and his new wife, Princess Faustine," Caladynn said.

Runa and Cathal bowed, but Morydonn and Faustine looked at them with the distaste one reserves for vermin. Morydonn did not speak, but simply walked away. Faustine followed her husband's example.

"I see Morydonn hasn't changed," Cathal commented sadly.

"Did I do something wrong?" Runa whispered.

"Of course not dear," Cathal replied. "Morydonn hates magic. That extends to us."

Caladynn sighed. "I'm sorry, friends. Morydonn's rudeness is unforgiveable."

"We rarely see them. They usually reside in the northern capitol," Sorcha said.

Cathal shrugged. "Don't worry about it."

"Your heart is generous, Cathal," Caladynn replied.

"Will you announce Koll's fate at the reception?" Cathal asked.

Caladynn nodded. "The public will hear too. The town criers are going into the streets as we speak."

"What happened?" Runa asked.

"Koll was found guilty," Caladynn replied. "That is no surprise. He will be executed in three days. That is the news of duty. Now, on to happier subjects, Cathal. You'll be glad to know that Selyf the Bard will entertain us today."

Cathal brightened. "I remember Selyf! He performed here years ago, before the Sorcerer War. He told marvelous tales, and his singing was remarkable."

Mellypip looked forward to hearing a real bard. He loved stories.

Maybe it would help push the specter of Koll from his thoughts. He even wished for Belwyn's word lessons.

"Come say hello to our friends, Selyf!" Caladynn called, summoning a tall, thin man from a nearby table.

Selyf joined them, dressed for performing in a midnight blue robe with runic symbols embroidered in red on the borders. He carried a staff, though Mellypip sensed no magic from it. His weathered face, graying ginger hair and dark eyes were striking. Selyf bowed his head and smiled warmly. "Cathal, it's good to see you again."

"I've offered him a post at my court many times," Caladynn enthused. "He always declines, with regret of course. He's a master storyteller! I often envy his freedom too."

A girl of not more than five years with a mass of wavy black hair and brown eyes walked up to Selyf. She carried a small drum and stick. Selyf picked her up and kissed her cheek. "This tiny jewel is my daughter, Raven! She's also my apprentice. She beats the drum in time as I speak."

"You're a fluffy wampu!" Raven giggled. She did not pull or tug, but stroked his fur gently, prompting a loud purr from Mellypip.

"I bet you do a wonderful job keeping time on the drums," Runa complimented her, brushing back her hair, revealing delicate pointed ears. "Are you part Ilyrran? So am I!"

Sober, Raven nodded. "My mama was tribal. She's gone away now."

Selyf gently put her down. "Since we have already had our lunch, why don't you try the desserts? Have whatever you desire!"

Raven's tiny face lit up again. Sorcha took her hand and helped Raven pick out some choice cakes.

"She's beautiful," Runa commented.

"She knows it too," Selyf said with a laugh.

"I'm sorry for your loss," Cathal said.

Selyf's eyebrow arched. "I'm no widower, Cathal. My grief is different. My wife Veda was born of the nomadic tribes who never accepted Ilyrra as their homeland. I met Veda when they offered me a ride one day. We fell in love. Veda gave up her tribe to marry me, but the call of her people was too strong. She returned to them when Raven was only three."

"How could she leave her daughter?" Runa asked, stunned.

"Marriage outside the tribe is not accepted, especially to one not of their race," Selyf explained. "A half-breed child has no status in her tribe, so Veda left her with me. We all live with the past. It gives us a future or curses us. I chose a future with my daughter."

"A good choice," Cathal said looking at Runa. "I too made a similar decision, fifteen years ago."

Jadon whispered in Runa's ear. "I think we may sit together now that Opaline is occupied with Prince Ulric. Should I stomp or hum on the way?"

"You realize I'm armed," Runa warned with a smile, hefting her staff.

Confronted with food heaven, Mellypip forgot about Jadon's ring and Koll's shadow for a brief spell. Rosy servings of baked salmon with a creamy dill sauce and buttery potatoes seasoned with rosemary were savory. Chilled fruits in crystal cups were served after the main course before dessert. Also, everyone, including Mellypip had their own loaf of bread and a tiny crock of butter stamped with the royal seal of a regal horse's head. Mellypip though he would burst when he finished. He feared Belwyn would chastise him if he belched.

I'm worried, Runa said through the bonding. *None of the others are here.*

Grandpa Cathal knows why, but he isn't telling.

Dessert plates were carried to each table. The varieties made Mellypip's head spin—apple and blackberry pies, strawberry cakes dosed with heavy cream, cream puffs, and tarts of all kinds, including something new called banana custard. What was a banana? He would have to investigate that.

"What's that?" Mellypip pointed to a plate of new sweets a servant placed before them. "I want some!"

"Drobba puffs," Sorcha answered. "The frosting is coated with toasted coconut, imported from Zeli. Please try some. It's delicious."

"Thank you, Your Majesty." Runa nodded, smiling, piling several little puffs on her plate.

Take more! Mellypip advised.

Don't be greedy, Runa replied.

Selyf the Bard performed after the meal. Selyf's tale carried Mellypip to the dusty past of the Bloodstone Age, filled with tales of love, death, loss, sacrifice, and victory. He regaled them with the ancient legend of Queen Upala, Thema's first queen and her defeat over Obsydia. Mellypip even forgot he had a drobba puff clutched in his paw. The bard used his staff to add effect, swinging and rapping it to add impact. Raven's subtle drumbeats followed the rhythm of Selyf's words, building to the tale's epic conclusion. After he finished, applause resounded in appreciation.

Mellypip wanted to be storyteller now. He was sure it would add prestige to being a ranger mage. Belwyn told him once words had power, but he never understood it until now.

After Selyf's performance, Cathal and Belwyn casually drew Runa and Mellypip away to the shade of an old oak. Jadon was overly curious, so Cathal motioned him over too. He subtly waved his hand. "Act natural. I've cloaked our words, though the magic is invisible to others. I'm telling you, Jadon, because you will be helping protect the house tonight. Your father will give you more information when you get back to the house. I won't be coming with you. Koll dies tonight."

Runa hoped her demeanor looked natural. "But the king said three days."

"It's a ruse. Even this reception is a front. Half the nobles here are armed guards. Koll has allies and we know they're here somewhere," Cathal explained. "Between now and Koll's execution, we are watching Koll and area around the prison."

Jadon looked at the guests. "Is this why none of the other mages are here?"

Cathal nodded. "Caladynn assigned dozens to guard Koll, but we know swords aren't always effective against sorcery. Ryen and Darcus are flying over the city and neighboring forests to alert us if they spot anything suspicious."

"Do you really think there's a real danger?" Runa asked. "We dragged Koll across the wilderness for weeks without any trouble."

"Yes," Cathal confirmed. "My spy in Urgonclaw sent a message that Xabral was seen in Kra'zum and was even received by Zhelon Thor himself."

"Since when did you get spies?" Runa asked, confused.

"They worked for Ramirez; the former archon whom Koll had murdered. Since we've returned to Thill, they've been sending their secret messages to me here at the Sorcerer House. That's why Myrsalian's poor calling crystal became so damaged."

"I knew that blasted snake would be trouble," Belwyn added. "Xabral will have recruited Koll's followers. Those morons see Koll as a prophet for the dark trinity. They will die for him. They will kill for him. So, we can't take any chances. If Koll escapes, there'll be several hells to pay. He won't just walk away. Koll will come after all of us."

Cathal took Runa by the shoulders, his voice hardened with worry. "Be careful. Your actions ruined Koll's plans. He's vindictive. He's obsessed with Panthara too, which adds to the trouble pot."

"Panthara is helpless," Runa agreed.

"I'll keep watch over Runa and the others," Jadon promised.

"And I'll be there to supervise you," Belwyn added. "With Cathal watching Koll at the prison, I'll be at the house guarding you and Furball."

Cathal pressed a finger to his lips and the invisible shield she detected vanished.

Mellypip's worry did not vanish. Runa sensed his discomfort and stroked his fur.

Don't fret, Melly. I can defend myself. And Jadon will protect us. Act normal.

It's hard to act normal when evil is stalking you, Mellypip replied.

CHAPTER NINE

Runa carried a cloth-wrapped plate up the stairs. "I'm going to take some dessert to Iona and Panthara. Don't you want to visit Iona?" Runa asked Opaline.

"Perhaps another time," Opaline replied carefully.

"Iona's been asking about you," Runa added pointedly.

Opaline hung her head. "I know. I'm a terrible person. I just can't deal with Panthara, even though she is a silent statue. I still want to throttle her. I can't help it. I'm going to change into something practical to help Mother. She wants me to learn about casting wards. It will keep me busy while I try not to think about, well, you know."

"Koll and Xabral?" Runa finished.

Opaline nodded quickly.

Runa ran up the stairs and stopped at Iona's room and after a moment's hesitation, knocked with her foot, since her hands were full.

"Come in," Iona's soft voice answered as the door magically opened.

Iona was combing Panthara's long black hair. She was unveiled, her pale beauty luminous in the fading light. The ancient customs of the Necromancers were mysterious and Runa burned with questions but refrained from intruding.

Runa carefully placed the plate on the table. "I brought desserts from the feast. I chose a variety, since I did not know what you liked."

Iona put the brush down and lifted the cloth, inspecting the delectable samples of cakes, drobba puffs, and tarts. "How wonderful. It all looks quite scrumptious. Thank you, Runa."

Resting on his perch, Amun nodded his beak in approval. "You were kind to think of us."

"Azmadu, come out and sample some treats Runa has brought us," Iona called.

The crill lizard poked his head out from under the bed. His black satin eye-patch was askew as usual. He sniffed the air and waddled out. He accepted a tidbit from Iona's hand. The Necromancer stroked his blue and green head. "There, now let's see if we can coax Panthara into trying some."

"Has she spoken at all?" Runa asked.

Iona shook her head. "Panthara is still a captive of her past I am afraid. I will take her home with me. I live in a cave nearby. It's a sacred space, painted with the ancient images of mystery. Perhaps there I can heal her soul wounds."

Confused, Runa shook her head. "Soul wounds?"

Iona smiled patiently and offered a piece of cake to Amun. "Her soul is wounded. Koll and her insane mother hurt her for years, but a Wraith Guardian touched her. You cannot glimpse the mysteries of the Eternals without being scarred."

"Will she ever heal?" Runa asked.

"I do not know," Iona said. "Though I sense there is something else you long to say."

"Koll dies tonight."

Runa glanced at Panthara, but there was no reaction, as though the words were nothing.

Iona nodded. "Then we must be very careful and watch over each other until the Otherworld has taken him."

~ * ~

Mellypip donned a blue dishtowel as a cloak and proudly guarded the house with his staff. Mellypip took his duty as familiar guardian seriously as he patrolled each room.

"How is the great ranger mage?" Sirah asked, passing him in the living room.

"The front door is secure and bolted," Mellypip replied. "All is well. Did you lay down lots of wards?"

"Oodles," Sirah assured him and went upstairs.

Mellypip decided to patrol the house again. Belwyn's warnings about Koll left him uneasy. The house seemed so vast and empty without the bustle of the sorcerers. Even the crystal chamber was still. The few here tonight were huddled away. Opaline and Taran were helping Sirah. Runa was with Iona and Panthara. Jadon was outside patrolling the grounds. He hoped Rono was not scared. The poor gryphon was quite delicate. He must check on him before bedtime, not that he would sleep tonight.

Mellypip ventured into the large kitchen and found Dabiro and Pointessa sitting on the large round table, playing chess. Low-lit lamps and a few hanging light crystals brightened the room with a soft golden glow. A cup of fragrant tea and a tempting plate of lemon cookies were by Pointessa, and a pewter mug of ale rested next to

Dabiro. The chess board was checkered in shiny brown and white, and the wooden pieces were polished and stained a walnut color, and carved to represent kings and queens, knights, and other odd things Mellypip found very confusing.

"What are you doing?" Mellypip asked as he leapt up on the table. "I thought you were going to the prison to guard Koll."

"Belwyn thought we should stay. With a house full of young innocents like you, Runa, and Opaline, both Cathal and Belwyn thought it prudent if a few of the familiars stayed here," Pointessa said. "Plus, Panthara is here."

Mellypip nodded, holding his staff closer. Koll was Panthara's teacher, and she betrayed him. He may try to hurt Panthara and anyone who stood in his way. Runa was uneasy but oddly protective about her half-sister, so that was another worry for Mellypip.

Pointessa offered Mellypip an iced lemon cookie, which he accepted with glee. He liked iced cookies, plus eating helped calm his nerves.

"Can I play?" Mellypip inquired, munching his treat, curious now about the game with pretty, wooden toys. Belwyn and Cathal often played chess, but it all seemed too slow to be any fun. Maybe chess could be more creative? He wondered if he could play ranger with them.

"We're playing a serious adult game, wampum." Dabiro grunted, pondering his next move.

"But can I play?" Mellypip asked again.

"No," Dabiro snapped, paw reaching for a knight.

Mellypip's long fluffy tail swished and knocked a piece over. The badger glared at him. Mellypip carefully returned the wooden figure to its proper square.

"Go away," Dabiro ordered.

"Oh, leave Melly alone, grumpy puss," Pointessa warned. "You're so irritable."

"Why is he staring at the board?" Mellypip asked. "His eyes look like they're going to pop out of his head."

"Bugger off," Dabiro said, paw still poised to move his piece.

"He thinks he's being clever," Pointessa answered. "If Dabiro can't decide on his next move the sheer tedium will make me descend into such a wretched boredom no spell would be able to save me from it." She glared at Dabiro. "Just choose already!"

"Stop pressuring me!" Dabiro growled, still hunched over the board, paw still poised over the same piece.

"I thought games made you relax," Mellypip commented.

Dabiro grunted and glared at Mellypip. "Maybe you could check the house for stray dust bunnies, if you're brave enough!"

"What do you mean dust bunnies? Why would I need bravery for that?" Mellypip asked. "And what are dust bunnies?"

"Dust bunnies...surely you've heard about them." Dabiro's voice was ominous as he leaned closer. "Didn't Belwyn teach you? Warn you? Shame. It's a curse of magic! Very tragic."

"You're going to hell," Pointessa warned.

"No, Belwyn didn't tell me about the dust bunnies," Mellypip replied.

Dabiro looked around conspiratorially and then whispered, "Dust bunnies come to life when exposed to stray magical residue, you know. This is a house of magic, so the chances are very strong they will spring to life and infest the whole place. If not completely swept away and trapped in a special jar, they can take over everything; suck the magic out of everyone! Oh no! Look over there in that corner—"

Mellypip's head snapped around to look in the corner, unaware a spark of magic from Dabiro's paws sprinkled bits of dust and lint until they formed into several bouncing bunny shapes. He winced, having fallen for one of Dabiro's tricks. The dust bunnies sparkled and began to dance around and made funny little sounds as they hopped out of the room.

"Better find a broom and sweep, wampu," Dabiro advised, moving his knight at last. "Can't defeat those nasty dust bunnies any other way. If you don't stop them now, they will take over the whole house and suck out all the magic! Then we will be bereft of our gifts! Go now! Save us!"

"Belwyn warned me about you," Mellypip replied dryly, clutching his staff. "You did the same thing to Sanura when she was a kitten. I am not a newborn kit, you know. I have experienced life and adventure despite my youth."

"The little furball is not so gullible," Pointessa giggled.

Still, Dabiro's spark of magic caused a stampede of ephemeral dust bunnies running amok. "I guess I can clean up your magical mess," Mellypip said, secretly happy to have a moment's respite from thinking about Koll. He grabbed a tiny hand broom that rested on the bottom shelf of a pantry.

"Hell," Pointessa shouted. "You're going to the deepest fire pits, badger, and my prayers won't save you!"

"Bah! It'll keep fluffy occupied," Dabiro gruffly replied. "He's been walking around the house for the last two hours with that damned towel knotted like a cape and waving his staff."

Pointessa moved her piece to take his in triumph. "Checkmate!" she shouted.

"Damn," Dabiro groaned.

Mellypip chased after the dust bunnies, trying to sweep them up, but they kept hopping out of his reach. At least this was fun. He was also working up an appetite and hoped there were more lemon cookies.

Mellypip sensed something dark as he played his game, in the far corner of the dining room. His fur bristled and a faint sparkle in his peripheral vision alerted him, and he quickly turned to see. Nothing was there. Still, a cold shiver traveled down his spine. He approached closer, wishing he had his trusty staff and not a stupid broom. Suddenly, an ominous pair of dark eyes rose before him and mingled with the dancing dust bunnies.

He dropped his broom and stepped back from black floating eyes burning with wicked magic. Even the dust bunnies ran away screaming. The eyes glided toward him, menacing.

Mellypip cried out, "Belwyn! Pointessa! Runa! Help! Intruders! Creepy eyes dancing are coming at me now!"

~ * ~

Xabral slithered off the shoulders of the Rashurkeen warrior, impatient to begin. Dozens of Rashurkeen assassins waited in shadows, ready to follow his command.

Xabral surveyed the warriors with a cold stare. "The forces guarding Koll are heavy and well placed. Caladynn is not a village idiot. Security will be tight. Do not be afraid of magic fortifications. I will take care of that. You know what to do."

Swathed in black robes, his black raven familiar perched on his shoulder, the sorcerer Dagon stepped forward with a box in his hand, carved from shimmering ebonite, the lid decorated with large rubies.

"Dagon, are the eyes still watching in the Sorcerer House?" Xabral asked.

"Yes," Dagon answered. "I cast the enchantment myself. Using the eyes has delivered useful information. We discovered Koll's execution time tonight. We must act now."

Xabral nodded, his black and red scales glistening in the half-light. "Yes, they are so eager to execute my sorcerer. Infidels. They will suffer for their offense to the Dark Trinity when Obsydia is freed. I will gladly suffer this pain to free Koll."

Dagon's raven, Gethen, expressed concern. "What of the sorcerers? They will all be there waiting. Koll will be guarded by sword and magic."

"Bloodstone magic will be with us. It is vital to Koll's rescue. Dagon and I have chosen powerful weapons from Koll's personal collection of mystical dark relics, rare but still potent. Not even all the sorcerers in Aybarr can stand against what I have chosen. Not even Cathal. We will kill anyone who stands in my way to Koll. Time is short so we must move fast. If you fail and Koll dies, all of you will follow him to the Otherworld. Now we must begin the spell."

Dagon placed the ebonite box before Xabral. "Are you sure? This will be painful beyond imagining. It's not like shapeshifting. It is old diabolism from the Bloodstone Age."

"Good. Dark magic is what I need. I can endure the pain for Koll, if it is his best chance for escape—and for our revenge," Xabral replied coldly. "Now open the box."

CHAPTER TEN

Koll was conducted into the execution chamber by Captain Vasya of the Royal Guard, a mountain of a man with a grim face. Koll slowly marched to his death, bound by heavy chains, barefoot, stripped except for a loin cloth. The manacles around his wrists forged from sorcerer bane negated any sorcerous resistance. He appeared harmless. Cathal knew better. The damage that sinister sorcerer could wreak if he escaped would be devastating.

Koll remained the wellspring of Cathal's grief since they crossed paths a scant fifteen years ago, and now he would finally die. Cathal did not feel pity or even justice from this fact, only a strange and bitter relief. Because of Koll, his wife Yllia and daughter Rualla were murdered, Rualla's familiar Striker perished saving Runa, and even Ashur, whom Cathal blamed for many years for their deaths and the Sorcerer War, was Koll's first victim. In truth he had been dead long before they realized because a demon had possessed his body. All this tragedy because Koll sought the lost tomb of Obsydia.

Caliste took his hand and squeezed it. The presence of his adopted daughter was a balm he was grateful for.

Koll's executioner waited near the platform in the center of the room. The man's face was fully masked, a common practice for his grim occupation. His young assistant, an adolescent boy who carried his sword, wore a plain mask that covered the upper part of his face. A thick layer of straw was strewn around the executioner's platform designed specifically for Koll. The straw was there to absorb the blood.

"How did they remove the bane lock from Koll's neck?" Caliste whispered.

Cathal quietly leaned in. "Carefully. Even without magic, Koll is deadly. We made sure the manacles forged with bane were on his wrists before the guards removed his neck lock. It was necessary. The executioner would have been hindered by it."

Sanura shifted into her panther form and sat protectively at Caliste's feet. "Now he can strike off Koll's head with ease. Good. Because until Koll is dead, I'll never be able to relax."

"Are you worried, my sweet?" Caliste whispered, stroking her copper-colored fur. "The room is lined with warriors and our sorcerer friends for protection."

Sanura's deep purr was more like a growl. "I'm wary, that's all."

"Now you sound like Belwyn," Cathal remarked.

"Belwyn must be vexed he's not here to witness this," Sanura said.

"You have no idea," Cathal said with a sigh.

Cathal scanned the large room. A force of armed men lined the walls, including his sorcerer friends in disguise as guards. Handpicked by Caladynn, the space seemed a logical choice, located in the lower level of the palace with no windows and only one door. One exit could be detrimental as well as secure, but nothing was absolute where Koll was concerned.

King Caladynn entered, followed by his younger brother, Morydonn. Caladynn took his place next to Cathal and nodded his head in greeting. Morydonn ignored everyone and stood next to his brother with his arms crossed.

"I wish you would take the advice of a wise old sorcerer and stay away," Cathal whispered to Caladynn.

"You fuss like an old woman, Cathal. I appreciate your concern, but my people need to know I witnessed the death of this monster," Caladynn replied. "Besides, I wouldn't miss this for the world."

Morydonn remarked openly. "Perhaps you secretly long for a fellow sorcerer to escape justice."

Cathal ignored the blunt insult and bit his tongue, though a few of Belwyn's barbed insults popped into his head.

Caladynn coldly glared at his brother. "Your prejudice is not acceptable in my presence, brother." The king turned away from Morydonn and stepped forward. "Proceed with the execution."

Captain Vasya signaled, and four men lifted Koll and strapped him to the platform.

The air crisped with magical energy; a sinister element Cathal recognized. Sorcery had its own energy mark depending on the caster, but bloodstone magic, *diabolism*, was distinctive. Koll's magic was bound and useless, so where the hell was it coming from? His eyes darted around the room as he gripped his staff, his heart racing.

"I sense magic," Cathal gasped, raising his staff. "Damn it. It's the boy. I feel it vibrating off him. Stop the boy now! Get him away from the prisoner!"

A soldier seized the boy and dragged him away from Koll. Caladynn drew his sword, as did every soldier in the room.

"But he's my apprentice!" the executioner protested.

The boy grinned maliciously. "Your apprentice was delicious."

"Who is this, Cathal?" Eberr asked, removing his helmet.

"It's Xabral!" Cathal shouted. "Cuff him with sorcerer bane now!"

"But Xabral is a scorpion snake," Morydonn gasped.

"Just do as Cathal says," Caladynn boomed. "Bind that despicable familiar, no matter what shape its wearing."

Human Xabral's eyes glittered like black diamonds when they ripped away the cloth mask. The unnatural glow had little to do with the shift in Xabral's human shape. Cathal glanced at the floor and saw a piece of sorcerer bane lying in the straw.

Cathal grimaced. "Clever snake."

Xabral spoke with the gravelly timbre of his true voice, so odd in the face of youth. "Sorcerer bane has its uses. I was already transformed into a human, so the stone didn't unravel my shapeshift. It did conceal my bag of sorcerous tricks." A purple crystal flared in human Xabral's palm, and its burst of magic struck Vasya and several others who surrounded Xabral, but none were affected by the mystical assault. The magic simply evaporated when it touched them. Xabral frowned.

"Sorcerer bane does indeed have its uses," Cathal remarked dryly. "We knew this also."

Vasya chuckled as he lifted a leather cord from around his neck with a tiny ball of sorcerer bane at the end.

"We're all wearing it," Cathal said. "Except for me, to detect magic."

Two soldiers bent back Xabral's arms as Vasya quickly approached him with a ring of sorcerer bane. Xabral threw off his captors with an astounding display of strength. He fled to his sorcerer, Koll, and hurled a vial to the floor that shattered and released a cloud of black mist that filled the chamber in an instant. The noxious fumes choked everyone as they collapsed to the floor, choking on the fetid air.

Eyes and lungs burning, Cathal realized Xabral's toxic mist was a product of simple science, for the guards and his friends who wore sorcerer bane suffered from the gas, even Koll, who lay choking on the fumes.

"Cathal, look!" Caliste cried, holding on to Sanura. "The floor!"

Despite his agony, his gaze detected insects swarming around the execution platform. Cathal sensed the creatures were not normal bugs. Sorcerous energy emanated from them. He managed to throw a few bursts of fire and burn some of them. Coughing and blinded by the vapors, Cathal focused and produced a spell that evaporated the toxic fumes.

Cathal summoned a sword dropped by a fallen soldier to his grip. Koll was still strapped to the platform. Good. If he must be the executioner, so be it. He rushed toward Koll. Two ravens evolved from the bugs swarming in the spongy straw. One raven shapeshifted into a black-robed sorcerer, brandishing an ebony staff crowned with a raven's head. The other raven landed on the sorcerer's shoulder.

The strange sorcerer blocked Cathal's path and they crossed staves, bright flashes of magic emanating from their staves as they fought.

Xabral ripped open a pouch and scattered a black glittering powder that formed a dome to shield Koll. "Hurry Dagon!" Xabral shouted. "I'm running out of time!"

Cathal's grey eyes burned with disgust. "Dagon!" He knew that name. A war criminal who served Koll but had eluded capture since the Sorcerer War.

Dagon extended his staff, but instead of assaulting Cathal or the others, he aimed his sorcery at the swarm of bugs at his feet, a glowing red magic swept the floor, causing the damned bugs to shapeshift into Rashurkeen assassins. A lot of them.

"Oh, hell," Cathal groaned.

For a breathless heartbeat, the air was mute as the two forces faced each other. The glint of Thill and Rashurkeen blades gleamed in the dim light of the crowded chamber.

Caladynn shouted a war cry, charging the assassins.

Morydonn spat, stepping away from his brother and drawing a long dirk to fight an assassin.

Xabral glanced up at the raven on Dagon's shoulders. "Gethen, make sure your sorcerer keeps the wall strong until we leave."

The guards quickly rallied with their king. Eberr ripped off the amulet of sorcerer bane and tossed it aside, leading the other sorcerers against the Rashurkeen alongside the Thill warriors. Magic was essential now. Rashurkeen warriors were not immune to the blasts of sorcery or the blades of the guards. Jiana fought fiercely, dagger in one hand, magic pouring from the other. Myrsalian and Eberr took down several with magic before the invaders could strike. Sleep spells were very useful. Ulan and Riva flanked the king, wielding their staves.

Sanura was the only familiar present. She roared and her claws raked the assassins with savage force. A Rashurkeen distracted Sanura, stabbing his curved blade at Caliste, who barely evaded the strike, but the assassin was foolish despite his skill as a death dealer. Sanura in her panther state was over two hundred pounds of springy muscle. Sanura killed the assassin with swift precision.

Cathal summoned a shield and a flood of golden magic poured from Cathal's hand, beating against the shadowed dome as a Rashurkeen foolishly tried to attack his magical barrier. When he swung his sword, the energy recoiled and threw the assassin back. Cathal ignored him, focusing on destroying the dome protecting Koll and Xabral.

The Rashurkeen's vast numbers dwindled quickly against the onslaught, but Cathal knew they were no more than a brief distraction from Xabral's plans. It was hard to say how many had been slain or captured. Dozens? It was hard to tell from the carnage. Cathal knew they were fodder. A sacrifice for Koll. Nothing more. What Cathal wanted was behind that damn shield.

Seizures wracked Xabral's body and bulging black veins distorted his face. Xabral ripped at his clothes, exposing a crimson crystal embedded in Xabral's chest. Cathal knew what that damn snake was doing now. Cathal stopped firing at the dome and stepped back. When the others saw Cathal do this, they too backed away. Even the executioner cowered against the wall.

"What is that?" Liat gasped.

"A *Dark* gift," Xabral said. Black and red tendrils sprouted throughout Xabral's human form, darkening, and twisting. Xabral opened his mouth and cried out, the shrieks neither human nor snake.

"That's a hellstone in his chest!" Cathal spun around to the king. "Caladynn, get your men out of here. Now!"

Caladynn shook his head. "But Koll lives!"

Cathal gripped Caladynn's arm. "My friend, let sorcerers deal with sorcerers. I know what Xabral's becoming, and you don't want your men anywhere near it!"

"I've never retreated from battle, Cathal. If you stay so, do I," Caladynn replied stubbornly. "But I give full permission if anyone wants to leave."

No one left.

Caladynn stubbornly remained in the room, bloodstained sword in one hand. His brother Morydonn stood behind him, fear etched on his face.

"Fortify the shield," Cathal ordered.

"What!" Caliste gasped. "I thought we wanted to eliminate it?"

"Xabral is turning into a demon of some sort. I don't know what kind. We'll want to keep that shield up. It keeps them in as well as us out. If Xabral is confined, so is Koll."

Caliste glanced at her familiar. "Sanura, spread the word to the others, but keep it quiet. We don't want the enemy to suspect."

Cathal unleashed magic, his hands a stream of blue-grey beams that covered the shadowed dome with light. He needed all of his powers to combat what was coming and his staff was almost drained. The sorcerers joined him—Caliste, Liat, Myrsalian, Ulan, Jiana, Riva, and Eberr aligned their staves together at the shadow dome that protected Koll and his familiar.

The hellstone burned like a wicked star in Xabral's chest until it exploded with a burst of blinding light within the dome, swelling the mystical shield with potent force.

Xabral transformed in a haze of burning diabolistic power. His former human body, a product of shapeshifting, fell away, briefly exposing the snake's red and black scales beneath the illusion until the transformation took hold. He shifted and expanded to at least eight feet tall, shredding his clothes. No longer human or scorpion snake, but an abomination of the dark otherworld from bloodstone magic. Xabral's skin altered to leathery grey and sprouted long bird-like legs, muscular and strong, with feet sprouting three curved talons that scratched the floor. The body was misshapen and bloated with a narrow chest cavity. Two gangly arms with skeletal hands emerged and rested on the floor, and his neck elongated by at least three feet. A withered mask of a face framed by two drooping black horns offset blazing red eyes set deep into its malformed skull. Its vertical mouth opened, rimmed with long, sharp teeth and a narrow forked black tongue darted from its mouth.

Sorcerer and soldier alike gasped in terror at Xabral's demonic transformation.

"Keep adding the magic," Cathal warned, forcing them to focus on the task instead of the terror.

Dagon sliced away the leather straps that bound Koll to the table. He produced a ring of keys and unlocked the manacles around his hands and ankles. He could not remove the sorcerer bane from wrists. "Forgive me, Master. I can't undo the lock!"

Gethen shouted, "Never mind that! Koll must flee now."

"It does not matter," Koll replied, rising from his death bed and crawling to the back of the transformed Xabral. "Kill them for me, Dagon. Drop the shield."

Dagon gazed at Koll with devotion and released his shadow shield.

A dome had been formed above Dagon's shadow shield of light magic. Forged by the sorcerers to keep Koll and Xabral trapped; it remained strong.

"It's working!" Liat cried.

"Keep weaving the magic," Cathal warned, rays of grey-blue magic weaving with the others in a myriad of colors, trapping the demon and his master.

Xabral rammed against the dome, unable to shatter the sorcerous barrier Cathal and his allies wove that bound them within. Xabral thundered in fury. Dagon began throwing magic at the dome to break it down, but the shield was strong.

"Stand aside," Koll whispered to Dagon.

Dagon obeyed. Demon-Xabral seemed to glow dark as black flame dripped from his jaws. Then the demon inhaled, the narrow chest expanding vastly. Xabral exhaled a mystical black flame that dissolved parts of the shield. Cathal backed away, pushing everyone back.

"Get everyone away from the line of fire!" Cathal shouted. "Everyone down! Its breath is deadly demon fire."

Demon-Xabral opened his long vertical maw, the razor teeth bright as it exhaled a flow of black flame that burned away the shield. A guard in the crossfire was burned to ashes before their eyes.

Xabral roared, shaking the room and rushed toward the barred door, Koll clinging to his back. Caladynn scooped a fallen spear into his hand and hurled, striking Xabral's side. Xabral roared in pain but fled on swift feet. The men backed away from the demon's breath as he charged through solid wood, shattering the doorframe and wall. Most of the sorcerers and soldiers pursued Xabral and Koll.

Cathal knew it was a hopeless pursuit.

Dagon attacked Caliste and Sanura, whose backs were turned in the chaos as the others pursued Xabral and Koll. Dagon's black beam hurled Caliste and Sanura across the room. They slammed against the wall and fell to the floor. Dagon's dark magic had a burnt, fusty odor as he conjured a ball of burning blackness in his hand.

Cathal rushed to Caliste's side. Anger fueled his strength as he faced Dagon. He remained in front of Caliste and Sanura's unconscious bodies.

Dagon aimed his dark magic at Cathal. "Koll will praise me for killing you."

Dagon's raven flew above his sorcerer, cawing loudly. A mute spell quickly silenced the bird. Dagon's ball of darkness struck Cathal's chest, but nothing happened. Dagon raged. Cathal realized he was standing on an amulet of sorcerer bane and smiled.

Cathal moved and retaliated with a force of fiery sorcery that knocked Dagon off his feet onto a pile of dead Rashurkeen warriors.

Infuriated, Dagon attempted to turn his sorcery on the nearest victim, Caladynn. He must have lost his amulet of bane in the battle, and it scraped his arm. Morydonn stepped away from his brother, though he was still protected. Dagon laughed and before Cathal could stop him, he threw another deadly bolt of magic that struck Eberr, who jumped in front of the king, taking the blast. Eberr fell to his knees, but Caladynn gripped his shoulders to soften his fall.

Captain Vasya sprang at Dagon from the side, spry for such a big man. Dagon stumbled back and dropped his staff. The second he did that, Cathal scooped it up magically. Dagon attempted sorcery on Vasya, a useless gesture since Vasya still wore his amulet. Vasya grabbed Dagon's arm, pushing it high in the air with one hand and twisting it. Dagon screamed. The sorcery scorched the ceiling, charring the stone, but left Vasya unharmed.

Vasya plunged his sword into Dagon's body, terminating his wicked conjuring. Blood gushed from Dagon's chest as he plummeted to the floor. The raven flew to his dead master, screeching until an irritated Caladynn silenced it with a blow of his sword. A flurry of bloody black feathers hovered in the air.

Cathal's rage that Koll escaped threatened to overwhelm him but worry for Caliste and Sanura reclaimed his reason. He collapsed by their still bodies, trying to revive them. Caliste and Sanura lay in spectral sleep.

"Do they live, Cathal?" Caladynn asked gently.

Cathal nodded, concerned. "They still breathe, but dark magic has deeply injured them. We need more than a physician. We need Raghnall. How is Eberr?"

"Dead," Caladynn said softly.

CHAPTER ELEVEN

"Help!" Mellypip shouted. The spectral eyes glided toward him with menace, scattering the shimmering dust bunnies. Mellypip tried to beat the eyes back, but his staff passed through the things like air. How he wished his staff was weaponized with sorcery!

Belwyn swooped down in front of him in a flurry of grey and white feathers. "Stay behind me, Furball."

"It's not a dust bunny," Mellypip warned. "It smells evil and is probably carnivorous."

Belwyn studied the floating orbs. "I doubt if it will eat you. But I sense dark sorcery here. Damn."

Everyone dashed to help and were all soon quickly confronted with the unsettling dark drifting eyes hovering above the floor. Runa picked him up. Safe and warm in her arms, he allowed a comforting moment of security as he rested, though he could not look away from the creepy eyes.

"Damn, that's nasty," Dabiro murmured. "Hey, I didn't do that you know."

"Never said that you did," Belwyn remarked coolly.

The eyes darted around them, a swift trail of shadowy tendrils. Runa cast a ball of light and entrapped the aberration.

Arial's ears folded back. "What the blazes is that thing?"

Belwyn did not flinch. "Trouble. Coincidence with Koll's appointment with the executioner tonight—I think not!"

Pointessa's thorny back rose dangerously. "If that thing penetrated our magical wards protecting the house, who knows what it's relayed to the enemy."

Arial growled. "Or what else is lurking."

"Have you heard from Cathal yet? Is Koll dead?" Sirah asked.

Belwyn shook his beak. "Not a word. Search the grounds and the house. We stay in pairs. I'll try to contact Cathal."

"We should destroy it," Opaline stated shakily. "Who knows what its purpose is."

"Agreed. This evil must go," Jadon replied and a wave of blue-white drusai magic flowed from his hands, incinerating the sorcerous eyes.

Mellypip felt satisfaction in watching them vaporize. "I can help search for stuff."

"No. Stay with Runa." Belwyn's head swiveled toward Dabiro. "You were supposed to be watching him."

"It's not my fault nasty spy eyes infested the house!" Dabiro protested.

Mellypip refused to give in. "But I'm the one who discovered the sneaky eyes."

"And you begged for rescue like a newborn kit," Dabiro snorted.

"That's beside the point," Mellypip said. "And I'm not a baby."

Runa firmly tucked Mellypip under her arm. "You stay with me."

"But I found the spying eyes!" Mellypip succumbed to being coddled but sulked about it. He was miffed because it was *his* guard duty as ranger-mage which exposed the revolting thing. They searched the house inside while the *adult* sorcerers and familiars checked outside. Everything appeared normal inside. Mellypip squirmed, but Runa kept a firm hold.

When Runa peered into Iona's room, he glimpsed Panthara lying abed. Iona read next to her, with Amun perched on the back of her chair and Azmadu snoring at Panthara's feet.

They went downstairs and through the window Mellypip noticed Rono wandering in the backyard, head down, looking confused and frightened. Everyone was so busy they ignored him.

"Please! Let me check on Rono," Mellypip begged Runa. "You know how scared he gets."

Runa relented and set him down. "Alright! Stop wiggling! Very well, go see about Rono, but promise me you'll be very careful and come right back. Tell Rono it's probably safer to stay in the stables until the other perytons return. Assure Rono we will protect him. You can even bring him a cookie. There are some molasses cookies in the jar."

Mellypip nodded eagerly and made a dash for the kitchen first, taking a cookie from the giant cookie crock. He paused, and then decided to take two, for sharing, as they smelled quite yummy. He darted through the flap in the kitchen door with two large cookies clenched in his mouth. Rono's brown eyes lit up when he saw Mellypip and the gryphon rushed over to his little friend.

Mellypip removed the sweet from his mouth and held it up. "I brought you a cookie. You looked upset. What's wrong?"

"I'm afraid to be alone," Rono confessed, chewing his cookie. "I sense something bad. No one will tell me anything."

Rono lowered his head so Mellypip could crawl up to rest on top between his long-tufted ears. "It's alright, Rono. I'll keep you safe. I'm a brave ranger mage and you're my valiant flying gryphon. Nothing bad will happen. Runa says the other perytons will be back soon. We'll play tomorrow after a good night's sleep. It will be better when the sun is out."

Rono sighed. "I do love the sun. I doubt if I will sleep. It's lonely without the other perytons." The gryphon lifted his head, as though searching for something. "The darkness is alive. I feel its evil."

Mellypip was confused by his words, but his friend always had difficulty with his vocabulary. A great grey mountain owl swooped down, and Mellypip was sure Belwyn was going to chastise him for being outside; until he noticed the owl looked slightly different than Belwyn. He realized why when the owl shimmered into Cathal.

Before Mellypip could protest, Grandpa Cathal scooped him up. "We're going inside now, Melly. Rono, go to the stables. Do not be afraid, but we should remain out of sight."

Fear knotted Mellypip's belly, but he kept a brave face for his friend. "It's alright, Rono. Go to the stable. I'll ask one of the others to check on you later. We can play tomorrow."

Rono obeyed, but Mellypip worried about his friend. "What's wrong, Grandpa Cathal?" he whispered when Rono was out of sight.

"Everything I'm afraid, Melly. I need you to be strong and brave. Can you do that?"

Mellypip nodded vigorously, though he felt less brave by the moment. He entered a house of tearful mourning now. Several people were weeping. Runa had tears in her eyes when she took him from Cathal. The sorcerers who had gone with Cathal had returned with him, but Mellypip noted not all of the mages were there. They were disheveled and bloodstained. Eberr was missing, as was Caliste, Ulan, and Sanura. They all had a defeated look. Raghnall came down the stairs carrying his medicine bag, followed by Baldur.

He tugged at Runa's braid. "What's happened?"

"Koll escaped. Caliste and Sanura were injured," Runa explained softly. "Raghnall is going to the palace to help them. But, Eberr is dead. This is so terrible."

Caliste and Sanura hurt! And Eberr dead! Koll did this! Mellypip had not known Eberr long, but he was jolly fellow who cooked wonderful meals and gave him lots of treats. Pointessa was his bonded familiar! He could not imagine her loss! Unable to absorb it all, he sucked his paw, like he did as a baby.

"Caliste and Sanura won't die too—will they?" Mellypip mumbled.

"Of course not," Runa assured him, though her expression was troubled.

Mellypip hung his head. "Pointessa's lost her sorcerer forever."

"We must be strong for her," Runa whispered.

Belwyn's voice was grim. "Sirah and Dabiro are with her now. We take care of our own."

Opaline quietly made herself useful, bringing pots of hot tea and sandwiches into the dining room. "Do you think I should sit with them? Poor Pointessa needs her friends now more than ever."

Taran shook his head. "Not now. I think its best we leave them alone."

"Where's MacTabbish?" Opaline asked.

Taran sat down, putting his head in his hands. "He's with Iona, helping watch over Panthara."

Opaline passed him a cup of tea, which he absently took. "How did this happen?"

"The truth would give you nightmares," Cathal said. "Suffice it to say dark magic and assassins were involved.

Jiana shivered, holding Jasper tight in her arms. "Koll was all set for execution. We prepared for every contingency."

Liat looked grim. "Until Koll's allies showed up. What is a hell-stone anyway?"

Belwyn blinked. "It's from the bloodstone era. It temporarily transforms the victim into a demon. Nasty piece of diabolistic sorcery." He spun around to Cathal. "You never mentioned they had a hellstone?"

Cathal dropped his head into his hands. "I was trying to forget. Xabral used it. He became a demon, but that was only half the battle."

"I hope he's prepared for the price," Belwyn remarked. "Hell-stones leave a mark on their users. I hope he bloody suffers for it."

Cathal looked up, his anger and sorrow etched on his face. "Eberr is dead. He died protecting King Caladynn. He was very brave, but sadly, his bravery will be of little comfort to Pointessa."

"What about Caliste and Sanura?" Runa asked.

"Ulan remained at the palace to look after Caliste and Sanura until Raghnall arrives."

"We must find Darcus and Ryen," Jadon offered. "They should

be here now. They need to know Koll escaped. I'll ride out and search for them."

"Very good," Cathal agreed. "Be careful. I do not want to lose anyone else this night."

Jadon turned to go. Mellypip sensed Runa's fear and conflict at watching him leave. He wished in turn Jadon would tell Runa his feelings and give her the ring.

Runa, quick! Tell him goodbye!

But, Grandfather is watching.

Don't argue. He's almost out the door! Do I have to thump you?

"Jadon, wait!" Runa shouted and grabbed Jadon's arm, but words abandoned her when he looked at her. She bit her lip, feeling both mute and stupid. Jadon gently kissed her softly on the lips and smiled.

"Don't you dare die," Runa ordered.

"I promise," he grinned.

After Jadon left, Belwyn harrumphed loudly. "Cathal and I have enough to worry about without you kissing boys."

Runa stroked Belwyn on the beak. "I think you can handle such a mild crisis. Right now, I must take care of Caliste and Sanura."

"You will, but not tonight," Belwyn insisted. "We sent Raghnall and Baldur there ahead of us. Raghnall is an expert mystical healer. He will alert us of any changes. Don't fret. Caliste and Sanura are in the best hands."

Cathal agreed with Belwyn. "He's right. It'll be safer tomorrow. Koll has no intention of returning to the palace, but I do not want you leaving the house until morning."

"Wouldn't Koll just flee?" Runa asked. "He's a wanted man."

Cathal shook his head. "Xabral used a lot of firepower in his escape, a large amount of dark magic, as did the sorcerer Dagon he brought along. Dagon and his familiar died in the battle. A very tiny victory. Koll's still wearing manacles of sorcerer bane, which will prohibit his using magic for now and will slow his escape."

Grim, Belwyn was not so hopeful. "Until Koll gets them removed. Xabral planned for everything. I think the snake would remember to bring a locksmith since he knows magic will not remove those manacles. Sorcerer bane is immune to magic."

Cathal began charging his staff with spells. "And then there's Xabral. Despite the power of the hellstone, its effects are devastating. Xabral will be weak and vulnerable, as Koll may be. But we have no idea if any other sorcerers or assassins are waiting to carry them away. King Caladynn is sending every solider available out to hunt him down." Cathal turned to Runa and Mellypip. You two stay inside the house and do what I tell you. The rest of us will fortify the defenses. If Koll is going to strike against me or any of us, it will be tonight."

~ * ~

Rono was afraid. He wished he had more courage like Mellypip. Despite hours of peaceful night, he sensed something dark in the air. The other sorcerers had taken turns around the grounds, but this was different. You could not see it. He sensed it. Rono hated being alone. He usually had the company of the perytons, even the young ones, but they had been summoned to duty to patrol the skies. Darkleaf had kept him company, but Jadon took him to help find Ryen and Darcus. Darkleaf told him they would return soon. Rono put on a brave front, but it was so hard, especially when he sensed something wicked in the air. He longed for the comforting presence of Melly, who was always brave and fearless even if he was small.

Despite the commotion a few hours ago, the night was quiet in such a strange way. The sorcerers had cast new wards to protect the house. They took turns patrolling the property. Rono wished he were tiny, like Melly, so he could go inside. Gryphons are too big, so he waited in the stables like Cathal told him. Maybe the sorcerers could cast a spell on him and make him little. Then he could stay with Melly. He knew he was too big to go inside, but he wished they would ask. Rono longed for courage just as he longed for the sun's return to banish the shadows.

He left his stable and peeked outside. It was strange. The sky was bright with the twin moons and the stars shining, so why was it so dark in the garden? A rustling sound at the edge of the garden alerted Rono and he carefully peered out of the stable doors. Panthara walked right by him! He was relieved, but also worried. Panthara looked strange. She stumbled over a stone. Where was she going? Mellypip had told him Panthara was sick and could not be left alone. He knew Panthara needed help and decided to be brave.

He called to her, but Panthara was oblivious. He followed her, concerned and wary. He just hoped her annoying familiar was nowhere about. She walked beyond the garden, past the wards, past the rows of bushes bordering the backyard of the house. He intended to coax her back to the house. But, the spark of magic scented the air, so heavy a wave of dizziness made him sway. Sorcery was guiding her, he realized. He sniffed. *Dark sorcery.*

He worried for Panthara, who seemed so helpless. Terrified, he forced himself to be brave. He caught up with her a few paces beyond the bushes. A wispy golden rope of magic was tethered to Panthara's waist, pulling her forward. A cloaked figure in the distance was holding a crystal tome with the mystical rope drawing Panthara closer.

"Yes, come to me, Panthara," Xabral's voice hissed.

Rono froze. He did not see a scorpion snake, but remembered Xabral's voice and what it sounded like! Rono backed away and spread his wings for flight, intending to warn the others, but he could not move. The cloaked figure threw back the concealing hood. The face, which at first seemed to be a young boy, was gruesome and not fully human, with flaps of skin hanging like torn paper, exposing red and black scales beneath the human shell.

Xabral's snake eyes glared at him and he grinned maliciously. He pointed the crystal at him and magical ropes restrained Rono from fleeing. "You stay, gryphon. You will be useful at least."

Rono realized a golden rope of magic bound him, and though he struggled he could not break the mystical tie. His heart beat rapidly when a frightening figure emerged from the shadows.

It was Koll.

CHAPTER TWELVE

Koll took Panthara's hand and drew her close to him. He stroked her hair. She did not resist or even react, as though trapped in a waking sleep. Xabral scowled at Panthara.

Unable to fly or escape, Rono screamed out a warning.

Koll shook his head and pointed to the ground. "No one hears you, gryphon. We are outside the area of the wards and Xabral cleverly brought a silent crystal to mute any sounds around us. The wards the others planted are going off, but no one hears them—or you."

Terrified, Rono looked down at the crystal at Xabral's feet.

Xabral grinned, a macabre image with his damaged face. "We can speak in this small circle, even shout, and no one will hear."

Koll jerked his head back and Rono was forced to look into Koll's cold black eyes. "Listen to me now, gryphon. Surely even you know what a crystal tome is? Do you see this crystal in my hand?" Koll held a red crystal, like one would find in any sorcerer's collection.

Rono nodded. Mellypip often talked about all the crystal tomes Cathal had and how much Runa coveted them.

"This crystal tome has a different power. Its power is not silence, but death. This red crystal is the life of your precious friend, Mellypip. Yes, I know much about what went on in this house. My devoted familiar made sure special eyes watched everyone here. There are no secrets I do not know."

"Please let me go. I will not tell anyone. Please!"

"But why should I let you go when I have the power to bring you to heel. Let's call this crystal Mellypip's heart. I now hold power over his every heartbeat. If I shatter this stone, which I can do with a single word, your Mellypip dies."

Tears welled in Rono's eyes. "Please don't kill my friend."

"Then you must obey me," Koll warned. "You will be my ride to freedom. I will be your master now. Do not even try to alert the others, gryphon. Mellypip will die unless you obey only me."

Koll tugged at Panthara's arm, but she suddenly resisted. "Come, Panthara, we must leave now!"

Panthara stirred, blinked a few times, as though waking from a nap. When she looked and saw Koll standing before her, she did not rejoice but beat at him with her fists and kicked. "No! Let go of me! Go away"

Koll's stony voice chilled Rono. "You dare betray me!"

"Leave her!" Xabral pleaded. "I told you this was a waste! Panthara is not worthy of you. Your obsession with her will be our doom!"

Koll tried to pull her closer to him. "Panthara, you are not thinking clearly. Come with me now. I command you."

Panthara still resisted. "No! Let me go. I hate you Koll! I despise you! I'll never follow you again! Help!"

Koll mocked her. "Has your magic diminished as well? But I am touching you and wearing sorcerer bane. You can do nothing. Scream, Panthara. Go ahead. The silent crystal will not stop you. No one hears. You belong to me. Accept it."

"No!" she screamed.

Koll's grasp on Panthara loosened when he swayed and gripped Xabral's shoulder. Xabral cut the mystical ropes around her.

Fury contorted Koll's face. "Why did you do that?"

"Panthara is no longer one of us, Koll. She's a traitor. We must flee now! You're weak. Your discipline of mystic abstinence has taken its toll. It can no longer sustain you. We must go now!"

Panthara wrenched her hand free from Koll's grip. She pointed at the silent crystal, but nothing happened. She looked at her hands in confusion.

Koll's voice was bitter. "Have the wraith guardians taken your magic?"

Panthara's eyes flashed with anger. She bent down, snatched the silent crystal and hurled it across the path, breaking the circle of silence around them.

"You will pay for that one day," Koll threatened.

Panthara glared at Koll. "I have a lot to pay for. What? Your sorcerer bane stolen your magic?"

The mystical wards screamed as Panthara fled.

~ * ~

Jolted by the wards shrilly sounding off outside, Mellypip and Runa jumped off the couch; the ruckus disturbed Opaline who had begun to doze fitfully next to them.

"Stay," Cathal ordered, heading out the back door, with the other sorcerers and familiars following.

Azmadu, blue and green wings beating fast, flew down the stairs, Iona and Amun following. Iona's beautiful face was not masked by her usual veils, but it was furrowed with worry.

"My Panthara's gone, my Panthara's gone!" Azmadu shouted, frantic.

They heard Panthara's screaming outside and followed it.

Wait, Mellypip cried, chasing after her. *Cathal told us to stay.*

Not going to happen.

Mellypip rushed after her into the backyard. To his horror, he glimpsed Rono at the far end by the back road with Koll! The gryphon wailed as Koll held onto him with a stern hand. Someone was with Koll too. He knew it must be Xabral in his pseudo human shape when his hood dropped back, exposing a face of black and red scales mingled with bloody flaps of human skin.

Panthara was running toward them! She tripped and fell to the ground. Taran rushed to her aid and picked her up, carrying her inside.

Koll watched the others run toward him. He did not flee but watched them from a distance.

Koll's not running, he said to Runa through the bonding.

That worries me, she replied, taking Mellypip into her arms.

Xabral stepped forward and tossed a dark stone into the air. It traveled high, as though it were flying and then suspended in midair. The stone burst with black light and transformed into an orb of crimson flame that swiftly expanded into a colossal globe of fiery death. It tossed back the sorcerers with a blast of hot air.

The other sorcerers could not trespass the dark magic to reach Koll and Xabral, as it barred gentle Rono, who looked on helplessly.

"Oh hell," Felisia exclaimed, winging backwards as the rush of hot fire tossed her about.

"It is literally hell, my dear," Belwyn replied, diving to the tiny owl's aid and with broad strong wings, quickly guided her into the house for safety. "Stay!" he ordered and flew back to Cathal.

The globe of fire expanded before them to a frightening size.

"Everyone get back!" Cathal shouted.

Red magma dripped from the orb as it exploded in size above them. Cathal and the others summoned a shield across the whole property to prevent it from destroying them and their home. The size of the fireball increased, and its flames burned an apple tree to ashes and destroyed Sirah's garden.

Cathal's blue sorcerous waves encircled the globe of fire, forcing it back, further and further. But the globe expanded to a gargantuan size, exceeding the size of the house until it ripped apart Cathal's shell of light magic. A raging ball of fire descended, dripping red hot flames and spewing poisonous air that dripped and scorched the ground. The reek of diabolistic sorcery penetrated the shield, its odor acrid. The effects were caustic. Mellypip's eyes watered and burned. It was hard to breathe. He huddled close to Runa, gasping for air.

"Opaline, go away," Sirah cried. "You've no protection! You too, Runa! This sorcery is too strong."

Opaline jumped back when fragments of flame sizzled at her feet, but when it dropped on her arm, the flames merely slid off like beads of water.

"The flame is sorcerous and harmless to me as long as I wear my amulet!"

"But we can't protect the whole house with sorcerer bane," Taran shouted. He pushed his sister into the house. "Now go inside and stay out of danger."

Mellypip leapt out of Runa's grasp, desperate to rescue his friend Rono, but walls of flame on the other side of the blue shield stopped him from going any further.

Cathal dropped his staff and using his whole being; bright blue sorcery flooded from his whole body and circled the orb of deadly sorcerous flame that threatened them all.

Belwyn fluttered around Runa, driving her to a safer distance. The owl swooped down and picked Mellypip up by the scruff of his neck and dropped him in Runa's arms. The others retreated from Koll and joined Cathal and added to his shield of blue sorcery to push back the globe of flame.

"Rono is on the other side," Mellypip screamed. "Koll has him! He can't get away."

An explosion within Cathal's dome deafened Mellypip. Glaring red flames seeped through the blue shield Cathal had cast around it. Mellypip and Runa could barely breathe as the heat burned around them like hellfire. Forced to retreat into the house, they could only watch from the windows in panic as Cathal and the others tried to fight the dark sorcery. The inferno within the dome was searing and ripping through the barrier of Cathal's light magic that protected them.

The others were collapsing from the toxic sorcery, but Cathal and Belwyn remained strong.

"Mother!" Opaline cried when she wavered and fell to her knees. She rushed out, with Taran shouting as he followed, and picked up their mother and carried her inside.

To Mellypip's horror, Rono flew to the sky, carrying the cursed Koll and Xabral. Even through the chaos, Rono tearfully cried good-bye to him as he disappeared into the night. Mellypip pressed a paw to the hot windowpane, watching his friend fly away with the enemy.

"We need to extinguish that ball of fire," Belwyn croaked weakly now. "That's it. I'm getting the white. We need it. I don't care of it's the last one."

Belwyn flew into the house and within seconds flew out the window with a brilliant white crystal in his talons. He dropped it into Cathal's hand.

With a flurry of potent sorcery, the white crystal opened like a blossom; waves of bright magic exploded, dousing the fury of bloodstone sorcery at last. The pure sorcery swept the air clean and vanquished the orb.

Everyone collapsed with relief, breathing pure air.

"Rono's gone," Mellypip wept in a choked voice. "Koll stole him."

"Bah! That stupid gryphon would go with anyone," Dabiro grunted. He sniffed his fur. "Phew, but I stink."

"Take that back!" Mellypip demanded, wiping his red runny eyes with his paw.

"Or what?" Dabiro challenged.

Pointessa was suddenly between them. "Enough. We have more urgent business."

Dabiro hung his head and said no more.

"What happened with Koll?" Runa asked Panthara directly when they had gathered everyone inside. Quite sick from the effects, they could barely move, with swollen red eyes and coughing. Opaline and Taran brought cloths and cold water for their eyes. Liat and Myrsalian could only lie on the ground and moan, while Jiana applied cold wet compresses, though she could barely see herself. Riva sat against the wall, Buzzy holding a cloth to his face.

"When Raghnall returns, he can prepare some healing balm, but right now this will do," Sirah said.

"Where's he taking Rono?" Mellypip asked Panthara, hopeful.

Panthara allowed Iona to hold her. She spoke in shaky tones. "I don't know. I'm sorry. Koll and Xabral forced the poor gryphon!

Xabral was there, he was in a human shape, but hideous. I saw black and red scales through the slashed skin. He reeked of dark magic."

"You would know," Opaline remarked.

Panthara glanced up at Opaline. "Yes, I do know all too well. Koll came back for me. It's my fault. I know that."

"Why did Rono help Koll escape?" Dabiro grunted. "He's a big gryphon."

Panthara straightened and wiped her eyes. "Koll threatened to kill Mellypip if Rono did not help them escape! He had a crystal and said he had power of death or something. I think he was lying. No, I know he was lying. Koll is the sorcerer of lies. The poor gryphon cried and begged him not to hurt his friend."

"I told you," Mellypip muttered to Dabiro.

"We know Rono was a victim," Pointessa added softly.

"Did you even think to help Rono?" Opaline asked.

Panthara wiped her eyes. "I was just waking up. Everything was hazy. I was confused. I thought I was still in the cave in Mowad and the wraith guardians were coming at me. Then Koll kissed me and I woke up."

"He kissed you!" Opaline shouted.

"I hate him!" Panthara protested.

Opaline glowered at Panthara. "I blame you for this!"

"Opaline, don't," Sirah begged weakly, putting a cold cloth to her eyes.

"No," Opaline shouted. "She is not the victim here. We are! Koll would not have come here if it wasn't for you! It was bad enough he escaped the headsman's sword, but he came here for you. Eberr is dead because of him. Caliste and Sanura are lying critically injured. We all almost just died when he tossed burning lava magic on our house. Maybe you should have gone with him, Panthara!" Opaline said bitterly then turned and fled up the stairs.

"Go after her," Sirah whispered to her familiar, Arial. "She's very upset."

The white wolf nodded and followed Opaline.

Runa fetched fresh water for everyone. Cathal sipped slowly but was so weak he could not hold the glass. Dabiro hung his head and sat next to Pointessa. Jiana brought a bowl of cold fresh water.

"What was that horrible spell?" Runa asked.

"Bloodstone sorcery at its worst," Cathal answered weakly. "The ancients called it the Breath of Ahridum. It destroys utterly, and what it does not burn, it weakens and kills with poisonous gas. I told you two to stay inside."

"Sorry, Grandpa. I'm not an obedient girl," Runa sighed. "That white crystal Belwyn carried to you saved us all. It was more powerful than anything I've ever seen. I've seen that crystal glittering in your tome box since I was little."

Cathal smiled weakly. "That is why I always told you not to touch it. It is rare and a personal keepsake from when I was a boy. It's a relic from the Sapphire Age. A gift from my old master, Borel. We're lucky to have survived tonight."

"This is still bad," Belwyn said. "The store of dark magic Xabral brought speaks of a vast collection of bloodstone magic Koll must have in his possession. Think of what they threw at us tonight alone. I know Xabral would do anything to save his bloody sorcerer, but this speaks of dangers to all of us, and that Koll has other plans. The assassins and the use of his former allies is proof Zhelon Thor himself funded this escape. This is sinister power from the Bloodstone Age. Not even Koll has the power to create such powerful magic."

"Or maybe he has learned," Panthara said. "Koll possesses a large collection of bloodstone relics. Some of it is very potent sorcery he never allowed me to touch. He has scrolls and books from the bloodstone era too. He may have learned how to use the power. He had acolytes search for these ancient relics since I was a little girl, but he never told me much."

"You should all get some rest," Iona said. "We need to gather our strength, this war with Koll is not over."

Cathal nodded and forced himself to stand. "And war is what we must prepare for."

Iona looked at the familiars, nestled together in sorrow and pain. "We have all suffered this night. Pointessa and Eberr most of all. We can only pray Raghnall's healing can restore Caliste and Sonora." She looked up at Runa. "Help me take Panthara upstairs, please."

Runa nodded. "Of course."

Taran helped Panthara and Iona to their feet. "I'll take care of them, Runa. I need to check on Opaline anyway. Mellypip needs you right now."

"Opaline is so very angry," Runa whispered.

Taran shrugged. "Don't worry about my sister. Opaline just loves you and she gets overprotective of those she cares about, as do I."

Taran's gaze at Panthara was telling as he gently took her hand and guided her up the stairs. Panthara did not look at anyone as she passed, but Azmadu eagerly followed Panthara, jealous of anyone too close to her. Taran's familiar, MacTabbish, swatted him when Azmadu shoved against him on the stairs.

"What about poor Rono!" Mellypip cried.

"We will organize a search party," Belwyn said. "This is not over."

"We'll find him, Melly," Runa promised. "I'm so sorry. I promise we'll get him back! We'll search for him no matter how long it takes. We will never abandon him to a fate with Koll."

Mellypip looked up at Runa. "Rono told me darkness was alive, but I did not understand him."

"What are you talking about, Melly," Runa whispered.

"I think he knew something bad was close. I just thought he mixed up his words." Mellypip covered his eyes and wept. "Poor Rono is gone. Perhaps forever. Rono must be so scared!"

"It will be alright, Melly," Pointessa said softly.

"I'm sorry," Mellypip said his voice choking. "You lost Eberr forever."

"We have both suffered tragedy this night," Pointessa said. "It does not make your sorrow any less. We will be here with you, to help you. Like Runa said, we never abandon one of our own."

The other familiars quietly gathered around Mellypip and Pointessa. Jasper the tiger hare, Belwyn, Rosepetal the hedgehog, Buzzy the sloth, Felisia the elf owl, Pointessa, and even Dabiro, who huddled close to Pointessa. There was no more arguing, just wordless love that surrounded Mellypip as he cried. Runa cradled him in her arms, rocking him.

~ * ~

Koll and Xabral flew inside a dark mist, concealing them in their night flight. Most of the collection of Koll's magnificent bloodstone crystals Xabral brought had been depleted, but the use of this rare sorcery was worth the price. He had Koll back. Xabral even endured this flight for the sake of Koll. The idiot Gryphon continued to bawl like a baby, though he obediently flew them east toward the ancient land of Skarros.

Waves of pain gripped Xabral. The essence of the demon he had become for Koll had a high price. He had not been able to fully change back to his glorious true form as a scorpion snake. When

Koll had the sorcerer bane removed, he could help restore him. Dagon is dead now, so there is no one else. Koll suffered too, for he swayed and his body shook from the long denial of food and drink, which had finally taken their toll.

Xabral clung to his sorcerer, refusing to look down. "We should have used the bloodstone vengeance on them all, while they slept. The breath of Ahridum wasted! If you had not tried to summon Panthara, all of our enemies would be dead, including Cathal."

"It does not matter," Koll snapped. "She is dead to me now. One day Panthara will lie upon a sacrificial alter for her sins against me. I will personally cut out her heart."

Xabral was mollified by his words. "I will hand you the blade joyfully. We must get your manacles removed, so your magic may be restored to you. You must eat and regain your strength. We will forget about Panthara. Human females are worthless. *She* is worthless."

"That is true," Koll replied. "We have more important things to do."

"Yes," Xabral cried out, partly from agony and partly from the terror of flying so high in the sky. "We have a dark goddess to liberate. I know where she waits for us."

CHAPTER THIRTEEN

Belwyn was losing patience.

Raghnall examined Caliste and Sanura. He laid his hand on her forehead and concentrated. He rummaged through his damn medicine bag for crystal balls and herbs, while Baldur sat nearby, quietly observing his wizard. Caliste and Sanura looked so helpless. Sanura, back to her normal cat size, looked terribly frail and tiny. Her copper-colored fur was filthy and dried blood stained her muzzle and paws, the bleak remnants of her ferocious battle. Caliste's lovely silk gown was ripped and soiled, and dried blood stained her long braids. It angered Belwyn.

"Well?" Belwyn inquired impatiently, after what seemed an eternity.

"Give him a moment," Cathal begged.

"I don't like this," Belwyn grumbled.

"Have they been like this since the battle?" Raghnall asked.

Ulan looked like he was going to cry. An odd sight from such a big, powerful man. Belwyn hoped not. He could not deal with tears. Ulan looked exhausted and worry creased his face.

"They've been in this coma state since the battle," Ulan replied in a shaky voice. "They're cold to the touch and do not move, and their breath is shallow."

Cathal patted his shoulder. "Ulan, get some rest, my friend. Go back to the house. Rosepetal needs you."

"Go on, Ulan" Belwyn added. "We'll let you know if anything changes."

Weary, Ulan agreed. "If I must. But I will return soon." He bowed to the King and Queen, standing vigil nearby. "If I may have your leave."

"Thank you, Ulan," Queen Sorcha said with a nod. "Don't worry. We will take care of her."

Raghnall passed a small green crystal over their still bodies, which glowed weakly with spots of dim grey. "I know the court physician thoroughly examined Caliste and Sanura. On the surface, I detect nothing fatal, but because it's magical trauma, I must tread carefully for both their sakes."

Queen Sorcha paced around the enormous chamber, satin gown swishing with each turn. "Nothing will wake them. Hasn't there been enough death! Damn Koll! I could cleave that monster apart with my bare hands!"

Caladynn reached out and gently took Sorcha's arm to stop her pacing. He smiled with pride. "My Queen is as passionate in her hatred as she is with love! Perhaps I should have set you to guard Koll."

"Koll is the foul scum congealing at the bottom of the potion cauldron," Belwyn remarked sharply.

"Belwyn, patience!" Cathal warned.

"I'm all out," Belwyn snapped. "Our little girls are in a mystical coma, suffering from gods knows what dark magic and you want me to mind my manners."

Calm yourself, Cathal begged him.

I can't do that. You're the one who suffers in silence. Silence is against my nature.

Cathal replied in turn. *After centuries of you griping in my head, I know that.*

"Will they recover? Belwyn asked pointedly, perched on the footboard, talons digging into the glossy, elegant, wooded frame trimmed in gold.

Raghnall fumbled through his medicine bag. "I'm trying to discern the wicked magic Dagon used on them, but if you persist in pecking at me, I'll cast a spell on you, Belwyn. Right now, I can't decide if it will be a mute spell or a simple sleep spell."

"Stop bickering. We need to focus on Caliste and Sanura," Cathal said.

"Agreed," Belwyn nodded. "But we will pick this up later."

Raghnall covered them with a blanket and put on his cloak. "Now, I must go back to the Sorcerer House. This is going to take strong mystical medicine. I will need assistance too, with little things like passing potions and fetching tea."

We'll send Runa and Opaline back with you," Cathal suggested.

"Excellent," Raghnall said, oblivious. "As much as I love Baldur, he is rather clumsy with potion bottles."

"It's my enormous bear paws," Baldur remarked.

Raghnall gave his patients one more check. "I hear Taran is quite good in a laboratory."

"When he's not blowing it up," Belwyn added.

"Part of the pursuit of knowledge. Taran can help me with

some experiments and the girls can help me here. Come, Baldur."

"Are you staying with them, Cathal?" Belwyn asked softly.

"Yes, but go home with Baldur. I want to make sure Runa is safe. The girls will be safer here at the palace right now," Cathal said.

"Do you mean because Koll and Xabral almost incinerated the Sorcerer House with bloodstone sorcery?"

Cathal clenched his jaw and rubbed his temples. "Forgive Belwyn. When he's upset he tends to be crabby."

"I will be back later today," Raghnall said. "I want anything that sorcerer had. His damn staff and any mystical items you found on him."

"Dagon and what remains of his raven are in the dungeon room," Caladynn said. "Take anything you need if it will help Caliste and Sanura. The rest can burn without prayer. I'll have them sent to the Sorcerer House immediately."

"Thank you, Your Majesty." Raghnall bowed.

Morydonn marched entered the room and bowed. "Caladynn, you summoned me."

Caladynn embraced his brother. "Ah, thank you for coming so fast. I want a requiem mass arranged for the heroes who died, including Eberr. They will all be awarded the banner of heroism."

Morydonn was incredulous. "You want to honor Eberr, *a sorcerer*, as a hero?"

Caladynn's response was firm. "Yes! That man saved my life. He died a hero and he will be proclaimed one."

"Why honor them! Magic only brings more trouble to all of us!" Morydonn remarked bitterly. "The mages failed us. Koll walks free now. He should be dead. Rashurkeen assassins trespassed into our kingdom! Loyal Thill warriors died because this sorcerer failed—"

"Enough!" Caladynn commanded in a booming voice. "Cathal is my friend and my guest, so show him respect! He saved us during the Sorcerer War, at great personal cost. I should have executed Koll at once, so if there is blame it is on my head."

Sorcha glared at Morydonn. "Wait outside, Morydonn. My husband, the King, will join you shortly."

Morydonn closed his mouth, bowed stiffly, and departed.

After Morydonn exited, Caladynn once again tried to apologize for his brother, but Cathal only shook his head. Raghnall pretended to study the carpet.

"It doesn't matter," Cathal said. "You cannot change him. He hates magic and those who practice it."

Caladynn's expression became hard. "I should have executed Koll outright. The trial and its delay brought this trouble."

Cathal shook his head. "It's not your fault, Caladynn."

Cathal winced, sensing Belwyn's potent stare from across the room. *I know. You were right. I should have killed Koll in Mowad. I will remind you of that the next time we see Koll.*

~ * ~

Later that evening, Baldur waited patiently by Runa's door, his great bulk took up most of the hallway. Belwyn flew up the stairs, carrying a basket in his talons and glided down to the floor and set the basket down. He hopped over to Baldur.

"How's Mellypip?" Belwyn asked, landing next to him.

"He's heartbroken." Baldur glanced at the basket of drobba chip cookies. "Those look quite delicious. Mellypip should enjoy them."

"How's the research on Dagon's staff?"

"Raghnall extracted some malevolent sorcery for study."

"I just wish Mellypip would stop crying," Belwyn snapped. He leaned against the wall and sighed wearily. "I apologize. I don't do well when crying is involved."

Baldur sighed heavily. "You're not the cuddliest owl, are you?"

"Don't start with me," Belwyn warned. "I have enough trouble on my mind."

Baldur studied the owl with a serene gaze. "And still you remember to bring your apprentice a gift of cookies to ease his pain. You must care a great deal."

"Well, Furball loves anything sweet, especially drobba," Belwyn said. "Sirah made them. Baking is not my forte. I never knew he was so attached to Rono."

"They were playmates. Runa told me their favorite game was to play ranger mage. Mellypip was of course the valiant ranger mage. It's good to play. I suspect you feel a bit jealous of Rono."

"Nonsense. I'm Furball's teacher. It's my duty to instruct him in the ways of familiar magic. Jealous of Rono? Not even a little."

Baldur crossed his paws on his great bulk, studying Belwyn. "You're such a scary old owl. You carry the weight of the world on your wings. Mellypip loves you, but you are his guardian. Rono was like another child for Mellypip to play with. With Rono is gone, you need to be gentle with him. Maybe play a little yourself."

"I don't play well with others," Belwyn sighed.

"Try. You might surprise yourself," Baldur winked. "In the meantime, I will help watch over him."

Hinkleburr Crowyn walked up the stairs, a small basket tied with green ribbon in his hands, led by Jiana and Jasper. His two aides, Broda and Talwyn, followed close behind.

"Hello Hinkleburr," Belwyn said. "What are you doing here?"

"Just saying goodbye," Hinkleburr replied. "I'm leaving for Thema tomorrow, but I had to say farewell to my wonderful friends. I looked in on poor Caliste and Sanura before I came here. This is so heartbreaking. I will pray hourly for their recovery. We also brought a basket of flowers and cakes for Pointessa. Sirah took them for her, as Pointessa is grieving so. How is our Mellypip doing?"

"Heartbroken," Baldur said.

"Should we leave them alone?" Hinkleburr whispered. "I could just leave my gift."

"No, you should say goodbye. Mellypip would like that," Belwyn insisted.

Belwyn looked at the door, opening it slightly and peering inside. "Hinkleburr and his friends have come to say goodbye."

Opaline opened the door and hugged Hinkleburr, Broda, and Talwyn. "I will miss you! All of you."

The two aides blushed, but smiled brightly when Opaline kissed them.

"Yes, my charming princess, duty calls!" Hinkleburr said as he stepped into the room. Belwyn and Baldur followed Broda and Talwyn into the room. Hinkleburr's smile vanished when he saw Mellypip curled up in Runa's lap, sobbing, clutching his little blue blanket.

Runa stroked Mellypip's head. "Melly, Hinkleburr, Broda and Talwyn came to visit before they journey to Thema! See, they brought you a present!"

"I brought you a basket of cookies," Belwyn added.

"Very smooth," Baldur said.

"See, Belwyn brought us cookies!" Runa coaxed. "They're your favorite."

"It breaks our hearts to leave you like this," Hinkleburr said.

"I wish you could stay a little longer," Runa whispered.

"As do we," Hinkleburr said sadly. "The Sovereign of Ironia wants sharp eyes on the east, with Koll's escape, and commands we leave today. We will be well protected on our journey since Cathal has assigned Jiana and Jasper to protect us."

Jiana kissed Runa quickly on the cheek. "No tears. It's your grandfather's desire to keep eyes on key points of the kingdoms, and to watch for signs of that sorcerer Koll and what he's up to. I will keep our little friends safe. Thema is my home. I have missed it, but I will miss you more, little Runa, and Melly. You must visit us soon."

Jasper the tiger hare was on his best behavior, and did not snatch at the cookies, but waited politely for his turn.

"Melly was so brave today too," Runa said. "He didn't shed a tear when he sat with Pointessa for hours."

Hinkleburr knelt by Mellypip. "Dear Melly, I wanted to say goodbye, and to give you a present before I go." He lifted the basket. "See, there's a tiny notebook just your size, bound in a green leaf cover and the paper inside is a lovely creamy shade. There's a bundle of special writing styluses small enough for your tiny paws. You loved the storyteller Selyf, so I thought this might be a proper gift. I also added a special bag of nuts, coated in drobba! They're quite scrumptious."

Mellypip wiped his eyes, fingering the notebook. "I was going to tell Rono about Selyf the storyteller and his magical tales."

"Then you must write it, for Rono when he returns to us," Hinkleburr suggested. "Then you will not have forgotten anything, because it will be preserved in this little book."

Mellypip took the little basket. "Thank you Hinkleburr." Mellypip fondled the writing stylus in his paw. He wiped his eyes. "I wonder what I should write first, to tell Rono when I see him again."

"Write down a wonderful tale," Hinkleburr whispered, "of a brave ranger mage and his valiant gryphon."

Raghnall poked his head in the door. "Runa! Opaline! I just received word from the palace. Caliste and Sanura have taken a turn for the worse. We must go now."

~ * ~

At the palace, Sorcha sadly guided them to the sick bed. They had been bathed and Caliste was wearing a white linen shift, soaked with fever sweat. Both of them were shivering. More frightening, a shimmering black essence was being exhaled.

"What is that?" Opaline exclaimed, rushing to her friend's side.

"When did the black mist manifest?" Raghnall asked.

"About an hour ago," Sorcha answered.

"Magical injuries like this are tricky, my dear." Raghnall examined them, checking their eyes and pulse. "Fortunately, we have the staff Dagon used. I was able to glean remnants of the dark sorcery from it. I just wish I had more time. Now, keep out of my way, your majesty," Raghnall said.

"My wizard is not accustomed to court etiquette," Baldur apologized.

King Caladynn led his worried wife to the door. "Let them do their work, my dear. We will be in the next room, Wizard Raghnall, should you need anything."

Raghnall nodded, scratching his ginger beard. "Bring me two blue crystals. Hurry now."

Runa rushed to pick up Raghnall's medicine bag. The leather satchel reeked of herbs and magic. She looked inside and moaned, "How do you find anything in this bag?"

Mellypip's nimble paws helped rifle through a myriad of items that sparkled—thick glass balls filled with mysterious smoky essences or ripe with pungent green herbs or pale flower petals rolled around, crystals of every conceivable color were scattered among empty potion bottles. Finally, he pulled out two blue crystals.

"Bring them. Don't dawdle!" Raghnall ordered.

"You medicine bag is a shambles," Opaline grumbled, taking the crystals from Mellypip and handing them over. She then took his bag and carefully emptied it onto the fine carpets and spread the items out in a neat and orderly fashion. "Next time, we can find something."

"Thank you. It did need cleaning," Raghnall said as he proceeded to charge the crystals with beams of wizardry. Raghnall placed a crystal on Caliste's head and the other on Sanura's side. "These will help cool their fevers while I figure out what to do next."

Runa stroked Caliste's cheek. Mellypip sensed a wave of shadows travel up Runa's arm. Darkness, hot and wicked, pulsated through Caliste's veins. This black dusty essence was like a poison that contaminated the body. Runa and Mellypip in their mental union, both felt the sting of its evil. An angry flash of Drusai light pushed it back for a second. Runa let go and stumbled back. Cathal rushed to steady her.

"What is it?" Cathal asked.

Runa steadied herself. "I saw images of black mercurial flecks inside Caliste. It's like mystical residue of the malicious sorcery that hurt them. My Drusai light instinctively fought back, I think. It forced the shadows back with it. I could feel it."

"I sensed it too," Mellypip said. "Wicked sorcery alive and hurting them from the inside. Runa's light did hurt it."

"That's dangerous," Opaline shivered. "Maybe you shouldn't touch them until Raghnall has cured them of this."

"Opaline is right," Raghnall confirmed. "You're not a trained healer. You could infect yourself if not careful. From what I extrapolated from Dagon's staff, this residue is of bloodstone sorcery. Taran was a great help to me with this when I was working. Your brother has an excellent scientific mind by the way, Opaline. So useful for mystical healing and research."

Opaline's expression was neutral. "Taran does have a fine mind —for science."

Raghnall's face lit with hope. "Runa needs to refrain from actually touching them. She might become infected with the bloodstone magic. We will force out the darkness with light."

Belwyn agreed. "It must be a controlled form of light, powerful enough to flush the malignant shadows out without hurting them or you, missy!"

Raghnall chose a narrow crystal wand from the neatly arranged objects Opaline laid on the carpet. It was a foot long and devoid of color. "This will do nicely. We must flood their bodies with mystical light and then force out the dark sorcerous deposits. This will do both functions. It will also trap the malignant magic." He closed his eyes and gripped the crystal cylinder, sending his magic into it until bursts of wizardry glowed with intense light.

"Come here, Runa," Raghnall commanded. "Help me charge this crystal with more light. As much as you can summon. It does not matter if it is drusai or sorcerous. You too, Cathal. Do not worry if it is not enough. My wizard light will add to it."

"Could I help?" Opaline asked with hopeful eyes.

Raghnall patted Opaline's cheek. "I know you wish to help, dear, but your powers are very volatile."

Opaline nodded, though she was obviously disappointed. "I understand."

Runa comforted her. "I'm sorry. Your sorcery is just so strong. When you have more training, you will not need that amulet of bane."

Opaline sighed. "I know. I know. Practice. If I am to help my friends, I must take that to heart."

Cathal's magic filled the crystal first and then Runa summoned her Drusai and sorcery light. The crystal wand in her hands glowed with cool blue-white light and radiated bright power.

"Incredible light you have within you, Runa." Raghnall had to shield his eyes as he took the wand from her. He waved it up and down Caliste and Sanura and mumbled an incantation. The light began to flow into their bodies like a shower of radiance until the last rays were absorbed into their bodies.

"It looks like a bath of sunbeams," Mellypip gasped in awe.

When the crystal wand was emptied of its brilliance, Raghnall mumbled more words, and a wave of magic flashed around Caliste and Sanura. They glowed with intense brightness for a moment. Then the hollowed crystal sucked the black waves of aberrant magic from their bodies into the wand. The crystal absorbed the foul wispy fragments until the wand was dark as pitch. Then the glow around the sorceress and her familiar dimmed.

Caliste and Sanura opened their eyes.

CHAPTER FOURTEEN

Runa draped a shawl around Caliste's shoulders and covered her lap with a blanket.

"Stop fussing over me," Caliste insisted, petting a dozing Sanura, the cat was content to be cocooned in the soft wool on her lap. "You're the one who needs rest and pampering." Caliste cupped Runa's chin in her hand. "You have circles under your eyes, and I know you're not sleeping."

"I'm fine," Runa insisted.

"No you're not," Opaline contradicted. "You toss and turn. Sometimes you cry out. So does poor Mellypip because you're dream bonded." She stubbornly returned Runa's stare. "What? You sleep three feet away from me. I'm also suffering under eye shadows from your nightly turbulence."

"We're all having trouble sleeping," Runa pointed out.

Opaline nodded and chose a pastry from the platter. "Eberr's funeral was so sad." For a moment they were silent. "Poor Mother is so distraught. I know she hasn't slept a full night since he died. He was a good and loyal friend to us both. He was brave. Eberr risked a lot to smuggle letters for us. Pointessa must be bereft, yet she is stoic in her grief. It breaks my heart. But still, you need to find out why your dreams are so terrible. It's not normal, even for a mage. It worries me. That's not just my vanity speaking."

"I know. Grandpa thinks the nightmares have to do with my Drusai blood and some kind of dream seer ability, but he's not sure. So much has happened. Let's just enjoy the sunny garden and our tea. I'm fine."

Mellypip chewed on the tip of his writing stylus. *You're lying. The bad dreams about the tree of bones torment us. We are not fine.*

I know. I'm sorry baby, but we can't worry everyone. Dreams don't actually hurt you.

Speak for yourself, Mellypip replied.

Belwyn sniffed. "It would be more enjoyable if Koll and Xabral hadn't destroyed half the garden."

Opaline frowned and put her teacup down. "And Eberr had not died. I'm grateful the king and queen gave him such a beautiful funeral and honored him as a hero, but it's unjust and tragic a good man is dead while Koll still breathes air."

Belwyn twitched his ear tuffs. "I vow to you, Princess, Koll and his damn snake will not be enjoying air for long. Add some more sugar to my tea, please. And is Sanura going to sleep all day?"

Caliste checked Sanura, snoring softly under the blanket. "She's just resting. My precious Sanura is stronger every day."

"Wouldn't know it to look at her," MacTabbish remarked as he stretched, and then flopped on the cool green grass. "I think Sanura might still be feeble. All she does is sleep."

"Quothe the king of sleep," Opaline said.

"I'm a cat, that's what I do," MacTabbish countered and rolled over. "But Sanura is also ignoring me."

"And you hate to be ignored," Opaline added.

Sanura opened her eyes and blinked lazily. "Opaline, please remind MacTabbish that I am not in heat."

"I'm available in case you change your mind, love," MacTabbish replied.

"Tomcats." Sanura sniffed with disdain and went back to sleep.

Mellypip tried not to think about Runa's nightmares and scribbled in his childish scrawl on the pretty paper. He would write out a sentence or two, and then close his eyes, as though deep in meditation.

"What are you doing, little brother?" Baldur asked.

"I'm memorizing what I wrote, so I can recite it later with flawless precision," Mellypip answered. "That's the new word Belwyn gave me today—precision."

Runa smiled proudly. "He's in bard training."

Opaline handed him a pastry smothered in nuts and honey. "Will this help our great bard concentrate?"

"Thank you, Opaline." Mellypip replied. He savored the roll's nutty sweetness.

"Did you read the chapter I outlined yesterday in *Practice Magic for Young Familiars*?" Belwyn asked.

"Yes," Mellypip nodded, and then his ears drooped. "Well, I tried to read it. It's hard to study now since…well, you know."

"Tell me," Belwyn finished for him. "I won't peck."

Mellypip put down his stylus. "It's been scary. Runa's bad dreams and Koll's escape. Eberr's death. I miss Hinkleburr too. And Jiana. I even miss Jasper chasing me. Now Riva is leaving tomorrow. Grandpa Cathal is sending him to the Ivory Kingdoms. I'll miss

Buzzy, even if he can't chase me."

Belwyn nodded his beak. "I agree. There have been some frightening changes in our lives. You are still so young."

"Was it scary for you when you were an owlet?"

Belwyn sighed. "You have no idea, but that's a conversation for when you are older."

"Isn't Taran joining us for tea?" Runa asked.

"Taran is busy," Opaline replied tersely, dropping several cubes of sugar in her tea and stirring with fury.

"Busy or mad at you?" Runa pressed.

"Both," Opaline confessed.

"They had a big fight about Panthara again," Mellypip added.

Opaline gave Mellypip a stunned look.

Mellypip shrugged. "What? Your shouting was heard in the next kingdom."

"He still hasn't forgiven me," Opaline said. "I tried to apologize about the other night when Panthara woke up from her wraith coma. That dissolved into an exchange of hot testy words which ended with him storming out of the room. He hasn't spoken to me in two days. He's locked himself in his laboratory. I'm sure he's concocting something horrific to punish me in there." She relentlessly stirred her tea. "Alas, I am Opaline, destroyer of relationships."

"Brothers and sisters are supposed to fight," Runa said soothingly, hugging her friend. "Do you hate Panthara because of me? You don't have to, you know."

Opaline threw up her hands. "I can't help it, Runa. She vexes me on a level I cannot fathom. I picked a bad time for a fight too, since I hoped Taran would accompany me to visit Ulric's sister. Ulric loves *his* sister Danu and her word counts for a lot with him."

"Give Taran time to cool off, lass," MacTabbish advised, rolling over on his back, exposing his furry orange tummy to the sun. "He'll soon forgive your shrewish taunts."

Opaline scowled at MacTabbish. "How generous."

"The King and Queen adore you," Runa assured her. "They have no objections to Ulric courting you. I'm sure Princess Danu will love you too. Taran just needs time to calm down."

"They are wonderful to me. However, Morydonn and his wife, Faustine, look at me like I'm a troll," Opaline quipped and then she paled and dropped her spoon.

"Oh dear, don't start fussing about Gorvanus and the troll thing again!" Runa begged.

"I know, I know, don't worry," Opaline replied, though she winced as she downed her tea in one gulp.

"Morydonn and his wife hate mages of all castes," Belwyn pointed out. "Not that he is very likeable. Don't take it personally."

"Sounds like those two have more in common with my father," Opaline remarked. "Did you know Princess Danu gave up the crown to become a nun? She was the heir, a crown princess! Sorcha and Caladynn were shocked last year when Princess Danu begged them to let her take the veil. They all miss her terribly. Imagine! A royal family that loves one another! Ulric had to adjust from being a freewheeling prince with little responsibility to being the future King of Thill." Opaline's face brightened and grabbed Runa's hand. "Come with us, Runa! The Abbey is not that far! I need a friend to keep me calm. We'll be surrounded by guards galore for safety. We plan to stay at the Abbey for a few days only. Surely Cathal will approve. We'll have the Queen herself as chaperone."

"I think it's a marvelous idea," Caliste agreed, sipping her tea. "You need some distraction, Runa, and wholesome fresh air!"

"Alright! I'll ask Grandpa, but only because I don't want you to shame yourself in front of royalty."

"Thank you!" Opaline exclaimed, biting into an iced cinnamon bun.

A loud, high-pitched humming sound came from the house. The sound was so unbearable they had to cover their ears.

"Damn crystal," Belwyn groaned.

They rushed into the house and ran to the crystal chamber. The calling crystal was pulsating and turning several colors. Myrsalian and Liat maintained a safe distance from it.

"Don't trust it," Myrsalian warned.

Raghnall stormed into the room. "What the blazes is going on. Can't you silence that cursed thing?"

"I thought you fixed the calling crystal?" Felisia asked.

Myrsalian flung his hands up. "I did!"

"Grandpa, there's something wrong with the crystal again," Runa shouted.

The crystal finally fell silent. Suddenly, an ethereal blue dove sprang from its core. It flew past Opaline, though she tried to catch it.

"What's that?" Runa chased after the luminous dove as it flew into the living room.

"It's a private message," Cathal replied, rising from his chair. The ethereal blue dove stopped and hovered before Cathal. It clutched a small white scroll embellished with gold writing in its misty talons and dropped it into Cathal's hands. Then the magical bird vanished, leaving a spray of soft colorful lights in its departure. Cathal opened the scroll and read its contents. His expression changed from curious to sorrowful.

"What is it, Cathal?" Raghnall asked.

"It's a message from Neelam," Cathal replied.

"Neelam? The Mage Chieftain of Ironia?" Raghnall exclaimed with surprise. "Well, what does he say?"

"Ambera is dying," Cathal replied. "I must go to Ilyrra at once."

~ * ~

Cathal was ready to leave within an hour of receiving word about Ambera. He was quiet and tense as he prepared for his journey.

Much to Mellypip's shock, the rangers and perytons also gathered out front preparing to leave with him for Ilyrra.

"Did you know Ambera?" Mellypip asked.

Runa shook her head, dismayed. "I don't remember her, but Grandpa said she blessed me when I was a baby. Ambera must be very important for Cathal to leave like this. Even the rangers and perytons are leaving us. I know she was once the Drusane of Ilyrra. Some have called her the mother of Ilyrra."

Cathal kissed Runa on the cheek. "Be a good sorceress now. I love you. I will return as soon as possible."

Runa threw her arms around him. "I love you too, Grandpa! Please let me go with you."

Cathal shook his head. "With Koll on the loose, it's too dangerous. Here you have Caliste, Sirah, Raghnall, and even the King and Queen looking after you. While I'm there, I will ask the Drusai about your nightmares and dream seer magic. I cannot bear seeing you suffer."

"I will be alright, Grandpa. I know you'll think of a way to fix me."

Redstorm the peryton spread his broad crimson wings and lowered his head before Belwyn. "Perhaps you should perch now and get comfortable, instead of disturbing me when I am trying to concentrate on where I'm flying."

"I think you're being teased, Belwyn," Darcus remarked with a grin, strapping on his sword.

"Well, isn't that why perytons have antlers?" Belwyn asked with mock innocence.

"What do I tell King Caladynn?" Myrsalian asked.

"Tell him the truth," Cathal replied. "I was summoned to Moonthorne because Ambera of Ilyrra is dying. He will know it's important. Tell him I promise Koll will not disappear into the cracks. Tell him the Archon gives his word."

"It's about time you accepted your fate," Belwyn said. The owl glanced down at Mellypip. "Be a good familiar and keep your sorceress out of trouble."

"I will," Mellypip promised.

Darcus heartily embraced Runa and ruffled Mellypip's ears. The wampu leapt to his shoulder and hugged him one last time.

"If you ever need me, I will be here," Darcus promised and mounted Redstorm.

"We will both be here," Redstorm added.

The other perytons, though eager for home, bade a sorrowful goodbye to their friends. Mellypip would miss the majestic perytons. They had become like family, Silverthorne, Starwynd, Dawnfire, and Dovetail, were a comforting presence. They had been kind and protective of Rono too.

Runa embraced Ryen. "Safe journey and Light's Blessing. I will pray for Ambera."

"Thank you, Runa. Light's blessing." Ryen mounted Silverthorne and nodded to his son, Jadon to follow.

"Light's Blessing, Jadon," Runa whispered, chewing her lip.

"Be brave," Mellypip added, hoping Jadon would finally give Runa the pretty wooden ring he crafted.

Jadon rubbed Mellypip's large round ears and grinned. "My little friend, look after your sorceress well. I will remember about being brave."

"What are you two talking about?" Runa asked, suspicious.

"Ranger matters," Mellypip replied with such gravity Darkleaf snickered.

Jadon kissed her and for a heartbeat, Mellypip thought Jadon was going to reach into his pocket and give Runa the beautiful wooden ring. Instead Jadon mounted Darkleaf and flew into the sky to join the others.

Cathal glowed and shapeshifted into a grey mountain owl. He and Belwyn took flight and followed. The peryton's broad wings quickly gathered speed as they soared through the sky and soon were out of sight.

Alone, Runa and Mellypip watched the sky until sunfall.

~ * ~

Grimm Darkrunner stood on the bluff overlooking a desert of black sand. The troll scrambled down the dunes, as though joyful in this dismal hell. But then, what would a troll know of anything good?

Grimm was reluctant to follow. "This is my destiny? Follow the troll into starvation and oblivion into that barren land. What wisdom is there in this mad pursuit?"

Midnight turned to Grimm, his ghostly shimmer bright against the night sky. "You will meet challenges, but you will not be alone. It is not for me to question the gods."

"I will happily question them."

"This journey is necessary, not only for your own fate, but the fate of others. Enemies lurk in those shadows, to be sure, but you will also find a friend."

"What friend would live in that hell?"

"You will find out soon enough, Grimm."

"What is this wasteland called?"

"Skarros," Midnight answered.

"It is a dark place. I sense great evil happened here."

"Yes, but once it was a place of shining beauty. Darkness himself destroyed it in his jealously. The true name of this land has been long forgotten. It holds many ancient secrets. Trust me, Grimm. You must go there."

Grimm glowered but said nothing and followed the wretched troll into the desert.

CHAPTER FIFTEEN

Koll tossed dry weeds into the circle of stones and shot beams of hot sorcery until fresh flames kindled. Acrid smoke rose from the burning pile, and the meager hearth blazed into defiant flames. Koll rubbed his fingers to loosen his joints. "It is gratifying to use my sorcery again. I missed the heat when magic surged through my hands." He touched his neck, blistered from weeks of wearing the accursed sorcerer bane. "We're fortunate to have found a locksmith who is a devoted follower of the Dark Trinity on our way. No one will ever bind my sorcery again."

Xabral stretched out on a long flat rock. "I missed our bonding of thoughts. I was so lonely without you."

Koll walked the ancient terrain, unable to keep still since he was freed from his captivity. His new black robes billowed in the cold desert wind. He welcomed the primal touch of the elements. "Fear not, we shall never be parted again, Xabral. I promise you."

"I will make you keep that promise."

"Have faith, beloved familiar. We evaded our enemies and reached this feral land of promise," Koll said. "One day my enemies will pay for what they did, especially Cathal, who desired my death more than anyone. If Cathal knew our secret, he would never have turned me over to Thill justice, but would have killed me in Mowad."

"Do not say such things!" Xabral cried. "I came too close to losing you forever."

"Forgive me," Koll said, brushing sand from his robes. "We shall think of better things. A thousand years ago on this holy ground, *Her* temple palace rose above the black sands in triumph. I know we will find her."

"Remember, Zhelon is adamant about results this time," Xabral warned. "He is weary of our relic hunts which bear no fruit. He says if we fail again the sacrificial altar will be our reward."

"I have faced death before on such an altar," Koll replied. "I can still recall the feel of warm blood that steamed on the dark stones when I was laid there. How my sorcery first manifested before the blade struck me. And then I saw Obsydia's face in my mind! I knew I was chosen to be her deliverer. When I free her, Zhelon will kneel before me and beg forgiveness for doubting me." Koll stroked his scales with tender care. "How are you feeling, my poor sweet?"

"Some of the agony has faded, but I'm still weak. It took so long to shed the remains of human shape. Being human was very exhausting--and dirty. No wonder you humans need to wash so often. I yearned for my clean glossy scales and pretty fangs when I was ensorcelled. This pain is from the *hellstone*. The transformation into a demon was as raw and agonizing as it was exhilarating. The power was unearthly. It did not last long, but its effects have debilitated me I fear."

"It was a dangerous gamble, Xabral, and I regret your suffering. The combination of both was risky. The hellstone's effects complicated your return to your true lovely snake form."

Xabral laid his head in Koll's lap. "Once freed, your sorcery helped restore me. I don't regret it. It enabled me to free you. I grieve for your former apprentice, Dagon, and his raven. Why are deserts always so cold at night?"

"Warm yourself by the fire," Koll suggested. "I need to research the scrolls you found."

The scorpion snake slithered closer to the fire, hoping the warmth would ease his chill and soothe his scales. "Bloodstone sorcery has a bitter after effect. I understand you a little better though."

"In what way?"

"Being human. It was a strange sensation to walk, smile, to have warm blood and...*body hair*. Don't be insulted Koll, but I found it repulsive."

"You should eat. A hearty meal will help restore your strength," Koll suggested. "The days of hard travel have been exhausting for both of us."

"I am hungry," Xabral agreed listlessly. "Hunt for me. Please Koll."

"I will return soon with your dinner," Koll promised. "Rest now, my sweet snake."

Koll's eyes searched the bleak landscape of the wastelands until a desert vole darted across a rock. He pointed his finger and stunned the vole with a red flash of sorcery. He walked over and picked it up, enjoying the atmosphere of this ancient, mysterious land. The twin moons were dark tonight, as though they had vanished from the sky, and clouds shadowed most of the stars. He tossed the vole to Xabral. "Here's a fine meal. A nice fat vole. Don't worry. It's only dazed. I know how much you hate dead food."

"Thank you, Koll," Xabral said. He devoured the vole, savoring the feeling of living warmth. Koll joined him, eating a modest portion of bread and dried meat. He sipped from the water skin, careful not to waste. After Xabral's meal, he did feel better, but he was still bored and cold.

"Maybe we ask for help from Zhelon. I know we do not need slaves to dig, though it might be gratifying. You have your sorcery again, after all. We could both benefit from a proper rest in a comfortable environment."

"We will go home after we have found the temple and can prove to Zhelon we were right. Now let me study," Koll warned.

Xabral flattened his scales on the rocks and sulked. "I know we are on a holy quest, but roughing it is not to my taste. I miss the lush food and vibrant atmosphere of Urgonclaw."

"And the plump edibles the temple cook provided whenever you had a twinge of hunger," Koll added. "Years of such opulence have spoiled you, Xabral."

"Well, at least he did not have to *cook* my meals," Xabral giggled. "I usually preferred them alive and kicking, with a dash of salt." He coiled into a ball of scales, and stared at the fire until the monotony made him restless.

"I wish I had something to distract me," Xabral sighed. "I no longer have Azmadu to pick on. That idiot gryphon provides some amusement, but he's too easy to shake up. Rather high strung."

"Xabral," Koll interrupted, "This scroll is important. Please be silent. Get some sleep." Koll resumed his study by the firelight.

Xabral flicked his tongue and glanced at the terrified gryphon bound to a leafless, emaciated tree. He weaved gracefully across the sands and over the rocks toward the gryphon. He coiled when he reached Rono and lifted his head, flicking his tongue and shaking his stinger. He cast a vicious stare at the gryphon. "I can eat you any time I want."

Terrified by Xabral's threat, Rono backed away, kicking up sand. "Koll! He's doing it again! Make nasty snake go away!"

"Xabral! Stop teasing the gryphon. I'm not in the mood. You know how stupid it is."

Playful and malicious, Xabral shook his barbed tail and pleaded. "But it's *fun!*"

Sloppy tears rolled from Rono's large brown eyes and his choking sobs filled the night air. "Go away, mean snake!" retreating against a large boulder. Tied to a dead, skeletal tree, Rono was trapped, because Koll had cast a binding enchantment on the rope, so Rono could not break free even with his formidable strength.

"Are you chilly tonight, Rono?" Xabral taunted. He slithered closer. "Want to cuddle?" he invited, pointing his stinger at him.

Xabral enjoyed it when his victims were cornered so he exploited the gentle nature of Rono. It made the torment that much sweeter. Xabral doubted the idiot could remember to fly unless reminded of it. "Behave! We can kill Mellypip with a mere thought! Mellypip will be a pile of ashes if you anger us." Gryphons were so dense. It gave Xabral a giggle to threaten him, though it was a fleeting levity.

The gryphon only became more hysterical. His cries could have cracked the sky. The weeping was beginning to bore Xabral now. Worse, his amusement irritated Koll.

"Enough," Koll shouted. He threw down the scroll and marched over to them. He untied Rono, tossed aside the rope, and shoved him. "Leave! Miss your friends, gryphon? Go! Try and find them, if your tiny brain can even navigate out of the wastelands before you starve to death or die of thirst! Leave! I am sick of you. Go! And the crystal was a lie. I could not kill your friend with it. You were stupid!"

"But Koll, who will I torment?" Xabral whined.

"You're doing a splendid job tormenting me!" Koll shot back. "I am trying to free a goddess and bring darkness into the world, and you are acting like a hatchling!"

The gryphon cowered in terror when Koll touched him. The sorcerer's black mood terrified Rono. The sorcerer dragged him along the sands and pointed, "See the sky? Fly. Go on! Fly or I will slit your throat myself!"

"Yes, slit his throat, slit his throat!" Xabral chimed, shaking his stinger.

The earth rumbled and the sand shifted beneath them. The gryphon cried out yet did not take to the sky. *Perhaps Rono did forget how to fly*, Xabral wondered.

The world shuddered. The ground around them crumpled before their eyes, forming long jagged craters. The gryphon finally opened his wings and hovered above the heaving earth in terror. Koll was tossed across the quaking earth until he gathered his wits and floated above the roving sands.

With a terrified howl, Rono flew away. His weeping filled the night sky as he fled his captors. But the earthquake kept Koll and Xabral absorbed. The withered tree Koll had tethered to Rono was pulled beneath the hungry sands. Great rocks jutted up, carving an ugly landscape. Rumbles of foul vapors exhaled from the raging underworld. Flames gushed from the cracks while the ground beneath Xabral opened like a ravenous mouth to devour him.

"Xabral? Where are you?" Koll shouted.

Xabral fell into oblivion. In his plight, a brief ironic thought intruded his panic. He was not bored anymore. When Xabral hit the bottom with a thud, he continued to travel as he descended deeper into the maw. Finally, he stopped sliding and the earth ceased thundering.

It took a moment for Xabral to recover from the shock. He blinked and looked around in the darkness. He was not injured, just shaken and dizzy. But it was bloody inconvenient. Now he would have to crawl out of this pit! No wait, he would not need to. He had a sorcerer that could use magic to carry him out of this dank hole. From above, he heard the faint echoes of Koll crying his name.

I'm down here, Koll. Just look for the deepest pit, Xabral called through the bonding.

A shadowy glimmer caught Xabral's eye. Through the falling dirt and rocks, a glimpse of bloodstone and red marble gleamed in the darkness, exposing bits of archaic majesty. His vision noticed an opening which went deeper, tempting him to go down into the abyss further. A surge of shadowy bliss filled his being. Something important was buried here. He tasted and smelled the aroma of evil on the air with his tongue and trembled with joy.

Xabral. Where are you!

Continue down, just follow my thoughts. I found something, Koll. Ahridum himself must have opened this path to guide us. I sense evil, Koll. Pure and ripe evil! She is here. I just know it!

Magic eased Koll's descent into the broad abyss which had taken Xabral deep into a mysterious opening the earthquake had uncovered. Koll floated down into the depths, casting light on his staff to see with more clarity as he followed the steep path where Xabral, anxious and elated, waited for his sorcerer to rescue him. When Koll found Xabral, they examined the large opening, which could go deeper into what they hoped was the great ancient complex they had hunted for.

"Could it be her ancient temple palace? Or perhaps the great citadel of Ralnazzar, the demon city?" Xabral asked, waving his stinger. "Goblins and trolls lived there! Obsydia had handmaidens too. They were *Shades* from the demon realm."

Koll brushed away the concealing dirt and rubble to reveal more bloodstone and marble. "We may have found Obsydia's Temple!"

"Do you think so?"

"Yes. I am sure of it now."

"What about the gryphon!" Xabral cried. "What if he tells where we are? We should hunt him down and kill him."

"There is no way that moronic gryphon can reveal where we are. He will die flying around lost, blubbering until the heat kills him. Forget about him. He served his purpose. Now we must do the work of Darkness. Do not fear! We've been shown the true way. Now let's see how far we can go."

Koll stepped through the hole, his staff's illumination forming shadows in the dusky tunnels. "The way is clear. Come, Xabral."

Koll and Xabral followed the dusty path. Xabral slithered with joy, feeling his energy return. Together they traveled into the depths of the old palace. Cautiously they traversed the archaic halls and passed wondrous architecture of glistening obsidian and smoky bloodstone. They slowly moved through the labyrinth. They traveled with ease past any fallen pillars or great iron doors which might have barred their way.

"The mysteries of a lost age are around us, whispering secrets of kingdoms long turned to ashes, filled with delight and power," Koll whispered with awe.

"I feel it," Xabral sang, his tongue flicking in and out, "the ancient and wicked past." He glanced up at his sorcerer, his snake eyes bright in the dim glow. "I especially love the wicked part."

Koll traversed, guiding by the glow of his staff. Xabral enjoyed the image of his face at the top. Debris of dirt and rocks blocked their way, but Koll's magic dispersed all obstacles. Koll's ebony eyes glowed with triumph when he examined a new wall in a wider corridor, exposing a large battle carving of black marble. "This must lead to the chamber we saw drawn in the scrolls. Oh, see the detail of the army led by demon warlords!" Koll said.

"Adventurous days long gone. We were born in the wrong age," Xabral said with a sigh. The aura of evil made his scales itch with delight, until an earth shudder troubled the snake. The aftershock was unsettling, but here surely the Darkness would protect them from harm.

Koll caressed his fears away. "Have faith, my darling snake, fear not. She will not let us perish. We are her saviors who will lift her to the bloodstone throne where she will reign supreme!"

The chambers and corridors echoed of old glories, where blood flowed from mortals to quench the thirst of Ahridum. The sands of Skarros only cloaked her temple but did not spoil it. Once deep within the arcane halls, they traversed with little to block their pilgrimage. Some pillars and walls had collapsed, but on the whole, it was remarkably well preserved. Wealth gleamed around them, even in this state of archaic abandon. Deeper in the old temple, immense doors barred their way, broken off from the hinges. The dangerous weight bowed against the cracked walls. The doors were forged from ebonite! The precious black metal so rare kings balked at its price. Hundreds of carved ruby skulls framed a mask of ethereal grace molded from the same shimmering ebonite, which could only be of Queen Obsydia, staring with eternal eyes.

"Do you think this is *Her* true likeness?" Xabral whispered.

"It must be," Koll answered.

Excited, Koll's sorcery lit the torches lining the walls. They blazed with a dark blue and crimson flame, illuminating her sacred halls with a shadowy veil. Koll extended his hand, and a burst of crimson sorcery propelled the doors into the air. He restored them to their proper place so they could stand with pride again. After all, they bore the image of Obsydia, and should not be blasphemed. The great doors once again were attached, rising in their glory over fifty feet high. The burnt metal sizzled and smoked as Koll's sorcery repaired the doors. Then he raised his hands, and the magnificent doors opened wide.

They passed a hallway to a wider chamber, where a bright light almost blinded them. Koll shielded his eyes as he looked around, and to his surprise braziers still flamed with dark promise, a deep blue and red flame like the sconces in the hall. This new dazzling light was not born from shadow, unlike the rest of the palace which emanated shadows pure. Even in the intense glare, he could make out the lofty ceilings of onyx and on the domed ceiling an immense painting of Ahridum looked down upon them.

Xabral slid past the doorway behind Koll. "What is that cursed brightness?"

Corpses of war lingered in this silent tomb, remnants of the final battle. Some were skeletons of demon breeds, like goblins, holding crude swords and axes in bony grip. Some remains were human. Worshippers and nobility of her court perhaps? The bodies of those who served *Her* lay where they fell a thousand years ago, mummified by the dry air and clothing decayed by time, though their jewels sparkled on withered bones.

At the far end of the great room, this cruel Light beckoned them. As they drew closer, they could make a crystal over seven feet tall on a dais of black marble. The crystal's brilliance was like the sun, its essence of purity a sacrilege within this hallowed hall. Within the mysterious lustrous prison of the crystal was a woman, a woman of ethereal and flawless beauty.

"Koll! It's Obsydia! For centuries, the myth of light holding her captive was common, but I did not realize it was so literal."

"I see her now! How she must have suffered!" Koll said with amazement.

Koll cast a shadow over the whole area so they could look upon her, though it did not dim the brilliance of the strange crystal. "The shadows make it almost bearable. This crystal of light throbs with a life of its own! It's not of mortal origin. What source of magic was conjured so powerful it defeated a goddess. Oh Xabral, look at her! It is beyond dreams to see her noble face! It is the face I saw when I was a boy on that altar!"

Xabral, flicking his tongue, could smell her life within. "She lives! Unlike mortals, the scent is pure. No mortification defames her immortal body. She is perfection!"

Indeed, Obsydia's splendor was of the darkest conception. Gowned in deep scarlet with a high-winged collar that circled her head like a crown, the gown clung to the perfect curves of her body. No mortal could possess the beauty of her face. Full sensuous lips, arched black brows and high cheekbones formed a face of super-natural grace that possessed not only beautiful, but ethereal power of the Dark Eternals. Her hair was truly shadow that floated about her face, just as the scriptures said. She glowed with the essence of the Otherworld, where flesh burned away and spirits revealed their true visage. The heavy-lashed eyes were still closed as though in sleep, but Xabral sensed her pain—and her *awakening.*

Koll circled the crystal tomb. "Xabral, this is the face that destroyed a thousand kings. Skin pale as death, a crown of shadow, and lips red as blood!"

A moan escaped the ruby mouth, and eyelids lifted to reveal silver irises that gazed at them like fire moons.

"She wakes!" Xabral exclaimed. Her exquisite beauty enthralled both snake and man. When she moved her head, shadow floated about her face like a storm cloud. Xabral sensed other things too, anger, frustration, evil, wickedness.

"Who disturbs me from my sleep of pain?" her voice commanded, filling Xabral's soul with dizzy delight.

Koll knelt before the crystal. "I am Koll the Sorcerer! I have come to free you, my Queen and Goddess."

"I am Xabral! I serve you too!" the snake added, flicking his barbed tail to get her attention.

Her glorious voice pierced the crystal of her prison like a phantom. "I am She, Daughter of Ahridum. I am Queen of the Bloodstone and Maiden of Shadow. I am Obsydia. I have waited for you, Koll the Sorcerer."

CHAPTER SIXTEEN

A giant of a man, Captain Vasya, supervised the fifty soldiers as the royal party enjoyed their quiet journey and wonderful surroundings.

Well, I feel quite secure with a whole army protecting me, Runa commented to Mellypip.

Don't forget you have me to protect you, Mellypip added, sitting on her shoulder, proudly holding his little staff.

They traveled the rim of the vast Thill forest, and the smell of fresh green earth was invigorating. Once outside of the city, Runa relaxed. The woodlands revived memories of home.

This is so enchanting. I miss our forest and our wonderful tree tower. Runa sighed with longing. She noticed how sweet and attentive Prince Ulric was to Opaline. *Look Melly, perhaps they are really in love.* Runa thought about Jadon and how much she truly missed him. She blushed when she recalled Jadon's kiss on her lips. Her fingers brushed her lips, wondering.

"Enjoying the scenery," Queen Sorcha asked, riding up alongside Runa, startling her out of her silent revelry.

"Yes, Your Majesty," Runa replied. "You have such a beautiful country. Thank you for inviting me today."

"We're delighted to have you," Sorcha said, her smile devoid of the usual artifice royal persons wore for people.

"Are you having fun?" Runa asked Mellypip.

Mellypip scratched his tummy, holding his staff in his other paw. "I'm enjoying the pretty trees." A blue butterfly floated by them, brushing against Mellypip's nose, which made him giggle. "I like this adventure. Horse stinky though. Not its fault, but stinky. The trees are very old in these woods. Being a wampu, I love trees. I'm writing a poem about trees. We live in a tree tower at home, but your castle is ever so nice."

Sorcha laughed. "Why thank you, Mellypip. I would love to hear your poem when it is completed."

A peal of Opaline's laughter and the sight of Prince Ulric taking Opaline's hand as they rode side by side tugged at Runa's heart.

"I am pleased my son found a match in Opaline," Sorcha said, as though reading Runa's mind. "Ulric does not offer his heart easily.

In fact, this is the first woman who has captivated him. I do not give my blessing so easily either. I felt much the same way when I met Caladynn. So I am willing to see where this progresses."

"Even though she's a sorceress?" Runa asked.

"I know Opaline and Sirah have concerns. It would be unusual, but not unprecedented in Thill history. My brother by wedlock sadly has contempt for anything magical."

"Opaline is only sixteen," Runa said. "I worry about her, even though I am younger."

Sorcha smiled. "A great king in the distant past loved a beautiful sorceress. He married her, and they were happy. This king loved her so much the people accepted her. She was as good and kind as she was beautiful. They were blessed with only one child, a son. The son was sorcerous, like his mother. This concerned the King. There was also enmity in the royal family. The family was jealous because if this Mage Prince became King, he may rule for a thousand years! What if he was wicked or cruel? What if no one else got to be king or queen? The King worried for his son and the people. But the Prince eased their fears, and promised to be fair and just. He would rule for only a short time and then step down from his throne. The Prince claimed he would never demand centuries of tribute, but only to do his royal duty to his kingdom. He did become King when his father died, and ruled for only fifty years. A paltry sum when considering how long mages live. The people loved him. As promised, he abdicated and gave his throne to his niece. He retired from public life not long after and disappeared to begin a new life. The land was not harmed by a mage being king."

"Sounds like a fey tale," Runa remarked, and with a grin added, "In fact, it is a fey tale! I read it when I was little."

"Legends and myths spring from the seed of truth," Sorcha said. "Who can say it did not happen? The name of the original country is lost to memory, so why not let me claim it for the happiness of my son. This could be just a passing romance, but a Queen must be prepared for all contingencies. Thill does come first, but I will never sacrifice the happiness of my children. Opaline's blood is also royal and she has a brilliant mind and loving heart to match her beauty. I can think of no one better to tame my son's wildness and guide his hand as king." A raffish smile lit Sorcha's face, "It will also gall Emperor Tarsicius to no end, but that's just a bonus."

"The story about the ancient king and his sorceress bride is told in many lands, so why not Thill! I want Opaline to be happy too. She's my best friend. You know, we could say this legend happened when Thill was a new country. It was founded by the twelve great tribes of Thill after the Bloodstone Wars a thousand years ago. So much chaos in those days, so much lost to history's pen!"

"You're a clever girl Runa," Sorcha complimented her. "Yes, we can make this work, and I usually get my way."

Captain Vasya halted the party and rode up to Sorcha's side. He looked troubled, though Captain Vasya never looked cheerful either. He bowed his head briefly, and stated in his deep voice, "Forgive my intrusion, my Queen. The scout returned and says the bridge has collapsed. The storms a few weeks ago must have washed it out when the river flooded."

"Oh dear," Sorcha said. "We will have to take the old forest road."

"Will it take long, Your Majesty?" Runa asked.

"No, my dear," Sorcha said uneasily, "but it will not be a pleasant journey. And please call me Sorcha."

"I don't understand," Opaline said.

"We will have to pass through a part of the forest which has been cursed since the Sorcerer War," Ulric said.

Mellypip clung to Runa's head. "What do they mean cursed?"

"Koll's dark magic destroyed it," Ulric replied "It's dreadful to see. Mystical healers tried to restore it for years. Priests and shamans have exorcised it and blessed it. Nothing has healed the land. There is a barrier of thorns no one can pass."

"Ulric, is it safe?" Opaline asked. "I've been witness to evil sorcery and the consequences do not end with the end of an incantation."

Ulric's warm smile was like the sun and he kissed Opaline's hand. "Magic or not, I would never let anything happen to you."

"Perhaps we should turn back, Your Majesty," Captain Vasya advised, his frown prominent beneath his drooping brown mustache. "That blighted land is rife with evil."

Sorcha stubbornly shook her head. "No. I want to see my daughter and I will not let this stop us. The other way will take half a day. We'll continue on but will ride quickly until we pass the wretched place."

"As you command, my Queen," Captain Vasya bowed.

Mellypip watched for trouble. At first, he was showing off, but he began to sense something…vile. He clung to Runa's shoulder, intent on protecting his sorceress.

When the party first approached the damaged area, Runa shivered, chilled by the image of the wasted forest, she almost choked at the sight. Mellypip wished he had worn his ranger cloak, though it was just a dish towel.

"Bad magic," Mellypip wheezed, sitting her shoulder, holding his little staff close to ward off evil.

"The trees look quite old, but chalky and pale. Void of natural life," Opaline remarked.

Mellypip remembered the dreams he shared with Runa about a cursed forest. Fear tugged at him, and he clenched his staff. "Captain Vasya is right. We should go back. Now."

"Melly, close your eyes!" Runa advised. "It might make the passing easier."

But Runa, it is like our nasty dream! Remember the wasted forest! Melly warned.

Melly, I'm part Ilyrran, and the disease of this place would have an effect on me. Maybe this is what I dreamed about for days! This poor scarred square of earth! This place explains those dreams.

You are being rational, Mellypip replied. *But I don't think rational is right choice at this time. We need to flee. I sense very bad things.*

I won't spoil this for Opaline, Runa insisted to Mellypip through the bonding. Feeling faint, she took a drink from a water bag.

Runa, are you sick? Mellypip asked, concerned. He had to admit he felt wobbly too, and the air here made his tummy queasy.

Just a bit woozy. The others, not even Opaline because she wears the sorcerer bane, don't feel the aura of this place like I do.

Runa was right. When Mellypip looked at the others, they were tense or even afraid, but no one else looked physically ill. A different wave of magic washed over him. He looked down and Runa's staff glowed. Then Runa suddenly pulled away from the others toward the forbidden path. Mellypip tugged at her sleeve but she was oblivious. She clutched her head and bent over in the saddle, wailing in pain. Something tormented her with fresh malice.

Runa, what's wrong! Mellypip cried in her head.

Concerned for her charge, Sorcha, rode up to her and took the horses reins. "Runa child, can you hear me? Captain, quick! Help me get her off the horse. Everyone stop!"

Opaline's face was pinched with worry when she joined them.

"She looks terrible! Ulric, help her!"

Runa was weeping hysterically now, rejecting anyone's attempt to touch her. Mellypip was at a loss. Opaline was confounded.

Sorcha eyes flashed with anger. "It must be these haunted woods! The dark mystical residue is tormenting her somehow. Captain, you were right, we must turn back! Hurry! I am so sorry, my dear! We're going back."

"No!" Runa screamed, and jerked away when Sorcha took her arm.

Ulric tried to lift Runa from her saddle, but Runa was possessed with madness. Runa's sorcerous push shoved Ulric and Opaline off their mounts. Opaline and Ulric rolled to the ground. Soldiers surrounded her. Runa summoned her staff from its holster on the saddle. It still shimmered with light as she fought off the men. Her skill with the staff was well taught but ill-used, as she injured several soldiers in the fracas. Mellypip was knocked off the saddle in the chaos, and tried to return to Runa, and avoid the nervous stomping of the horses around him.

"Runa stop!" Mellypip shouted. "Let us help!"

Driven by an unseen force, Runa turned the horse around and rode into the cursed forest; but even the horse recognized its wicked blight and skidded to an abrupt stop at the boundary of the grim woods. The horse reared up in terror, refusing to trespass into the grim shadows. Runa leapt off the horse and marched into the woods with demented fervor, dropping her bright staff. It rolled into the dry weedy ditch as its glow faded.

"Guards, stop her!" Sorcha commanded. "Knock her out if necessary, but do not let her go into the forest!"

Several soldiers tried to grab Run and pull her away, but her sorcery became potent and wild. A fling of her arm and her magic tossed several soldiers back to the road. Even Captain Vasya, who towered over everyone, was thrown several feet into the air by an angry wave of Runa's hand.

Runa, Runa, Runa, wait for me! Mellypip pleaded as he pursued his sorceress into the dead woodland.

This possessed Runa terrified Mellypip. Knots of fear jabbed in his belly as he followed her into the strange wild. The sun's light vanished in this grim wood. Runa stumbled over a fallen tree, and it was as though she fell through dry paper, as her body crushed it into dusty chunks. Runa pulled herself up and walked on. This forest was void of not only natural life, but any life! Even monsters would be scared of this place. She trekked deeper into the forest where the scent of old divination burned strong now. Death's cold hand lurked here. The hues of greens and browns which marked a forest's mantle had been wiped away by the residue of evil sorcery. Tree bark was bleached dead white. It was as though the woods had lost its soul. The forest loam was piled with fragments of bones, which was very odd; until he realized they were once blades of grass.

Mellypip dashed after her. *Runa wait for me.* Then a thorny wall loomed before them. A wall of chalky grey thorns over thirty feet high surrounded the rest of the forest as far as they could see.

No Runa! Stop! Bad nightmare! Mellypip cried into her mind, trying to reason with her.

Runa collapsed to her knees and pulled at the thorns barring her way, tearing at her flesh. Fresh drops of blood spilled to the parched ground. Sobbing, she summoned bolts of sorcery and finally blazed wildly through the wall of thorns. The smell of her magic was the only wholesome thing here. Runa ran through the charred corridor toward the mystery. Bits of thorn scratched at her face and tore at her clothes. Mellypip followed her on the harsh bramble-covered earth, clenching the little staff in his mouth, his paws pricked and bleeding.

The stench of old sorcery reeked here, spawned from something wicked. Panting and weak, he kept after Runa until they finally passed through the tunnel of thorns into a wide clearing. There they met their nightmare.

A tree of bones greeted them.

The size of the tree of bones was immense, towering over them. Its rickety boughs weighed down with black leaves tipped with red thorns. Its bleak canopy shaded a wide area over the desolate waste.

Runa stopped her fevered march. "Surely, bones conjured from hell pits fashioned this looming menace." She looked around, shaking, "How did I get here, Melly? What happened?"

"You ran here and I chased you," Mellypip panted. "I think we're in trouble. You hit some guards and yelled at the queen."

"Oh no," Runa gasped. "Look!" Runa rushed toward the twisted tree and dropped to her knees. She flung her arms around the trunk of yellowed bones in despair.

Mellypip dropped his little staff and limped over to Runa's side.

"Oh Melly," she whispered. "Look at them."

Exhausted and terrified, he finally saw what the tree held captive in its bony grave and why Runa embraced it.

Bound to the tree's base were two women—or what had once been women. They were statues of smooth bone! They looked a lot like Runa! Mellypip had seen the miniature portraits of Yllia and Rualla enough times to recognize them. The two people bound to the tree were neither stone, flesh, nor bark, but made of smooth polished bone.

"Mother! Grandmother!" Runa wept, leaning against the images. The scent of old divination burned their eyes and noses. "Melly, this is how the demon killed them." She wept. "Grandfather doesn't know. How could he know a demon lied to him! They have been here since—"

"Runa, come away," Mellypip begged, tugging at her skirt. The statues of Yllia and Rualla were too heartbreaking to look upon. Mellypip knew they were not just statues, but Yllia and Rualla's bodies, cursed by bloodstone sorcery into bone.

Runa fingers caressed the smooth bone cheek of one. A drop of Runa's blood marred the pristine bone face. Fresh grief tormented Runa, knowing their fate had been worse than any death she could have imagined.

A flash of light stunned Runa and Mellypip. Runa's body glowed like a star and a burst of thunder shook them. They were bound together and held by the grasp of some strange magic, as fragmented images flooded Runa and Mellypip's consciousness. Trapped by forces stronger than they could fight, they shared a vision of the past.

Yllia and Rualla struggled against the red beams of magic that confined them to this ancient oak tree. It was a true tree then, with crusty bark and deep green leaves. It was night and torches were lit around the tree. Two men were there. The demon Ashur, who stole Ashur's body and life, and Koll! Koll was there! He walked toward Yllia and Rualla. He touched the cheek of each with a black dagger and drew little drops of blood. Xabral coiled at his feet like a lover, enjoying the brutality. Koll unrolled a scroll and touched the bloodstained dagger to the page.

"Yes," the demon Ashur approved, "blood for the spell must come from the living, not the dead."

"I have done it as the ritual demanded; now we must finish this and leave," Koll said. The scroll Koll held was embossed with a large bloodstone. It glowed

with red light as Koll read the incantation. In their strange state, Mellypip and Runa were helpless observers. Mellypip saw the strange symbols on the scroll. They were not even mage speak, but sensed they might be from a demon tongue.

In the distance, lay a baby crying in a basket. Runa! The baby was Runa! Mellypip could not breathe for the fear. Then a red panther slipped by the demon and Koll, hidden by shadow. It was Striker, Rualla's familiar. Striker was wounded, a crossbow bolt buried in his side. A moment of sorrow passed between Rualla and the panther; then the massive cat grasped the wailing bundle in its jaws and carried her away. He saved Runa! The panther fled into the night with his stolen treasure.

"You are not my husband!" Rualla cried. "I thought you had gone mad, but this is too much! He would never do this to me! What did you do to my husband, Ashur?"

"You are right madam; I am not Ashur," the demon taunted. "Some call me a demon. I hold dominion over his body now, though Ashur's memories still exist in this shell. I just wish I had bedded you like he had!"

"They will find us," Yllia shouted with anger.

Koll laughed. "No one hunts for the dead, lady." He picked up a metal urn. "We will deliver this to Cathal, with the ashes of three people inside. Well, two people, as the ashes of a baby take very little room." He held up rings of silver and amber. "I will place your wedding rings with the ashes, along with the rattle for added pain. It should be a memorable gift."

"It will be easy to kill a man with nothing to live for," the demon Ashur said. "We will find the map to lead us to her!" The demon Ashur looked around and cried, "Where is the baby!"

"Striker must have stolen Runa!" Xabral said. "I thought you said you killed Striker!"

"Striker will not get far," Koll said.

"The baby amused me," Demon Ashur ranted. "Like Panthara, she will make a handmaiden for Obsydia, or maybe even a sacrifice. Now we must journey. I will show you where Obsydia is hidden."

Even though it was a visual memory of a time long past, Mellypip could smell the arcane evil of this demon magic. Words of ancient magic Koll summoned filled the wampu's ears, strange words he did not understand. Rualla and Yllia cried out as their flesh petrified to unnatural textures and colors. Rualla grasped Yllia's hand as the magic altered them, flowing like water over their bodies. Even in this moment of doom they faced death with unbending courage. Their eyes, so green and full of life like Runa's, mutated to pale bone like the rest of their bodies.

The damage did not end there, for the rabid demonic conjuration was feral and spread throughout the forest, killing everything in its path.

"Now we hide them from prying eyes," Koll said as they walked away, Xabral coiled around his body.

"Why?" demon Ashur asked as he followed him.

Because this is a sacred and private sacrifice to Obsydia. One that I shall keep secret against Cathal, who is my greatest enemy.

A good distance away, Koll tossed black crystals to the dead earth. Thorns sprouted from the crystals and multiplied around the tree of bones.

Koll looked at his handiwork. "This sacrifice will surely please Obsydia! I offer it to the darkest of all hearts, Obsydia, Goddess of the Bloodstone."

The vision vanished. They were alone in this wasteland again until two voices in unison cried one desperate word, "Alive!"

Mellypip gasped for breath. Runa winced with pain and anger.

"They're alive! How could they be?" Runa cried.

Scenes of the past dissolved into a plight of chaos. The mystical trance which enthralled Runa still bound her to the tree of bones forged from demonic knowledge. Its cruel essence seemed hungry as Runa struggled to break the spell.

Mellypip called into her mind, *Let go Runa. Let go! Come back to me!*

Melly, Melly, help me, Runa whimpered.

He held her fevered head and concentrated, drawing her from the brink, until the dark cord which chained her to the cruel past finally snapped and Runa fell to the ground in convulsions. The bright light shrouding Runa's body finally faded, Runa and Mellypip collapsed together at the base of the tree. Hollowed out and weak, they lay, unable to move.

The single cry of Yllia and Rualla haunted them.

Alive.

Then strong hands lifted Mellypip from Runa's side. Mellypip was vaguely aware of Prince Ulric holding him, stroking him gently with warm hands. Mellypip weakly glanced down to see Opaline cradling Runa's head in her lap.

Runa wept bitterly as Opaline held her tight. "My mother and grandmother have been trapped here since the war. They're not dead, dear gods, they're not dead. They've been trapped here for years! Alone. Without hope." She lifted her head, green eyes veiled by pain. "Koll did this to them."

CHAPTER SEVENTEEN

Ambera's tree tower grew on the edge of Moonthorne, a modest home overlooking the river with broad leafy boughs shading the water; long, exposed moss-covered roots snaked down to the riverbed to rest in shallow water. The usually serene dwelling was surrounded by mourners congesting the woods around Ambera's home. To protect Ambera's privacy, Raven Wing Ranger solemnly guarded her tree tower. Security increased when the Oak and Rowan of Ilyrra arrived to see her one last time.

"Looks like the whole city is camped around here," Darcus said observing the multitude of sorrowful faces gathering across the narrow river. The undercurrent of whispered prayers mingled with the sound of birds. "Ambera must be very important to these folk."

Cathal looked across the river where people gathered in prayer or silent tribute. "She is the mother of this nation, and an old friend I will miss dearly."

"Why was it so dark last night?" Darcus asked. "The moons and stars were shadowed by clouds. I didn't like it. My sister Eshra would accuse me of being superstitious, but a bad foreboding was in the air last night. I couldn't sleep a wink."

"I cannot speak for the heavens, but I didn't sleep either."

"I'm sorry you're losing a friend, Cathal. Ryen told me you were close."

"She is an old friend and a teacher. She guided me after my teacher, Borel, died. She officiated at my wedding to Yllia. She blessed my daughter Rualla when she was born, and she blessed Runa. I never thought I would be visiting her deathbed."

Perched on a small log, Belwyn murmured in disgust, "I hate the term deathbed. It's morbid to wait for someone to pass. And who came up with that phrase anyway? Deathbed! Stupid humans."

Cathal crouched down next to Belwyn, resting his staff in the crook of his other arm. He stroked his beak. *I will miss her too. The world will be a darker place without her light.*

Belwyn harrumphed and looked away. "Have you checked on Runa yet?" he asked avoiding further discussion of death.

"I spoke with Raghnall on the crystal at the Ranger Tower. Runa and Opaline are going to visit Princess Danu at the Abbey. Raghnall assured me Queen Sorcha was chaperoning. I think it might do Runa good to get out of the city too. Her bad dreams and all this madness have been difficult for her."

"Runa's been a bit pale lately," Darcus commented. "She's a strong girl though. She will come through this and you will figure things out, Cathal. You usually do."

"I was too preoccupied with Koll," Cathal said.

"All of us were," Darcus replied, frowning. "I wish I had just killed him when we found him unconscious in that cave. Justice would not have faulted us. The gods would forgive such a minor slight."

"We all share that sin—regret," Belwyn added.

Jadon edged his way through the crowds toward them. "Ambera is asking to see you now. The Oak and Rowan are just departing."

"Thank you, Jadon," Cathal said.

Belwyn settled on Cathal's shoulder and they walked up the small hill. Cathal and Darcus met Ryen at Ambera's front door just as the Oak and Rowan were leaving. The crowd hushed and bowed before the royal couple as they passed.

"Light's Blessings," the Oak and Rowan greeted Cathal and Belwyn. They looked grief-stricken. Niall's golden presence was subdued by the deep grey damask robe he wore. Talaith was beautiful even in sorrow, rich brown hair was simply plaited, and her leaf green eyes were moist with tears. She wore a blue gown which rivaled the sky's beauty.

"Ambera would approve," Cathal complimented her, taking her hands and bowing. "I know that shade of blue is her favorite color."

"Talaith inclined her head and smiled sadly. "Thank you, Cathal. I chose it to honor what gives her joy, rather than lament her with somber mourning."

"We are pleased you could make the journey to see her," Niall said. He nodded to Darcus. "I am also pleased our newest ranger has returned to the fold. Welcome home, Darcus."

Darcus bowed. "Thank you, Oak Niall."

"Ambera desires Darcus and Ryen join Cathal and Belwyn," Talaith said. "She says it's important."

"You are confused Darcus, that the Mother of Ilyrra wants to see a man she has never met?" Niall asked, noting the bewildered expression on Darcus' face.

Darcus nodded uneasily.

"Ambera has a talent for doing that to people." Niall said. "It is also a mark of honor, Ranger Darcus."

"Hurry inside now," Talaith urged, "she grows weaker each moment."

Ryen turned to his son. "Ranger Jadon, join the guard at Ambera's door."

"Thank you, Father," Jadon said with earnest gravity. "I am honored to serve the Mother."

They entered the tree tower. The earthy aroma of apples, vanilla, and nutmeg scented the room. Light crystals were scattered about in generous profusion, some used as weights on stacks of papers. The heady smell of herbs and the remnants of baking bread still filled the house. No odor of death lingered yet.

A Drusai healer sat by the door to Ambera's bedroom. She wore a simple green gauze robe and veil. She rose and opened the door for them. Darcus stationed himself quietly in the back of the room against the wall when they stepped inside. Her bedroom was a clutter of homey chaos. Scrolls and books crowded shelves and bookcases.

In a narrow bed by the window, Ambera was tucked in with a deep blue quilt embroidered with pale moons and stars. Propped up on large pillows encased with snowy white linen, the edges embroidered with light blue flowers. Ambera's eyes were closed, and her long silver hair was in a single thick braid. Her ivory skin was pallid, and wrinkles seamed her face. A flash of memory from many years ago filled Cathal's mind, when Ambera united Yllia and Cathal in marriage. Ambera's skin was smooth as butter and her hair a vibrant walnut brown. She had been a beacon of vitality and it distressed Cathal to see her life slipping away.

Neelam the Wizard was by her side. Another familiar face from the old days. He had been a stern mentor whose sharp gaze missed nothing. He was also a loyal friend. His snow eagle, Surya, regally perched on Ambera's bedpost.

"We are honored the Mage Chieftain of Ironia has come to pay his respects," Ryen whispered as he bowed.

"You needn't speak in hushed tones," Ambera said in a thin voice. "Talking won't scare death away you know."

Cathal and Neelam clasped hands. "I had hoped you would be here."

"We got here the day before you did, boy," Neelam replied.

A thousand years have passed, and he still calls me boy, Cathal moaned to Belwyn.

Comforting, isn't it? Belwyn replied.

"Enough formalities," Surya announced. "Belwyn, take your place by me. Sit down everyone. We have much to discuss."

Belwyn opened his beak, but a glance from Surya closed it.

Surya always did make me feel like a downy owlet, Belwyn communicated to Cathal.

Comforting, isn't it? Cathal replied.

Neelam is grayer now, though his vibrant red hair still outnumbers the grays—unlike you Cathal, Belwyn noted with acerbic observation.

The Dwarven Wizard was still sharp of eye and just as impatient with fools. "Well, what you are waiting for? Go on! Sit boy," Neelam commanded. "There's a stool under that pile of scrolls, Ryen. As leader of the Rangers, Ambera wanted you here too." He snapped his fingers, sparking a flame and lit his pipe. "Don't be shy, Darcus. We won't bite." Neelam motioned toward the stalwart warrior to come closer. Darcus moved closer to the bed, though reluctantly.

"The smoke is not wholesome," the healer scolded from the doorway as Neelam puffed. The smoke filled the room with the aroma of cinnamon.

"He can puff on his pipe if he wants to," Ambera insisted, her eyes still closed. "I asked him to. A proper man smokes a pipe, young lady. Remember that when you choose a husband. I always enjoyed the earthy smell of a fine tobacco. Now be a good girl and wait outside while the adults converse."

The healer bowed, submitting to the daunting task of serving the Mother of Ilyrra. "If anyone gets weepy, I will banish you from my sight," Ambera warned after the healer left.

"I wouldn't dare," Cathal replied. He went to her bedside opposite Neelam and sat on the wobbly stool. Cathal kissed her hand and Ambera opened her eyes.

"Now that's how you greet a lady," Ambera said with a smile.

The bright coppery shade he remembered was dimmed by her great age and illness, but still beautiful. She laughed at Cathal. "Heavens, why are you so gray? Ryen mentioned you used sorcery to turn your hair all silver. Foolish boy. Why?"

"I'm not a boy," Cathal protested. "I'm over a thousand years old, though both of you make me feel like a seventeen-year-old apprentice again."

"Oh, to banish those memories of skinny awkwardness and clumsy magic," Ambera whispered. "Yet, after your teacher Borel was killed by Obsydia, you took his place in our magic circle to fight an evil which almost consumed our world."

"Cathal thinks grandfathers should be silver," Belwyn said. "Apparently that's a mark of wisdom. He may be silver, but I am not betting on his wisdom."

Ambera gingerly touched his hair. "In a couple hundred years your grey will sprout naturally. Be patient. Age comes to us all. No need to rush it."

Cathal's hair and short, neatly trimmed beard sparkled. The silver vanished, replaced by dark brown hair, though Belwyn noted a few traces of grey were visible. "Better?" Cathal asked.

She shifted her head on the pillow. "Yes. I glimpsed Runa when she came here some weeks ago on a mad rescue mission to save your hide! You were with her, Darcus. Yes, I know what happened. She had a hodgepodge of hopeful heroes at her side and a wide-eyed baby wampu as her familiar. Runa's still only a child, yet they all look-ed to her to lead them. Much like you, Cathal. Pretty as a flower too. Runa is as wild and stubborn as Yllia was. Good. It will keep you on your toes."

"You should have talked with Runa," Cathal said. "She would have liked to have met you."

"Bah! What young girl wants to be bored by dull wisdom from a frail old lady? I was pleased to see Runa full of fire and purpose. I never cared for pasty shy girls. Waste of breath." She looked across the room. "You! Darcus! My, what a feral looking warrior you are! Ryen says you are one of us now. Step closer, Darcus. My eyes are too old to see you clearly without magic or a magnifying glass."

Darcus walked to the foot of the bed. Hs dark hair was scruffy as usual and the rough scar over his right eye shadowed his face, but he looked natural in his Raven Wing uniform. The black high-necked tunic, the boots and armor made of Ilyrran oak leather, and the mossy green vest, trousers, and cloak were simple, yet on Darcus looked quite gallant.

Ambera studied Darcus for a moment and smiled with satisfaction. "Ranger Darcus, a human boy serving the Raven Wing of Ilyrra. Imagine that!"

"I'm hardly a boy," Darcus grinned.

"By my standards, you're a boy, but I'll grant you're a hearty one.

Good thing you shaved your beard though, Darcus. Ilyrran men can't grow beards, so you'll look more like one of us. You are a rare man. Savage as a beast and noble as a king. I like you, Ranger Darcus. You will confront unexpected challenges of the heart that will confound your hardened warrior spirit. I hope you live up to my praise. I despise being confounded you know."

Darcus answered, "I will do my duty, Lady Ambera. I always do."

Ambera was pleased. "A fine answer. I never thought to see one of your race take the oath of Raven Wing again, yet here you are. Perhaps that is another sign."

"Stop it now, Ambera," Cathal soothed. "This is not the time to debate the next battle of ages."

"I'm dying, so I'll say what I please," Ambera insisted. "My time is short and I don't want to be late for my passage to the Otherside because you quibble like children. I've always wanted to meet the Eternals and ask them to explain their mistakes to me." She winked at Darcus. "Most of us Ilyrrans can live a couple hundred years, if we're lucky, but we mages live a lot longer. We are not immortal though. Cathal is over a thousand, and so is scruffy old Neelam here. But don't get too jealous. It can be a trying and lonely existence, especially when you see silly folk making the same mistakes over and over again. I am the oldest living Ilyrran. *The Ancient Mother*, they call me. I wonder who will wear that harebrained title when I pass into spirit. Poor thing, whoever it is. Such a fussy title. It brings images of runny porridge and infirmity. Personally, I prefer something more sensual."

Neelam squeezed her hand. "You helped deliver your people and the world from darkness. You became the mother of a nation. And you were a fine-looking wench. A good testimony to your life."

"It wasn't in my plans to mother a nation," Ambera scoffed. "The Eternals are amused when mortals make plans. They like to shuffle things around to spice up the journey." She closed her eyes again. "I am tired. Tired of seeing uncertain futures and reliving the past. I was once Ambera of Elfshara, when my race was called the Elfsharan--until Obsydia ruined our land with her demon army and diabolistic sorcery. We relinquished our race name and our ravaged country after the defeat. We could never return to the home of our birth. I became Ambera of the Fallen People, nomads fighting the demon armies, and then I became Ambera of Ilyrra, when we made our new home here after the fall of Obsydia. I have lived through three Ages. The Sapphire Age, the time of my birth and youth. Then the Bloodstone Age erupted when Ahridum hurled a dark star upon our world. I grew up hard. I lost everything. My country, my family and my man. The Bloodstone Age did not last long, but the evil left deep scars in the soul of the world, as it did on my heart. Kingdoms were destroyed, mountains shot hot lava at the sky and the oceans heaved with violence. Multitudes died of starvation in the long winter that followed that cruel blast. A winter which lasted years until light was just a distant memory. Then came this age, the Topaz Age, the time of healing. Our Topaz Age is one of light, but it has been dimmed because *her* darkness still stains the earth."

"She cannot die by mortal hands or by magic, but she cannot escape. We made sure of that," Cathal assured her.

"Pour me some rose wine. I want to taste a drop before I die," Ambera whispered. "Then I will say what is important."

"The healer said you shouldn't have any," Neelam grinned.

"I'll have my rose wine. Let's toast my bones now, before the dirges get boring," Ambera winked.

Neelam poured them all cups of rose wine and passed them around. Cathal lifted Ambera's head and helped her sip the potent drink.

When she was done, Ambera sighed. "Now I have the strength to tell you why I wanted all of you here. I must speak truth without riddles now. Darcus and Ryen, did you know we three were the ones who trapped Obsydia the Bloodstone Queen?"

Darcus raised an eyebrow and remarked to Cathal, "Keeping secrets from me, old mage?"

"And from me as well," Ryen said. "We knew three mages destroyed Obsydia, but their names were never spoken.

"Not destroyed," Ambera corrected. "Trapped the she demon in a prison of light. Which is the problem—trapped is not dead."

"Many folk think what happened all those years ago was not all real," Surya said. "Spells were forged to prevent Obsydia's followers from finding her lost temple buried in the sands! Some even believe Obsydia was just a powerful sorcerous queen who used dark magic."

"We have been called the Mage Trinity, the Scions of Light. In truth, we were three desperate mages battling a war against evil and got lucky. There were cults that worshipped the Dark Trinity and consider Obsydia a goddess," Neelam added. "The truth has faded over the centuries. Things have changed. There are rumors in the temples of Ahridum. Whispers of a deliverer."

"Those whispers milled about for centuries," Cathal said. "Now it is a true threat. Koll declared himself Obsydia's deliverer. After we captured him in Mowad, I was in communication with a spy the previous Archon, Ramirez, had watching the high temple in Kra'zum. Now Gabriel is spying for me, as he had for his father. He was sending me messages."

"You never told us," Darcus said.

"After the incident in Mowad with Koll, I realized the threat to free Obsydia was a possibility. Even if Koll cannot free her from the prison we created, he can use her as a template to mount a dark holy war. I haven't heard from him since before Koll escaped his execution, and I fear Gabriel may be dead. Koll is obsessed with Obsydia and his hunt for her tomb is well known. It was the indirect cause of the Sorcerer War. It also caused the deaths of my wife, daughter, and her husband, Ashur. Many a follower of the shadows have hunted for her lost temple. Now Koll is free and I could not stop him."

Ambera looked at Cathal with compassion. "You did nothing wrong, my boy. To this day, the deaths of your family haunt me, as I did not foresee their peril, but only a shroud of shadow and bone I could never see through. You can only do so much against blood-stone sorcery and Koll's familiar had an ample supply of the deadliest spells which he used quite liberally. I know Koll is what the Dark Eternals have concealed long before we even became aware of him. They have plans for him. You must take care. Once we were three, Neelam, Cathal, and myself. We defeated Obsydia the Bloodstone Queen. We used the combined magic of our three castes to entomb her in a crystal of living Light. The secret to our success was a gift from the Winged Fey who provided powerful magic that sealed the ritual. Once imprisoned, her temple palace was consumed by the sands of Skarros. We thought it would keep forever, but I warn all of you now that prison will shatter! I have seen Obsydia free of the Light. A new darkness is coming!" Ambera wailed.

"Hush, Ambera! Obsydia is trapped forever," Cathal assured her. "We did this. The Winged Fey promised it would be enough to hold her."

"When dealing with a spawn of Dark Eternal origin, anything is possible," Neelam warned.

Ambera's hand shook and she grasped Cathal's arm. "What we did to Obsydia will not hold her much longer! Her dark prophet will rescue her from light's chains. The Topaz Age is ending. Like the Bloodstone Age, it is only a transition leading to something else. The world had only known Ages of Light until Ahridum twisted things." Ambera paused and Neelam tenderly took her hand. She breathed with difficulty for a moment, and then continued. "A new age is coming. The next war, that will bring the new era, will affect our world for all time. If Darkness wins, then all the future eras will be of Darkness and if Light wins, all the future eras will be Light. This is not the mutterings of senility! I warn you with this truth to save us all. I was Drusane! The Seer of Ilyrra. Araema and Rhone have shown me this truth in dreams. This is my truth. My time is done, but you are not! You were there, Cathal and Neelam, when we trapped that bitch of darkness! It was only a trap, and evil is good at escaping traps. You must all be strong! Else, we are all doomed to the dark."

"I promise," Cathal cried. "We all do."

Ambera closed her eyes and let out one last exhalation of life.

The healer rushed to Ambera's bedside, sensing the passing of her charge, and wept at its confirmation.

Neelam, a dwarf of over four and half feet, had the bearing of a giant as he stood. With tenderness he laid his hand on Ambera's brow and prayed aloud. "Ambera of Ilyrra, Light's Blessing guide your way through the Gate of Souls. Go to the paradise where heroes dwell, for there was none braver than you. The burdens of this world can pass to others now. Your soul is free, Ambera. Farewell."

Ambera, Mother of Ilyrra, was dead.

Jadon entered the room and bowed. "I'm sorry to intrude, Cathal. I don't know how to say this gently. A message from Raghnall says Runa found your wife and daughter, or what remains of them, in the cursed forest outside of Aybarr. His message was wild, but Runa insists they are not dead. That is all I know. I am sorry, Cathal. You must return at once."

CHAPTER EIGHTEEN

A tree of bones.

Cathal could not dispel the image from his mind. How could his Yllia and Rualla be trapped in a bone tree for fifteen years? Numb through and through, Cathal could not even feel the wind through his feathers as he dipped low in the air and glided down to earth.

"Watch your wingspread," Belwyn warned, swooping down by his side. "Else you'll fly beak first into the mud."

"I know what I'm doing," Cathal replied.

"Of course you do," Belwyn replied.

Cathal noted the stubborn owl had not taken his eyes off him the whole journey. Neither did Neelam and Surya. No one left him alone since Jadon told them about the tree of bones in Ambera's tower when she died. What about poor Runa? What had she suffered facing this terrible truth in the forest? He was not there. He was supposed to take care of her. She was still a child. Why is it he never knew? Did Ashur's demon deliberately keep this secret, and deceive them with the ashes for some other bizarre purpose? A thousand more questions loomed. A thousand more questions that did not have answers crowded his mind until he thought he might explode.

"What are you thinking?" Belwyn asked,

"I'm surprised you haven't pried into my mind to find out," Cathal replied.

"I could you know," Belwyn said testily. "Watch it!"

"Damn it!" Cathal shouted, making a sloppy landing on the road.

Belwyn dropped by his side and said, "Told you so."

"You're trying my patience, Belwyn," Cathal warned.

"An angry response is better than nothing," Belwyn replied. "You've been a ghost since Moonthorne."

"I am not breaking down," Cathal insisted.

"I'm not saying you are," Belwyn said.

A large company of Thill soldiers waited at the edge of the cursed forest. Cathal shimmered back into his natural human form and dusted off his tunic and trousers. He looked around.

"Why have they summoned so many soldiers?" Belwyn asked, perching on his shoulder.

"That's why," Cathal answered, pointing his staff at the road, to the scattered groups of people that huddled together on the outskirts of the forest. Some were praying aloud some were staring with sharp curiosity. "Let's hope they have enough common sense to stay out of those woods."

"They are people. You give them too much credit," Belwyn replied.

"Even I would be afraid to step into the cursed woods. But some might, and that's why the guards were there. To protect what was inside and the fools that pry too deeply," Cathal said.

Neelam landed next to him and shed his snow eagle form in a glimmer of golden light. He marched toward Cathal, clutching his staff. His physical size did not diminish his commanding presence as he surveyed the area.

Surya perched on a fallen log, looking at the rim of the dead forest with tremulous apprehension. "These woods are a nightmare made real," she commented with a shiver.

Cathal walked toward Captain Vasya. "Take me too them."

"Yes, Lord Cathal," Captain Vasya said.

"We tried to find it from the air," Neelam said. "But the aerial view is blocked by strange grey mist, roofed with dead branches and thorns."

The stalwart Vasya turned to Neelam and looked down. "Forgive me sir, but who are you?" he inquired.

"I'm an old war companion," Neelam replied tersely, looking up at the giant with equal tenacity. "I'm here to offer moral support."

"This is Neelam, Wizard and Mage Chieftain of Ironia," Cathal said quickly. "His familiar is Surya."

"Mage Chieftain," Vasya bowed, "we are honored."

"Just Neelam will do, my good man. I don't care for pompous titles. Now lead on, my giant friend." Neelam marched toward the woods, his staff keeping time with the rhythm of his quick steps. "Let's see what this thicket of hell is hiding."

"He hasn't changed," Belwyn commented.

"Where is Runa now?" Cathal asked Vasya, trying to focus on the journey. His stomach sickened as he walked deeper into the parched land. He was glad he had not had any breakfast.

"Runa is safe at the Abbey, Cathal," Vasya said, striding along on long thick-muscled legs, a sword clenched in his large hand. "The Queen herself is looking after your granddaughter. They're all at the

Abbey waiting for you. Raghnall and Lady Opaline are there too. Caliste just arrived, but she too stopped to see this tragedy, though we warned her."

"My wife raised Caliste," Cathal said. "She was a sister to my Rualla."

"Caliste and her cat could not stop weeping afterward. I should not have let them see that cursed tree. A lady should not be exposed to such things. It is not proper. I have refused any strangers passage here."

"Thank you, Captain, we appreciate your diligence. How are Runa and Mellypip recovering?" Cathal asked.

Vasya stepped over a dead log. "Raghnall says Runa will recover from the shock. Her tiny wampu was quite brave. I think the little fellow sensed something before the rest of us did. He protected his sorceress in this hell. You should be proud, Belwyn."

"I am," Belwyn agreed.

"Also, do not worry. Be assured Her Majesty has requested a company of men stand guard around these woods. We know you would want your privacy protected. Too many people have already heard of this tragedy. I do not understand why folk intrude on another's sorrow. It is not proper," Vasya said, frowning, making his brown mustache droop more.

"People always nose in where they don't belong," Belwyn said. "It's human nature. I am often glad I'm not human."

I do not know if I can take this? Belwyn said to Cathal through the bonding. *How did Runa endure this?*

We must, Belwyn. Think also of what poor Yllia and Rualla suffered here. Cathal kept his face neutral as he walked, but he wanted to break down. *Runa! It tears my heart she had to see such a thing.*

The potent reek of evil made Cathal dizzy. His head throbbed and his eyes watered. When they finally came to the wall of thorns that surrounded a large section of the forest, the sight was terrifying. Only the narrow corridor Runa's sorcery had burned through had traces of a clean wholesome scent. Cathal walked through the pathway of thorns; his chest tightened and his stomach knotted into a ball, but he walked on.

"You holding up, boy?" Neelam asked, keeping step with Cathal.

"I'm holding Neelam," Cathal replied. "I cannot promise anything else."

"You're doing better than I would," Neelam said. "If my beloved and daughter were trapped for years in this grim arboreal menace, I'd be a raving lunatic."

"I'm sure I can accommodate you later with a fit," Cathal whispered, feeling his heart twist as he stepped into the clearing. He had been warned about what he would find here.

They reached the grove, and the tree of bones that shaded the area with deathly boughs. Cathal looked at the vast tree, stunned by its terrible, ugly beauty. The bones that thickened the trunk and the jagged bones that spread out from the tree's canopy were ivory with a yellowish tinge and drooped with black leaves tipped with red thorns. When he saw the image of Yllia and Rualla at the base of the tree, frozen and lifeless, it was a blow that sucked out his breath.

"What demented sculptor carved these images," Cathal whispered. The pain he felt all those years ago when he was told they were dead revived with such virulence Cathal's whole being was a raw wound of pain.

"Cathal, this is not the worst of it," Iona said, stepping from the shadows. Iona, veiled in her black with silver runes dangling from her veil, stood at the base of the tree. Only her ice blue eyes gave any wholesome color to this stark landscape.

"Iona, how long have you been here?" Cathal asked with difficulty.

"Three days, since Captain Vasya fetched me to examine them. After I touched the tree and sensed their souls, I did not want to leave them alone, Cathal. I could not. They sleep, but are sometimes aware, I think. Runa was right about them still living, in some fashion. My necromancy detects two souls trapped in this bone terror. They are still with us, Cathal. I am aware of their souls within. I am so sorry."

"I don't know if I should rejoice or cry," Belwyn said. "Yllia, and my little Rualla, they are truly alive?"

"Their souls are trapped here. Whether or not their bodies can survive if we can manage to free them from this dark sorcery, I do not know. Iona's blue eyes were bright with tears. "Cathal, I am so sorry."

Cathal, stunned with grief, was immobile. He could only stare at the still images of his wife and daughter. He noticed their hands were clasped together; in that final breath they managed to cling together.

Neelam walked toward the aberration. "Cathal," he said, "this is beyond us all. I do not know if anyone could survive such a metamorphosis. This is not any normal magery, but demon magic. It's Bloodstone diabolism. I haven't seen anything like this in a thousand years."

"There is more you must know," Iona said. "Runa will tell you, but you should learn it now. Runa needs to recover from this horror and reliving it each time she tells is not good for her. It is true the demon that possessed Ashur was here when this horror was done, but from what Runa saw in her vision of the past; Ashur's demon did not do this. It was Koll. Koll did this to them."

"Koll?" Cathal's whisper was so cold, even Belwyn wanted to flee to the heavens.

Neelam looked at Cathal with concern. "Cathal, are you still with us?"

Cathal was deaf to all the voices around him. He stood there before his wife and daughter, staring at their frozen beauty.

Iona started to go to Cathal, but Neelam stopped her. "Comfort him later," Neelam advised.

Belwyn looked at the others and commanded, "Go."

The owl guarded Cathal as the others, even Neelam and Surya, left the grove of terrors. Vasya gently took Iona's arm and guided her through the long path of thorns, Amun on her shoulder.

Cathal knelt before the sad bone statues of what were his wife and daughter.

Only when they were alone did Cathal's pain and rage explode. Belwyn waited, patiently with stubborn love until it was over.

CHAPTER NINETEEN

Skarros, the Wasteland.

Grimm Darkrunner howled at the dismal sky. Night's bitter chill stripped away the day's insufferable heat. He hated this wretched landscape. The two moons only dimly illuminated the sky and even the stars seemed absent here. Resting on the rocky outcrop overlooking the Wasteland, he tracked the troll in the distance. The troll's speed increased since crossing into this forbidding desert. Weary, Grimm stopped to rest his sore, irritated paws. He did not know how much longer he could go on like this. His rib bones protruded beneath his filthy black fur and exhaustion seared him to the bone. Grimm wondered if at least water could be found somewhere in this forsaken wilderness his father called Skarros.

Midnight had warned him few animals lived in this place. On his trek, an occasional stray tiny lizard would dart across the sands or a lumbering beetle would crawl up from a dusty grave. Meager meals indeed, yet he took what little the desert offered. Grimm resented being pushed here by his ghostly father to a desolate land of nowhere where death walked. He breathed in the odor of peculiar, unnamable essences that followed the troll now…dark spectral things. He did not investigate these strange entities. Grimm had enough problems.

A pitiful shriek interrupted Grimm's thoughts. Could that be food? It was not a human cry, and it was definitely *not* the troll. Hunger urged him toward the sound, and unfortunately, toward the foul-smelling troll as well.

He jumped from the rocks, following the frantic wails across the sands. He climbed another hill to a stony protrusion that overlooked a narrow, dry riverbed that had not seen water in centuries.

Below, a black gryphon screamed in terror, fighting back feebly against the troll's tusks and claws. Grimm spotted the gryphon's torn and bloody wing and pity overwhelmed him. Unable to suffer the cruelty any longer, the wolf jumped from the rocks, landing on the troll's back. The thrill of the attack filled Grimm with fresh strength as he ripped away chunks of fur from its back. The troll howled and ran away.

The wolf stood his territory and won. The taste of the troll sickened his stomach. He spat out tufts of troll hair and turned his attention to the gryphon that cowered before him. It was indeed a strange looking creature. His father told him about other mystical beasts. Gryphons had the body, hind legs and tail of a lion; the head and front legs were those of an eagle, tall ear tufts, and a sturdy pair of wings finished this jest of creation. His father told them gryphons were fierce; but Grimm saw only a wounded creature shaking with fear.

So much for dinner.

Grimm sighed. "Do not fear me, Gryphon. I will not eat you."

A glimmer of hope lit the gryphon's eyes. "Do you promise?"

Grimm had not expected the creature to understand him or he it. He was merely being polite. "How do you understand my words?" Grimm asked.

"I'm a gryphon. We are magical. All mystical creatures share the same tongue. You must be magical too! Are you a familiar?"

"I am told this, yes."

"Who is your wizard or sorcerer?" the gryphon asked shyly.

"I have none," Grimm answered. "I'm alone. My father spoke of your clan but did not include their magical status." He moved closer to the gryphon and noted it was thin and the inky feathers dusty. "Who do you belong to?"

The poor thing hung his head. "They are so far way! I brought a sorcerer named Koll here, but he was not my keeper or my friend. He made me bring him. Bad man. Scares me. His familiar is worse! A mean snake named Xabral! Cruel snake picked on me all the time. Koll and Xabral were going to hurt my friend, Melly, so I obeyed them.

"Who is Melly?"

"A familiar, like you," the gryphon said with a sniffle. "Melly is very brave. He's a valiant wampu ranger-mage."

"A wampu brave? A ranger-mage?" Grimm remarked. "He must be…unusual."

"Oh, he is! I miss Melly so much. He helped take care of me. There were so many I loved. There was Darcus, Runa, and the owl Belwyn who was bossy but nice. Princess Opaline always brought me apples. The perytons were kind. I liked them all, well, except for a badger named Dabiro. He was very cranky. We stayed at a magical house. We were a family. Melly was my best friend. I was not cramped in stables all the time. They never yelled at me or scolded me when I forgot things. I got to run in the yard and fly. I love to fly." He glanced sadly at his wounded wing and then looked at Grimm. "Why don't you have a mage? You must be a very valiant familiar. You scared off the troll. Couldn't you find someone powerful and nice?"

"I have lived alone since I was a cub," Grimm answered. "I know little of these strange mysteries. I was born in the wild. I am alone."

"That is sad," the gryphon said. "It's not good to be alone."

"What is your name?" Grimm asked, hoping to distract the gryphon from further talk of loneliness.

"I'm called Rono. I have a much longer name my old keeper gave me, but I cannot always remember it. Rono, Rono, oh! Wait! Now I remember! It's Quoronos! But everyone calls me Rono. I am free with my friends. Before I was just property."

"How long were you the property of people?"

The gryphon shook its head. "Not sure. I was born free, on an island with tall palm trees that shaded warm beaches. I remember an ocean so blue and lots of fruit trees. When you shook the trees fruit dropped to the ground and we ate it. When I was still a baby hatch-ling, gryphon wranglers caught me in a net. They brought me to a strange land. They weren't nice to me. They withheld food and water unless I did certain things on command. Sometimes they would hit me with a whip. Later, a man named Hemio bought me and took me away. He was much nicer, but too busy to see me much. Princess Opaline was good to me though, and always brought me goodies and would scratch my head. Then I met Runa and Mellypip. They said Hemio went away, but I could stay with them. Now I have lots of friends. I miss the magic house. They were all so good to me. Some think I am stupid, but I am not so dumb. I sense evil. Evil is strong here." Fresh sobs wracked the gryphon. "I can't find my way home. Now my wing is broken."

"Where are this Koll and Xabral?" Grimm asked. "If they are wicked, they should be avoided."

The gryphon trembled. "They went down the scary hole after the earthquake. The sorcerer Koll was trying to find a goddess he called Obsydia."

"Why didn't you fly away when the troll attacked?" Grimm asked gently.

The gryphon hung his head. "I was sleeping in the shelter of these rocks. Troll pounced on me. Mean creature, just like snake. I remember that troll. He was a human until Opaline turned him into a troll when he tried to kill her, but it was an accident. We never speak of it because it upsets her." The gryphon looked at the wolf with trusting eyes, "Will you be my friend?"

Grimm's heart raced. The gryphon's connection to the troll was no accident and for the first time, he had a flicker of faith in his father's promises of fate. Overcome by the innocence of the creature, the tether of a friend, a companion, warmed Grimm's heart. "Yes Rono, I will be your friend. My name is Grimm Darkrunner. I am an outcast with no pack, and a familiar with no mage, but I will be your friend."

Rono shyly moved closer. "I like you, Grimm Darkrunner."

"You're welcome, Rono." The wolf studied the landscape. Gusts of flame issued from the ground in some places, and it was dangerous to even walk here. They needed shelter. A cave somewhere, to make a proper den. He also needed to find out where the troll went. The gryphon was too fragile to leave alone for too long.

"You are thinking too hard," the shimmering black wolf chided as it walked toward him.

"Where the hell have you been?" Grimm barked, annoyed at his sire's casual intervention after he had done all the work.

Confused, Rono looked at Grimm. "Who are you talking to?" he asked, looking around.

"My father's ghost," Grimm replied. The wolf did not know how to lie or use subterfuge to cover the unexplainable forces that ruled his life. He simply told the truth.

"The troll found the lair. You need to follow, but do not make yourself known to what is there," Midnight warned. "We must keep an eye on what is happening, so be silent."

"Who is in this lair?" Grimm asked bluntly.

"The gryphon knows them. Koll and Xabral have found *her*."

"What can I do? Rono says this Koll and his snake are evil and cruel, and very powerful. If I cannot make myself known or fight them, why did I even come here?" Grimm argued.

Midnight glowed, circling him. "This is beyond evil. It is the threat of Darkness, not the night which is natural. This is Darkness spawned of an Eternal. We must observe, Grimm, which is why you must watch silently for now. Our quest is knowledge."

Grimm relented. "Then take me to this terrible place. While I risk my hide, perhaps my father's spirit can find us a safe cave somewhere?"

Midnight's eyes narrowed. "You are demanding of late."

"It's a simple request," Grimm countered. "Rono needs care and protection while his wing heals, and we must find food."

Midnight laughed. "Gryphons are not known for being brilliant."

"Leave him alone," Grimm said firmly.

"You're very protective of one you have only just met," Midnight observed.

"You shouldn't be so cruel to the innocent," Grimm reprimanded him.

"As you wish," Midnight replied.

Midnight guided them a few miles to where a great chasm had opened up the earth. Grimm looked at Rono. "Wait here but hide if you see anyone or anything."

Rono nodded and sat down to wait a safe distance from the hollow.

Grimm leapt into the crater, following the scent of the troll.

He trekked deeper into the abyss, filled with dread more terrifying than anything he sensed above ground. The bottom of the pit opened to a corridor. Grimm stepped inside, wondering why he was so mad as to go into this pit of hell. These ancient halls whispered of great evil best left undisturbed. This temple celebrated evil, finding beauty only in darkness. The residue of evil still clung here. Grimm's fur bristled with fear as he passed blue flames on the walls, held by something his father had once explained as torches. *Men are strange to play with fire.* Grimm breathed in the air, detecting strong enchantments.

He came across many parched bones, unsure if they were human, animal, or demon. Fear gripped his vitals even more strongly now. The troll's ugly shrieks echoed in the cavernous underground. He followed until the speech of man gave him pause. Silent, he crouched down and peered inside the great chamber, but kept to the shadows.

A tall crystal of immense beauty was partially covered by a cloak of sheer black material. Even so, the light was blinding. It hurt to look at it, but there was clean warmth from the light which Grimm found oddly comforting. The light was not evil, but it held a captive, for within its blinding brilliance he saw the image of a woman. *She* was not good. His instinct warned him she was also not truly human. Perhaps this was the Eternal his father spoke of? Despite the purity of the crystal, her evil radiated so strongly it struck him like a blow. The troll was there too. It groveled at the base of the crystal, covering its eyes with its paws, drooling on the floor.

The woman spoke. "Koll, see what has come to worship me. I think I have a new pet."

A tall man fearlessly approached the mad troll. His hair and eyes black as coal, but Grimm sensed his heart was even darker. He did not like him.

"Koll, you shaved off your beard," the woman said. "Good. It pleases me. I do not like men with beards."

"I do all for your pleasure, Queen Obsydia," Koll replied with a bow. He looked down at the pathetic creature. "I know who this troll is. It's Gorvanus, the feeble sorcerer who worked for me in Tiamet. He was transformed into a troll by Princess Opaline, an untrained sorceress, a fact that eluded all of us until it was too late. Gorvanus tried to assassinate Opaline for Prince Levandius. Her sorcery cursed him and now he's a troll. Serves him right for being so incompetent."

Grimm was taken back when he heard the name *Opaline*. He remembered the gryphon mentioned her. Was she truly part of his pack? He remembered the underlying mark of magic he sniffed when he first saw the troll, that pure stroke of beauty he detected beneath the foul. Could this Opaline be the source of that light?

"Gorvanus the troll has come in devotion. The first of our minions." Koll waved his hand in front of his face, his expression sour. "However, we must do something about his aroma."

"Good luck with that task," a snake said as it slithered happily toward the sorcerer. It was several feet long, with red and black scales and a vicious looking stinger. "Gorvanus is not so pretty now!" the snake taunted, waving his stinger. "Can I kill him, Obsydia?"

Rono spoke of a mean snake named Xabral who served Koll and tormented the gryphon. He was accurate in his description.

Obsydia could move her head, but the rest of her body was still as a tree. "I think not. Gorvanus can provide us with amusement." Obsydia's scarlet mouth curved into a wicked smile. Grimm realized her hair was not any kind of hair or fur he knew of. It was a shadow of mist floating about her face. Her silver eyes glittered as she spoke, "I see his past. Gorvanus…so greedy in his human life. He had no scruples. Fragments of his human life torment him, mingling with his beastly state. I find that pleasurable."

"Gorvanus could be a good watchdog if trained," Koll observed.

"I have no intention of housebreaking a troll," Xabral said. "And he is no longer Gorvanus. Such a wretched idiot does not even deserve a name. Let's just call it Troll."

Obsydia's ruby lips curled into a chilling smile. "His mind, what little is left of it, is open and exposed as a sliced pomegranate. The little seeds of his life are vulnerable to me. I can control him with ease, as I always have with my demons. This prison holds me captive, but I have many Eternal gifts, else this torture of excruciating light would have scorched me to ash a thousand years ago. I have slept for centuries, waiting to be released. I long to sate my hungry heart with the blood of my enemies and bring darkness to the world forever."

"How can I free you?" Koll asked. "All the sorcery I've tried failed to break this prison!"

"You cannot Koll, for all your great power, this is beyond sorcery. We must summon help from the Otherworld, the shadow realm of my father, Ahridum. Only then can we shatter this living Light.

"Living light?" Koll asked.

"Yes, it is alive!" Obsydia proclaimed. "My Eternal powers saved me from the oblivion of madness its torture would have wrought. The three mages who cast me into this prison, I hope they still live, so I may torment them when I am finally free. Alas, even a mage's life is limited, and death may have claimed them by now."

"Who trapped you, Queen Obsydia?" Koll asked. "If they do live, I shall cut their hearts out."

Obsydia's silver eyes darkened. "Ambera of the Fallen People, Neelam the Wizard, and Cathal the Sorcerer!"

"Cathal was one of the scions of light!" Koll cried, stepping back. "If it is the same man, my greatest enemy is yours as well. Yes, they still live. Ambera is very old now and near death. The other two must have been much younger than Ambera when they did this to you and are still vital. I promise to kill them for you."

"No, I want them brought to me after I have my freedom. What I plan to do to them will be worse than any death. I will, however, permit you to watch."

Xabral shook his stinger. "Goody."

"What of the Winged Fey?" Obsydia asked. "Their blood and tears spiced their enchantment that has trapped me for a thousand years."

"They vanished after the Bloodstone Wars," Koll replied. "No one has seen their kind in a thousand years."

"They are not dead," Obsydia replied. "They are immortal and have the essence of Eternals running through their veins. They cannot find solace in death. My sovereignty is restricted to this mean jail, but I am still the Bloodstone Queen. This bright tomb that is my bane must be broken. Then I shall take my revenge. Then I shall take the world for my father, Ahridum. Once I sought to kill all the mages in this world. I was commanded to snuff out all magic, anything that challenged my sovereignty and threatened the Dark. A seer at my court once told me a sorcerer would be my deliverer. I killed her for such blasphemy. Now I know her words were truth. You are my chosen one, Koll. Free me from this prison and you shall sit at my feet as my warrior priest. I give you the promise of an Eternal." She glanced down at the scorpion snake, "You shall be my beloved pet and assassin of infidels."

Xabral bowed his head, eyes full of adoration. "Yes, my goddess."

Obsydia spoke longingly, swaying her head. "I long to feast on the warm red nectar of life and taste death cool in my mouth again. Hearts shall be ripped out to honor my radiance. The temples will run red with the glory of sacrifice. I will cloak the world with blood. I shall destroy the light, so only my darkness reigns in majesty. Gather my worshippers in this grave of shadow. Bring them to me. Sacrifice to me."

Grimm was sickened by her malicious words, but in his disgust was reckless too. He must have made a noise because the snake sniffed around, tongue lashing in and out, trying to seek out what else has crept into the abyss.

Xabral hissed, head bobbing. "Something else is here."

Caution urged Grimm to flee back to the world above, where terrors were solid and mortal, born of hunger and tiredness, but fear rooted him.

"Run, run, you fool!" his ghost father barked, appearing behind him.

Freed of his paralysis, Grimm fled. He followed his path back to the surface. He struggled up from the pit. Bone tired, he scrambled to safety and lay there panting in the sand. Rono waddled over to him and nudged him tenderly.

Midnight shimmered before him, "She sensed you, fool. We must take care in the future. Did I not say our quest was important, my son? I have found us a cave; if you have the strength to follow me."

Weary, Grimm lifted his head, "I really hate you sometimes."

A dark thing scuttled past them and descended into the pit.

Grimm jumped up, despite his aching tiredness, and the gryphon frantically flapped its good wing in panic.

"*What was that?*" Grimm growled, his ears flattened and body crouched down.

Midnight cocked his ethereal head sideways and replied, "I think it was a goblin. A young one too. Damn, haven't seen one of those since the Sorcerer War. Best tread with care Grimm, for if the demons are crawling out of their holes now, things could get ugly sooner than I thought."

"Have I mentioned that I hate you?" Grimm asked.

The gryphon's good wing drooped.

Grimm shook his head and growled softly, "No. Not you, Rono. My ghost of a father. Come, let us flee to shelter. Quickly."

CHAPTER TWENTY

Opaline paced impatiently in a circle by the front gate. Abbess Odelia hurried to join her, her girth jiggling beneath her voluminous robes as she adjusted her askew turban. She carried a cloak on her arm.

"Goodness," the Abbess said breathlessly. "It's so chilly this morning. You should not be out in this blustering wind without a cloak, my dear. You'll make yourself ill."

Opaline had not even noticed how cold it was. She accepted the cloak. "Thank you, Abbess."

"Have you slept at all?"

Opaline stopped her relentless orbit and shrugged. "I can't sleep. I thought I should watch for Cathal. I needed the air anyway."

"How's Runa?" Odelia whispered.

"Sleeping again, thank heavens. I finally convinced Sorcha and Ulric to get some rest. How can I sleep when my best friend is suffering so?"

Odelia tucked her plump, sturdy hands into the wide sleeves of her plain blue habit, breathless from her short sprint. "Poor child! It's terrible for an innocent girl like Runa to suffer. Come inside. How can you be sure Cathal will arrive today? They are traveling from Moonthorne. That's so far. Are they riding perytons?"

"No, they're flying. And there they are!" Opaline shouted, pointing to the sky.

Odelia craned her neck, her expression quizzical. "Where? I see only birds."

Four birds flew over the gate. The flock was not normal, for it was comprised of two snow eagles and two owls. They swept down and landed before Opaline and Odelia. A brief shimmer clouded them, and then suddenly there was only one owl and one eagle, for the other two shapeshifted back into human form.

Opaline recognized the pain behind Cathal's stoic expression. It was a mask she knew all too well. Her father never revealed his emotions, even in private and never to her. Opaline did something she could never do with her own father. She threw her arms around Cathal and embraced him tightly for a moment.

"Thank the gods you're here," Opaline cried. "I am so sorry, so very sorry."

Cathal returned her embrace for a heartbeat and took a deep breath before they parted.

"Thank you, dear. You were there? You saw?" Cathal whispered.

Opaline wiped angry tears from her cheeks. "Yes. It was heart-breaking. If I had the power to kill anyone, it would be Koll for what he has done—and that death would be a bloody one."

"Dear Opaline, such dangerous words from a delicate princess," Odelia exclaimed, pressing fleshy fingers to her quivering mouth.

"Opaline is not that delicate," Belwyn remarked.

"I'll take that as a compliment," Opaline replied.

Cathal regained his stoic face. "We flew here as fast as we could. Thank you for looking after my girl."

"Cathal, what's happened to your hair?" Opaline blurted, staring at Cathal's dark hair and beard.

Cathal self-consciously touched his head. "It's hard to explain."

Belwyn alighted to Cathal's shoulder. "Never mind that for now. We'll happily explain after we see Runa."

In her emotional state, Opaline hardly noticed the Dwarf Lord who arrived with Cathal. His hair and beard vibrant red with touches of grey, and garbed more like a warrior than a wizard, wearing brown oak-leather and bracers, and a sword with a large sapphire set into the hilt was strapped to his back. The snow eagle perched on his muscular arm and his staff was evidence of his wizardry. Opaline knew many royals, nobles, and warriors throughout her life, and recognized a man of true rank and power when she saw one. You could sense that off the man even if you were a village idiot. "Who are your noble companions?" Opaline inquired with a side glance.

"Sorry," Cathal said quickly. "May I present the Mage Chieftain of Ironia, Lord Neelam. He's an old friend."

"Just Neelam will do ladies. My familiar is called Surya," Neelam answered with an elegant bow. "We appreciate your hospitality."

Odelia opened her hands in the traditional welcome. "Welcome to our humble Abbey of Araema, honored guests. I am Abbess Odelia. I am happy to serve. Your rooms are being prepared in the guest house."

"Thank you, Abbess. Take me to Runa now," Cathal whispered.

"Of course, I'll do it. Follow me," Opaline said.

"Thank you, my dear," Odelia said gratefully. "I'll have some fresh hot soup and bread brought when they are ready."

"That will be most welcome, Abbess," Neelam nodded. "Blessings on your holy house."

Abbess Odelia rushed away on silent, tiny feet. Neelam picked up his pace to follow his companions into the Abbey.

"How are Runa and Melly really?" Cathal asked with concern, briskly walking.

Opaline kept pace with Cathal's stride. "With the dark sorcery she experienced, honestly I am worried. What happened there was complicated. It's hard to explain. Physically she is well. The strange magic which affected her at the tree of bones is a mystery and rather hazardous. Caliste and Danu are sitting with her right now. Raghnall has been monitoring her condition."

"He's a fine healer," Neelam said, steps matching their speed.

Opaline guided him through the Abbey's immaculate and silent corridors. They arrived at Runa's room and Opaline knocked softly.

Danu opened the door and stepped aside, "Thank the Goddess. Welcome, Cathal. We're relieved to see you."

"Princess Danu, it's good to see you again," Cathal acknowledged.

"I am just Sister Danu now. I will be down the hall if you need me," she whispered.

"Thank you," Cathal said.

They all looked up but did not speak at first when Cathal and Neelam stepped inside. The sparse room had only a wooden chair, a chest and bed. Tucked in bed was Runa, Mellypip curled up at her side. Caliste doted on them, tucking her blankets while Sanura watched over Mellypip. Raghnall read a scroll nearby and Baldur, his great mass taking up a good deal of the tiny cell, sat by the small open window.

"She's sleeping soundly. Peacefully sleeping," Cathal whispered in awe.

Caliste quietly walked up to Cathal and kissed him on the cheek. She lifted a brown lock of hair. "Good. I think enough magic has concealed truth for these many years." She nodded to Neelam. "I'm glad you are here too. We need all the help and friends we can muster."

Neelam kissed her slim hand. "Charmed as always, Caliste. How's she healing?"

"Better," Caliste said softly. "But it has been such a shock."

Cathal went to Runa's bedside. He kissed Runa on the forehead and gave Mellypip a tender stroke.

"Is she alright?" Cathal whispered. "Truly? What I saw was a nightmare, but Runa also experienced a mystical episode there. What happened?"

Raghnall crooked his finger to draw Cathal and Neelam away from the bed.

"What is going on?" Cathal asked tightly. "Tell me."

"Don't fret. Runa is doing much better. Her dreams which plagued her have finally vanished, Cathal." Raghnall quickly bowed. "Welcome Neelam, Mage Chieftain."

"Hail Raghnall," Neelam nodded. "Now get on with it."

Flustered, Raghnall explained. "Runa's experience was two-fold. The darkness of the curse on the forest and your family. I know you've seen the wretched tree, so I don't have to tell you what it's like, Cathal. Runa was a wreck when they finally caught up to her. So was poor Melly. She saw what happened to Yllia and Rualla in a vision. She witnessed the bloodstone sorcery which Koll summoned from Darkness. She even witnessed Striker rescuing her. Somehow, Yllia was able to communicate those last moments to poor Runa. The effects of such a catastrophic encounter are always difficult, but Runa has no training in her dream seer abilities and it took its toll. Runa suffered a fever for a night and is very weak, but the interesting thing is, ever since she found Yllia and Rualla in that blasted hell of a forest, she has been sleeping peacefully! No nightmares or visions! Just gentle deep sleep."

Baldur agreed, shifting his great furry bulk. "I have monitored her emotions. My empathic powers would have detected any turbulence in her slumber. The facts are not forgotten. She remembers what happened and what she saw."

"Baldur's right," Opaline whispered. "She wakes a little every few hours or so, starving. We feed her soup, bread, drobba—whatever she asks for. She is ravenous! Then after she eats her fill, she goes right back to sleep. Runa's asked about you each time she's awakened, she just never stays awake long enough to hear our answers. Mellypip is the same way."

Raghnall looked at them. "I never knew even wampus could eat so much!"

"Oh, I do know," Belwyn hooted.

"We've all taken turns sitting with her," Caliste assured him. "I promise you Cathal, she has not been alone for a moment since the dreadful incident in the woods."

"She had trouble sleeping ever since we crossed into Thill's borders!" Cathal said. "Nightmares plagued her! What happened in the bath when we arrived and that terrible imagery. Of course! Now I know why."

"She sensed Yllia and Rualla," Neelam finished for him.

"And when she finally came close enough to them physically, she snapped," Raghnall said. "She turned into a mad woman until she found them. Then after the vision at the tree of bones, Runa and Mellypip collapsed."

"It makes sense," Belwyn said. "We all had trouble sleeping, if you recall. It was a side effect of what was happening to Runa. But the brunt of the trouble was on Runa, and through the dream bonding, Mellypip. But why only her?"

"Her Ilyrran blood!" Cathal said. "Perhaps she sensed them calling to her? Her Drusai abilities were not disrupting so much as actually working. They were attempting to contact her."

"Indeed," Raghnall agreed. "After the terrible incident in the woods, Runa revealed to us her nightmares about a tree of bones. Now we know why. Her excessive sleeping now is to make up for the lack of sleep she suffered. I think in a few more days she will be normal again. It's like being drunk, and now she has a mystical hangover, so to speak."

Neelam clawed at his beard, thinking for a moment. He looked up at Cathal and said, "I think perhaps Yllia and Rualla were more active in their last moments before Koll's deviltry consumed them. Perhaps it is not only Runa's new drusai abilities, but the combined effects of a mystical beacon Yllia and Rualla managed to conjure in their last moment. She has both sorcerous and drusai magic, which is quite rare."

"But why did no one sense it all these years? Why is it I never sensed it?" Cathal asked, pacing up and down.

"You have no Ilyrran blood, but Runa does," Surya pointed out. "Plus, Runa is bound to them by blood and since her drusai abilities are growing, perhaps the combination of her sorcerous talents has given her this unique ability."

Raghnall nodded and leaned on his staff. "The aura of the forest was congested with so much dark diabolism; no one could have found them. Mammoth walls of thorns encircled the tree of bones, concealing them from discovery. No one knew they were there. No one could. Not even you, Cathal. Remember, you returned to your home in the west after the war. Runa was too far away to sense them.

Plus, she was just a baby at the time. She could not have known either, if my theory is correct, until now. Her drusai powers are new, remember? I believe that, in combination with her blood tie, drew Runa toward Yllia and Rualla to the cursed tree imprisoning Yllia and Rualla."

"I thought they were dead. For fifteen years, I thought my wife and daughter were dead. Now I learn they have suffered a fate worse than death."

"There is something else you should know," Raghnall said. "Something Runa told me in a rare conscious moment yesterday. She said—"

Opaline gestured to them impatiently. "Come quickly. Runa is awake."

"Grandpa? Is that my grandpa?" Runa mumbled, sitting up and rubbing her eyes.

Cathal spun on his heels and rushed to her side. Mellypip was yawning and rubbing his tummy. Cathal sat on the edge of the narrow bed.

Opaline said quietly, leading the others out the door. "We'll leave you alone." Everyone left the room to allow Cathal and Belwyn privacy.

"We will bring a tray of soup and bread, and lots of drobba pudding for dessert," Caliste promised as she closed the door.

~ * ~

Cathal gently took Runa's hand. They mutely sat there, devastated and in shock. Wrecked by emotion, haunted since seeing the tree of bones, neither knew what to say. Their familiars were close and silent, protective, suffering from sorrow and the upheaval of truth.

Just talk to her, Belwyn advised after several moments.

Runa's little face was so pale, and her hair a mass of tangles, but she seemed stronger than he expected. It eased his heart to see her. "How are you doing, sweetheart?" Cathal asked, brushing away a stray lock of hair from her eyes.

"Hallowed. Sad. Hungry. Angry." Sitting in a cross-legged position, Runa finally gazed at Cathal with confusion. "Grandpa, why is your hair dark?"

"Long story,' Belwyn said and perched on the headboard. "How about you, Furball? How are you feeling? Can I get you anything?"

"Tired," Mellypip grumbled and cuddled closer to Runa. "I hate Koll."

"We are all bonded in that," Belwyn agreed.

"Are you hungry?" Cathal asked, remembering what Raghnall said about her appetite.

"Yes, but before I eat myself into another heavy nap, I need to tell you something. I'm not sure how much Raghnall has told you."

"He told me enough," Cathal said gently. "I'm so sorry you had to suffer, sweetheart."

Runa shook her head. "No, I am glad I did. If I had not, they would still be alone. We must save them. They have slept for all these years in that evil place, waiting for someone they could summon to free them. My grandmother's drusai magic protected them, but it was not enough to break the curse or free them."

"We will do everything we can to rescue them," Cathal assured her.

"Mother is still alive. I sensed her too, but she is fading."

"We will save them," Cathal assured her.

"You don't understand. We're almost out of time." Tears welled in Runa's eyes. She leaned against Cathal, her body shaking. "Grandmother showed me so much when I was bound to them, but this was the hardest. If they are not freed soon, their souls will not be able to pass to the Otherworld. That curse trapped not only their consciousness but their souls. The bloodstone sorcery must be broken. We must release them. Even if we can't save them, we must save their souls."

Cathal grasped her shoulders. "I don't understand sweetheart."

"If we cannot save then and they die while cursed in the tree of bones, their souls will be bound to that tree forever."

"They won't be. I promise," Cathal replied fervently.

"Koll did this to him. I saw Ashur, but it was not my true father. It was the demon who possessed my father's body that was there. But the ritual was performed by Koll. He did it as a private sacrifice to his dark goddess. It was a deliberate act against you, but a strange secret, to please his Obsydia. What kind of person does that?"

"Koll," Belwyn answered grimly.

Cathal rocked Runa, like he used to when she was tiny. "We'll work this out. I promise. We are magic too, remember? We will save them. If I must summon every mage on the continent, steal every scroll, crystal, and spell, I will save them. We just need time."

Mellypip clung to Runa as she buried her face in Cathal's shoulder. "No! You don't understand. They are dying," Runa wept.

As Runa cried and Mellypip felt helpless to comfort her, he sensed a mystical presence, Mellypip dared to glance at Runa's staff in the corner and the faint imprint of Striker's eyes glowed in the shadows.

CHAPTER TWENTY-ONE

Prince Levandius pitched about in his filthy bed, cringing from the sunlight streaming through the narrow window. He kicked off the sheets. "Someone close the bloody drapes!"

The naked whore next to him stirred in her sleep. He opened an eye to covet her flawless body for a moment; well, almost flawless, except for the hideous temple slave brand that marred her thigh. His tongue felt like a wad of cotton and his stomach was queasy. The stale odor of sweat and urine did not ease his lamentable condition. "Get up, wench. I need a bath and change of linens. And close the damn curtains." He finally kicked her out of bed and she landed hard on the floor. She cried out in pain, but Levandius ignored her discomfort. "Bring more good wine too! Surely the Temple of Rygon can afford a decent vintage. I am after all, the honored guest of Zhelon Thor."

Suffering the penalty of smoking dream herbs with her master, she stumbled blindly toward the door. After she left, the sun's cruel beams continued to assault his dry, bloodshot eyes.

"Stupid whore! I told you to shut the drapes!" He squinted against the torment until he forced himself out of bed and closed the velvet drapes, blocking out the cursed light. He stripped off his damp tunic and staggered to the washstand and splashed water on his face.

"So stands the Crown Prince of the Ivory Kingdoms," a deep voice said from the shadows. "Dishonored, disinherited, and in exile. Once you were a prince, now you are a pathetic wretch squandering his time with depravity."

Levandius sluiced water from his face and spun around on shaky legs. "Koll, is that you? Where are you?"

Koll stepped from a dark corner like a phantom. Levandius jumped back in fear. Koll looked strange, transformed, and his eyes gleamed with a strange radiance. Levandius reached for a fresh silk robe and put it on. "Where did you come from? How dare you come to me like this! And shouldn't your head be on a spike somewhere?"

Koll stalked toward Levandius. "How dare you fall into sin when the salvation of Darkness summons you."

Panicked, Levandius backed away, knocking the water bowl and pitcher to the floor. Koll grabbed him by the collar of his silk robe and with deft precision, hurled Levandius into the dark abyss.

Levandius howled his horror as a tunnel of shadow carried him along. He was still screaming when he fell through the shadow into a strange chamber that glowed with deep blue light. Levandius slid across the cold marble floor until he finally stopped and lay there, shivering. He bolted up as his stomach heaved and vomited colorless liquid.

A foul-smelling hulk of shaggy gray and sooty fur hovered over him as he wiped his mouth. Levandius yelped and scooted away from the troll. It squatted before Levandius with a wounded look in its red eyes, drool dribbling from its tusks.

A broad strange mirror loomed over him, over ten feet high and the frame ornately carved from ebonite. Indecipherable runes were cut into the shimmering metal. Clusters of jewels—onyx, black diamonds, rubies, and bloodstone decorated the exquisite frame. The mirror's nebulous glass was sorcerous and shifted its element with a breath. The smoky glass reflected his sickly features, then it transformed into a shadowy liquid that swelled dangerously until it finally dissolved into smoky mystery.

"This mirror is not the make of mortals," Levandius whimpered, crawling away from it.

"No, it is not," Koll's voice echoed as he stepped through the mirror's vapors, a cruel shade. "This mirror is *The Eye of Shadows*." The surface solidified into glass again. "It was forged in the darkest realm of the Otherworld. Demons brought it to this world to serve a great queen, a goddess made flesh, born of Eternal origin. Rejoice Levandius, for at last you have a noble purpose in life."

Levandius cowered in a fetal position on the floor. "And what is that damned troll doing here?"

"Don't you recognize him? Koll inquired. "That's poor Gorvanus, or what is left of him after your sister Opaline turned him into a troll. Well, you did command Gorvanus to kill your sister, didn't you? You underestimated Opaline. She turned Gorvanus into a troll. It is glorious though, what Opaline did. Amazing what untrained raw sorcery can manifest when emotions run wild. It is a shame Opaline is pure-hearted. What a waste."

Levandius spat. "If I'd known she was sorcerous, I would have gotten rid of her sooner."

"Hindsight is a useless tool," Koll remarked coolly.

"Where are we?" Levandius whimpered.

"We are in Skarros, the Wasteland," Koll answered. "It had another name once, now lost to the ages. This is where Ahridum unleashed a dark star to bring about the Bloodstone Age and to signal *Her* coming. This is holy ground. This is her ancient temple palace, hidden for a thousand years since the fall of the Bloodstone."

Koll clapped his hands and two Rashurkeen warriors stepped from the gloom and dragged Levandius to the center of a large chamber. They dropped him before a strange object. Jet-black velvet cloth covered a man-sized crystal of terrible brightness. The glare of the massive diamond, even with the cover of the cloth, tormented his swollen eyes, ravaged by dream herbs and wine. Levandius scrambled to run but Koll's heavy hand pushed Levandius to his knees. He crumbled at the base of the crystal, knees searing with pain from striking hard marble. The aura of darkness at this core of brightness made his soul tremble. Finally, he gazed up at *Her.*

The ethereal magnificence of her face stunned him. Garbed in a deep crimson gown with long sleeves and a high winged collar that matched her blood-red mouth, she was beyond beauty. Awestruck, unable to look away from her. Silver eyes measured Levandius with cool contempt. A dark cloud sprang from her scalp. She was wickedness in its most alluring shape.

"Who is she?" Levandius choked and blinked, trying not to look.

"Behold Obsydia, Goddess of the Bloodstone and Queen of this world," Koll proclaimed.

"Dear heavens, she's real!" Levandius cried, squirming away.

"No…not heaven," Koll corrected him.

Zhelon Thor's firm hand on his quaking shoulder prevented Levandius from crawling away. The High Priest knelt before Obsydia, voice and face rapturous. "Hail Obsydia, Blessed of Darkness, Daughter of Ahridum."

"I don't understand," Levandius sniveled. "I'm afraid."

Zhelon tone became sinister. "You should fear Obsydia. Good. All should fear HER truth for Obsydia is the divine shadow. You are unworthy—yet you have been called to serve HER. Be grateful you are not called to sacrifice." Zhelon's gaze returned to worship Obsydia, uncaring of the crystal's cruel glare of sun that trapped his shadow queen. "Koll has found her at last! He was truly her chosen deliverer. Tonight, sacrifices at our temples shall commemorate this blessing. Blood will run wild to honor Obsydia's return."

Shivering, Levandius looked around the large chamber that was so ominous and full of strange evils. Enormous braziers of ebonite burned with blue flames, yet many areas of the chamber were dark and fathomless. Black and red marble pillars soared to support a high domed ceiling. At the heart of it was a symbolic painting of Ahridum, faceless yet terrifying. Beneath him was a smaller painting of a raven-haired woman who writhed in agony as though the image were alive. Perhaps she was? Reality disbanded here.

Rashurkeen assassins and temple guards were stationed everywhere. No escape, Levandius winced. Even the Rashurkeen, whose cult was death, looked frightened and small; the temple priests mouthed silent prayers, dread stamped on their faces.

In the deepest shadows, strange inhuman eyes glowed! They were not the orbs of wild animals, but something more sinister. What watched them from the dark recesses of this temple? A murky, erratic shape darted close to Levandius. His guts knotted with terror. It brushed against him and then vanished back into the darkness. "What was that?"

Obsydia laughed. "Just one of my pets."

Koll circled Levandius, his robes sweeping the cold floor. "There are many wonders here. Numinous power forged from the Otherworld, like the mirror we traveled through. We will launch a crusade of darkness that will change the world! Join our brotherhood, Levandius. Join and prosper! Deny us and perish."

"What must I do in this brotherhood?" Levandius asked.

"Bow to Obsydia. Worship her as a living goddess," Koll said simply. "What other faith in this world was given a goddess made of immortal flesh that we might worship at her feet? Pledge faithfulness to Obsydia. Her beloved brother is Rygon, God of War, so you would not be committing heresy. It is all in the same Eternal family." Koll's voice softened as he pulled Levandius to his feet. "The divine of the ages summons you to arise with us, fallen Prince."

"Is he even worthy to join us?" Obsydia asked coldly. "His character is recreant and his body is soft."

Xabral rested his head on the marble steps. "No, but we can shape him. Blessed Obsydia, it's true Levandius is delinquent of honor and courage, but his bloodline is flawless. I find such inadequacies a common theme among noble families. Through him your new empire will rise."

Levandius shook his head. "I'm an exiled prince. Father banished me. I'm disinherited,"

Zhelon smiled. "Swear fealty to our cause and we will restore you to your lost throne. Tarsicius will die. Who wears his crown is up to you. Yours can be the new hand to rule the Ivory Kingdoms. Be grateful you have a place in this world where there are only victims or victors. Which shall you play?"

Levandius shakily glanced up at the dark goddess. "What do you want me to do?"

Obsydia's lips curled into a smile. "Worship my glory and I will give you a true purpose. You will rule a great empire!"

"The coming war is pivotal," Koll added. "This war will determine the fate of light and dark in this world."

"Such things are beyond me," Levandius said.

"Of course it is," Obsydia said. "This world is now a battleground of the Eternals of Light and Dark. All the worlds are our clay, as you are *my* clay, lost prince. The battle for supremacy of Light and Dark predates the creation of the moons and stars, the world and sky. If you knew the truth, you would crumble to ash. I am She! Obsydia, daughter of the Eternal Ahridum!" Choose! Your love and devotion shall not go unrewarded, for I will be the mother you never had. Death claimed her at your birth and fate denied you the solace of a mother. I will love you as your father never could," Obsydia whispered tenderly. "I see your bitter heart. I see the love Tarsicius had for a concubine! A temple slave who stole his affection from you! She bore him children who usurped you! You were a child born of a loveless political marriage. The first-born son he so quickly abandoned for his bastard children, all for a temple whore!"

Levandius face twisted with hatred. "Sirah! Sirahnami! That whore! I rebuffed her feeble offering of maternal love! I hated her."

Obsydia nodded. "When Sirahnami bore Tarsicius twins, they became the bright moons of his world. Not you. As years passed, Sirahnami's children flaunted their bright minds and beauty, while you, the heir, struggled alone."

Levandius nodded. "I was the oldest. I should have been first. I punished them when I could! When I discovered Sirah's magic, I told Father! I thought he might have had her executed, but she was banished instead. He sent her to a secret prison. She escaped though, the bitch. I was the one who deserved praise for exposing her. He did not honor me for my loyalty."

"Tarsicius did not realize your worth," Obsydia agreed. "He deserves death and oblivion for that alone."

Levandius rocked back and forth, hugging his knees. "I waited and watched! When Taran's sorcery finally appeared, I exposed him. Father banished him too, but he had tears in his eyes. Just like Sirah! Tears for them, never for me! I was glad they were gone."

"Of course you were," Obsydia agreed. "A crown can never be shared. Join our crusade of darkness and you shall rule! Death will pluck your father's soul and deliver it to Rygon for punishment. You will rise to be Emperor."

Obsydia's silver eyes enthralled him. Even his headache vanished. Feeble and selfish long before dream herbs and wine polluted him; he relinquished his soul for a throne. "I will obey, Queen Obsydia." The petty soul of Levandius swelled with bitter hunger. "I will finally wear the imperial crown! I will take revenge on Opaline and Taran! I shall offer them in sacrifice to you! The whore Sirahnami will suffer death too! I will personally carve her heart out for you." He looked up at Obsydia's terrible beauty. "Yes, make me Emperor. I swear fealty to you. I offer my body and soul for your pleasure, my Goddess."

"Then you shall be rewarded," Zhelon approved.

"Bring the ring," Obsydia commanded. "Let us seal our pledge with a token of my love."

Koll and Zhelon Thor bowed and went to the shadows. When they returned Koll handed a small red box to Levandius. Zhelon Thor opened it to reveal a ring of bloodstone set in ebonite. Levandius noticed both Zhelon and Koll wore the same ring.

"Hold out your right hand," Zhelon commanded solemnly.

Levandius extended a shaking hand, slick with sweat. Koll grasped it to hold it steady. Zhelon whipped out a small dagger. Levandius jumped at the sight. The curved blade gleamed in the dusky light. Fear pulsed through Levandius when Zhelon nicked his throat with the sharp tip. He yelped, feeling the blood trickle down his naked chest. Zhelon coated the ring with his blood and then put it on his third finger. Levandius grimaced with pain. The ring burned his finger. When Koll released him, it took a moment for the burning to subside. Levandius tugged at the ring, but it would not budge.

"I can't get it off," Levandius cried. "Why won't the ring come off?"

"Be brave, Prince Levandius," Koll soothed. "We too offered

our blood to sanctify the vow to serve Obsydia. You are one of us now. Be glad, for your heart shall go on beating, while the hearts of others will be torn out on altars of stone."

"Does this ring have...powers?" Levandius asked.

"Yes," Koll said. "We can speak through the dark jewel and come here through the mirror with the right incantations, even if not mage born or demon."

"Really? Now what?" Levandius was enchanted by his new ring now, until Obsydia's powerful voice snapped him from admiring it.

"Koll has been chosen to take those first steps toward my liberation," Obsydia replied. "He is going on a sacred quest to the Obsidian Tower."

"I have not heard of this place," Levandius said.

"It is not of this world," Obsydia answered. "Go now Koll. They await you."

Xabral slithered down the steps, but Obsydia summoned him back. "Stay with me, my sweet serpent. Koll must endure this alone."

Koll bowed to her and stroked Xabral's scales. "Be patient. I shall return soon."

Koll mounted the steps of the altar and disappeared into the Eye of Shadows.

~ * ~

Grimm rose from his hiding place behind the great doors that had Obsydia's face carved onto it. He could hear plain enough, but it had grown too risky to come here. The congregation of so many people there now made Grimm uneasy; but so many smells from so many folk also prevented anyone detecting him. The strange creatures that began to gather in this pit also disturbed him. Grimm ran down the crumbling hallways away from the chamber of hell. The dark corridors were well lit now-not that Grimm needed the light. He possessed excellent night vision, a gift of his wolf clan. The evil in this place made him sick and he longed to be away, even in the desert heat.

The sun was setting when Grimm crawled out of the pit and headed toward the haven of the cave. The small cave was about five miles from away, but his speed, both as a wolf and a familiar, propelled him swiftly to his makeshift den. The strain on his strength was rough. When he stopped before the cave's mouth, he almost collapsed from exhaustion.

"Hello, Grimm," Rono said, sticking his head out of the opening.

"Hello, Rono," Grimm replied weakly.

Rono's feathered ear tufts twitching with excitement. "Come inside! Quick! I have present for you."

Grimm pulled himself up and entered the cave. Three dead snakes and a lizard were piled together on the sand.

"What is this?" Grimm asked.

"Dinner!" Rono exclaimed. "I did it for you. I hunted them all by myself when you were being heroic in horrid hell pit." He looked down at the pile. "I liked hunting. Especially snakes—*hate* snakes. You looked so hungry and skinny I thought I would help feed you. The snakes are scorpion breed, but I bit off nasty stingers so they are safe to eat now. I know you need strength to fight evil. Eat!"

"Thank you, Rono," Grimm said gratefully. "We will eat together."

After they shared their meal, they huddled together in the dark cave. The night turned cold after the intense heat, but for the moment they were fed and content.

Grimm rested his head on his paws. "Rono, tell me again about Princess Opaline."

"Oh yes, Opaline's very nice. Her hair is sunshine, all pretty and golden. She smelled like sweet flowers."

As Rono continued his tale of Opaline and his friends from so far away, Grimm listened, imagining for a moment he was part of Rono's strange magical pack.

CHAPTER TWENTY-TWO

Panthara walked the Abbey's garden, enjoying the scent of the lush roses. She liked the garden. It was safe and quiet. The nuns were kind and did not pry. Even so, Panthara longed for the security of Iona's presence. She was hesitant to follow Iona here from the Sorcerer House, but she insisted, feeling Panthara would be too vulnerable if left alone. The cruel truth is she was vulnerable. *Vulnerable without magic.* Since she woke from her waking sleep, Panthara realized she was not only alone in the world for the first time, but bereft of her magic. She could deal with losing her crown more than her sorcery. All she had was a kind necromancer as a shield from her past sins.

The bustle of activity following Runa's macabre discovery of the tree of bones shielded Panthara from notice. Opaline was too busy taking care of Runa to confront her. Still, she sensed Opaline's animosity. She knew Opaline and Taran argued about her. Taran assured her they had made up. Panthara did not want to see them fight. Not over her.

Panthara's imagined the hatred and distrust they must feel whenever they saw her. So Panthara kept her distance. She was grateful for the blessing of being invisible in the chaos, except for Taran.

Taran did not leave her alone, and secretly she was glad of it. She welcomed him, and him alone, in her circle of oblivion. Without Taran she would have no knowledge about what was happening. As with Iona, he provided a cloak of protection from the others. He did not judge. He did not punish.

The Wraith Guardians had already punished her. She shivered when she recalled their touch. She did not remember anything else until she woke up.

Will I have my magic again? Am I being punished?

Azmadu flew over to her, breaking her tormented thoughts. He landed in the grass. His eye-patch was crooked. He moaned pitifully, flopping down at her feet. "Not fun anymore."

"Stop pouting, Azmadu. It's not the end of the world."

The crill lizard snorted and hung his head. "I'm not pouting. The sisters don't like me."

"You spilled a whole kettle of soup," Panthara said.

"I didn't mean to make a mess. Just wanted a taste. Now the sisters banned me from the kitchen."

"You won't starve," Panthara assured him. She knelt down and stroked his crested head tenderly. "The sisters like spoiling the familiars. Even overly curious flying lizards who tip over pots of soup get treats."

Taran waved to her as he ran toward her. "I thought I would find you here," he said breathlessly. "Cathal arrived with Neelam, the Mage Chieftain of Ironia. Runa is awake again. Just in case you were wondering."

Panthara smiled faintly. "Thank you, Taran."

"You know, you could even ask to see her," Taran suggested.

"No," Panthara whispered.

"You are Runa's sister," Taran said.

"Runa doesn't want to see me," Panthara insisted. "Our blood bonds are through serendipitous fate."

"You're still sisters," Taran said. "True, you had a rocky start. I often want to throttle Opaline, but that's natural."

"But you never tried to kill her, did you? Speaking of Opaline, does she still despise me? Plot my doom?" Panthara inquired lightly.

"We simply decided not to discuss you, for the sake of family survival," Taran replied.

"I'm a forbidden subject?" Panthara asked. "Charming."

"You're a sore spot," Taran said, a little impatient. "We were, however, discussing Runa—your sister."

"Where's MacTabbish? I thought I heard him snoring in the chapel earlier."

"He's sleeping in the library now. Panthara stop it! I mean it!"

"Is Iona still…at that terrible place?"

"The tree of bones? Yes, I think so," Taran nodded. "Have you seen it?"

"No. Iona would not let me," Panthara said.

A moment of silence fell between them. Taran lifted Panthara's chin. "I will ask this only once. I will believe your answer. Did you know about Cathal's wife and daughter—about the tree of bones and what it held?"

Panthara looked up at Taran. "No. Why? Don't you believe me?"

"I believe you. Because in Runa's vision she saw Koll perform the ritual that cursed her mother and grandmother. Koll did this to them—not the possessed Ashur. He used an ancient scroll with a bloodstone and he dedicated this horror to Obsydia and—"

"Koll? You said Koll did this," Panthara interrupted him. "Is that what Runa saw in her vision?"

"Yes. He used some ancient scroll, at least that's what Runa saw in her vision. Neelam, the Mage Chieftain, is uncertain of what kind of curse it is too. He's the fellow who arrived with Cathal. That Dwarf is quite an intense man."

"Tell me everything," Panthara demanded.

"Why?" Taran asked.

"Listen!" she begged. "I've known Koll since I was a little girl! He was my teacher! I'm also privy to at least some of his secrets. I know where he has hidden most of his most powerful spells. Koll has a vast collection of relics from the Bloodstone Age. He had a treasure trove of them he had collected for hundreds of years. You think he can carry them everywhere? The great temple in Kra'zum is where he keeps most of them. He has a private apartment there. If it was a bloodstone scroll, there is only one place he has them secreted away. I know where. Any hope of saving Cathal's family lies in that. If we find that original scroll—"

"What do you mean?" Taran asked.

"I mean the original scroll Koll used to create the tree of bones might be used somehow to reverse the curse!"

"Then let's go see them together. Tell them what you know!"

"No!" Panthara protested. "They all hate me. They won't believe anything I say anyway."

"They might." Taran grabbed her hand and pulled her toward the abbey doors. "This also might be a way for you to make amends." Azmadu growled, flapping his little reptilian wings as he pursued them.

"I hate you," Panthara said.

"My sister says that quite often," Taran replied dryly.

~ * ~

Captain Vasya was frustrated, mammoth arms crossed over his chest. "I ordered him to go back. He refused to heed my warnings! When I tried to stop him, he became quite defiant and rude. I never knew he could be so hot-tempered. Mage or not, I never expected such disobedience from him! I was stunned, especially...well...since he's always been such a timid fellow."

"That's alright, Captain. I should have known he would come." Cathal wearily leaned on his staff. "What else did he do?"

Vasya burrowed his thumbs into his sword belt and grunted with frustration. "Forgive me, Cathal. He even used magic against me! It's not proper to fight *me* with magic! I have no magic in my blood."

Cathal sympathetically patted Vasya's broad back. "I will handle things from here. I apologize for any trouble he caused you, Captain."

"I am sorry, Cathal, that you must suffer to go in…there again," Vasya replied with a solemn bow.

Old wounds being ripped open seem to be the theme this season, Belwyn said.

I should have known he would come, Cathal remarked sadly to Belwyn.

"Thank you for sending for me. I'll take care of things from here," Cathal told Captain Vasya.

"Thank you, Cathal." Captain Vasya bowed and returned to his duties.

Cathal walked the chalky path of the cursed woods. The sickness mages suffered here was eased by the chunk of sorcerer bane Cathal gripped in his hand. His staff struck dead earth as he marched on. When Cathal entered the tunnel of thorns, he tried to brace for the coming pain of seeing Yllia and Rualla trapped in that wretched tree of bones.

Finally, they stepped from the long tunnel of thorns into the grotesque grove. Cathal faced the tree of bones and blinked back tears confronting the tragic frozen beauty of his wife and daughter. Iona and Amun were there, watching over Yllia and Rualla; but two others had joined her in a vigil of sorrow. Cathal wiped his face with his sleeve and took a deep breath. A bright patch of color was out of place in this forest of death. A bouquet of lush sunflowers was laid at Rualla's feet.

"Sunflowers were her favorite," Liat said, sitting cross-legged a few inches from Rualla. His long black hair hung in his face, but it did not conceal his tears.

"I know," Cathal said gently, walking up to him. "Come back with me, Liat. This isn't good for you."

"I was a coward when Rualla lived. I lost her to Ashur," Liat whispered. "I never spoke of love. Never offered my heart when there was a chance. I lost her then. Then I lost her to death, and I grieved. Now I am losing her again." Dabiro huddled closer to Liat, head in his lap.

"I understand your pain," Cathal whispered. "Rualla would not want you to suffer like this. Come away with us."

"I lost her because I could never speak of my love. I lived in mute sorrow for years. I failed to save her from Ashur's demon years ago. How can I leave her now?"

Cathal knelt next to Liat and squeezed his shoulder in sympathy. "You must, because it would be her wish. We must work to free them now. I need your help to do this, Liat. She needs your help."

He sent his thoughts to Belwyn. *He never stopped loving her. I never knew how much until now.*

Give him time to absorb this cruelty, else he will cling here in grief and wither like this forest, Belwyn replied.

"Do we free them to die—or to live? Liat asked.

Cathal shook his head and looked up at their pale bone features. "We don't know."

"We need to cling to hope," Belwyn said.

"What do you suggest?" Cathal asked.

"Shave your beard," Belwyn stated simply. "Yllia loathed men with beards. Ilyrran men cannot even grow beards. For centuries you were clean-shaven. I think you looked more elegant beardless myself. Humans don't always look good with face fuzz."

Cathal rubbed his chin, feeling the short, trimmed beard. "I thought I looked rather distinguished."

"You thought silver hair made you look wise too, but I know better," Belwyn said. "If Yllia and Rualla are restored to us, I know your wife would not appreciate a furry face."

"I've had this beard since Runa was a baby," Cathal said.

"You look like a rumpled badger," Belwyn said.

"I'm right here you know," Dabiro growled in response.

Liat brushed back his hair, glancing up at them suspiciously. "You're trying to bait me back into the circle of the living. Dabiro is the one that likes to argue—remember? Let me stay. I will join you later. Now, I need my sorrow." He turned away from Cathal to gaze up at Rualla's face. Dabiro laid his head in Liat's lap and refused to move.

Iona looked up at Cathal and shook her head, her silver chains jingling on her heavy veils. "He needs to mourn her again, Cathal, as you did. I will watch over him."

"Can you send him to the Abbey at sunset," Cathal asked.

Iona nodded. "I will make sure he arrives."

"You come too. I don't want you in this place alone too long," Cathal insisted. "Walk with me back to the road. We must talk." They walked back arm in arm. Amun remained behind to watch over Liat and Dabiro.

"How is Panthara?" Cathal asked when they were far enough away.

"Is Panthara evil or good?" Belwyn asked. "We're all wondering, you know."

"Belwyn!" Cathal said, aghast.

Iona tilted her head. "It's quite alright. I think she is afraid she will be sent away. Her mother was a cruel and unstable woman, and Koll's influence, well, being raised by a priest of darkness would not be good for anyone. The Wraith Guardian's touch still concerns me. Taran has helped to draw her out of her shell a little. Panthara is uncertain of her future and ashamed of her past. She has lost everything, including her magic."

"Are you sure about that?" Cathal asked.

"Yes. I think it is a side effect of the Wraith's touch."

"Is the crill lizard still afraid of me?" Belwyn asked hesitantly.

Cathal cocked his eyebrow and looked at his familiar. "Belwyn, you took Azmadu's eye in battle. Your relationship is going to be rocky for a long time."

A winged stone flew across the road toward them. Cathal paused, feeling a little defensive, until it stopped and hovered before him. He saw a note tied to the stone and plucked it form the air. He untied the ribbon and read the note.

"What is it?" Iona asked.

"It's from Taran. Come. Iona, please fetch Liat, and no arguments this time. We all need to go back to the Abbey right away."

"What's happened?" Belwyn asked.

Cathal's grey stare was chilling. "It's about Panthara—she knows about Koll's collection of relics. And where they are hidden."

CHAPTER TWENTY-THREE

Koll emerged from the shadows to stand on the edge of a gray and desolate sea. Winds pungent with salt buffeted his body. Heavy clouds gathered in a dismal sky. The arcane mirror had brought him to this gloomy seashore at the rim of the world, where not even a seabird or stray crab hinted at life.

"I am chosen by dark prophesy. I am the savior of Obsydia! I summon the tower of her birth to rise."

A booming thunderclap shattered Koll's ears and a great gale swelled in the sea. The once placid waters heaved with violence and foamy waves rose wildly in the fetid air, though now the brackish odor was replaced by a fiery sensation. The sky split with lightning as smoky red shadows blocked out the faded sun. Night's dominion blotted out all light, for not even the moons and stars graced this austere sky. Torrential rain burst from the sky and the violent tempest drenched his being. The earth rumbled and heaved, pitching him across the sands. Then the raging tremors ceased, though the ocean still churned and heaved. He pushed himself up on his elbows. His mouth and nose gritty, he spat out wet sand and pushed back his hair to see the raging mysterious currents boil.

Then all the winds and waters stilled, as though hushed by a god. Koll could hear the thunder of his heartbeat. In the distance, a circle of black fire rose from the sea. The dark ring of fire began to rise and swirl, spawning scarlet storm clouds and jets of lightning.

The Obsidian Tower soared up from the ocean's depths. It erupted from the waves like a spear of darkness, rising hundreds of feet above the ocean, a spiral of shadow, never seeming to stop its rise from oblivion. The waters roiled again from its mystical upheaval. Koll watched the tower arise with wonder and when it finally stopped its climb, it glowed with Eternal power at the heart of the maelstrom. Koll breathed in the glory of it, filled with exhilaration. He bowed before the terrible presence, weeping with joy.

When he finally looked up, a ferry of crimson glass with webbed sails glided above the choppy waves, guided by gray-robed figures, their faces concealed by heavy cowls and hoods. A single lamp glowed with ethereal crimson light as they piloted the strange craft to the beach. There they waited in patient silence until Koll walked toward them. He entered the ethereal vessel, and knew he had achieved his destiny, but missed his beloved Xabral to share in this great moment.

The hooded ones sailed with silent skill to the dark tower. The Obsidian Tower was glorious. Storm clouds rimmed the top of the sphere, unleashing thunder and lightning. The transcendent ride was calm despite the tempest's wrath. The hooded beings did not speak nor could he see past their hoods to glimpse their faces...if they had faces. When they reached shelter inside the strange fortress, the hooded ones docked at the moorings and climbed stones steps shiny with wetness. Koll followed.

Within the haven of the tower, the hooded beings led him up a winding staircase of stone steps glittering with chips of black diamonds. Long narrow openings hinted at the storms raging outside, but within this fortress no mortal element touched these strange creatures. Finally, he was before polished black double doors carved with strange runes that opened with mystical grace. Koll followed the hooded ones into a staggering chamber where gigantic braziers of ebonite burned with red and black flame.

With reverent solemnity, Koll's silent prayers were offered to his Queen. *Darkness blessed me and brought me to this sacred tower, forged in the Otherworld. This was Her birthplace. Where Obsydia was conceived and first breathed life. Now I stand in the same hallowed halls.*

Koll wondered if his weird guides were mute until they began to chant. He kept a respectful distance, afraid to disrupt their ritual. From the shadows floated more hooded beings. They glided above the immaculate black and crimson floors. In the distance, he heard the faint echoes of screams.

Koll touched an ebony column; it towered over a hundred feet above him. He ran his long fingers along the smooth surface and wondered about the strange runes of the forbidden kingdom carved into it! Its aroma and touch were hot with Otherworld origin. But not even his vast knowledge could translate these strange symbols. He looked up at the ceiling which narrowed and curved upward into a spiracle. The open space revealed fragments of the storm in the sky above, but the wrath did not scorch these shadowed halls. Koll studied the walls of the chamber, which seemed absent of form or substance, but woven of a fathomless night void of starlight. What if he touched this darkness? Would he be consumed or transformed?

At the end of the room a raised altar of gray stones glittered with jewel dust. At the shrine's heart a ghostly black flame burned from a hole in the floor. The gray-robed hooded beings formed a circle on the altar around the burning flame, holding high goblets of black glass. They chanted words Koll could not comprehend, for theirs was the natural language of demons in their most sacred state. *How many mortals have heard this secret tongue? Did ancient Lilith experience this before Ahridum touched her womb and filled it with Obsydia?* The archaic words echoed with raw power, and these powers were channeled into a purpose of which Koll was ignorant. He could only watch and be patient. Obsydia had warned him not to interfere, for all would be as it should.

Koll counted thirteen hooded ones around the altar. In unison they stopped their mysterious canticle and one by one they poured the contents of their goblets onto the flame of the holy platform. It was blood. He recognized the smell. He had witnessed blood offerings on the sacrificial altar since he was a boy, but what these strange creatures were doing was different. This ritual went beyond an offering.

It was a summoning.

The altar's smoky flame did not sputter and die with the red flow, but instead flared high with searing flames. Koll inhaled the profound power, but even he had to shield his eyes from the fiery burst. When it faded, black smoke danced on the holy mound around the flame until it molded into a shape. A human-like shape, but its scent was supernatural. Another burst of shadow gave it substance and evoked a newborn demon woman on Dark's penetralia. The silent hooded guardians stepped back along the shadowy walls.

On the altar lay a demon woman in serpentine glory with bands of glittering jetty fabric tied with seductive promise around her hips and breasts. Her essence was crepuscular with translucent ruby-red skin; long black hair clung to her supple body with curly ripples, and her large eyes were misty pools of darkness with flame-orange irises and framed by arched brows and thick lashes; her nails were shimmering black and long. Her face was oddly youthful with rounded cheeks softening her sharp bone structure. She smiled at him, revealing smooth white teeth.

The demon woman rose and stepped down from the altar. Her movements were jerky and stiff, unaccustomed to her renascent body.

She approached him on shaky legs, ignoring the strange guardians. A wicked smile curled her black lips. "Koll the Sorcerer, welcome to the Obsidian Tower. We have awaited your coming. You were to be sacrificed on Rygon's altar, but Ahridum chose you to free his daughter. Rygon did not mind giving up his sacrifice, for he missed his sister. You are blessed, as few puny mortals are. We have missed Obsydia's wicked heart. Ahridum desires his only daughter to be released, for he cannot even look upon her bereft captive body because the despised living *Light* contaminates her. We must shatter it, for the shadows are lonely without Obsydia."

"I am lifted by your words demoness," Koll bowed. "That is my life's quest."

"Long has Obsydia been an isolated prisoner. Alone in the light without the succor of Darkness. So sad." She circled Koll, sniffing him, touching him with greedy fingers. Her hands tingled with the essence of the ancient mysteries. "You are mortal born, despite your sorcery. Magic is a mere seedling of glory. A tiny vestige of what created the universe. You are still a weak mortal though. Impure. Death has brushed you many times, yet you elude the reaper of souls. Ahridum desired you to live. Maybe that is why the Gate of Souls has not taken you to your judgment. Beware if you do pass through Death's gates, Koll. The Wraith Guardians are still annoyed with you." She smelled him again. "Your heart is black as pitch. You will do, I suppose. Ahridum has sent me to you, so you must be worthy—for a human."

"My purpose," Koll replied, "is to free Obsydia. I am amazed though, for I have never seen a demon pure from Ahridum's realm?"

She shrugged and continued to move around the chamber, exploring, touching, and smelling. "I am amazing, aren't I? Ahridum has many realms in the Otherworld. I am from one of them. My being, my true essence, is from the Dark Netherworld where demons dwell. There are so many realms, many secrets. Do not seek to know them all Koll, for they burn." She walked with tender steps and her joints eased as she grew use to her newly-made body. It was both so human and demon at the same time; she was fascinating to watch. "The ancient guardians offered the blood of human women with sacred flame of darkness to summon me to this place. But there is more to it, of course." She pointed to the hooded beings in the shadows. "These guardians know all the old magian laws and secrets a mortal will never know. Not even the most powerful sorcerers will ever possess their power. Not even you. They are devoted servants of the Dark. They brought Lilith to this place long ago, so Ahridum could seed her with Obsydia's grace. Lilith became dust, but Obsydia was born." She stopped and looked at Koll again. "Tell me Sorcerer, am I beautiful?" she asked seriously.

"You are wicked splendor," Koll complimented her. It was true. Her lithe body was armed with dangerous curves that could turn a man idiot. Her demon beauty was a rare vision. Koll had seen many pictures in old books and scrolls of demons that once tread the world in the last age. Many were hideous and brutal. Yet Obsydia was true to her reputation for having the fairest demon handmaidens.

She sighed and touched her cheek. "It will do. As my true self, I could not stand before you. You could not bear such glory. No mortal could. Here I am...polluted with mortal stain to serve the Dark. Poor Koll, if you saw my true shape, you would wither and howl. You would risk the sad fate of Obsydia's mother. Lilith saw Ahridum in her mind's eye when she became His dark bride. She came here to be wedded to a god. The sacred wedding was sanctified in this very shrine. His Eternal touch filled her scrawny human body, filled her with the blessed darkness of Obsydia. Poor Lilith. She only remembered the terror and pain. She died within moments, right after she birthed Obsydia into the loving hands of these guardians. Lilith's body became a husk scoured of flesh and soul. Obsydia fed on her in the womb. She suckled at her soul until it was gone. Lilith sacrificed all for love." She smiled. "No Gate of Souls for her. Lilith was loved by Ahridum so much he destroyed her. That is great love. Absolute oblivion." She glanced at him, smiling. "What do you fear, Koll? Do you fear me? Do you fear Ahridum's love? Do you fear Darkness?"

"I have no fear of you," Koll said. "Ahridum I fear always, as is right. The Dark I fear too, but with love."

"Good. Fear of Ahridum is good."

"And you? Are you lethal to touch?" Koll inquired.

She slid her hands across her body seductively and sighed. "I can take pleasures. My touch will not kill, but I may kill a few anyway. That too is pleasure. Demons take, they do not ask—as you take, Koll."

"Can you free Obsydia? Is that why you were summoned here."

"I am Her new chief handmaiden, as Obsydia was granted in her glorious reign. She had thirteen handmaidens then. They died from blades of cruel light. They were foolish demons. I am not so foolish. More handmaidens will come later. Now, I will help you free Obsydia from her terrible bondage. The Scions of Light trapped her, but we will free her."

"Scions of Light?" Koll inquired.

"The three mages chosen to cast the enchantment of Light."

"What shall I call you, demoness, for convenience sake? Do demons of your domain even have names?"

"Call me Chimera. That will do. Your human tongue could not speak my true name. This mortal world is not to my liking, but I serve Ahridum, Eternal Lord of Dark Chaos. One cannot serve Ahridum and be weak of heart. I do not have a heart." She glanced at Koll. "You must take care, Sorcerer. Do not become weak. Ahridum's punishment would be more than your insignificant soul could suffer. Few mortals receive such gifts as you."

"Why does Ahridum act now? I searched for Obsydia for nearly three hundred years! For a thousand years she has been trapped!"

Chimera's sharp sidelong glance silenced Koll. "Because this age is dying. A new era waits. We must make it ours. Forever. Ahridum desires Obsydia's freedom to regain their supremacy. Bring back Darkness."

"Could nothing have been done before now?" Koll asked. "Could Ahridum not free her? She was his beloved daughter."

Chimera shook her head. "No. They punish her for failure, I think. Obsydia lost the Bloodstone War. The age of Darkness was lost when Light won. A token period of penance was required before the mercy of his shadow embraced her again. Ahridum hates failure."

Chimera paused; her brow furrowed with thought. "Great difficulty," she said with a nod. "The spell was not just mortal, but it had a dangerous dose of blood. Blood that had been created by the Eternals of Light sprinkled in their conjuration. Sly tricks to hurt Obsydia."

"Do Eternals have blood?" Koll asked.

Chimera touched her flesh. "I have blood now, but in my home, in my domain of demons, we have no blood. I cannot describe my true essence to you. You'd never comprehend. But my essence in mortal form needs blood. The Light interfered with our plans. Now we must interfere. To free Obsydia, we need the essence of true Darkness to break the cursed Light. Much magic and ritual. Sacrifices must flow like a river. Need darkest magic."

"Then we will begin at once. We should bring Obsydia here to the tower until she is freed."

"No! Foolish sorcerer! The light that curses her would be blasphemy here! Sacrilege against the darkness! She cannot come here."

"Then what shall we do?" Koll demanded.

"Only when the Light that holds Obsydia is finally dead and she is liberated, will she be granted her tower again! She will remain in her old temple palace for the moment. But we must keep her safe. I will care for her as I create the ritual. That is my purpose for coming here. Mortal hands are not enough to conjure what we need and we need many things."

"What do we need to free Obsydia from her prison? Tell me!"

"Blood and flesh from the original weavers of this cursed magic. Their blood is vital to shattering the Light."

"Then blood and flesh I will gladly take," Koll promised.

CHAPTER TWENTY-FOUR

Mellypip stared at Runa's staff in the corner all morning; scrutinizing the panther eyes carved beneath his wampu image, both expectant and frightened they would glow again. Striker's presence was strong now, stronger than when Runa's conjured her staff from the willow-oak shading Striker's grave. He did not mention this to Runa, because there was enough magical mayhem going on.

Runa suddenly picked him up. "Come, Melly. Grandfather has called a meeting."

"You should still be in bed," Mellypip told her. "You're infirm."

"I'm much better," Runa insisted. "I am even staying awake today. I'm not even hungry."

"What about your staff?" he gasped, bouncing in her arm as she carried him out of the room.

"It can stay in my room. I won't need it."

Runa ran down the hall, passing armed guards who mingled with the sisters. "The Abbey is abuzz with so much activity."

"Poor Abbess Odelia is in a perpetual state of fluster," Mellypip sighed. "As I will be if you keep bouncing me like a ball."

They rushed to the large communal hall where the sisters usually shared their quiet meals. *Was there a sorcerer left at the Sorcerer House?* Mellypip wondered. Ulan, Taran, Liat, Myrsalian, Sirah, and Caliste, took their places with anticipation, their familiar's next to them. King Caladynn and Queen Sorcha sat near the head of the table. Surprisingly, Panthara sat next to Iona. Prince Ulric sat next to Opaline, a safe distance from Panthara.

Something important is happening, Mellypip sent to Runa.

Cathal and Neelam entered, Belwyn and Surya regal on their arms. They stood at the head of the table together and bowed.

Cathal welcomed them. "Thank you for gathering in such short notice. Before we speak, allow us to add a shield of protection." Belwyn hopped off his arm and settled on the table, as did Surya.

Neelam raised his staff of twisted wood, and the eagle head carved at the top burst with green light that covered the whole chamber. Neelam's eyes glinted with satisfaction. "Now, no one will be able to spy on us."

"Grandfather, what's happening?"

Cathal lifted his hand. "Patience, my dear. There is something I had not expected. First, this morning Myrsalian informed me Gabriel finally sent a message."

"Whose Gabriel?" Opaline asked.

Cathal sat down and laid his staff on the table. "He was the spy watching things in Urgonclaw, in the capital of Kra'zum. I feared he may be dead, but he has contacted us with grave news."

"I know Gabriel. What does he say?" King Caladynn asked.

"As do we," Taran said. "We have not seen him since the former Archon's funeral."

"You were not meant to," Myrsalian said.

Cathal looked unhappy as he relayed the message. "Gabriel says strange things are happening in Kra'zum. There are great celebrations and bonfires in the street. According to Gabriel, sacrifices have increased. Zhelon Thor claims their goddess will rise soon. The original plan was to see if Xabral had returned to Kra'zum. Gabriel was originally coming here to see Koll executed, but received new information about Xabral recruiting Zhelon to help Koll. He was on his way here, but says he was delayed. Gabriel rescued some temple slave girls who helped him and was delayed. After Gabriel learned about Koll's escape, he immediately returned to Kra'zum. There was nothing at first, but then priests cried out from the altars Koll had found Obsydia. They mourn Obsydia's prison of light."

Neelam grimaced. "They could not know this, unless Koll has found her."

"Gabriel warned me he has a large price on his head in Urgonclaw now, since he killed several priests while disrupting their blood sacrifices. He says he managed to save some of them, mostly children. He cannot return until he finds a safe place for them."

"Good for Gabriel, I say," Belwyn added.

Cathal continued. "I agree.

Queen Sorcha's disgust was unrestrained. "That monster Koll is in Kra'zum? Then we will send an army! Shed their blood!"

Cathal shook his head. "Gabriel didn't see Koll there, but Zhelon is revering Koll as a dark saint now. They have been in contact."

"Gently, my love," Caladynn cautioned her. "We will have our vengeance. "I thought Obsydia was a myth. One of the many shadow tales from the era of the bloodstone."

"Obsydia is real," Cathal confirmed. "I know, because I am one of the three mages who imprisoned her a thousand years ago."

I wasn't expecting that, Mellypip gasped in Runa's head.

"Grandpa!" Runa blurted. "You never told me this!"

"He never told me either," Caliste added. "Why?"

"These were war secrets," Neelam said bluntly. "A thousand years ago, we created a ritual which required all three magics of drusai, wizard, and sorcerer to trap her in a crystal of light. The Bloodstone Era was ruled by an immortal no one could kill. It took years and a powerful enchantment with an added gift from the Winged-Fey to seal it. They helped scribe the ritual, along with our leader, Borel the Sorcerer. Obsydia had him assassinated, but not before we had completed the ritual."

"The Winged-Fey, they are real too?" Sorcha whispered.

Neelam nodded. "To fight an immortal, you need an immortal. For a thousand years, we kept this secret. Cathal, Ambera, and myself performed the ritual that ended the Bloodstone Wars and defeated Obsydia."

"Skarros is a barren land, so there was no danger of anyone living there," Cathal added. "Not even caravans pass into that territory."

"Afterward we imprisoned Obsydia, we planted many spells to block prying sorcery and relic hunters; we thought it would keep her hidden. Every century or so, I would go there to make sure and add new spells to conceal her old temple beneath the sands. Well, now Obsydia has been found and we must deal with it."

Runa was incredulous. "What about Grandmother? Did she know anything about this?"

Cathal's smile was unexpected and steeped with memory. "Oh, your grandmother Yllia was there, fighting Obsydia's armies with the other allied nations which joined us, riding a fire dragon. Yllia was magnificent."

Dragons! Mellypip cried in Runa's head. He was eager to hear more about the dragons, but Neelam rapped his staff on the table when words and emotions threatened to dissolve into chaos.

"Cathal, you owe me a long story and a lot of ale," Caladynn insisted.

"We have two problems which need immediate attention," Neelam said. "First, if Koll has truly found hell-bitch Obsydia, we must make sure he doesn't release her. The enchantments we used were powerful, forged from Light, but we cannot take chances. I'll take Zhelon's and Koll's heads before anything else happens. The second problem is how to liberate Cathal's family from the curse Koll invoked, especially without harming them."

"We tried to take Koll's head," Caladynn remarked bitterly.

Neelam's sharp gaze was unsettling. "Do not be hard on yourself. You were obeying the law, which gave Koll's allies time to strike. I am not bound by such restraints and can be quite lawless when it comes to dealing with enemies."

"Can we save them?" Runa asked eagerly. "We don't have much time."

Cathal's exhaustion was evident. "Panthara told me about Koll's treasure of mystical relics from the Bloodstone Age. He keeps most of them in a special chamber in the great temple. When Panthara heard about Runa's visions at the tree, she told me Koll's original bloodstone scroll could most likely be there. If it is there, I will steal it and formulate a ritual to reverse the curse. If it is the original scroll used, we may be able to save them. I am going today."

"Going to Kra'zum!" Runa cried. "It's too dangerous."

"Walking into Rygon's Temple is no easy task," Caladynn pointed out.

"Can we trust Panthara's information?" Opaline asked bluntly.

Panthara remained in her seat, her hands primly folded on the table, not a flicker of emotion revealed on her beautiful face.

"I think we must give her a chance," Iona said.

"I understand your trepidation," Panthara said. "But my unfortunate history with Koll may be your salvation to help Cathal's family."

Cathal turned to Panthara. "Are you sure Koll kept his relics in the temple?"

She took out a folded piece of parchment. "Yes, Koll would trust nowhere else. I've drawn a map from memory and marked a path to his personal suite of rooms and where the relics are concealed. I know which wards he used too. I doubt he changed them, so I can tell you what to do to deactivate them. Koll took me to the temple in Kra'zum only once, but I remember it well. He showed me a secret door in his chambers. Within is a room filled with artifacts—scrolls, stone tablets, ancient bottles with strange magical runes, statues, and crystals. He glorified in them and touched them with tender care. If he used this scroll you speak of to summon a terrible curse, as a secret sacrifice, he would keep it there. I remember an onyx case bound with crimson ribbon on a small pedestal in the center of the chamber. The onyx and ribbon are part of the ritual for secret sacrifices. Perhaps the scroll you need is there."

"What is a secret sacrifice? Caliste asked.

"When they offer something of great price, but do not reveal what or who it is, not even to a priest." Panthara lowered her head. "It usually involves taking a life."

"My job will be to ensure Obsydia remains locked in her prison," Neelam said. "I'll go investigate Skarros while Cathal fetches Koll's scrolls."

"You cannot go to Skarros alone," Cathal protested.

Neelam shrugged and lit his pipe. "I'm better suited for it, Cathal. You'll have enough troubles in Urgonclaw. Koll mucking about with Bloodstone diabolism and traipsing about in Skarros— that irritates me. We cannot take chances, not with Ambera's dying words ringing in my ears. If Koll's collection of Bloodstone relics has a chance at shattering the magic, we must stop him. Killing him would be even better of course." Neelam puffed on his pipe. "At least my plan is simple. Go to Skarros and make sure the she-beast is still captive. You face bigger troubles in Urgonclaw. Are you sure you can't wait until I get back, Cathal?"

Cathal dourly shook his head and glanced at Runa. "No. We cannot wait. I believe in Runa's vision."

"Sorcery is not our only talent," Sirah suggested. "We wear disguises of course. Perhaps a nomadic chieftain or warlord from Ithuli or Ucara? If word is spreading Koll found Obsydia, then the faithful would make pilgrimages. It would be hard to disprove our claims. A rich pilgrim offering gifts to Rygon's temple is common, often rewarded with a meeting with the High Priest in the inner sanctum. Offer gold and jewels as personal gifts for the High Priest, or me perhaps?"

"Mother!" Opaline and Taran cried out in unison, horrified.

"No! No! No!" Myrsalian protested, jumping out of his chair. "Sirah, you're not thinking clearly!"

"Zhelon Thor is a monster!" Opaline cried. "He visited Tiamet often enough to visit Father. I spied on his obscene conversations when I used the secret passageways. He boasted about killing innocent victims and called it religion!"

"Opaline is right," Panthara said. "Zhelon is a horrid man who loves sacrifice. When I visited there with Koll, I saw how he treated his poor handmaidens. He is vicious and cruel. It would be dangerous."

There was a momentary hush.

Will the world go boom if Panthara and Opaline agree on anything?
Mellypip asked Runa.

*I'm not sure, but for once Opaline is looking at Panthara with something
other than loathing.*

Is that good or bad? Mellypip asked.

Sirah quite calmly waved away any protests. "I'm the only logical
choice. I could be a gift to Zhelon Thor himself, along with a generous pouch of gold and gems. It would be custom for the High Priest
to personally give thanks and invite you to supper. You could take
advantage of easy access and find Koll's trove of relics. I know
Rygon's Temple quite well. I grew up there, remember?"

Myrsalian burst into tears. "I would never see you victimized
again, even in a ruse."

"There now, Father," Sirah said softly. "Don't cry. I will never be
a slave again. Thanks to you and my sorcery, I'll never have to fear
again." She kissed Myrsalian on his forehead.

"Sirah, I would never forgive myself if anything happened to
you!" Cathal told her.

"I know temple customs," Sirah said. "True, I haven't been in
Rygon's temple since I was fifteen years old, but it will be to our
benefit. Who will remember me? I never knew Zhelon Thor. I don't
think I would be recognized unless Tarsicius or Levandius were
there, but the Emperor is staying in his kingdom since the civil war
with his son." She fingered a lock of Myrsalian's long hair, frowning.
"Father, you should color your hair black. Not many redheads reside
in the desert kingdoms. I would be considered an exotic treasure,
since slaves come from many cultures, however."

"Ask Cathal about changing hair color," Belwyn suggested.
"He's a master at it."

"You could come along and help, but you must watch your
temper," Sirah cautioned.

"You can't risk such a thing!" Opaline begged.

"Rygon's cult attracts the worst type of monsters," Sirah agreed.
"The human kind. I was luckier than most. My beauty enabled
survival in a den of bloodthirsty fiends. They like their women slaves
to look pretty while they mop up the blood."

"Mother!" Opaline shivered with disgust. Ulric took her hand
and kissed it.

Sirah calmly touched Opaline's cheek. "Truth is hard, my daughter. I am much harder."

"Can you pass for a slave now?" Neelam asked. "You walk and speak like a queen, not like a broken temple slave."

Sirah's smile was chilling. "I can fake it. Women do it often enough. I faked humility as a slave, though every waking moment I longed to kill my keepers or at the very least escape. I spat into many wine cups and plates, knowing they would drink and eat from my hand. Even a lowly slave has their tiny triumphs." Sirah lifted her skirt and exposed the ugly brand with Rygon's symbol on her thigh, two inches long, in the shape of a scythe. "I still bear the brand of Rygon's slave. I am your only choice."

"Your suffering must have been great, lady," Neelam remarked soberly. "I would not expose you to such terror again."

"Thank you," Sirah replied, dropping her skirt. "But, this brand will give our lies an illusion of truth. I was just a baby when I was sold to Rygon's temple. My poor father is distraught. For years he thought both myself and my mother perished in an attack when Urgonclaw army invaded our village. I lived, but he did not know for years, and he still carries guilt. He has no need to. I am going."

"I must go with you," Arial added. "My camouflage magic can conceal me. Warlords also keep wolves and lions for pets and protection. I will not permit my sorceress to go into a den of butchers unprotected."

"What about us?" Runa asked.

"Oh no! You will stay here at the Sorcerer House," Cathal said firmly.

"Grandpa!" Runa protested.

Cathal's steely gaze silenced her. "No protests are permitted, young lady." He pointed his finger. "That goes for Opaline and Taran too. This is a job for more experienced adult mages. This is no fool adventure."

"I should go with you," Liat offered.

"No," Cathal said. "You will go with Neelam to Skarros. Ulan will make a fine warlord, however."

"I don't need anyone," Neelam protested.

"You need someone to watch your back," Cathal insisted.

"How can you be sure you have the right scroll, even if Panthara is speaking the truth?" Opaline asked.

"I remember the Bloodstone language," Cathal replied. "I will be able to recognize the curse from what Runa described. Ambera's dying words warned us of Obsydia's return. I wish I could say they were the ravings of a dying woman. Darkness is coming. I will not wait for it to knock on my door."

A resounding banging on the door and the familiar voices of Jadon and Darcus on the other side prompted Neelam to deactivate the shield.

Darcus and Jadon pushed the doors open and marched into the hall amid a flutter of blue veils and royal guards. They were filthy, disheveled, and looked very angry.

"It's alright," Cathal assured them. "They're friends."

The nuns and soldiers silently stepped away and left the chamber, closing the double doors.

Runa's heart beat very fast, both with joy at seeing him and dread as to why he was here. *Melly, it's Jadon! He's back! And so is Darcus!*

"I fear why too," Mellypip whispered aloud.

"The Oak and Rowan sent us," Darcus shouted. "Forgive our intrusion. We have been flying nonstop to reach you. We went to the Sorcerer House first, but the King's guards at the Sorcerer House sent us here."

"What the hell happened?" Belwyn asked.

Revulsion passed over Darcus' features and his scarred eye twitched. "Ambera's grave was violated."

"What?" Neelam shouted, striking his staff hard on the floor.

Darcus grimaced. "It sickens me to share this tale. Three priestesses, whose duty it was to watch over Ambera's grave the first three nights after her burial, were murdered. I was among the honor guard. I heard their screams and ran to help. When I reached Ambera's grave, they were already dead and Ambera's grave was opened. Little bits of her flesh and hair were cut away." His eyes burned with hatred and his voice was hoarse with emotion as he spoke. "Koll did it."

Cathal was livid. "Koll violated Ambera!"

Darcus nodded. "I found him standing over her grave with a jar in his hand. The poor priestesses were dead at his feet. I rushed him with my sword! He should be dead! I had Koll cornered against the trunk of an old hawthorn tree, but right before I plunged my sword into him, he melted into the shadows and disappeared! He was gone! Damn him! Gone!"

"I think darkness is knocking," Belwyn said.

CHAPTER TWENTY-FIVE

Levandius watched Tarsicius as he slept in his bed. Moonlight glowed through the long glass windows and the late summer breeze carried the smell of the sea. Everything was deceptively peaceful. Tarsicius suddenly opened his eyes and reached beneath his silk pillow and unsheathed a long dagger.

"Did I disturb your rest, Father?" Levandius asked, stepping from the shadows.

"What are you doing here?" Tarsicius spat, gathering his wits. "I'll have those guards' worthless heads!"

"Cannot a son beg for forgiveness? Entreat to kiss your withered royal hand and be embraced back into your circle again?"

"You can ask," Tarsicius spat, "but I will not grant it."

"But Father, I missed you so," Levandius murmured softly. "Have you no yearning in your heart for your only true son. You cannot keep holding mock funerals for children you banish, though I heard you gave Opaline a splendid funeral. You even wept as her empty coffin was carried into the royal crypt. All those empty coffins crowded in the family vault. If only folks knew of your dirty secrets!"

"Get out!" the Emperor demanded. "Unless you desire to be the first Imperial Prince of the Ivory Kingdoms to be executed by his own father, get out!" He threw off his satin covers and jumped out of bed, still clenching the dagger in his hand. "I exiled you! You're forever banished for treason! You should be grateful I spared your miserable life! You should kiss my feet for such clemency! Guards! Guards! Come quickly!"

"They are sleeping, Father," Levandius said.

"Sleeping?" Tarsicius inquired suspiciously.

Levandius shrugged. "Dead actually."

"Assassination is it? Royal slaughter in the dead of night. Are you so greedy for my crown you would stain your hands with my blood?"

"All kings are stained with blood. You taught me that when I was five," Levandius said.

"And you're stained with vice! You will never understand the cruel burden of royal sacrifice; the sacrifices I made for my kingdom.

I can't even give the crown to—"

"Taran? Your favorite. Taran is a sorcerer," Levandius mused. "By your own laws, that makes it illegal for him to rule, so your bastard must do without. I have new allies. I will bring a new age to the Ivory Kingdoms. I will be Emperor! You, however, will soon be rotting in the royal necropolis next to all those empty coffins! Should I place your coffin next to your true dead wife and queen, or would you prefer the whore's false tomb?"

"Foul wretch!" Tarsicius spat. He raised his dagger to strike, but Levandius sidestepped him. A cloud of dark surrounded Tarsicius. Suddenly, he could not move or speak.

Chimera stepped from the shadows. Her demonic beauty stunned the Emperor. Koll appeared, a shade himself, black eyes glittering, with Xabral coiled around his body like a lover.

"You took your sweet time," Levandius snapped.

Koll's icy stare made Levandius look away. "I am not your minion, Levandius. I serve a higher power. *Never* forget that."

The mute Emperor struggled to raise his dagger, but the demon's hex kept him bound in the smoky bedevilment. Chimera knocked the dagger out of his hand. Tarsicius was moribund in the darkness and he knew it. Fear and regret replaced his anger now as she caressed him.

"Be grateful the stupid Emperor is helpless," Chimera scolded. "The prince needs to learn manners." She glanced at Koll lovingly. "Let me teach him? Please!"

"Later," Koll whispered impatiently. "Do the deed."

"Yes. Finish this," Levandius insisted. "You promised I could watch him die."

Chimera slowly licked her lips. The demonolatry which enthralled him prevented his movement as she stroked his short-cropped pewter hair and gazed into his blue-gray eyes that now watered with tears long kept imprisoned. She turned away and took a vial of black glass from her hip and uncorked it. "You must drink this nectar," she cooed as she poured it into his mouth. He choked but she made sure he swallowed the vial.

"Is that all?" Levandius demanded.

"Patience," she hissed.

The shield around Tarsicius vanished. He paled and clutched his chest, eyes bulging.

"Is he suffering?" Levandius asked eagerly.

"Yes," Chimera said with a smile. "My special demon poison seals his doom with death."

"Good," Levandius said, watching his father falter.

Tarsicius collapsed to the carpeted floor. His hands reached out, not toward Levandius or even Koll, but instead crawled to his bed and groped beneath the plump pillows with frantic need, though the useless dagger lay close on the floor. The struggle for life ceased and with a final strangled breath, Tarsicius, Emperor of the Ivory Kingdoms, was dead.

Levandius' boot prodded the corpse of his father, as though to make sure he were truly dead. "Now, I am finally Emperor. When they find him in the morning, the physicians will believe a heart attack or stroke killed him. Then soon, a messenger will arrive in Urgonclaw to offer me the Crown Imperial. I will humbly accept."

"Your desire to be Emperor is now fulfilled," Koll said. "Remember the price, Levandius."

"I am finally Emperor," Levandius declared again, though his voice was hollow.

Chimera smiled and lifted Xabral from Koll's arms and draped him around her naked shoulders. "I adore Xabral, Koll. His black and red scales compliment my beauty. May I keep him?"

"No," Koll replied impatiently, and took Xabral from her greedy grasp. "Xabral is my familiar, not an accessory."

Xabral looked into Chimera's eyes. "You're pretty," he said with giddy affection.

Levandius noticed a small gold disc clenched in his father's other hand. He snatched it from his fingers. It was a locket; he opened it. Inside was a portrait of Sirahnami.

Bitterness twisted his expression. "All these years he kept her picture! The whore! He hid it in his bed, and gazed at it when he was all alone like a lovesick fool. Even in the end, he loved her more than me! She will be punished one day. The concubine and her bastards will die in the coming war. I will see to it."

Levandius dropped the locket by Tarsicius' head. With childish resentment he crushed the locket under his boot heel and walked away from his father's lifeless body.

~ * ~

Koll stepped through the eye of shadows with Chimera. They made their obeisance to Obsydia.

"Is it done?" Obsydia asked.

"Yes, my Queen, the old emperor is dead."

"I shall return to my cauldron." Chimera bowed. "See how Ambera's flesh is simmering."

"You are a devoted servant," Obsydia complimented her.

Koll endured the glare of the light, circling the crystal. "So much is at stake now. How did three mortal mages trap a goddess whose father is the source of all shadow and chaos? You have told me fragments, but what was the truth? Please, tell me."

"I will do more. I will show you. It was more than magic, more than a conjuration. Come closer, Koll, and bring your sweet pet, Xabral. Lay your hand upon this cursed crystal and witness the final battle of the Bloodstone Wars and the fall of my glory."

Koll laid his hands upon the crystal, which seared his flesh, and he could almost taste the element of the Light which spiced it. Xabral coiled about his feet, joined his mind to share this vision. His body convulsed as the past streamed into his mind.

The vast gates of Obsydia's palace opened. From atop the battlements, black-robed Warrior Priests, once human men, now demons with red, lidless eyes, unleashed even more legions onto the sun-scorched battlefield. Throngs of fur-clad bestial-looking men wielding rough forged axes and blades, while the roars of hulking trolls, crazed in their bloodlust and held in check by wiry goblins controlling their chains, filled the harsh, dry air.

The Allies of Light clashed with Obsydia's legions. For the first time in history, dragons permitted riders upon their backs; fighting together as one. They fought against Obsydia with the armies of men and mages.

Fire Dragons swooped low, the sun sparkling over their crimson scales as they summoned their fiery magic, spewing first hot bolts, then sheets of flame over Obsydia's aberrant forces. Swinging around for another pass, the dragons gobbled up remnants of Obsydia's forces, snapping burnt and smoldering bones in their powerful jaws.

Green Earth Dragons, bodies iridescent in the desert glare, descended upon the human elements of Obsydia's army, spraying a green mist that quickly hardened into a thick, leafy cocoon, trapping her soldiers within. Shadow Dragons followed, the small but clever tunnel diggers of the Dragon Clans, who burst up from beneath the hot sands, rending the surviving enemy without mercy.

Silver-scaled Ice Dragons, their icy blue eyes freezing with hatred, breathed their icy mist, blanketing the field. Ghostly moon dragons supported Warriors of Light, driving back the hordes of Obsydia's armies, giving them time to withdraw, while Blue Mist Dragons dazed the enemy with their powerful breath that caused confusion and forgetfulness, and Sun Dragons summoned the light of the desert sun to their golden scales, blinding Obsydia's forces.

Far from the madness of battle outside, three mages and their familiars stalked the shadowed corridors of Obsydia's temple palace: Ambera of the Fallen People, Neelam, Wizard of Ironia and Surya the snow eagle, and a young inexperienced sorcerer, Cathal, and Belwyn the owl.

Shade, Obsydia's chief handmaiden, confronted the mages in the throne room. Thirteen handmaids circled them; robed in red silk, their ebony eyes glittered in the firelight.

Shade warned them. "Fool mages! Did you think you could trespass into this sacred palace unless Obsydia desired you?

"We come for Obsydia," Neelam countered. "Not to banter words with her demon lackey."

Other members of Obsydia's court stepped from the gloom. Some nobles of her circle; jeweled and garbed in rich silks, sinewy goblins guards appeared, gripping heavy serrated blades, and Obsydia's black-robed priests.

"What are they waiting for?" Cathal asked in a choked whisper.

"They wait for me," a melodious, feminine voice replied above them.

They craned their necks to see. On the domed ceiling above the throne of ebonite was a life size portrait of Obsydia. Her silver eyes blinked.

Cathal sucked in his breath and stumbled back. "Obsydia's portrait...It's alive!"

Obsydia stepped from her own painting, and as her corporal form floated to the floor, her demon handmaidens knelt as one in reverence, their resonant voices singing a hymn praising her. Obsydia sat gracefully upon her throne and studied the intruders.

"Three infidels creep into my palace," Obsydia began in a mocking tone, "with nothing but dirty magic. A drusai witch, a wizard, and a boy sorcerer! You are the Scions of Light? I thought your plans would change, since I killed Borel and his lion familiar, Torrin. The greatest sorcerer of your caste and you replace him with this weak boy."

Koll smiled when he saw tears well in Cathal's eyes.

"Hello hell-bitch," Neelam threw back his concealing hood. "Remember me?"

"Neelam!" Obsydia hissed. "I thought you dead when I killed Borel and his cat!" A brief spark of fury clouded her dark beauty.

Neelam smiled with frosty calm, "Oh, I wouldn't miss this. I owe this to Borel." He sheathed his sword. "Steel won't do us any good, now."

Cathal and Ambera likewise sheathed their weapons.

"Kill them!" Obsydia commanded in a soft voice. "Kill them all!"

The demon guards charged, their high-pitched shrieks echoing through the chamber.

"Now!" Neelam shouted.

Each of the three mages took a smoky crystal from their pockets and hurled them to the floor. The hollow crystals smashed like glass, releasing a thick green smoke. The first to fall to the mystical poison were the goblin guards. The vapors spread quickly throughout the throne room. Nobles and priests alike clutched their throats, gasping for air, succumbing to a painful death within a few breaths. Only Obsydia and her demon handmaids remained unaffected.

"Why didn't the poison kill the handmaids?" Ambera demanded.

"Because they're true demons from the Otherworld," Neelam snapped.

Obsydia, having watched most of her court fall dead, grew enraged. In her fury, she summoned a ball of black flame, hurling it at them.

The trio of mages raised their joined hands and sent a surge of combined magic to block her attack. Two strains of magic, light and dark, collided violently; fusing before it exploded with an ear-splitting roar. The impact tossed the mages across the room.

Obsydia remained untouched by the blast.

Cathal struggled to rise and Belwyn fluttered around him, pecking at him to get up. Ambera leapt to her feet, hair wild and smoking at the tips, but her bright copper-colored eyes remained determined. Neelam regained his footing with amazing speed, rushing to Cathal's side, pulling him to his feet.

The handmaidens drew long, narrow blades of obsidian glass from beneath their robes, and closed in on the mages. Spears of mystical white energy shot from Neelam's outstretched fingers, impaling the handmaidens and knocking them off their feet. Ambera cast a glowing dome of protection about them, just as Obsydia hurled another fiery sphere.

Ambera's dome held against the assault—deflecting Obsydia's smoking black fire and the razored blades of the demon handmaidens. The shield began to crisp and wither beneath the angry queen's onslaught.

"Hurry!" Ambera cried.

"Almost there!" Neelam answered, retrieving a round diamond of intense brilliance the size of a large apple from his pocket.

"What can you do, fool?" Obsydia sneered. "I am immortal. You cannot kill me. Only another god has such power."

"I don't need to slay you, Obsydia," Neelam closed his eyes in concentration. "But I can make you suffer an eternity for your sins."

"You? Make me suffer!" Obsydia laughed. "I, who was sired by an Eternal, I am the immaculate conception of Darkness. A goddess made flesh to rule this world."

Obsydia's bombardment against the trio grew stronger, the waves of fiery darkness intensifying until the dome sizzled; thin fissures spread across the mystical protection.

Neelam plucked a small vial from his pocket. Inside, a silvery essence shimmered, more light than liquid.

He uncorked the vial with his teeth, spit out the cork, and poured the liquid over the diamond. Each mage touched the diamond with reverence. The thunder of dark flames pummeled mercilessly against the protective dome.

"The conjuration prayer," Ambera urged. "Now!"

The mages joined hands as they began to chant the prayer spell with every ounce of passion their voices could muster.

"Ancient Eternals, show compassion for our plight. Fuse our magic with this blood of Light. Bind this wicked queen with your Grace. Forever banish her to endless night. Circle this Bloodstone Seed and remove her darkness from our sight. Bind her forever with your Light. We summon—"

The diamond glowed with the brightness of the sun.

"Drop the shield, Ambera!" Neelam commanded.

Ambera hesitated, stricken with fear.

"Now!" Neelam ordered.

"If we die," Ambera shouted back, "I swear I'll never speak to you again!" The mystic shield abruptly evaporated, leaving them utterly vulnerable.

The three mages touched the diamond as their renewed chant resonated throughout the vast chamber. The diamond radiated with a blinding light. The shadows of the opulent room dissolved against the magical blaze of pure radiance. Obsydia's demon handmaidens wailed in despair, shielding their eyes against the brilliance.

The great diamond pulsated, transforming into a living heart of Light. A stream of wholesome, blue-white light shot from its center toward Obsydia. Her black flames dissolving into wisps of ash as the jewel's radiance passed through them.

The demon handmaidens gathered around their unholy goddess. Though demon-spawned, they were not immortal. Shade was the first to die from light ripping through her body. The handmaidens howled in agony as each succumbed to death; their flesh ripped asunder by the purity of Light.

Obsydia stood alone.

The pure Light broke into countless tiny stars, and reformed about the dark queen, like bees buzzing about a hive. Obsydia screamed in pain as the iridescent Light enveloped her body and the sparkling cocoon trapped her. Light flowed from the diamond, and with each bright strand, it grew smaller and smaller until nothing remained, and the three mages let go. Neelam was first to *end the chant. The essence of Light formed a glowing chrysalis that imprisoned a dark jewel in its heart—Obsydia. Still living; yet trapped forever in a living tomb of Light.*

"We did it!" Cathal breathed. "We really did it!"

"Don't celebrate now," Belwyn cautioned, "it's not over yet."

The palace shuddered violently, knocking the mages to the floor.

"See?" Belwyn circling him wings flapping frantically. "What did I tell you?

Another quake and the chamber floor tilted. Cathal slid toward Obsydia's crystal tomb, close enough to see her silver eyes burning into him with her hatred; the only power left to her now.

The walls of the palace shook again, when the great double-doors burst outward, torn from their hinges as Neelam struck them with continual waves of violent purple wizardry. Cathal scrambled away from the cocoon.

"Time to go!" Neelam shouted above the roar of falling stone. "Everyone out!

They sprinted back down the hallway, dodging falling stone and collapsing pillars. Walls cracked and tumbled, blocking the way. Desperate, they turned down another corridor, following a weakening glow of what seemed to be sunlight, until they reached a shuttered balcony.

Breaking through the shutters, revealed a perilous spectacle high above the still raging battle. Fissures opened and swallowed the remains of demons, returning them to Hell. Another severe jolt formed another fissure. It rent the earth, heaving chunks of bedrock into the air. The army of light was forced to flee as their enemy was consumed.

The Bloodstone palace sank into the bowels of the angry earth, entombing Obsydia into oblivion.

Koll fell back from Obsydia's crystal, the knowledge burning in his brain. Shivering, he sank to the floor, Xabral coiling around him lovingly.

"Now you have seen the truth of my fall from grace," Obsydia said.

Chimera joined them, ignoring Koll's prostrate form. "This new ritual I am creating must have elements of Light and Dark. After we have appeased the Light Gods in the ritual, we must shatter it, but only a weapon forged in the Dark Realm will work."

Obsydia's eyes flashed. "Then we must find Rygon's Scythe. It's a powerful weapon, touched by my brother's breath in blessing. It was forged in the Dark Realms."

"That would suffice," Chimera agreed eagerly.

"I was the keeper of it. I made a gift of it to my first warrior priest, Solem. After he was slain in Thema, I laid it in his tomb for safekeeping."

"Then Koll must fetch it," Chimera said.

CHAPTER TWENTY-SIX

Mellypip scribbled intently in his notebook, long whiskers twitching, pausing for a breath to think before resuming his writing. He found the sorcery chamber more comforting, since it was so like the one in their old tree tower. The aura of light magic lingered here, giving him a sense of security in a time of chaos.

"What are you doing, Melly?" Runa asked, entering the room, still in her nightgown. "You're up quite early."

Mellypip tapped his stylus against his furry brow. "I'm composing a story for Pointessa and Rosepetal. They are so sad. Pointessa's loss can never be healed because Eberr is dead, but I still want to make her smile. Rosepetal misses Ulan terribly since he decided to leave her here when Cathal took him on the secret mission. I was going to write about the Winged-Fey, but that tale is too sad. So I am writing about your quest to make a potion that did not explode or turn our tree tower pink."

"We could all use a smile. I don't think Opaline has slept since her mother and grandfather left."

"You're an early riser today." Caliste smiled as she joined them in the room."

"Sun's up now." Runa stretched and sat in the window seat. "Any message from Grandpa? Are they in Urgonclaw yet?"

Caliste shuffled though a stack of papers on the table and shook her head. Sanura was asleep in the windowsill, oblivious. "No. We cannot risk contacting them yet either."

"I think Sanura has been hanging around MacTabbish too much," Mellypip commented. "Is napping contagious?"

"Please let me go see my mother and grandmother," Runa begged.

"No, dear, it is too dangerous. Raghnall and Iona are with them."

"And Panthara and Azmadu?" Mellypip asked cautiously, whiskers twitching.

Caliste arranged colorful crystals on the shelf. "They are with Iona this morning."

Runa hugged her knees close and looked out the window. "I hate being left behind. I'm not the only one. Redstorm was furious when Darcus left him here."

"Redstorm is cranky," Mellypip confirmed. "He curses as well as Darcus too. I learned lots of new words."

Baldur lumbered into the sorcery chamber. "Anything you can say in public?"

"Not without getting my mouth scrubbed with soap, but they are fascinating phrases I may use one day in my bardship," Mellypip replied.

"He was quite vexed when Darcus did not take him along," Caliste said. "But a peryton would not be easily explained in Urgonclaw."

Runa jumped up, a bundle of frustrated energy. "This place feels like a prison now. King Caladynn has so many soldiers guarding the tower. We can't go anywhere. Will we ever be safe again?"

"Your Grandfather once faced the dark daughter of Ahridum. I think at some point he can manage to bring Koll to justice—or death. Speaking of learning, I'm planning some lessons for you and Opaline. Your magical education has stalled since, well, since everything happened. Sirah wants me to ease Opaline into practicing magic. I thought some simple crystal training would be good for her. She is so reluctant to even try. Poor girl is afraid."

"It's called troll fear," Mellypip remarked. "Oh, that is a good tale too. Rono will love to hear it when they find him."

"I think Opaline is ready to practice her sorcery," Baldur said. "I just saw her in the kitchen. She removed her sorcerer bane necklace and was weaving magic over the dough."

Runa's eyes widened. "What do you mean weaving magic?"

Baldur rolled onto the carpet. "Only that she thought practicing on flour would be less harmful. Opaline told me she was casting a charm to get the bread to rise with sorcery. She thought it would be simple and a nice surprise."

Runa rushed toward the door with Mellypip scrambling at her heels. "Opaline is a terrible cook, and her sorcery is anything but simple."

"But I have a feeling we are going to be surprised," Mellypip added.

Opaline's cries echoed as they hurried down the stairs toward the kitchen. Opaline had fled into the living room, face and hands speckled with flour, wringing her hands.

Taran, sleepy-eyed, stumbled down the stairs, MacTabbish flopped across his shoulder. "What's going on?"

"What happened dear?" Caliste asked calmly.

"I thought I would make scones for everyone," Opaline replied shakily. "I had an urge to attempt some simple magic spell to practice, to make my mother proud." She pointed toward the kitchen door. "But it went all wrong!"

Caliste opened the kitchen door and stepped back. Mellypip scuttled behind her and gasped. The entire kitchen was overtaken by an enormous ball of dough, expanding in size with each second. The yeasty smell was comforting, but the giant blob of dough was intimidating.

"Look Runa," Mellypip pointed. "We can feed the world!"

"Sister, sorcery and cooking are not your strengths. Where's your necklace?"

"In the kitchen somewhere."

"I'll take care of this," Caliste said patiently.

A loud boom shook them.

"I think your bane necklace finally touched the enchanted dough," Taran grinned.

Runa sat next to Opaline and patted her hand. "Your effort was valiant, but I think you should be supervised when you practice your sorcery. Or try to cook anything."

"I'm a failure," Opaline sniffled.

"No, you just need to study, with supervision," Runa consoled her. "If you don't, you'll never learn to control it. That pendant of sorcerer bane is helpful, but it can become an object of dependence prohibiting your magical development."

"I know, I know, but I could hardly perform my sorcery when I lived in Tiamet," Opaline shrugged. "The ring of sorcerer bane protected my secret for so long, I found it hard to be without it. When I lost it, I thought I could manage and finally begin to learn to express my gift, but my magic keeps spurting out when I don't mean it to. It's always in some devastating fashion too. Do I need to remind you of Gorvanus—a wicked sorcerer to be sure, but I turned him into a hideous troll! I didn't even mean to do that! Must I mention the baskets of Runa's hair in the closet that magically sprouted several yards and gave her a nasty headache when I was just brushing it?"

"We all have bad days," Runa consoled her.

Taran rubbed his eyes. "I take it the kitchen is plastered with dough and we don't have tea?"

"I'll restore the kitchen and bring us tea," Caliste promised. "These are the days I am grateful to have magic."

Taran knelt before Opaline and took her hand. "Stop crying. Your problem is your demand for perfection. It's your curse, Sister. You had to excel above anyone at your studies, and then your perfect clothes, perfect horseback riding, perfect hair and skin, perfect at learning languages, handwriting perfect. When we were children, you would spend hours mastering your penmanship. But, if you couldn't be perfect, you didn't pursue it. Remember the trouble you had with archery?"

"My teacher recovered," Opaline objected, wincing.

"But you stopped doing it when it became difficult and you could not easily achieve perfection."

"Are you saying I give up?" Opaline accused.

"You shine at many things, Sis, but not everything can be mastered quickly."

"You just need to trust yourself," Runa added. "My potions use to explode."

"I'm writing an opus about it," Mellypip interjected.

"When Grandfather brought Mellypip to me and we bonded, things began to change. It got better."

"How can I ever be granted the honor of a familiar when I can't even do a simple spell?"

"Practice," Taran and Runa intoned simultaneously.

Taran stood up and stretched. "Just don't make me eat your cooking."

Opaline smacked him with a pillow.

Taran grinned in response. "Besides, I need help in my science experiments. I have been researching with sarod metal, and it only neutralizes magic when forged with iron. I think if it can be fused with other metals, it could even enhance sorcery."

Runa furrowed her brow. "I'm confused. How? I thought sarod metal itself prevented magic."

"That's just it! Sarod metal by itself is not the bane. It's only when it's blended with iron that it has those properties! With other types of metals, I am finding the results are quite different."

"What do you mean?" Runa asked, fascinated.

"Some metals enhance the magic or alter even it," Taran said excitedly. "Which is why, Sister, you need to start practicing more. I need an assistant for my experiments."

Opaline's eyes widened and her skin paled. "After the last explosion in your mystical lab? No! I prefer to live a little longer, thank you."

Mellypip crawled into Opaline's lap. "But you just created monster dough, so I think you're even. It has fed my ambitions and will make a wonderful tale. So it wasn't all bad."

"Runa, why don't you ask Jadon if he would like some tea and scones," Caliste suggested. "I restored both dough and kitchen to normal. Opaline can assist me with making tea. I will make the scones. I think she can manage the tea without tragic incident."

Elated at having a reason to talk to Jadon, Runa tucked Mellypip under her arm. "That's a wonderful idea."

"Why do humans need a reason to talk to someone?" Mellypip asked as they went to the back door.

"Hush Melly! I want to seem normal," Runa whispered.

Mellypip harrumphed. "Normal? Love leaves humans anything but normal! And I know you want to do that kissing thing. Must I fetch my staff to protect your virtue?"

"You're sounding more like Belwyn," Runa commented with an arched brow. "That may not be a good thing. And my virtue is fine."

Mellypip knew Jadon had been told by Cathal and Darcus to protect Runa. Mellypip also knew Jadon's true feelings for his sorceress. It was torment to keep the pretty wooden ring Jadon made for her a secret too! He must reconsider the next time he promised to keep secrets. Promises are trouble.

Just outside the stables, Jadon was grooming Darkleaf. Redstorm was sulking.

Mellypip waved to them, tale swishing excitedly. "Hi Redstorm! Hi Darkleaf! Opaline just blew up the kitchen."

"That sounds serious," Redstorm said.

"But not surprising," Darkleaf added.

"The kitchen is fine," Runa said. "There were complications with dough and magic."

Jadon's blue eyes lit with joy. "Good morning, Runa, Mellypip."

"People," Redstorm sniffed. "Jadon, just tell Runa you like her and mate."

Runa's cheeks flared and Jadon stopped in mid-brush, mouth open. Mellypip jumped down from Runa's arms and bounced over to the crimson peryton. Redstorm lowered his rack of antlers so Mellypip could climb up and sit on top of his head.

"Well, I don't think that went well," Mellypip whispered to him.

"I tried," Redstorm snorted.

Both Jadon and Runa finally burst out laughing. Jadon took her hand and leaned into her. He was just about to kiss her when they heard the guards shouting from the front of the house. They jumped apart and Jadon pulled Runa behind him and drew his sword.

"Mellypip jumped from Redstorm's back onto Runa's shoulder.

"Stay here!" Jadon said, rushing toward the sounds of chaos.

"Not on your life!" Runa replied, following.

"Cathal was right!" Jadon shouted. "You do need to be watched."

"Is that the only reason you stayed!' she cried, running after him.

Jadon skidded to a stop to avoid being struck by a soldier flying through the air. The poor fellow dropped to the ground unconscious. Runa slammed into Jadon and they fell over. Mellypip rolled to the green grass but leapt up quickly. Darkleaf and Redstorm followed them around to the front of the Sorcerer House, ready to fight.

Everyone rushed out of the Sorcerer House to see the giant of a man swinging his staff against Caladynn's soldiers.

A strange man in a ragged brown tunic was throwing soldiers around like they were rag dolls. He was tall, thick-boned, and muscular. When a soldier charged the stranger, he simply picked the fellow up and held him over his head like a twig. A clouded leopard was nipping at stranger's heels, crying, "Stop it! Please, just calm down."

"I want to speak to Cathal!" the stranger shouted.

Jadon pulled Runa to her feet. They watched the powerful man fight off a small army until they finally circled the stranger with swords and staves.

"I warn you," the stranger mumbled. "I rarely use my sorcery against non-mages, but you gentleman are pushing my patience! Where's Cathal? I need to see him!"

"Wait! It's alright! He's not an enemy!" Taran shouted.

MacTabbish was actually awake and ran alongside Sanura, who shapeshifted into her panther shape for battle.

The guards surrounded the stranger, who held a staff of dark wood, the top carved with the likeness of the clouded leopard who pawed at his leg with impatience. A rakish smile broke on his face. In the early morning light, his features were rough but handsome, with shorn dark hair, broad jaw, and a strong nose.

"Stop fighting!" Taran shouted. "Are you completely mad?"

"He's not evil?" Opaline asked, pointing in confusion.

"Nope—just trouble," MacTabbish confirmed, sitting down on

the grass next to an unconscious soldier.

"I love it when you do that, lass," MacTabbish said to Sanura.

"Back off," Sanura warned, tail swishing.

The guards reluctantly backed away at Taran's insistence.

The stranger bowed and stumbled. "Taran! Is that you? Good boy. These misguided fools tried to keep me from coming inside. I need to speak Cathal. No man shall stop me."

"You're blind drunk!" Taran scolded him, gripping his arm when he fell to his knees. He helped him to his feet. "You could have told them who you were!"

"I apologize for his behavior," the clouded leopard moaned. "I also apologize for the assault on the King's soldiers."

Gabriel spun around and waved to them. "Sorry mates! All a silly misunderstanding. Lovely to meet you." He bowed deeply.

"Who is he?" Opaline asked Taran.

"He is Gabriel the Sorcerer," Taran answered. "The clouded leopard is Namir, his familiar. He's the one Cathal sent to Urgonclaw to spy. I've actually known him for years."

Opaline shook her head in disbelief. "This drunk is the rescuer of children, slayer of murderous dark priests, and the scourge of Urgonclaw?"

"You've heard of me?" Gabriel bowed. "I am honored, most lovely maiden. Sorry to be such a bother." He belched loudly and the stench was overwhelming. He straightened and gazed at Opaline with bloodshot eyes. "Why, you're the prettiest girl I've ever seen."

Opaline stepped back and wrinkled her nose. "You're the drunkest."

"I wholeheartedly agree!" Gabriel replied. Then he collapsed at Opaline's feet. "But the most deadly. Just ask that bastard Zhelon Thor! His vicious priests won't be killing anymore children. Well, not forever, not until that cursed bloody temple is demolished and I have Zhelon's head on a spike. I am sorry I did not kill them all, but I tried. I blew up his altar. It made a pretty boom sound when I blasted it with my magic stick."

Magic stick?" Opaline inquired.

"His staff," Namir replied.

"You saved some people. What happened to them?" Caliste asked, kneeling next to him.

"Got them to safety across the border. They are in a safe house. So many children crying. But they are protected now. There were also some fine wenches I saved too. They were most grateful. Such pretty little things. I got delayed."

"By a bottle?" Taran asked gently.

"By several," Gabriel confessed. "If you'd seen what I've seen, you'd drink and never stop. I have a bounty on my head now. Twenty-thousand pieces of gold! Offered by Zhelon himself. I plan to go back and see if I can raise it to fifty thousand."

"Once again, I apologize." Namir nudged at his sorcerer with concern.

"Let's help him inside," Taran said. He and Jadon reached down to pull him up.

Caliste waved them away. "I'll do it. With flick of her finger sorcerous blue beams of light coiled around Gabriel, lifting him in the air toward the Sorcerer House.

"This is the man who spied for Grandpa?" Runa asked in a low voice.

"He's certainly no gentleman," Opaline added.

Taran leaned in and whispered. "Be kind. Gabriel has suffered much. Not only was Gabriel risking his life spying in Kra'zum, his father was Ramirez, the last Archon Koll murdered."

CHAPTER TWENTY-SEVEN

Darcus urged his horse forward to pay the proper tribute for the honor of entering Kra'zum. He wore a patch over his scarred eye, which added to his stature as a hardened veteran of Rygon's war cult.

A city guard with rough-hewn features in black leather and a greasy red turban weighed the pouch of gold coins in his hand with prolonged assessment. Finally satisfied with the tribute, he waved them on. "Welcome to the great and sacred city of Kra'zum. Move along."

"Hadeon the Desert Wolf, majestic Warlord of the thirteenth tribe of Ucara, thanks you," Darcus replied tersely. "Too bad that hefty bag of gold wasn't real," he said after they rode a sufficient distance.

Cathal's eyes glinted like steel. "They will find it a useless bag of sand tomorrow. Visitors like a nomadic tribal chieftain, flanked by bodyguards and his personal female slave, are not subject to scrutiny, but we should move with caution."

Their clothes were simple but concealed them from enemy eyes. Turbans and face scarves were common. Cathal and Myrsalian took further precautions to subtly alter their features and coloring. Myrsalian's disapproving face was not only covered by a long beard, but he had enchanted his red hair to black and darkened his fair skin to a deep olive. Cathal's new black beard, beaky nose, and bushy eyebrows were sufficient illusion.

"I feel ridiculous in these trappings," Arial grumbled as she walked alongside the horses, leather armor strapped to her head and back, as the warlord's pet wolf.

"Hush my dear," Sirah warned. "We will attract suspicion if people hear a wolf speak."

Ulan adjusted his white turban. His usual colorful silk caftans and sandals had been discarded for stark white linen robes and elaborately tooled brown leather armor and arm-bracers, and heavy dark brown boots.

"You are quite dashing as a warlord, Ulan," Sirah complimented him.

"If you had voted for me as chieftain in the beginning, we would not have wasted so much time." Ulan played his part to the hilt as Hadeon the Warlord. He also adopted a beard to conceal his features and cut a powerful image with his height and imposing musculature; the tall ebony-skinned man with the deep voice and kingly features was a natural for the part of the visiting eastern warlord.

"I never knew this was such a large city," Ulan commented. He subtly brushed his hand to his nose. "Or that it smelled so vile."

Sirah glanced at Cathal with kohl-lined eyes. "I think Cathal's beard is a bit overdone. It's so big and bristly."

"Is that a practical assessment?" Cathal inquired.

"It is a woman's assessment," Sirah replied smoothly.

"My face is too well known," Cathal replied. "I'm not exactly well liked here you know."

Sirah was covered head to toe in thick-woven black silk, as would be expected of a rich man's concubine; only her brown eyes were visible. "At least my public costume was easy," Sirah said. "I just wished it weren't so damn hot."

"Your private costume is what worries me," Myrsalian hissed.

"Do not worry so," Sirah whispered. "We must be prepared for all contingencies."

"I hope Redstorm forgives me," Darcus said. "That stubborn peryton was downright angry about not coming."

"We heard you arguing before we left," Sirah said.

"We all did," Ulan added sadly. "I know your troubles, Darcus. Poor little Rosepetal couldn't stop hiccuping when I left. I feel wretched leaving her behind. At least you and Myrsalian have Belwyn and Felisia with you, and Sirah has Arial."

"They are miffed too," Myrsalian said, "as now they must remain hidden. They can fly and Arial can blend in, but little Rosepetal would be at risk here. Warlords do not keep adorable hedgehogs as pets."

Cathal pulled down his face scarf to scratch his beard, which stuck out with kinky curls. "Redstorm can't step a hoof into Urgonclaw without raising a ruckus and he knows it. He's grown attached to you, that's a mark of great honor, especially from a seasoned war stag like Redstorm."

The dry afternoon heat enhanced the pungent stench of the market. Human sweat, animal dung, incense, spices, smoke, and slabs of meat at the butcher's tables. The combination of it all sickened them a little. The more wholesome odors of flowers, vegetables and fruits lined rows of merchant stalls in the outdoor market added some solace when they passed. Married women carried large woven baskets for their shopping, their somber robes and veils billowing in the afternoon wind. They moved with swift economy; eyes downcast but with sharp tongues for the haggling merchants. Some highborn matrons swathed in rich silks were accompanied by their young daughters, virgins in snowy white robes, only their bright eyes evident as they learned to bargain from their mothers. They picked their way across the filthy streets to avoid stepping into horse dung. A few prostitutes strutted along the streets or lounged in doorways, wrapped seductively with strips of red gauze, their uncovered faces masked with heavy face paint.

"So much of it seems so…normal," Ulan commented with surprise.

Sirah took a long drink from the water bag and passed it to Cathal. "Despite the fact the Dark Eternals are worshipped here, and human sacrifice is a way of life, people still have to buy bread at the market, have babies, sweep their floors, and bargain for a good price on oranges."

Ulan pointed and whispered. "What about that woman? Why isn't her face veiled? She is surely no street whore."

Sirah saw an old thin woman in the market, her narrow face creased with wrinkles and dark eyes angry, arguing with a melon merchant. "She is past the age of childbearing, has been spared sacrifice, and is honored now as a teacher of young maidens. If a woman reaches such a great age and loses her blood flow, she is considered a wise woman and may show her face in public." Memories of Sirah's early life in this bleak land burned in her eyes. "The role of women is well defined in Urgonclaw by ancient traditions since the Bloodstone Era. The caste system is ironclad. Priests and Warriors come first. Nobles and wealthy merchants second, and everyone else is at the bottom. That is for the men. For a woman, her place is determined by her family, and her role in the marriage bed, the birthing bed…or the sacrificial altar. And slaves are less than nothing."

"You are a brave woman and have suffered much," Ulan replied with genuine awe. "Yet they did not wound your spirit. That is still pure, Lady."

"We are wasting time," Myrsalian grumbled, spurring his horse toward the towering steppe pyramid of Rygon's Temple.

Ulan became concerned and turned to Sirah. "Is Myrsalian

upset with me?"

"No," Sirah said shaking her head. "It's being here in Urgonclaw that has him on edge."

"I hope he can pull this off," Cathal whispered. "He has been in a foul mood since we crossed the border."

Sirah's worry was evident in her eyes. "This is hard for him. Just watch him and make sure he doesn't do anything foolish."

They rode to catch up with Myrsalian.

What the hell is going on down there? Belwyn demanded through the bonding, taking Cathal's attention off Sirah and Myrsalian.

My, you're cranky. Sorry Belwyn. Anything we should be aware of? Where are you?

Felisia and I are on top of the temple just like we planned—remember? Nothing unusual. Just the normal muck of smelly humans and unsanitary piles of refuse in alleys. Annoying chanting. I hate it here.

So do we, Cathal agreed, glancing at Myrsalian.

The Temple of Rygon loomed over the ancient city, a hungry shadow of dark stone built from ancient design. The steppe pyramid rose high above them as they craned their necks to see its dark glory. The paintings covering the walls, though beautiful, were filled with grim and frightening images of ancient battles of myth and legend. Temple Guards in red and black robes lined the entrance, their scimitars polished and sharp.

"What is that?" Ulan asked. "There is a town caller handing out something."

They rode up to the man and Cathal took the offered leaflet he was passing out. Cathal moaned when he read it. Cathal showed them a poster with a rough drawing of Gabriel's face and his long list of crimes and blasphemies. "It's a wanted poster for Gabriel. Twenty-thousand gold pieces, dead or alive."

"I hope there are no sacrifices today," Myrsalian said hoarsely.

"As do I," Cathal said. "I fear I would be added to Gabriel's wanted poster."

"We all would," Sirah added.

Finally, a black-robed priest came down the steps to greet them. His head was shaven, and a faint mask of red ochre painted around his eyes.

Ulan played the part of a devout pilgrim, his hands lifted with false praise. "I am Hadeon of Ucara, Chieftain of the thirteenth tribe of Kushlea. I come to prostrate myself at the holiest of all temples and seek the blessing of the Dark Trinity! Word has reached us that Obsydia has been found by Koll the Sorcerer."

The priest greeted Ulan with a deep bow. "Welcome to our temple, Warlord. We rejoice in these dark blessings. Koll is truly the dark prophet."

"I offer thanks with my meager offerings," Ulan proclaimed. Jewels were poured into the greedy priest's hands and overflowed onto the street.

"Welcome, Great Chieftain Hadeon of Ucara. Come inside and worship. A blessing awaits you," the priest invited, though his hard bright eyes were on the gems he gathered into the skirt of his robes. "A royal guest is always welcome within the walls of Rygon's Temple. Zhelon Thor is in residence, so you are fortunate you may receive his personal blessing and advice."

~ * ~

The trappings of the High Priest's reception hall were rich. Hadeon was carried in a litter while the others walked behind. A private audience was granted thanks to his rich offerings, though they were surrounded by guards and priests. Masks of Rygon were hung on the walls in gold or ebonite. Death images of skulls were everywhere in carvings and wall paintings, contrasting with the elegant sheer silk curtains. Polished floors with rich carpets dotted the room; bronze braziers burned with fires. Slave women worked quietly in the background, carrying trays of fresh meat, wine and fruit for the guests. All were young and beautiful, unmarred except for the symbol of Rygon's scythe branded on their thighs.

Ulan reclined on thick pillows, his personal guard of Darcus, Myrsalian, and Cathal flanking him. Cathal stood behind, while the other two knelt, hands on the hilt of their scimitars, as Sirah taught them. Ulan was a consummate actor. He played the part of a rich chieftain with skill and nuance. Sirah knelt by Ulan's feet; head bowed.

Finally, Zhelon Thor swept into the chamber, golden hair flowing down his back and his blue eyes intense as he extended his hands in greeting, a great honor for a foreigner. "Welcome to the Temple of the Dark Trinity."

Ulan grasped Zhelon's hand only briefly and bowed deeply. "I am humbled and honored by your gracious hospitality, High Priest Zhelon Thor. I have longed to make a pilgrimage to the greatest of

Rygon's Temples. My life has been devoted to the sacred three, Ahridum, Father of Shadows, and his children, Rygon, Eternal of War, and Obsydia, the Bloodstone Queen, the living goddess."

Zhelon reclined on a couch of red velvet across from Ulan. "Soon shall Obsydia be freed! We are fortunate to live in these times."

Ulan nodded with solemn piety as he reclined against the plush pillows. He suddenly gasped and put his hand to his chest, as though terribly distressed. "Zhelon Thor, forgive me! I forgot about the casket of black pearls I brought for you! They were harvested from the Isini Sea! They are my personal gift to you." He turned to Cathal and Darcus, snapping his fingers. "Quickly fools! Go check the packs on the horses. You must have left it there! Forgetful morons! Return at once else I shall offer you as sacrifice!" He turned back to Zhelon, "Please forgive me. My bodyguards serve me well with blade and sweat but are useless at anything that requires thought."

"You are most generous, Chieftain Hadeon," Zhelon nodded. "Pearls from the Isini Sea are rare and precious. In our scriptures, Ahridum's Obsidian Tower rose from those wild waves to receive Lilith. There she became His dark bride and give birth to Obsydia, our Immortal Goddess."

"I've often read of that sacred moment when Ahridum blessed Lilith with tears in my eyes," Ulan added, voice choked with emotion.

Arial sent a dry message to Sirah. *Ulan should have been an actor, though he is milking the scene.*

Yet Zhelon Thor seems to be lapping it up, Sirah replied cooly.

~ * ~

After Darcus and Cathal bowed and marched out of the chamber, they started down the steps and then veered down another hall until they came to a narrow back staircase.

"I hope Panthara's map to Koll's suite is as good as Sirah's plans to the temple," Darcus muttered as they climbed several flights of stairs.

The effort strained Cathal, who paused for a moment in the hallway, breathing heavily. "My legs are going to feel this tomorrow."

Darcus laughed and pushed him along, "Come on, old mage."

"Are your legs made of iron?" Cathal asked bitterly.

They reached the proper floor. They counted the doors until they reached the chamber marked on Panthara's map. Cathal took a velvet pouch out of his belt. He opened it. There were several small crystal tomes humming in his palm in a variety of colors—blue, orange, gray, and a dark red one. He chose the blue and it glowed, the waves of magic penetrating the wide wooden door.

Darcus stood behind him, scimitar drawn, impatient. "What the hell are you doing anyway?"

"Checking for traps," Cathal whispered. "No magic in the door." He turned the latch and it was locked.

Darcus pulled down his mask and laughed. "Normal locks are also effective against intruders, oh wisest of sorcerers."

Cathal grunted. "If I wanted sarcasm, I'd summon Belwyn. It's easy to forget about those normal locks." He shot a beam of magic into the door and it magically opened. "But easy enough to rectify." They stepped inside the empty chamber, the narrow windows lighting the room clearly.

Cathal pulled out Panthara's floor plan from his sash. "She said the secret door would be on the wall tiled with gold and black design. This must be it." Cathal cast a magical shield around himself and Darcus. "Just in case he planted some surprises."

Cathal counted to the thirteenth tile from the floor and pressed the starburst pattern in the middle. "There it is." There was an audible click and the secret door popped open.

"Any traps?" Darcus inquired.

"There was a gaseous flame trap as Panthara said, but I eliminated it."

"That would have been unpleasant," Darcus said. "Ever thought about being a thief?"

"My moral code would get in the way, but I would outshine all thieves." Cathal opened the narrow door and stepped into the dark room first. Darcus followed, sword raised.

Cathal cast a light spell, illuminating the room to reveal its secrets. They gasped in unison. As Panthara promised, there was a treasure trove of many rare items from ancient times: luminous crystals burning with dark promise, smoky bottles of wicked mystery, and stacked in neat rows in special racks along the walls, were hundreds of scrolls!

"There's the onyx box she spoke of," Darcus pointed.

"Panthara told the truth," Cathal whispered. "Look at all of this! Darcus…Darcus?" Cathal spun around to find Xabral holding Darcus in a trance, rising high on coiled scales.

"Be still or your friend dies," Xabral threatened, pointing his stinger at Darcus.

Xabral's magical trance held Darcus frozen, his hand still on his scimitar, body in mid-turn, ready to attack. "Remove your facade, Cathal; it does not suit you anyway."

Cathal's magical disguise of a bristly beard and beaky nose evaporated. Xabral reveled in his power, flexing his stinger at poor Darcus.

"You are foolish to seek my sorcerer here," Xabral ranted on. "I think I will poke your thief friend anyway just to punish you for such insolence!" He jabbed his stinger at Darcus.

But the stinger did not penetrate.

"He should be suffering!" Xabral wailed.

"My spell shields him," Cathal replied calmly. "We are both shielded, snake."

Xabral jerked away to flee, but with lightning speed a wave of deep blue sorcery burst from Cathal's body, striking both Xabral and Darcus. The blast threw Darcus back safely from Xabral and he rolled across the room. Xabral smashed against the wall and dropped to the floor. Cathal's magic sizzled on his scales.

A string of cursing indicated Darcus snapped out of his daze. He snatched up his scimitar and scrambled to his feet. "Slithering worm-beast from hell! I'm gonna make a belt out of him."

Cathal shot another sorcerous bolt at the fleeing snake; magical hooks lifted Xabral into the air and pinned him to the wall. Darcus stalked toward the snake, swinging his blade, but Cathal pushed him back. "Wait, Wait!"

"Why!" Darcus demanded, his scarred-eyed twitching.

"Because this might be to our advantage."

Xabral hung helpless on the wall, hissing his fury, shaking his stinger. The glowing half-moon orange hooks pinned the nine-foot scorpion snake quite firmly to the wall. Cathal unsheathed his scimitar and pressed the tip into Xabral's scaly neck. "Darcus, take the onyx box on that pedestal Panthara described. Bring it to me."

Xabral stopped struggling. "You know of the secret sacrifice? The scroll will not do you any good unless they are alive within that bony tomb." Xabral's eyes glinted with mirth as he studied Cathal's face. "Yes, they must be alive! Oh, that makes their suffering more intense! Koll will be delighted to learn that! Poor Cathal, is your magic so weak you cannot free them?"

Darcus grabbed the onyx box tied with scarlet ribbon and handed it to Cathal. His sorcery lifted the lid and revealed a scroll inside, wrapped around a black wooden rod with bloodstones gleaming at each end. Cathal extended his hand and the scroll flew into his grasp.

"There! Now you have your precious scroll! Go away!" Xabral spat. "It won't do you any good, since it's in demon language. The demon Ashur taught Koll the proper dialect and you don't know it, Sorcerer. It's useless to you!"

Cathal smiled darkly. "Don't be so sure."

Darcus studied Cathal's face. "You're not going to let him go are you?"

"No…I'm not," Cathal assured him. "I have other plans for this vile snake."

"This better be good."

"Oh, it will be," Cathal assured him. His hands flashed with purple magic, the light blinding as it enveloped the snake's body in a hot glow.

Xabral screamed.

Chapter Twenty-Eight

"Zhelon is growing restless," Myrsalian observed in a low voice, kneeling by Ulan's side.

The musicians played softly in the background, food and drink had been shared, but Zhelon and Ulan had run dry of small talk.

Sirah leaned against Ulan's knee to offer him more grapes. "We need to distract Zhelon," she whispered in his ear.

"What's taking them so long," Ulan whispered back.

"Cathal and Darcus must need more time," Sirah said.

"What should I do now?" Ulan asked.

"Offer me to Zhelon," Sirah suggested.

"Are you sure that's wise?" Myrsalian whispered through clenched teeth.

Sirah fed more grapes in Ulan's mouth "We must take that risk. We need to keep Zhelon's attention on us."

Ulan leaned forward, cupping his large hands. "Great Zhelon Thor, your hospitality has been beyond measure. There is another gift I wish to offer. My slave, Isada, if you find her acceptable."

"She is well behaved," Zhelon observed. "What are her talents?"

Ulan exhaled with joy. "The talents of my little Isada are immeasurable. She is not worthy of you, of course, but she is a beautiful dancer. She trained in Rygon's Temple in central Ucara. She was a gift from the local High Priest for my birthday last year. I loathe parting with her, for she is an obedient woman, but sacrifice in all things is the first commandment of Rygon. I vow her dancing can turn a man's bones to butter."

"A generous gift indeed," Zhelon noted, staring at Sirah with interest. "I will judge if her dancing is graceful, but first I must rule if her beauty is worthy of my temple. Show her to me—now."

Ulan's voice boomed as he shoved Sirah forward. "Go to your new master, slave. Display the charms Rygon blessed you with! Do not shame me before his Holiness after I praised you so lavishly!"

Sirah stood in her heavy black robes and with bowed head knelt at Zhelon Thor's feet.

"Show me your beauty, slave," Zhelon commanded.

Graceful as a swan, Sirah rose and unhooked her veil and cloak.

With one fluid movement she cast off her black garments as the day sheds the night. Gasps of lusty approval resounded in the chamber. Sirah was a beautiful woman. Zhelon's face waxed with desire as he studied her face and body. Dressed in a girdle of beaded orange and yellow silk that hugged her hips; sheer orange veils that fanned out into a skirt exposed her long slim legs. Her taut belly was bare and a bodice of matching glittering fabric covered her breasts. Golden bangles covered her upper arms. Her abundant red hair only enhanced her luminous skin and amber eyes.

"Your former master says you served in Rygon's Temple in Ucara? Show me your brand," Zhelon ordered.

Sirah gracefully put her foot on his knee and leaned in seductively.

Arial, curled up at Ulan's feet, warned her through the bonding. *You're being too bold Sirah!*

No. I know this type of man. He wants weak, pliant women but despises them at the same time. I must show him fire and strength; else he will dismiss me without interest. He may even kill me.

Sirah pulled back the sheer chiffon veils to expose her branded thigh. "Do I please you, dread High Priest?"

Zhelon gripped her leg as he examined her brand, and then moved his hand across her thigh. "Your face and body are perfect. You have passed the first test. Now dance for me!" Zhelon clapped his hands and commanded, "Musicians, play! The Dance of Dethia. A trained temple dancer would know this sacred dance."

Sirah walked to the center of the room, raised her hands, and tilted her head. Sirah did know this dance, for she performed it for Tarsicius when she was a slave of only fifteen in this very temple. Her beauty and skill as a dancer enthralled an Emperor enough to buy her on the spot and take her from this bleak hell. The symbolism of Dethia was ancient and Sirah had been schooled in its ritual, since as a young girl she showed a talent for performing. This skill kept her alive in these halls of death, for as slaves lost their youth, the altar of sacrifice loomed.

Sirah was surrounded by priests and warriors eager to watch her perform, but she did not even glance at them. She focused only on Zhelon Thor. Drums beat with a slow and sensuous measure, followed by soft flute and gentle cymbals. Her body swayed to its sultry pulse and her slender arms gracefully weaved an invitation to passion. As she danced, the rhythm gradually quickened, growing more vibrant and demanding in its cadence. Zhelon gazed at her with rare lust as she moved fluidly across the floor on bare feet, her golden anklets jingling to her steps.

"By the gods, she is magnificent!" Ulan whispered to Myrsalian in wonder. "I never knew a woman could do that with her stomach. It ripples like—"

Arial's growl and Myrsalian's sharp elbow jab to Ulan's ribs silenced him.

The music's pace accelerated with Sirah's heated moves and the men salivated with lust at her seductive promise. This dance was passionate, but also sacred here. Sirah enthralled with wild and sensual movements, but she was not lewd. She moved like a queen, for indeed she had been queen in all but name in the Ivory Kingdoms, until her sorcery exiled her.

Captivated by her mythic dance, the temple guards howled their lustful fury and drummed their spears on the floor in tempo to her hot ballet; the priests clapped with every passionate sway of her hips. Sirah leapt across the temple floor like a defiant goddess, as Dethia had demanded Ahridum's touch, until the music reached its crescendo. She danced with flawless grace, her steps symbolizing Dethia and Ahridum in the mysterious Realm of Shadow Eternals, the mystical bond of desire that birthed Rygon in the dark flames of Ahridum's Well of Chaos.

The double doors burst open, disrupting the finale. The musicians faltered in confusion as Imperial Dragon Knights of the Ivory Kingdom marched into the chamber. The sudden intrusion of soldiers broke the spell. Sirah fell to her knees and bowed her head to the floor.

"All kneel before the Emperor of the Ivory Kingdoms," an Imperial Knight proclaimed as he marched into the chamber.

Is it Tarsicius? Sirah thought to Arial.

Levandius walked into the chamber, dressed in deep black satin and wearing a crown of gold on his flaxen hair. Behind him was a figure cloaked and hooded in red velvet.

No. It is Levandius. This bodes trouble we did not plan for.

Zhelon raised his arms to the heavens. "This is a great day! Behold, our deliverance is at hand! Our indenture to the Ivory Kingdoms has ended. Emperor Tarsicius of the Ivory Kingdoms is dead! Long live Emperor Levandius!"

Sirah covered her face with her hands to hide her grief.

"To celebrate his new reign, Levandius has decreed Urgonclaw a free state and restored my rightful title of Priest-King of Urgonclaw," Zhelon declared.

Levandius relished the cheers for a moment before he raised his hand to silence the throng of admirers. "A new era dawns this day. Urgonclaw shall ever be a friend to the Ivory Kingdoms. My devotion to the faith shall not be like my father's, but as a true devout son of the Dark Trinity. I shall begin my reign with a sacrifice of thanksgiving with Priest-King Zhelon Thor at my side."

Myrsalian's face contorted at the word, *sacrifice*.

"What now?" Ulan whispered hoarsely.

"We leave, but we kill them instead!" Myrsalian replied.

Ulan grabbed Myrsalian, his heavily muscled arms holding the mage back. "Take care," he warned. After a tense moment, Myrsalian calmed down, though Ulan kept a firm grip on him.

Levandius noticed Sirah kneeling on the floor. "Who is this comely whore?"

"A gift from Hadeon of Ucara, a visiting pilgrim," Zhelon answered. "She was dancing for us when you arrived. It was magnificent."

"It is rare for Zhelon to compliment a slave. There is something familiar about you," Levandius observed. "What is your name, slave?"

"Isada," Sirah answered, keeping her head bowed.

"No…that's a lie," the figure in the crimson cloak accused. A gloved hand pushed back the concealing hood and a red-skinned demoness smiled down at Sirah. "That's Sirahnami, you fool! The exiled concubine witch your father so loved he kept her picture in a locket! Chimera sees her deception."

Levandius unsheathed a dagger from his belt. "Sorcerous whore!"

He moved to stab Sirah, but she evaded his clumsy strike and rolled away. With a wave of her hand she pushed him back and forced him to the floor. He turned purple with rage and raised his blade again, but the dagger flew out of his hand into Sirah's firm grip. Howling with rage, he beat the floor with his fists like a spoiled infant. "Kill the whore! What are you waiting for! Kill her!"

She levitated, narrowly missing the sharp points of several spears thrown at her. They hit the richly carpeted floor instead. Sirah's angry eyes she glared down at Levandius. "You always were a vicious brat!"

"They must all be sorcerers! We are deceived! Infidels! Defilers! Slay them you fools!" Zhelon commanded.

Rashurkeen surrounded Ulan and Myrsalian with scimitars. Myrsalian shapeshifted into an elf owl and flew up to Sirah's side. Ulan scuttled away as a tiny hedgehog. He weaved through the confused legs of the soldiers and evaded the poke of their sharp weapons.

Sirah spun around in the air and shot a protective ray of golden sorcery around Ulan just as a spear came down on him. Still in his hedgehog form, he squeaked and darted under some pillows. A mysterious rash of biting afflicted the guards, distracting them away from Ulan. Arial acted unseen, her magical ability of invisible stealth allowed her freedom to help the sorcerers and nip a few behinds. Ulan hobbled toward a scimitar and shape-shifted back to his human form. He raised the scimitar in one hand and the small stick in his sash expanded to his staff in the other. He charged the soldiers, cutting them down with blade and magic.

Felisia and Belwyn soared through the windows. The guards hurled spears at them, but the weapons bounced off the shield Felisia formed around her little body. Belwyn's telekinetic magic snatched swords out of hand and pushed guards away. Arial dropped her camouflage and attacked Levandius, locking her jaws around his throat.

"Get this beast off of me!" Levandius whimpered.

"Brilliant girl!" Sirah shouted as she cast a protective shield around Arial, who held Levandius' throat in her powerful jaws.

"Stop!" Zhelon commanded, and the fighting terminated.

"Let us go free and unharmed," Sirah offered, "and my wolf will not kill Levandius."

"I do not bargain with heathens," Zhelon replied coldly, looking up at her with calm blue eyes. "A shame. You danced so well."

Levandius lay with Arial's teeth firmly gripping his neck, stunned by Zhelon's cool reply. "Bargain, you idiot! I am the Emperor of the Ivory Kingdoms! Save me!"

"Your whining is upsetting my familiar," Sirah warned.

Arial growled for emphasis and Levandius fell mute, though his terror was evident in his bulging eyes.

~ * ~

"This better work," Darcus said, rushing down the stairs, glancing at the small sack Cathal carried over his shoulder.

"If it doesn't you can gloat to your heart's content later," Cathal replied.

We have trouble, Belwyn's warning came.

What happened? Cathal replied, stopping Darcus with an anxious gesture.

Levandius showed up. Tarsicius is dead. We are exposed. And there is a strange demon woman with him that unnerves me.

Demon woman?

Yes, catch up. Our cover is blown and has gone straight to the Underworld in a hand basket. Oh, and did I mention Arial has Levandius by the throat? Did you at least get the scroll?

Yes, Belwyn.

At least you didn't muck that up.

"What is it? Darcus asked, his voice constricted,

"Trouble," Cathal whispered.

An Imperial Dragon Knight fled the reception hall and was running toward them. He raised his sword at them. "Hold there!"

Darcus extended his scimitar, ripping off his turban and eye-patch. "Out of my way."

The Knight held his sword steady. "Stop in the name of the Emperor!" After a heartbeat the knight's stunned voice whispered, "Sir? Captain Darcus? Is that you?"

Darcus stopped and stepped back but held his scimitar ready. "Korun?"

The man removed his helmet. His wavy black hair was slick with sweat and his face confused as he stared at Darcus, obviously torn. "Oh sir, Levandius is Emperor now! Tarsicius is dead. Pol and I arrived with the Imperial escort to take Prince Levandius back to Tiamet to claim the throne. Now there has been an attack upon him." He looked his former commander up and down. "What are you doing here?"

Darcus looked at the young soldier. "Korun, there's no time to explain. Just stay out of my way."

"But sir, how can I do that?"

"We can't wait," Cathal commanded.

Darcus spoke in a gentle voice. "Go back, Korun. I never saw you. I give you one chance. You must choose orders or what is right."

They walked past Korun into the chamber, scimitars drawn. Darcus glanced back once. Korun was gone.

"Who was that boy?" Cathal asked.

"One of my former comrades," Darcus remarked sadly.

The Rashurkeen and priests all had swords or spears pointed at their friends but did not move further to attack. Arial's firm position on top of Levandius guaranteed that for the moment, but it would not hold for long. Sirah was floating a good twenty feet in the air, and the familiars were fluttering around her, except for Ulan, who held a backup blade over Levandius.

"You won't escape," Zhelon said in a cool voice. "I do not show pity on heathens who violate holy ground. Infidels suffer death in this holy place."

Sirah angrily glared down upon the High Priest. "Then we have a problem."

Behind you! Belwyn cried in Cathal's head.

The cloaked figure emerged from the shadows behind Cathal and Darcus, holding a black dagger. Darcus thrust his scimitar into the demon's body.

She laughed and hurled Darcus across the chamber. She removed the blade without even a flinch and dropped it. Cathal faced her, the scimitar in his hand shifting into his staff. He fired gray beams of sorcery at her, but they dribbled off her like beads of water. She did not even recoil, and then her hood fell back, exposing her scarlet skin.

"Demon!" Cathal charged.

"Sorcerer!" she countered. The demoness' swift dagger sliced at Cathal's cheek and hair. Then she vanished into the shadows.

Stunned, Cathal touched his bloody cheek. Belwyn flew down to Cathal's shoulder. "Okay, that's a sign to leave when demons are running amuck."

Cathal turned to Zhelon. "Tell Koll I send my regrets."

Zhelon was calm, despite Levandius whining at his feet. "You cannot escape, Cathal. My temple is filled with hundreds of soldiers, loyal to the Dark Trinity. Even with magic, how can you fight them all?"

"Like this," Cathal answered, plucking a red crystal tome from inside his tunic and flinging it at the wall.

It struck the heavy, thick, stone built centuries ago to withstand heavy military assault. The crystal exploded with the intensity of a blazing scarlet sun and the impact shook the chamber like a colossal attack of thunder. The air grew thick with mystical residue and conjured a powerful wind that forced everyone to fall for cover. Even Zhelon Thor was knocked to the floor and shielded his eyes from the powerful wind gusts that charged the room. When the sorcerous vapors cleared, there was a massive hole in the wall large enough for a small army to pass through, yet there was no dust from broken stones choking the air or rubble clogging the path. There was simply a great perfect and round hole in the wall of Rygon's impregnable temple.

"Impressive," Belwyn remarked.

"Thank you," Cathal replied.

Green beams of green sorcery flowed from Ulan's hands, knocking several guards backward off a large carpet. The carpet fluttered and rose in the air, shimmering with enchantment and escape. "Hurry everyone!" Ulan cried. He jumped onto the sorcery-charged rug, the tassels extending into long shimmering reins as Ulan guided it toward the gaping hole in the wall. "Time to depart this cursed place!

They all climbed upon the carpet. Sirah and Ulan deflected the weapons that threatened their friends.

Sirah cried to Arial. "We must go now. Let him go."

"Levandius is dangerous to my pack," Arial challenged, keeping her jaws locked around Levandius' soft neck.

"Chimera, save me," Levandius whimpered.

Chimera stepped though the shadows and punched through Sirah's magical barrier, grabbed Arial by the scruff of the neck and tossed her across the room. The assassins threw spears at the helpless wolf, but Sirah's hasty magic summoned a new shield around her familiar before they could strike her. Her sorcery lifted the stunned wolf out of harm's way, the weapons bouncing off the glowing magic, and guided Arial toward the safety of her arms. She embraced her dazed familiar with relief.

"Hold on!" Ulan cried. "It's going to be a wild ride."

The carpet carried them out of Rygon's temple and across the sky.

CHAPTER TWENTY-NINE

Neelam pushed across the hot sands of Skarros with his mage staff. Surya flew overhead in the cloudless sky, her plaintive eagle cry echoing across the desert.

I know you hate it here, girl, Neelam called through the bonding.

I always did, you dunderhead, Surya replied.

"No matter how many centuries pass, I'll never get use to this hellish place," Neelam grumbled aloud, glancing back at his companions, Liat and Dabiro, to make sure they were keeping up with him.

"Been here often have you?" Liat asked, huffing with effort as he trailed behind, swathed in robes and a turban against the unrelenting sun, his staff sinking into the sands with each heavy step.

"I've been here more often than I wanted to, but it was necessary. We three use to split the responsibility. Ambera grew too frail over time. The last fifteen years Cathal was a hermit living in the forest with his granddaughter after the Sorcerer War and the tragedy of losing his wife and daughter took its toll on him. Generally, once or twice a century one of us would make sure Obsydia was still trapped. We mined protective spells throughout the whole area around where Obsydia's palace was to deflect any nosy evil folk from digging *her* up. Those spells are gone now."

"What do you mean?" Liat asked.

Neelam marched at an increased pace. "I mean my spells are gone."

Liat wiped sweat off his face as he struggled to keep up. "How? And aren't you tired at all?"

"Aren't you a bit young to get winded so easily," Neelam remarked.

You do love to show off, Surya teased. *Maybe we should rest—for the children's sake.*

They're young. They'll get over it.

Liat shaded his filthy face from the harsh sun. He pushed on, struggling to keep up with the Dwarven Wizard. "I see why they named this abyss the Wasteland."

"It had another name once." Neelam reached the edge of a vast chasm and walked the edge, pondering the damage. "This wasn't here before."

"It could have been an earthquake. That would explain the change in the landscape," Liat said.

Neelam squatted and scratched his beard. "See there? The ground around the edges of the deep voids has shifted from sinking sands to hard-packed, burnt, cracked earth." He touched the edge of a gaping fissure which weaved several miles and frowned. "These scars are not naturally made, not by any normal earthquake. Ahridum's hand is in this. I sense the mystical energy. You can rest here awhile if you're tired, boy. I won't be too far."

"Stop calling me boy," Liat shouted over the wind, catching up with Neelam. He looked over his shoulder. "Come on, Dabiro, just a little bit more. Then we can rest."

Dabiro shuffled along, a foul look on his dusty face. "I'm hot, I'm thirsty, and I wanna go home!" He plopped down and refused to move, sand caking his fur and crusting his eyes and nose. "My poor paws are raw from these blistering sands."

"I know, Dabiro, but we traveled here by magic and gryphons. We've only been walking for a few hours," Liat responded gently.

"Cruel hours of damnation!" Dabiro pouted.

Liat finally walked back to Dabiro and picked the badger up, shifting his bulk in his arms as he carried him. He stopped behind Neelam and knelt down, still holding Dabiro, who grunted softly, nose buried in Liat's shoulder.

"Conjure some ice!" Dabiro begged. "Please. My paws are burning."

Surya glided to the earth and landed on a small rock. She looked at Dabiro quizzically. "Can't you summon frost or some such silliness?"

"Not the same as cubed ice my Liat can conjure," Dabiro said sniffing. "I can summon frost or fire, but I am also exhausted. And my power is not silly. What's your fancy power?"

"I summon light and shadow," Surya replied.

Dabiro grunted. "That's not so impressive."

"You have not seen Surya's light," Neelam countered. "And pray you never experience her shadow casting."

"I'll conjure ice for your poor paws if you promise to stop complaining for…perhaps an hour?" Liat bargained.

"Done," Dabiro agreed, holding out his paw for his sorcerer's cooling magic. "Familiar abilities are just tidbits anyway. I'm better at ramming the enemy anyway."

"I heard you have a hard skull," Surya said.

"Tough as iron. I'm strong—stronger than even that bear, Baldur. Easy to be tough when you're the size of a mountain. And why is it the puffy wampu got the ability to become a giant? He can't even use it much yet. It's wasted on such a meek critter. That power would be useful in a warrior's paws."

"Are you jealous of little Melly?" Liat asked.

"No...why would you think that?" Dabiro replied.

"No reason." Liat's fingers glowed and in the palm of his hand some ice appeared, and he rubbed the badger's paws with it. When he was done, he rubbed a cube across his own face, leaving streaks of black sand.

Dabiro settled in Liat's lap, somewhat appeased by his sorcerer's ministrations. "Why did we leave the gryphons behind anyway?"

"Does your badger understand the concept of stealth or secret infiltration?" Surya asked with pointed irritation. "They're waiting right where we left them. No worry. You won't have to walk home."

Neelam shook his head as he concentrated. "Something is wrong. I sense supernatural interference—Ahridum's baleful hand is in this. The Lord of Darkness is ever a thorn in my backside. Let's go. We are close to where her temple palace once stood."

"How do you remember where her palace was if it is has been sunken in a desert for a thousand years?"

"Some things you never forget, boy."

Liat uncorked his water bag and allowed Dabiro to slurp his fill first. "So, this is where Obsydia was defeated?"

"Yes. Obsydia is imprisoned beneath these sands in a crystal of living Light, the kind forged from Eternal origin. There was no other way to do it. Don't fear her name, boy. Her name isn't powerful. She was, but not her name." Neelam pulled down his face scarf and took out his water bag. Surya flew to Neelam's arm, which was wrapped in heavy leather bracers to cushion her talons. He poured water in a small tin cup for Surya and then took a long drink to slack his own thirst.

"Has this land always been so barren and evil," Liat asked.

"It was not always so," Neelam said sadly. "Once it was much different."

Liat took another drink, admiring the sword strapped to Neelam's back, a fine example of Dwarven craftsmanship. "That's a splendid sword you carry. The sapphire in the hilt is striking too. Who made it?"

Neelam's sword was strapped to his back for easy access, and he unsheathed the weapon, holding it out for Liat to admire. The sun glinted on the sun-warmed steel. Liat was duly impressed, and though the sword was little more than a long dirk or a short sword for a man of Liat's height, it was still an elegant weapon forged with the Dwarven technique they had guarded for centuries.

"Thanks boy. It was made for my father when he was a young warrior wizard. My clan, mage or not, were always warrior trained. The blacksmith who made it has been dead for well over fifteen hundred years. The sapphire was my father's addition, in remembrance of the Sapphire Age. This blade has been my ally in many battles."

"Your father was born in the Sapphire Age?" Liat inquired, amazed. "That was a long time ago. It must have been a wondrous time to live, if the legends are true."

Neelam sheathed the sword and crouched, his hands sending waves of sorcery across the sands. "I wouldn't know. I was born after. My father died fighting evil in the first years of the Bloodstone Age. He remembered a better world. I never knew a time when the world was peaceful. When I was born, Obsydia reigned. She was the goddess of the weak-willed and wicked. Nature became cruel and a bitter winter descended for many years. Many died from starvation as much as war in those days. My knowledge of the Sapphire Age comes mostly from my parents. Kingdoms prospered. There were few wars. The three castes of mages—Wizard, Sorcerer, and Drusai, worked together to expand their understanding of magic and the universe…until the shadow of Ahridum decided to make our world a battleground." Neelam walked along the rim of a deep chasm, concern masking his face.

"What truly ended this great era?" Liat asked.

Neelam grunted. "Most of the histories were gathered after the fact. Unfortunately, I think they toned down the death and violence. But I know this: Ahridum hurled a dark star upon our world. It fell here in this land, where once white towers soared above blue rivers and a lush green forest. It was the nexus of the mages. Overnight this peaceful land became a death pit, and the Bloodstone Age was born. Whole kingdoms were destroyed in its wake. Volcanoes erupted, mountains crumbled, and oceans heaved in the wake of evil. Some say the Eternals warred again, and our world was caught up in their storm. Years of harsh winter strangled our world. I was born in that era of darkness, same as Cathal. I think Ambera was the last mage who was alive before the Bloodstone. Now she's dead. All living memory of the last true age of Light is dead."

Liat wiped his brow, squinting in the bright noonday sun. "Now I find myself standing where Obsydia ruled."

"Make you feel small, boy?" Neelam asked.

"A bit," Liat confessed.

"A thousand years ago, her temple palace was the black jewel of this desert. But its beauty was deceptive, for it was a place of wicked conjuring and sacrifice." Neelam pointed, "Over there, in the south, a gate of bones led into Ralnazzar, the demon city. I fought many battles here. I lost friends here too. That's the worst thing about war. Good people die and there is nothing you can do about it. Grief is a constant companion." Neelam looked around, his eyes wistful. "This is a wretched hell pit, true, but I have one or two happy memories of this place."

"Like what?" Liat asked, perplexed.

"I met my wife here," Neelam said. "Well, come along, boy, time to see if the she-bitch is still locked in her crystal cage."

"Wait! I smell something bad," Dabiro grumbled.

"Now you sound like Mellypip," Liat grinned.

"Hey, my sniffing skills are way better than any wampu," Dabiro said proudly.

"The annoying badger is right," Surya remarked, perched on Neelam's arm. "But I smell more than people. I smell demons!"

Liat gasped, glancing around. "What do you mean demons? Real demons?"

Hideous faces, maws agape to emit howls, revealing rows of needle-like teeth, burst from the sands like dark beetles. Bulbous eyes squinted with hatred, and their sinewy gray-skinned bodies in ragged leather armor, their bony hands clutching heavy serrated blades or long iron spears.

"I think that counts as real," Neelam replied.

Surya took flight above the madness, her snowy wings bright in the sky. Liat and Neelam drew both sword and stave.

"What the hell are those creatures?" Liat gasped.

"Goblins," Neelam confirmed. "Don't worry, they can die. They are earthly born demons."

"Good to know," Liat gulped. He shot waves of green sorcery at two goblins charging him. The magical force catapulted the goblins across the sands like ugly dolls.

Dabiro's claws dug into the sand, growling deep in his throat. Neelam's staff sent a blast of silver sorcery which tossed the goblins back hundreds of feet. More crawled up the sandy tombs, their blades glittering in the harsh sun.

Surya flew over the charging goblins, casting her luminous light across the creatures. Her mystical beam disrupted the goblins attack with both its intensity and purity. The creatures spun around in confusion, wailing, and covering their faces. The cloak of luminescence stalled them, but more goblins emerged from their sandy graves.

This was a trap, Surya's voice cried in Neelam's head.

And that remark helps us how? Neelam shot back.

Dabiro charged a goblin, ramming it over the edge of the fissure, but the badger's speed was out of control and he rolled over and dropped into the pit with the goblin.

"Dabiro!" Liat cried. He levitated Dabiro high from the goblin's reach, though it leapt frantically.

A goblin emerged and jabbed his spear into Neelam's thigh. Disoriented, the wizard spun around and fell to the ground. He gripped his leg, gnashing his teeth as he cursed.

Surya swooped over the goblin's head, casting shadow that cocooned the demon, blinding its senses and disorienting it. It howled and fell to the ground, cowering.

Out of nowhere, a black gryphon flew above them, shouting with joy, "Liat! Dabiro!"

"That's not one of our gryphons!" Surya cried.

"No, it's Rono!" Liat shouted.

Rono hit the ground, kicking up sand as he skidded, putting himself between Neelam and the goblin. Another goblin tried to retrieve the spear from Neelam's leg, but Rono forced it back with sharp talons.

A goblin jumped Neelam from behind. Neelam's lost his hold on his staff and sword as he rolled across the sands, fighting. The goblin snarled and Neelam punched it in the face.

Surya nose-dived for the goblin, her talons raking the demon's flesh. It swayed and jerked but held its grip on the wizard. Then a blur of black fur and sharp teeth rammed itself between Neelam and the goblin. Surya let go of the goblin as Neelam rolled away and sprang to his feet, and the pain in his leg exploded. The wolf killed the creature, blood dripping from his jaws. Neelam cursed vividly; the spear still imbedded in his leg. He gritted his teeth, extended his hand and summoned both staff and sword back to his hands.

Another goblin tried to sneak up on Neelam and the black wolf pounced and snapped its neck, and then with savage force attacked another advancing goblin. Dabiro joined the wolf in fighting off the creatures. In the chaos, a goblin scuttled across the sands toward Neelam, but instead of attacking, the creature extracted the spear from Neelam's leg then burrowed back into the sands.

Then it stopped. The goblins had retreated to their hiding places. After a hazy moment, Neelam realized their enemies were dead or had gone back into hiding. Caked with blood, sweat and sand, he staggered to a rock to sit, gripping his wounded leg. "Damn goblins are running amok like cockroaches here. What the bloody hell!"

Liat dropped next to Neelam. "Let me take a look at your leg. We need to stop the bleeding. Is it just me, or were they focused on you? They almost ignored Dabiro and me." Liat ripped off his turban and began to bind Neelam's leg.

Surya fluttered down to perch on Neelam's shoulder.

"How's the leg feel?" Surya inquired.

"Hurts like a demon," Neelam said.

"How witty," Surya replied dryly.

Dabiro ran up to his sorcerer, shaking sand from his fat body. Rono hovered near the group.

Liat patted the gryphon's head. "Rono! Everyone's been so worried since Koll stole you, boy. Mellypip and Runa will be relieved you're safe."

"I've heard about you, Rono," Neelam nodded. "My name is Neelam and my familiar here is Surya."

Tears of happiness welled in the gryphon's eyes. "Hello! Hello! Friends! My friends have come! Even Dabiro is friend! We are rescued! I get to go home at last!"

Neelam limped toward the wolf. The wolf was nervous and looked at Neelam with haunted silver eyes. "Easy, there. You were very helpful just now, my friend. Who are you?"

"He's Grimm Darkrunner. He's my best friend next to Melly," Rono announced. "Grimm helped after I escaped from Koll. He saved me from stinky troll who broke my poor wing. Wing is better now, though it hurts some." He flapped his black wing to demonstrate. "See. A little crooked, but I can fly."

"He's been such a good friend," Rono said excitedly. "Come closer, Grimm! It's alright! They're good mages! I don't know the wizard, but he's good too. I do not sense evil." He turned to Neelam and said with pride, "We have been hiding here and spying for the Light."

Dabiro grunted and brushed sand off his muzzle. "Maybe heat stroke fried his senses?"

Grimm did not move any closer, so Neelam limped over to the reticent wolf. "That's a fine name, Grimm Darkrunner. Tell me about yourself?"

"I am a wolf without a pack," Grimm replied simply.

The black wolf was bloodstained, dusty, gaunt, and not trusting. Neelam approached carefully. "Thank you Grimm Darkrunner, for helping us. You have seen some hard times, I see. I sense magic about you too. You're a familiar. Where is your mage?"

"I have no mage," Grimm replied solemnly. "I am a wild familiar and belong to no one, but I have a duty to my spirit sire. I must warn you the Dark seeks out the blood and flesh of the three Scions. I do not understand its meaning, but I am supposed to tell you. That is what the goblins were doing—they wanted to steal your blood, Wizard. We were told you would come. I am sorry I did not prevent it." Then the wolf glanced to the side, as though listening to something, and returned his gaze to Neelam. "I bring you a warning about the sorcerer Koll, and the Bloodstone Queen, Obsydia."

They looked at Grimm with keen interest.

"Is Obsydia still in her prison of Light?" Neelam asked.

Grimm's silver eyes were solemn and his voice as sober as his name. "Obsydia is still trapped in the strange crystal, but she is not here now. Koll and Zhelon Thor took Obsydia away through the magic mirror a few hours ago. That was when my sire told me to find you. They are planning a ritual to free Obsydia. Everyone is in danger. A demon named Chimera was summoned from the Otherworld to achieve this goal. They used a mirror called the Eye of Shadows to travel, which is in the ruins below. There is a path to her old throne room. Chimera summoned goblins and other shadow beings to guard Obsydia's palace. And to hunt you. They knew you were coming here. They saw you in the Eye of Shadows."

Neelam stroked the weary wolf and offered him a drink of water. "We have a lot to talk about. Show me."

CHAPTER THIRTY

Mellypip bounded across the backyard toward the stable area. Darkleaf and Redstorm were exercising their wings in the early morning light. Jadon was busy filling buckets with grain, apples, and honey for the perytons.

"Light's Blessing, Mellypip," Redstorm and Darkleaf said. Redstorm stretched out his crimson wings, flapping them up and down. Darkleaf lowered his head so Mellypip could climb up.

"You're here early," Jadon said, carrying the buckets over to the perytons. The perytons enjoyed their breakfast as Jadon groomed them.

Mellypip settled on Darkleaf's soft blue back, plucking at the tufts of fur between his toes. "Runa and Opaline are both so anxious, they don't sleep much. Plus, Opaline snores. Runa is having weird dreams again, though not like last time. It's just worry."

"Is she alright?" Jadon asked, concerned. "Is she doing the meditations I taught her?"

"She is meditating a little, but she gets excited and can't focus. No one can concentrate." Mellypip chewed on his tail. "I miss Cathal. I miss Belwyn. I miss Rono. I even miss that big old slobbering bear, Baldur."

"I know you do," Jadon comforted him. "Raghnall needed Baldur to help him in the cursed forest. Belwyn is doing very important work with Cathal."

"I know. It's a secret sorcery mission. I plan to write an opus about it when it is over and they can talk about it. I am writing a special tale for Belwyn."

"Really? Does he know?" Redstorm asked.

"Not yet. I'm calling it *Ode to Belwyn*. I will be glad he's back."

"To spell check your ode?" Redstorm snickered.

"Be nice," Darkleaf chided him.

"I'm using the dictionary," Mellypip said, and then looked downcast. "So many people are going away on special missions. You're staying. Aren't you Jadon?"

"I won't leave," Jadon promised. "My father has assigned me here to help the mages with the threat of Obsydia. Anyway, who else would keep my secrets?"

"I keep your secrets too," Darkleaf teased.

Jadon leaned against Darkleaf, stroking his peryton's back. "I know you do. I wanted to come back and help Cathal fight Koll. The desecration that monster did to Ambera infuriated me. She was the mother of our race, the founder of Ilyrra. And Runa needs me. The tree of bones has hurt her. I couldn't bear that she suffered so."

"Did you tell your father you loved Runa?" Darkleaf asked.

Jadon nodded. "My father says I am too young to fall in love."

Mellypip jumped across Darkleaf's rack and leapt to Jadon's shoulder. "You *love* Runa! Really?"

Jadon put his fingers to his lips. "Shoosh! Not so loud! I am not ready to tell her yet. There is so much happening now more important than us. Promise me you won't say anything until I do, Melly!"

"But Jadon, Runa must know! Secrets are bad! I know she feels love too! I didn't mean when I said Cathal would turn you into a toad."

Redstorm snorted. He lifted his head, crunching an apple in his teeth. "People are the strangest when it comes to the mating ritual. If you wish to breed, Jadon, forget about delicate flowers and gifts! Roar to the heavens and proclaim Runa your mate."

Jadon gasped at Redstorm's bold remark. "Breed? Breeding?"

"Redstorm is very elemental," Darkleaf remarked, rolling his eyes.

Prince Ulric poked his head out the backdoor and smiled mischievously. "Hello Jadon! Join us for breakfast! Hurry up, Melly! Caliste is making drobba chip pancakes!"

"Coming!" Mellypip called back, swishing his long fluffy tail. "Come on, great ranger! Pancakes make you braver."

Disgruntled, Jadon tucked Mellypip in his arm, shaking his head. "I should never talk to the animals. They show me no respect."

Mellypip bounced along in Jadon's arm. "I should never talk to silly people, especially when they never listen to my fuzzy wisdom."

Pointessa greeted them at the backdoor. "Hold and wipe your feet."

Jadon obliged with a smile.

"Make sure Melly leaves no paw prints either!" Pointessa pressed, barring entry with a cranky expression and raised quills.

Jadon held Mellypip out for Pointessa's inspection. She gazed at his furry paws and finally nodded approval. "Very well then, you may come inside. After all, I can't have you tracking in dirt when the floors are freshly scrubbed."

"The floors were clean yesterday. Oh, did Opaline try to do magic again?" Mellypip asked.

Pointessa followed them into the Sorcerer House. "Well, a certain sorcerer was sick…everywhere. Runa just made fresh coffee too, Jadon. Hurry before it's gone."

"Morning, Runa," Jadon said when they entered the kitchen.

"Morning," Runa smiled.

Opaline poured coffee into a large cup in front of Gabriel, slumped over on the table, moaning. "Am I dead?" he croaked.

She wore a sun yellow cotton dress, but she made it look like the most regal of gowns. Opaline put down the coffee pot and shook her head in disgust. "No, you are not dead, Gabriel. You do reek of ale. I suggest a bath after breakfast. A thorough bath. In fact, take several."

"How long has he been like this?" Prince Ulric asked.

"Since he arrived," Caliste replied. "He's suffering quite the hangover. We won't discuss the side effects of excessive drinking that had me magically scrubbing down the Sorcerer House in the middle of the night. Thank heavens I'm a sorceress."

Opaline added a generous splash of milk to the coffee. "For nourishment, as I doubt you've consumed anything but alcohol for days. Drink up—but please keep it down."

An unintelligible moan was Gabriel's reply.

"Good morning," Namir the clouded leopard said, poking his head over the table.

Mellypip jumped down to the table. "Good morning. Why is your sorcerer so sick?"

"Ale," Namir said. "Last night, it was much worse though… much worse. I apologize for the trouble."

Runa scratched Namir's muzzle, looking intently at Gabriel's shaky and mournful condition. "This must be what Darcus calls a hangover."

"It is a gentle word for what my sorcerer suffers," Namir lamented.

"Has there been any word from Grandpa yet?" Runa asked.

Caliste placed a platter of warm pancakes on the table. "Yes, my dear, just a moment ago on the calling crystal he sent a very brief message. Cathal said they would be home safely though sooner than expected. He said he had some good news and bad news. Then the crystal began to flicker and the message faded."

"Anything from Neelam?" Opaline inquired, deftly cutting her pancake into perfect squares.

"No, but that is expected," Caliste said. "With our friends doing such dangerous work, we must wait in ignorance."

"That crystal does need some magical repair. It is always sparking or cutting out in the middle of the message," Opaline remarked. "These pancakes are heavenly. Pass the butter, please."

Gabriel moaned, shoving the butter crock toward her.

"These are delicious," Jadon complimented Caliste.

"Well, at least to those of us not decimated by alcohol," Opaline remarked, pouring coffee for her and Ulric. "Would Your Highness like sugar in his coffee?"

"No royal words," Ulric insisted. "Here I am only Ulric. I do not want stiff ceremony among my friends."

"You are here early this morning, Ulric," Caliste noted with a grin. "Do you have plans today?"

"Yes, as a matter of fact, I do," Ulric answered, sipping his coffee. "My mother thought Runa and Opaline would enjoy an afternoon in the royal gardens. She thought it would be a safe distraction from what is going on."

Caliste stirred more batter and magically flipped the hotcakes on the griddle. "That sounds like a fine idea."

"Will Faustine be there?" Opaline asked quietly.

"Don't worry about her joining us," Ulric replied. "She avoids keeping company with sorcerers. I do not know if it's because my uncle, Morydonn, dislikes them so or because she feels the same way. She's always been hard to read. I use to put it down to her shyness, but now I am not so sure."

"It's a shame they judge us because of our mage caste," Opaline said.

Caliste set a little saucer with a tiny pancake and a little cup of tea down for Rosepetal, sitting next to Runa on the table.

The hedgehog sniffed it appreciatively. "Thank you."

"Eat up," Runa coaxed. "We will play a game later."

Rosepetal nibbled a bite. "I miss Ulan. He loves drobba chip pancakes."

"We know," Runa said. "He'll be home soon. I promise."

"Can I try coffee?" Rosepetal asked.

"No, it's bad for you." Pointessa said. "Drink your tea, dear."

"We will hunt for grubs later with Pointessa," Mellypip promised. "Though I think apples would be more fun."

Forlorn, Rosepetal hiccupped once, but lapped a little more tea.

Pointessa waddled around to Runa's chair. "That's a good girl, Rosepetal. No need to hiccup or get upset. Those pancakes look good. Eat up like a good girl."

Pointessa had devoted herself to taking care of the little hedgehog. Mellypip helped too. Sometimes they played together, but Rosepetal's spiny body was too pointy for hugs. The morning was full of chatter until Panthara entered the kitchen, carrying a tray of empty plates and cups. The tension immediately tightened among everyone.

"Iona was exhausted. Raghnall and Captain Vasya insisted she get some rest," Panthara said evenly, walking to the sink and placing the dishes in the washtub.

"That's alright," Runa nodded. "Is she ill? Can we do anything to help? Do you want...pancakes? We have enough to feed an army."

Panthara shook her head. "No, thank you, we just ate. Iona just needs sleep. I thought some solid food would make her and Amun feel better." She looked at Opaline and quickly added, "Taran and MacTabbish are upstairs in his laboratory. He said they would be down for breakfast soon."

"Thank you," Opaline replied smoothly, staring into her coffee cup as though it were a crystal ball.

Panthara left the kitchen. Runa took Opaline's hand and squeezed it. "You did very well. I'm very proud of you."

Opaline speared a pancake onto her plate. "Well, as a princess I was trained to be diplomatic, no matter how much it pained me."

Ulric hugged her and laughed. "Oh, my darling, you're also kind and merciful, even though you can be very feisty, my Princess."

Ulric's teasing lightened the mood and Opaline laughed then kissed Ulric lightly on the cheek.

Opaline turned to Runa. "Speaking of feisty, you had a particularly bad dream last night. Is it another dream seer warning?"

Runa nervously cut up her pancakes into tiny pieces and dosed them with syrup. "Just fragmented images mostly. Even a sorceress with budding dream seer magic sometimes just has a bad dream. I do remember a very strange woman. Her skin was red and her eyes black as night! Then the dream breaks down into fragments. I remember nothing else. Poor Melly was cranky too. All my thrashing about knocked him off the bed. Poor baby fell on the floor.”

“My butt hurt,” Mellypip added, his cheeks puffy with pancakes.

“That was also the end of my beauty sleep for the night,” Opaline said.

“You are always beautiful, my love,” Ulric said with genuine warmth. Opaline blushed and ate her sweet cake with gusto.

“See. That is what you’re supposed to say,” Mellypip whispered to Jadon.

“What was that, Melly?” Runa asked.

“Nothing,” Mellypip said quickly. “Secret ranger stuff. May I have another pancake?”

“Oh, ranger secrets,” Runa smiled, scooping a little hotcake onto his saucer.

Gabriel groaned and slowly lifted his head off the table. He gazed around the other folk at the table and asked hoarsely, “Where am I?”

“The Sorcerer House,” Opaline replied coolly. “In Thill, city of Aybarr. You appeared here inebriated and attacked several of the royal guards when you showed up. Perhaps you would recall your activities with greater clarity if you cease drinking and find another task for your time,” she said pointedly, pouring more coffee for Ulric and then for herself. “Surely a sorcerer has better things to do.”

Gabriel squinted and blinked, trying focus. “I must agree, my golden princess. My father always said so, but then, I always disappointed him too.”

“I hate to ask about your time in Kra’zum, but how many did you rescue from the sacrificial altars?” Ulric inquired.

Gabriel slurped his coffee and tried to sit up straight. Deep shadows circled his eyes. “I think I saved twenty-five. There was a call to celebrate. A special mass for Obsydia. They were praising Koll as her deliverer. I thought I would find the bastard there. I was hidden in the crowd, cloaked and bowing my head in mock prayer. Namir was hidden in the folds of the cloak. There was a dull sermon. Then they brought in the sacrifices.”

“Dear gods,” Opaline shivered. “How could they?”

“They’re monsters and the worst monsters are always human, lady. Women and children were lined up before for the altar. Those damned priests had smeared red paint on their faces and called it a mass of glory and thanksgiving. Zhelon Thor himself was there. Children and women were huddled, crouching and crying as the temple guards shoved them toward the altar for slaughter. I fired my sorcery at him first. Then Namir and I were fighting our way out.

"Is Zhelon dead?" Ulric asked excitedly. "Is that terrible man dead?"

Gabriel's expression went dark. "No. Sadly, that man has the reflexes of a god, though his sacrificial altar of black stone is a smoking pile of dust and rubble. But I would rather have killed him. There were no bloodstains that day that the slaves had to scrub off because of sacrifice. The temple guards charged us with scimitars. Zhelon screamed for my head. I shot my sorcery at him again. His devoted priests used their bodies as a shield to protect him as they swept him away from my fury. I blasted guards and priests. Sorcery can be useful in dealing with murderous heathens. There were a lot of bright colors. I used all the sorcery I could summon and what was stored in my staff. Good old Namir, he raked a few of those bastards with his pretty claws."

"He used a lot of sorcery, and it did a great deal of damage," Namir confirmed proudly.

"How did you get everyone out?" Runa whispered.

"I couldn't carry all the children and the women were so scared. They could not run fast enough. People were hunting us. So I trans-formed them into little larks so they could fly out of the temple. Damn priests were furious. Sent more guards after me with scimitars. They did not last. Then the priests chased me, brandishing obsidian blades. Fools. They were easy to cut down. Their death screams were most satisfying. Then I shifted into a leopard like my Namir. I'm not sure what happened after that."

"Did you change them back?" Opaline asked, concerned. "The larks? The women and children?"

"Yes," Namir confirmed. "They were all safely restored. We took them across the borders to a special house. It's a secret religious order that looks after and finds safe places for runaway slaves, and escaped sacrifices. We have used them before. More recently for the slave girls Gabriel smuggled out when we were hunting for Xabral. Cathal thought if Xabral survived, he might find his way back to Urgonclaw."

"We know what Koll did to your father and his familiar, Derena," Runa said softly. "We are very sorry. Can we do anything to help?"

"Keeping him away from ale might be a good start," Namir suggested dryly.

Gabriel drank down the bowl of milky coffee and wiped his mouth on his sleeve. "I was in Zeli when my father died. I didn't hear about my father's death for almost a month. By then, it was a mess. I visited my poor mum. She's heartbroken. She was married to my dad for centuries. Been hard on her. I stayed with her for a bit. They buried my father and his familiar together. Poor little kitty. I'm gonna miss poor Derena. She helped me raise Namir." Gabriel slowly rose from the table. Standing straight he was six foot four. He stretched, touching the ceiling with his large fingers. "I was miffed I was not the hero who captured Koll, but was elated nonetheless. I was coming to witness the execution when I learned about Koll's escape. So I went back to see if Koll would go to Zhelon for sanctuary. I never saw the bastard. Or Xabral. But something bad is going on. They talked about Obsydia rising. They proclaimed Koll a dark saint. I had to leave and warn everyone. Then they were going to kill those children and the women. I had to get them away. After that, along the way I got waylaid in a tavern and lost my wits in a bottle. Several bottles."

"My grandfather will find Koll," Runa said with conviction.

"Who is your grandfather, girl?"

"Cathal," Runa said.

"Ah! So you are Runa! Yes, Cathal is a legend. He has good odds." He turned to Opaline, "And who is your pretty friend?"

"We already met. I'm Opaline. Sirah of Thill is my mother. I just poured you coffee."

"You're the little princess!" Gabriel laughed. "You look like a princess too."

"What is that supposed to mean?" Opaline asked.

"Nothing my sweet," Gabriel shrugged.

"I apologize," Namir said quietly.

"You do that a lot," Mellypip said.

"It is a requirement of late," Namir lamented, and laid his head on the table next to Gabriel.

"It's okay," Mellypip said, stroking the leopard's soft, thick fur. The clouded leopard looked so sad. "You can stay here until Gabriel is not so sicky. I will play with you later, if you want."

Caliste was looking out the window when her expression went from sympathy to shock. "Great Gods! I don't believe it." She bolted out the backdoor, black braids flying.

Everyone followed her into the large backyard to see Neelam,

Dabiro, Liat, and Surya emerging from the patch of shadows by the old hawthorn tree. Two others stepped from that strange darkness too. Rono the gryphon, thin, dirty, and scraggly, but it was Rono! The last to appear was a gaunt black wolf with silver eyes.

"It's Rono!" Mellypip cried, rushing toward his friend.

CHAPTER THIRTY-ONE

"The Royal Museum of Thema is almost as palatial as the palace," Hinkleburr observed to Broda and Talwyn, strolling down the opulent hall. "Will Queen Sarabia approve of my new suit?" He smoothed his rich brown velvet coat and silk vest woven with a delicate green leaf pattern.

"Indeed, most magnificent," Broda said.

"And look at all the magnificent ladies," Talwyn said, when an attractive female walked by.

"Behave now, my boys," Hinkleburr chastised with a chuckle.

"Why has Queen Sarabia summoned us?" Talwyn asked, keeping quick step with Hinkleburr.

"All she would say was an important object needed my expert knowledge. Oh boys, did you post the letters to our good friends in Aybarr?"

"Yes, Ambassador," Broda replied.

"And my letter to Lady Helga?" Hinkleburr winked.

"Yes, sir," Talwyn grinned. "We would never forget her."

The burgeoning romance between Helga, the exotic flaxen-haired daughter of the Ironian Ambassador to Thill, and Hinkleburr Crowyn, had blossomed despite their forced distance.

They stopped before the polished double doors and a royal guard immediately opened the door so they could enter.

In the private relic chamber, Queen Sarabia personally greeted Hinkleburr. "Welcome Ambassador."

"I'm delighted to serve," Hinkleburr bowed elegantly.

Jiana the sorceress was there, looking unusually groomed in a proper gown, though she wore a dagger in her belt. Jasper wiggled his nose, content in her arms. "Hello."

"Good to see you again, Hinkleburr," Jiana smiled broadly. She winked at Broda and Talwyn. "I hope you are enjoying my homeland."

Hinkleburr genuinely smiled. He admired the scrappy sorceress and her tiger hare. "Lovely to see you, Jiana, Jasper. Yes, we love it here. It is so warm and sunny. I pray you are all in good health." He turned to Sarabia to kiss her hand. "Charmed as always, Your Majesty. How fares Princess Hadrial?"

"My sister is in good spirits," Sarabia answered carefully.

Hinkleburr never knew how to speak about the Princess. She rarely attended court functions. As a child, she had been afflicted with a disease which partially paralyzed the right half of her body and her face, causing her eye and mouth to droop heavily. Bitter about her fate, Princess Hadrial often kept to herself, despite the loving devotion of her sister, Sarabia.

Queen Sarabia's brow furrowed with concern. "I am about to reveal something of a sensitive nature. Recently, my relic scholars found an artifact that concerned them. I asked Jiana to examine this relic and she detects magic but senses a dark origin. I must admit, I have fears about what we discovered in a lost tomb. What I am about to show you must remain secret. Unveil the weapon, Jiana."

Jiana gently put Jasper down on the floor. She stripped off the cloth to reveal a finely crafted scythe of black metal. The long curving blade was neither ebonite nor iron; but forged from some secret unknown element. It had a dim nacreous sheen, and weird runic symbols covering the long handle. With gloved hands Jiana carefully lifted the ancient weapon to show it off, and though the light crystals in the room were bright, they did not reflect off the weapon. At a certain angle, the scythe revealed a skull-like face embossed on the blade itself, though its shape was fleeting to the eye.

"It is definitely magical origin," Jiana said uneasily. "The very imagery of this weapon speaks of evil. I think its trouble waiting to happen."

Hinkleburr stepped closer. Though he was not a mage, there was a definite strong magical quality about the weapon—and an aura of the sinister. He was hesitant to touch it. The scythe had a malevolent quality. "The scythe is not of Ironian origin; I can assure you."

"The weapon has a wicked quality, so I hesitate to tamper with it," Jiana replied uneasily. "We believe it could be from the Bloodstone Era. It may even be a relic of legend. I think we should contact Cathal about this discovery."

Broda nodded nervously. "Bloodstone relics are known for their bad luck."

"Antiques should be less traumatizing." Talwyn agreed.

"I concur Cathal the Sorcerer should examine the weapon," Queen Sarabia said. "Though this artifact may represent a part of our history, it disturbs me. My mother always spoke well of the old Archon. We were grieved to learn Ramirez was murdered by Koll the

Sorcerer. He was a good man and made a fine Archon after Cathal stepped down. Still, I am pleased Cathal is once again guiding the mages. I want to ask for his help. There is a terrible rumor about Koll. In Urgonclaw, they claim Koll has found the lost tomb of Obsydia, the Bloodstone Queen. If it's true, Koll would want this weapon, and not as an antique."

Jiana gazed at the scythe. "It was found in a cave. A bloodstone decorated the top of a lone sarcophagus with runic symbols carved into the dark gray stone and crystals were encrusted all over it. They left the sarcophagus there to bring back later. Personally, I think they should reseal that tomb and place holy symbols around it."

"Was there a body in the crypt?" Talwyn asked, a little wary. "Was it *human?*"

Sarabia nodded quickly, but her dark eyes looked haunted. "Yes. The mummified remains of a man dressed in dragon armor."

"Dragon armor? That's sacrilege," Hinkleburr gasped.

"I know," Jiana shuddered. "It disgusted me too. It had been taken from a fire dragon, and the red dragon skin had been tooled with strange runes I cannot yet translate, though I believe it is in demon tongue. The body in the crypt had been decapitated and I found his head wrapped in linen with his body in the sarcophagus. The remains were mummified by the climate conditions, I believe. The scythe was with him in the sarcophagus, a sign of great honor. It's all very strange."

Sarabia's face was troubled, shadowing her exquisite beauty. "The man buried there was quickly entombed, which shows haste, yet the manner in which he was buried was also rich and elaborate. The coffin of this wretch is priceless by its historical implication alone, but its dark beauty is primeval and dangerous.'

"You think it's Solem of legend?" Hinkleburr asked.

Jiana and Sarabia exchanged looks and nodded.

"This weapon may have belonged to Solem," Sarabia agreed. "He was the Warrior Priest of Obsydia, which puts all of us at risk. Hinkleburr, I would ask that you and Jiana personally deliver this to Cathal in Thill. This would be a secret assignment. We cannot risk anything with dark power falling into Koll's hands."

Hinkleburr gasped. "The legends say Solem was once human, a warrior who sought to kill Obsydia. But she captured him and transformed into a demon with her kiss."

Queen Sarabia walked to the table and using the silk to buffer her hands from touching it, boldly lifted the scythe. "Once Obsydia's kiss turned Solem to the Dark, he became its siren. A thousand years ago, Obsydia's forces defeated our armies. My ancestor, Upala, defied Obsydia. She was a mere sixteen-year-old girl, a sheltered princess who had never used a knife except to peel an apple. Solem slaughtered her family before her eyes. He whipped her until she collapsed in blood and tears at Obsydia's feet. Upala had never seen death or cruelty before. Now she was surrounded by its horror. A lesser heart would have succumbed to madness, but Upala did not go mad.

"She prayed to Thema, her patron goddess, not only for courage, but to save her people from Darkness. Some say the Goddess herself breathed onto Upala's soul. Some say the Eternals were angry at Ahridum. The balance between mortal and Eternal was violated by spawning Obsydia. Whatever the reason, Upala was infused with strength she had never experienced before. She snatched the scythe from Solem's grip and struck off his head in a single blow. Upala's bold actions heartened the people and they too fought back. Forces led by their ally, King Kronus, finally arrived from the West to help. Obsydia's army was driven back. Our kingdom was redeemed from darkness. The scythe was spoken of in legend, but in Upala's writings, she never mentions what happened to it. She may have had a good reason for that. I fear my hunger for knowledge may have put us at risk."

"I believe that is the nefarious blade," Hinkleburr remarked. "I will be happy to serve you, Queen Sarabia. Cathal will know what to do."

"Thank you," Sarabia whispered. She put the weapon down on the table.

"I will send a coded message to Cathal," Jiana bowed. "I will arrange for our travel back to Thill."

Sarabia took Hinkleburr's hand. "You are a noble and true friend, Hinkleburr. As you are dear, Jiana. I will arrange for new identities for you all while you travel secretly. Be safe."

In the corner of the room, a glimmer of shadow blocked the sunlight streaming through the window. Koll the Sorcerer stepped through the shimmering gateway.

Jiana's warning cry was brief as Koll's harsh gesture sent her flying across the room before she could strike.

"Jiana! Jasper cried, dashing to her side.

"Guards!" Sarabia shouted, drawing a jeweled dagger tucked in her belt.

Jiana forced herself up and threw herself in front of the queen. She summoned a shield around everyone just as Koll's harsh gesture fired mystical black flames at them. Soldiers banged on the door as Koll's fire burned away her shield. Jiana breathed cold icy air at the fire, keeping its burning threat at bay. Jiana cleverly cast a second shield just beneath the one giving way, adding another layer of mystical protection Koll's sorcery was eroding.

With reverence Koll picked up the ancient weapon, as one touches a holy relic. He glanced once with malicious threat at Jiana, but quickly retreated back into the gloomy portal from which he invaded and vanished.

After Koll disappeared, Jiana vanquished her magical defense. Her stream of curses were only matched by those of her furious queen. Hinkleburr was shaken, as were his young aides.

"Alright, boys?"

"Sadly sir, we are becoming accustomed to magical attack," Broda replied bluntly.

The guards finally crashed through the door and rushed in swords drawn. The raw odor of dark magic choked the room.

"My Queen, what has happened," the soldier shouted.

"Koll happened!" Sarabia shouted. "And I fear he has a new weapon of sinister power."

~ * ~

Koll stepped through the Eye of Shadows. The ancient chamber was empty, since Zhelon had arranged to move Obsydia for her protection.

"Lord Koll?" A temple priest knelt before him in the ghostly chamber.

"Not even a goblin stirs in the shadows. Has everything been taken care of?" Koll asked.

"Obsydia is safe, away from infidel hands. The troll was taken away with the others, as the creature is very destructive when left unattended." The priest hesitated, then added in a shaky voice, "We waited for your return, Lord Koll. We expected you back as soon as you retrieved the holy scythe."

"First, I had to return to Obsydia's black tower. I had to present the scythe to the Hooded Guardians for blessing."

"And? Did you truly find it?"

"This is the Scythe of Rygon," Koll said, holding out the mystical weapon.

The priest gasped and gazed at it with awe.

"Where are the Rashurkeen guards?" Koll asked.

The priest suddenly looked uncomfortable. "Neelam came to us, as expected, but things did not go as planned."

Koll clenched the scythe in his hands, tempted to test it. "The mirror showed Neelam was coming here. It should have been easy. We summoned goblins to take Neelam's blood. We had Rashurkeen in the temple, should that have failed. You did not even have to kill the wizard. Did the goblins fail to get Neelam's essence? Where are the assassins? You didn't kill Neelam, did you?" Koll demanded. "The ritual will not work if the scions die by unnatural means."

"No, the wizard still lives as you command. But the wizard came into our chambers as though he knew the passage. He and another sorcerer killed all the Rashurkeen and some priests. They were not able to take any of Neelam's essence."

"You failed?"

"No, we have it, but the wretched goblin who took it in the desert will only give it to you. He would not let me touch it. Those things tend to bite. It's been waiting for you."

"Bring the goblin to me," Koll commanded.

The priest dragged the wounded goblin from the corner and dropped it before Koll. He savagely kicked it. "Here he is, goblin. Speak to your master."

Koll knelt by the dying goblin. The damage to its body was not by sword, but by teeth and claws. It opened its bulbous eyes and extended a shaking, gnarled hand.

"Have offering of...last...Scion." It opened its claw-like hand to expose a fragment of bloodstained cloth, with a morsel of red skin. Just enough. "The Dwarven Wizard you seek. He came. Just like beautiful Obsydia promised. They killed us. Sorcerer and Wizard fought us hard. Cut us up with cruel blades and magic. Familiars with vicious bites and claw. A gryphon and wolf helped the mages too. Not fair."

Koll scowled. "Rono! That damned gryphon! I should have slit its throat when I had the chance. But I know of no wolf."

"A black wolf fought us." The goblin's voice grew more faint and raspy. "Killed many of us. But I took the spear that struck the wizard's leg. I kept his flesh and blood, just for you, Master."

"Are you sure this is it from the Wizard Neelam?" Koll demanded.

"Yes," the goblin whimpered weakly. "Help goblin now?"

Koll seized the bloodstained cloth and replied. "Yes. I am pleased. You shall be rewarded, goblin." Koll rose and walked away. "Put it out of its misery."

The priest grinned and sliced the goblin's throat.

"The wizard and his allies escaped through the mirror. He knew how to use the mirror, Lord Koll. How did he know? I fought him myself—"

"And yet you live?" Koll inquired darkly.

"I offer my worthless life in penance!" he cried and bowed his head to the floor.

"I will take it after Obsydia is free and we have the celebratory sacrifices. Yours will be among the first hearts cut out. Blessed be the Dark."

Koll turned back to the mirror, the mystical Eye of Shadows, and concentrated on its power. He concentrated on his destination. Finally, the holy temple of Rygon in Tiamet appeared. He sought a chamber within its sacred halls until he found one with a deep mantel of darkness untainted by sunlight. Chimera was kneeling by the crystal tomb of Obsydia, which was shrouded in black silk to soften the glare of light in the room, though it did not abate Obsydia's pain. The mirror shifted from solid glass to a smoky veil, and Koll walked through. The journey was still unsettling, as though hands of shadow pulled him through a long, dark tunnel. He felt disembodied and light-headed each time he came through. The power was not designed for mortal use, not even a sorcerer. It was made for *Her*. Finally, Koll stepped into a place of solid mortality.

He knelt before Obsydia and bowed his head to the marble floor.

"Welcome back, Koll," Obsydia said. Were you victorious?"

Koll offered the scythe. "I was, my Goddess Queen. I bring this for you."

Chimera scolded him. "It's about time! I thought getting the scythe would be easy." She stood up, hands on her hips, in a sleeveless gown of black spider silk, more modest than her attire when first they met, though still barefoot. Her black hair curled wildly down her back as she marched toward Koll. She seized the scythe from his grip with greedy joy.

"You're welcome," Koll said dryly.

"Silly sorcerer," Chimera said. "This mythic weapon is not worthy even of you. Rygon himself forged it in the Dark Realms. It was a gift for Obsydia, not a mortal mage. What took you so long?"

"Solem's tomb had been opened and desecrated," Koll said impatiently. "Solem's body was still there, but the scythe was gone. Relic hunters had found it. Queen Sarabia had it in her possession. Fortunately, it was easy to retrieve. They had planned to conceal it from me. But I foiled their plans. I made haste, knowing time is important."

"Yes, yes, now we have Rygon's Scythe!" Chimera cried. She swung the weapon back and forth with effortless skill, and it made a humming sound as it danced in the air. "Yes, sacred is this weapon. I smell the smoky fires of the Dark Realms on its blade. But what of the wretch, Neelam? We need his blood! Where is it?"

"Do you mean this?" Koll inquired, dangling the bloody fragment of cloth before Chimera and Obsydia.

Chimera snatched it from Koll. "Ah, the old wizard was careless."

"Neelam carelessly killed all of our Rashurkeen in the process. Did you manage to take Cathal's blood?" Koll asked.

Chimera shrugged, turning the red-stained rag over and over in her hand. "Yes, of course I did. I told you he would come to Kra'zum. We had moved Obsydia to this temple first, just like we planned. They will never suspect us to have brought her here. Oh, Cathal was stunned to see me! I sliced his cheek. You would have laughed to see his shock. His essence is in cauldron now. Now we have Neelam's blood too." Chimera folded the bloody cloth. "Now we can appease the Light. We have the elements we need to begin the ritual. Now we just need to gather the sacrifices." She swung the scythe back and forth again, giggling like a child.

"Where is Xabral?" Koll asked. "I would have thought you would have him with you."

Chimera stopped swinging the scythe and pouted. "It's not Chimera's fault."

Koll ripped the scythe from her hands and kicked the demoness to the floor. He pressed the blade to her throat. "WHERE...IS... XABRAL?" he demanded.

Rygon's weapon pricked her scarlet flesh, causing rivulets of demon blood to flow. Terrified, Chimera raised her hands in supplication and fixed pleading eyes on Koll.

"Cathal took him."

CHAPTER THIRTY-TWO

The doorway of shade flickered and vanished behind Neelam and Liat as they stumbled through. Spattered with blood and sand, the mages dropped their bloodstained weapons and staves sizzling with magic to the dew-soaked grass before collapsing. Their familiars were equally disheveled from the remnants of battle and desert. Rono was the only happy one, elated at being reunited with his friends. The strange black wolf who came through with them nervously backed away from the advancing sorcerers and familiars welcoming them home.

Joyful being home, Rono's tears of happiness flowed as he relished the hugs and kisses of Runa, Opaline, and Mellypip, who scrambled up his front leg to hug him. "I missed my Melly! Missed Runa! Missed Opaline! I missed everyone! Being home makes me so happy."

Pointessa waddled over to Dabiro, who lay filthy and exhausted on the ground. "Welcome home. Wipe your paws before you go inside."

Dabiro weakly lifted his head and sniffed the air loudly. "Good to see you too. Hey, do I smell drobba?"

"Drobba chip pancakes, hot off the griddle. So mind your manners, badger, if you want any," Pointessa warned. "I'm glad you're safe," she added.

Dabiro sniffed and scratched his dusty belly. "I hate deserts. Why is it we always end up in a desert fighting bad mages? Don't evil folk like forests or cool lake country? I got sand burn on my poor paws."

"I know, Dabiro," Pointessa sympathized, lying next to him.

"What happened to you?" Caliste cried, kneeling by Neelam. "You're all covered in blood, and some of it isn't human judging by the smell."

"It isn't," Liat confirmed, taking the burden of Neelam's pack from him. "We fought goblins in the Wasteland first, and then some rather disagreeable assassins and priests in the temple."

"Real goblins?" Gabriel asked. "I thought they were extinct."

"Sadly they are with us," Liat replied. "And yes, they're far worse than the drawings in books. Plus, they stink! Gods, I need a hot bath and strong soap."

"What do you mean temple? You found Obsydia's actual temple? I thought it was buried deep in the bowels of the Wasteland?" Caliste asked.

Neelam winced, rubbing his leg. "It was, but the whole damn region has been ripped apart by earthquakes. There was a clear path to her underground temple. But that's not the problem. Koll found Obsydia and now she's gone. The evil bastard spirited her away. We have real problems now."

"Zhelon Thor was not exaggerating when he claimed Koll found their dark goddess," Gabriel said angrily. "Now he will slaughter more innocents for her glory."

Namir rubbed against Gabriel's leg. "Calm yourself."

"Who's the wolf?" Taran whispered to Neelam. "Can we trust him?"

Neelam glanced at the black wolf. "Yes. He's a friend. His name is Grimm and he not only helped us find the path underground to Obsydia's temple, he helped us fight off those pesky goblins and assassins. He also took care of your gryphon, Mellypip."

Mellypip looked at the large, grizzled black wolf with haunted silver eyes. "He did?"

Rono beckoned the wolf with his good wing. "Come on, Grimm! Meet my friends." He murmured to Mellypip and Runa, "Grimm is shy. He's a familiar just like my Melly, but he has no mage folk or familiars to teach him. He said he was born in the wild but has no wolf friends. Grimm and I hid together in cave." Rono's large brown eyes brimmed with fresh tears. "That's when I would tell Grimm about my magical family. I told him about playing ranger mage with Melly. Grimm protected me in the terrible desert. Because I got to meet my new friend Grimm, was not all bad."

"Has Cathal sent word yet?" Neelam asked, wincing when he moved his leg.

Caliste examined Neelam's leg, frowning. "Only briefly to say they made it safely out of Urgonclaw and are on their way home. This wound looks bad."

Neelam removed his scabbard and leaned back, holding his wounded leg, wrapped with a bloody scarf. He untied the gory rag from his thigh, gritting his teeth. "Iron spears tend to inflict nasty damage, especially when some stringy goblin yanks it out of you."

"It was pretty strange," Liat commented as he pulled off his filthy tunic. "We were outnumbered, but they didn't really try to kill Neelam. They did not care about me, but they focused on you, Neelam. When we met the wolf, he told us about what Koll and some red-skinned demon woman are doing. They had been spying on them. Imagine that? Koll is creating a ritual to free Obsydia from the crystal's enchantment."

"Demon woman?" Runa said nervously. *Melly, my dream last night had a red-skinned demon woman!*

Mellypip's thoughts back were equally nervous. *Your dream seer talents are not very comforting. Why can't you see nice things in your future? Why must it be some seething darkness? Does the future ever hold anything fluffy and nice?*

"We need to warn Cathal." Neelam grimaced and wiped his sand-streaked face with a kerchief. "We learned too late Koll sent his minions to take our essence for the creation of a bloodstone ritual to break the enchantment of the Light. If they free Obsydia from her prison, we are doomed. That's why Koll took Ambera's essence from her grave. They've got mine now too; if that goblin has enough brains to hand it over. Hideous thing carved out a big chunk of my flesh. Wish I'd killed it, but it scuttled away like a beetle into the sands. Didn't see the demon woman, which is one blessing. Pure demon breeds do not die easily. According to Rono and Grimm, this she-thing is a flame-skinned devil, summoned from the demon netherworld to serve hell-bitch. As if I didn't have enough to worry about," Neelam grumbled.

"Take care of that leg now, unless you want it to fester and risk amputation," Surya warned.

"She's right. It needs to be cleaned and properly bandaged," Jadon observed, squatting down by the wizard. "You need stitches too."

"See...I told you," Surya said.

Jadon's hands shimmered with a soft greenish light, and in a moment the swelling went down and the bleeding stopped. Neelam ground his teeth, but as the Drusai light spread over his leg, his jaw softened as the pain eased up from the healing magic. "That should make it better. I accelerated the healing, though you'll still have a good battle scar to boast about. I do recommend a few stitches and please keep it clean. Magic can't do everything you know."

"He will," Surya promised. "I will make sure of it."

Gabriel leaned against the backdoor, his face haggard. "How did you get back so quickly? I would love to know myself. Nice trick, even for the greatest of mages."

Neelam's expression blackened with disgust. "It's not a trick any of you would enjoy. We used a bloodstone relic from the old days. A mirror conjured in the Demon Netherworld called the Eye of Shadows. That's how we were able to come back here. If it were not necessary to return swiftly, I would not have used the cursed thing. It was still in her throne room where Obsydia was imprisoned. The last time I saw hell-bitch was in that chamber when we trapped her. I never wanted to go there again. Damn, it still galls me she's gone. I managed to send a magical word to our waiting gryphons in the desert to go back home. Didn't want them to end up as goblin food. Believe me—you don't want to step through the looking glass from the dark netherworld unless you have to. It's brimming with wicked power."

Gabriel raised an eyebrow. "You knew how to use the mirror?"

"From centuries past during the Bloodstone Wars, I learned a lot of things, most of them unpleasant," Neelam replied. "This was not my first time infiltrating in Obsydia's territory. We went through the mirror to get here, but—"

"You feel...*dirty* afterward," Surya added bleakly.

Melly nuzzled his face against Rono's soft black feathers. "I don't care how you made it home! I'm just glad you are back!"

Rono bobbed his head up and down. "I'm glad too. No more troll to worry about. After Koll got angry and sent me away, Grimm saved me in awful desert from nasty troll. He's very brave and noble."

"Troll?" Opaline whispered shakily. "What troll?"

"You know! The troll who used to be Gorvanus. He was in the Wasteland," Rono said. "That's where Koll took me after he escaped. Gorvanus was the bad sorcerer, remember? He tried to hurt you and Runa. The mean troll tried to eat me and broke my poor wing. Grimm saved me. The troll was drawn to Obsydia's wickedness. He followed Koll and Obsydia into hiding, so I don't know where he is now. Obsydia thinks he's a pet. Troll serves evil, so he deserved to be a troll. You shouldn't feel bad about it."

"From the mouths of gryphons," Taran laughed.

Anxious, Opaline rubbed her temples as though she had a headache. "How did that troll end up in Skarros?"

"Evil loves company," Dabiro grunted.

"But Grimm is good." Rono sighed, looking at the sad wolf.

Grimm the wolf remained silent and kept his distance, but when he saw Opaline, hope lit his eyes.

Prince Ulric pointed to Grimm. "The wolf is looking at you Opaline," he whispered. "See?"

"Grimm looks so thin," Opaline remarked with concern. "It was kind of him to protect you, Rono. Poor thing. He's so straggly and gaunt. So alone. Come here, Grimm. It's alright."

"Be careful," Taran warned, pulling Opaline back. "He's a wild familiar and he looks scared."

"His whole name Grimm Darkrunner," Rono added.

Opaline continued to approach Grimm, unafraid. "I don't think he'll hurt me."

"He needs to fatten up," Mellypip agreed. "Pancakes will help." He cautiously ran up to Grimm and sat before him. "Thanks for saving my friend. I'm Mellypip."

Grimm blinked and tilted his head as he looked down on the plump wampu. "You are the valiant ranger-mage Rono spoke of. He told me tales of your bravery."

Mellypip scratched his furry tummy and sighed. "Not as brave as you, Grimm."

Jadon put down a large bowl of water for the familiars. "Wild familiars are rare these days. Even so, what would a wolf be doing in the Wasteland?" Jadon fetched another bowl of water for the strange wolf, but Opaline took it from him and set it down a few feet from the reticent wolf.

Opaline's eyes brimmed with sadness as she met the wolf's silver eyes. "He seems so forlorn. Poor thing must have been very lonely, at least until he found Rono. Wolves live in packs, and he didn't even have that."

"Arial doesn't have a wolf pack," Ulric pointed out.

Opaline shook her head and took her Prince's arm. "*We* are her pack. It is different for familiars."

"Grimm saved me from stinky troll. My wing was hurt and I could not fly. Grimm promised to be my friend and not eat me. Wing better now, but it still hurts." Rono lifted his wounded wing and gazed at it sadly. "I think I fly crooked now."

"I think I can heal Rono's wing," Jadon offered, examining his damaged wing with glowing fingers. He nodded as his hands stroked the wing. "I sense it was not a complete break, which is good. The damage would be more pronounced and he would not have been able to fly so soon after his injury. Fortunately, gryphons are hearty creatures."

"I'm hearty and brave," Rono said with a nod.

"A little Drusai healing and your wing will no longer be crooked. It should help ease your pain too," Jadon promised. His hands glowed with Drusai healing magic, touching the wing gingerly and lightly. "All better, Rono?"

Rono cautiously extended his wing and flapped it. "No hurt now."

"Thank you," Runa smiled, touching Jadon's shoulder.

Darkleaf and Redstorm gathered around Rono. "You shall be made an honorary member of Raven Wing for such valor," Redstorm declared.

Darkleaf agreed, and nuzzled Rono with affection. "Yes, no gryphon has ever done what you have done. The Wasteland is a cursed and terrible place, yet you survived it!"

"The wolf knows we aren't evil, right?" Mellypip asked.

"Grimm is just shy," Rono whispered.

"Oh Rono, you must tell me everything so I can write your adventure," Mellypip insisted. "It will be epic!"

"I fought goblins and assassins too," Dabiro moaned. "No one's asking me about my heroic deeds for some epic."

Liat patiently ruffled the badger's fur. "Dabiro, just living with you is epic."

Surya shook her beak. "We will have epic trouble if we do not do something about Koll and Obsydia."

Neelam nodded and gave his snow eagle a sympathetic glance. Neelam pushed himself to his feet, steadier now after Jadon's healing touch.

"But Obsydia is still trapped in her tomb of crystal?" Ulric asked.

"Yes, but Grimm said they moved her using the Eye of Shadows. She could be anywhere. Obsydia has allies and worse—she has worshippers. You better advise your father, Prince Ulric."

Ulric kissed Opaline's hand, "I must go my love, and tell Father what has happened."

After Prince Ulric departed, Jadon's eyes burned with anger. "That's why Ambera's grave was violated. Koll stole her flesh for some wicked diabolistic spell!"

Runa took his hand and put her head on his shoulder. "I know, I know," she whispered.

Neelam picked up his staff and hobbled toward the backdoor. "The wolf told us all that has transpired in Skarros and I believe him. That's why we risked the Eye of Shadows to come home quickly and why I'm anxious for Cathal to get his butt back here."

Opaline turned her dazzling smile on the wolf and held out her hand, unafraid. "There, there," she said, "you're among friends now. Poor thing, you look starved! Want something to eat? Come inside. Grimm is a very interesting name. I am Opaline."

Rono exclaimed, nodding his head. "See Grimm! Opaline is so pretty isn't she? Just like I told you! He's wanted to meet Princess Opaline for a long time."

"He wanted to meet me?" Opaline gasped.

"The gryphon sure loves to babble," Gabriel grumbled.

Opaline's head jerked toward Gabriel. "Shut up! Rono is our friend. He's done many brave things too and he has suffered too! What have you done of late—drink a tavern dry?"

"My apologies, Princess," Gabriel replied humbly with a bowed head.

Mellypip could not determine if Gabriel was genuinely sorry or was mocking her. He looked at Opaline with dark eyes that were very much like the wolf's—hungry and sad.

"She's right you know," Namir said to his sorcerer. "We have vital information about Koll, our greatest enemy, because of Rono."

"I am also sorry, my familiar, for acting like an insensitive ogre," Gabriel said with bowed head. "My apologies to everyone."

"I cannot sense your magic," Grimm said to Opaline at last. "Where is it?"

"My magic?" Opaline gasped, surprised. "What do you mean?"

"Grimm says your magic is like sunlight," Rono said eagerly.

Opaline sat back on her heels and looked at the scruffy black wolf. "You think my magic is like sunlight?"

Taran crouched next to Opaline and grinned. "That wolf is smart. He knows a compliment goes a long way with my sister."

The wolf allowed Opaline to stroke his fur. Grimm gazed into Opaline's face, confused. "I sensed your magic on the troll. The troll was evil, but your sorcery was pure. Why are you hiding your magic?"

Opaline nervously smoothed the folds of her yellow dress, eyes downcast. "Well, I'm not really hiding it. I wear an amulet of sorcerer bane to control it, you see. My sorcery tends to escape me in the most unexpected ways. Ask my friend Runa. She has endured my magical mistakes."

Runa shook her head. "You really need to get over that! I wasn't hurt. I just required a haircut afterward."

"Then ask Gorvanus!" Opaline cried. "No, you can't—because I turned him into a troll!" She covered her face with her hands. "My sorcery is dangerous. Gorvanus was an evil, vile man who worked for Koll, but nobody deserves to be cursed into being a troll. I don't want to hurt anyone, but it happens. My sorcery tends to be a little... wild."

"Wild I understand," Grimm said. "I am wild."

Taran whispered to his sister. "Remove the sorcerer bane. Just for a moment. It's alright. I trust you won't enchant us into anything disgusting. The wolf just wants to sense your magic. Let him."

With hesitation, Opaline removed the sorcerer bane from her neck and dropped it into Taran's hand. Opaline then reached her hand out to Grimm, who sniffed and then licked her palm. "Now your magic is free."

"I think you have a new friend," Runa laughed.

"Are all these mages and animals part of your pack?" Grimm asked, looking at everyone.

"Yes, they are." Opaline laughed and rubbed Grimm's head. "This is Taran, my brother and Runa is my best friend. And now you're part of our pack too, Grimm. Let's get you something to eat. We have a larder full of meat. You can have the pancakes for dessert. My mother and her familiar will be glad to meet you too. Her familiar is a white wolf named Arial! I just know you will be great friends!"

Grimm followed Opaline, staying close to her side as she gently talked to him. "You will love it here. After you have eaten, I'll give you a bath. I hope you don't mind rose scented soap."

The crystal Caliste wore on a chain glowed. She touched it and smiled widely. "Yes!"

"What is it?" Runa asked.

"It's a message from Cathal. He made this before he left. The crystal's glowing blue, so they've made it home and all are safe. They should be here shortly!" Caliste and Runa embraced happily, Mellypip squished between them.

Rono observed Opaline and Grimm together. "I think Grimm is happy now. That's good. Grimm has been alone, except for his father's ghost."

Runa and Mellypip both gasped. "Ghost?"

CHAPTER THIRTY-THREE

Stunned, everyone stared at the glass jar on the dining room table, glowing with sorcery.

Runa suppressed a giggle. "I don't believe it. Is that really—"

"Yes, that's Xabral," Cathal confirmed, arms crossed over his chest.

Xabral, shrunk down to a mere five inches long by Cathal's sorcery, fought with fury against his confinement. The miniature scorpion snake's black and red scales glistened as he flayed his tiny stinger against the thick glass.

"He can't get out, can he?" Mellypip asked.

Cathal tapped the miniscule air holes shimmering with magic. "It's safe, Melly. I reinforced the jar with extra spells to prevent his escape and breakage. He's a vicious creature, even this small."

Mellypip solemnly sat just a few feet from Xabral's prison jar. "He is no longer the terrible nine-foot serpent fiend that reigned at Koll's side. If only you could do that to Koll?"

"I would pay to see that," Caliste grinned.

He's not so scary now, Mellypip said to Runa through the bonding.

Xabral is almost cute, if I did not know how evil that slithery varmint was, Runa replied.

Big or small, he's wicked and deserves many whacks from my staff, Mellypip proclaimed, staff firmly gripped in his paws.

Even so, you should not poke the evil one, Runa cautioned.

"What are you going to do with him?" Liat asked. "Ransom him?"

Dabiro poked his nose over the edge of the table and licked his chops. "Sprinkle him with a bit of salt. Perhaps roasted on toast?"

Hysterical, Xabral thrashed against the glass.

"Stop it, Dabiro," Cathal warned and sat down, never taking his eyes off the snake. "No, we hold onto Xabral until my family is released from the curse. If Koll tries to stop me, then I can use Xabral as a bargaining tool. I loathe this, but Koll has forced my hand. Even so, I would not willingly give him back to Koll unless forced to. Xabral is responsible for multiple deaths, including Eberr, when he helped Koll escape execution."

"I will never forget or forgive," Pointessa said.

"Nor should you," Cathal agreed somberly.

Runa hugged Cathal tightly. "I'm just grateful you made it back safely."

"We can credit Sirah's knowledge of the temple and Panthara's keen memory of Koll's chambers. Because of that we achieved our goal." He bowed his head to Panthara. "Thank you for your assistance. It made a difference."

"I am honored to help, Cathal," Panthara responded and bowed her head. "I hope your family is restored to you."

"Traitor!" Xabral accused. "Faithless witch! You turned your back on the Dark! Koll has not forgotten your betrayal!"

Panthara showed no fear or regret, only contempt as she confronted Xabral. "I have not forgotten Koll's lies and manipulation, Snake. Nor your cruelty to my poor familiar. So hold your forked tongue before I snip it off and feed it to Azmadu."

"Zhelon Thor will remember our visit for a long, long time," Ulan laughed, holding a very content Rosepetal in his huge hands. "My warlord performance was magnificent if I do say so myself."

"Grandpa, how did you make it back so fast from Urgonclaw? Neelam and the others just returned, but they used something called the Eye of Shadows. Did they have one in Rygon's Temple?"

Cathal shuddered. "Thankfully no, we didn't have to use such a dreadful device; however, some borrowed gryphons were quite helpful."

"Borrowed?" Caliste asked slyly. "And you didn't leave those poor horses in Urgonclaw did you?"

"Liberated," Cathal said with a wink, "with a bit of sorcerous infusion to speed the way home. I would never leave anyone behind, including our horses. I sent a message to the horses to leave and follow the same trail back home. They should be fine. Urgonclaw has no qualms about sacrificing humans, so I shudder to leave an innocent animal behind."

Taran's plump marmalade cat, MacTabbish, observed the oddity of a shrunken Xabral hissing with rage in his glass vessel. His orange eyes sparkled with mischief and his ears folded back. "I say, the snake is a wee bitty thing now. Poetic justice, if you ask me. Let me play with him for a spell, Cathal. Teach the vicious critter some manners."

"Xabral has many enemies in the familiar clan, but we need him unscathed…for now," Belwyn cautioned.

Xabral's minuscule voice piped from inside his glass prison, exposing tiny white fangs. "Infidels! Blasphemers! Defilers of the Dark! I'll have vengeance on you all! Just wait until Koll finds you! Not even the grave will protect you from Koll's wrath!"

"Silence, scaly!" Mellypip ordered and swatted the top of the jar with his little staff. "Bad snake."

Xabral coiled into a ball and sulked.

"Somehow Xabral sounds less intimidating with his wee squeaky voice," MacTabbish commented and reached his chubby paw out to swat the jar.

Belwyn's bright yellow eyes settled on MacTabbish with impatience. "Unless you want your furry rump pecked, please restrain yourself from tormenting the snake—even though it's tempting."

"We've got trouble anyway that surpasses a kidnapped familiar, even Koll's," Cathal grimly pointed out. "I couldn't leave Xabral there. Now with Obsydia spirited away and under the protection of our enemies, anything can happen. The enchantment we wove a thousand years ago could be undone if Koll can put together the right ritualistic spell, especially since there is demon woman named Chimera and the immortal daughter of Ahridum guiding his every step. They have access to the blackest sorceries and secrets. Our world faces doom from darkness, and we must stop it!"

Runa touched Cathal's cheek, where the demoness had sliced away a piece of his flesh. "Grandpa, you should clean that cut on your face. I think you need stitches too."

"It's nothing," Cathal insisted. "I feel foolish enough letting the demon woman close enough to nick me."

"How familiar that sounds," Surya remarked, perched on a chair.

"He never listens to me either," Belwyn added.

Neelam limped into the room. "Well, I am now fixed up good and proper." He leaned against his staff, looking at Surya. "Raghnall even gave me five stitches. Happy?"

"Thrilled," Surya answered dryly.

MacTabbish jumped down. "I think I'll find Taran. He's going to need me." Mellypip looked around.

"Where are Opaline and Taran?" Mellypip asked, looking around. "I just know they'll want to see teeny Xabral too.

"Taran and Opaline are with their mother," Myrsalian said. "You might as well know. While still in the temple, we learned Tarsicius is dead."

Shocked, Runa looked up at Myrsalian. "Opaline's father is dead? Oh, I know he was cruel to her and I did not like him, but I know she still loved him."

"That is true," Myrsalian agreed. "Tragically, Prince Levandius is the new emperor. From what we witnessed in the temple, he has chosen the path of evil and has allied forces with Zhelon Thor. Tarsicius treated my daughter with contempt when he learned she had sorcery years ago. He imprisoned Sirah in a sorcerer lock and cast her into a prison, until I rescued her. Tarsicius could not part with her nor accept her. Personally, I hated the man for this, and later, for the exile of my grandchildren. Despite all this, they need to know the truth. Sirah is breaking the news to them now. I know my daughter still loved him, despite everything, as did Opaline."

"I will be there for her," Runa whispered.

Cathal took a scroll from his coat with bloodstones at each end.

"Is that the scroll?" Caliste whispered. "Its design is exquisite. Pity it's so wicked."

Cathal stared at it with hatred. "Yes. I read the scroll to confirm it was the correct ritual. My language skills are a bit rusty when it comes to bloodstone tongue, but it's amazing what you remember. This is the original scroll, created during the Bloodstone time."

"I can't believe you escaped from Rygon's temple with that!" Neelam remarked. "Nice to know you haven't lost your touch, boy."

"That *boy* blew out a whole wall in the temple when we escaped," Darcus said proudly.

"It all sounds quite exciting and would make a wonderful story," Mellypip said, looking at Belwyn expectantly.

Belwyn blinked and patiently replied, "Yes Furball, I will tell you everything in great detail when we're finished undoing demonic curses and babysitting snappish scorpion snakes."

Mellypip swished his tail happily. "Thank you, Belwyn. I'm going to need a lot of writing paper for this one. My little notebook is almost full."

"Somehow it was easier when I gave you a weekly word for your vocabulary lessons," Belwyn moaned.

"Less annoying for us though," Darcus commented, grinning.

Runa touched the edge of the dark scroll and a flood of dark images made her dizzy and she stumbled back.

"Are you alright?" Jadon asked, gripping her arm.

Pale, Runa nodded and quickly wiped her hands on her skirt, as though fouled. "Grandpa, how can you bear to touch it with your bare hands? I sensed so much darkness from just that brief touch."

Cathal gingerly held the scroll. "Unfortunately, this is not my first time handling dark relics. I spent my youth researching blood-stone magic with my master, Borel, when we were seeking a way to defeat Obsydia. Your Drusai ability is also making you more sensitive, dear. Best not to touch it at all. My Yllia could not bear to touch them either, so it is a normal response. These magics have a strong effect on the innocent."

"Will the reversal spell take long to create?" Runa asked.

"I'm not sure, but it will be soon. We know the basics of what to do. We just want to be sure. Iona, Neelam, and Raghnall will help me. I'll do the full translation from the bloodstone tongue, which should not take too long, but its dangerous work to undo such a dark spell. It's going to be a complicated ritual. Undoing such a powerful and wicked ritual will be draining. Are you sure you want to be there, Runa? I know I can't stop you, but this is the worst kind of diabolism we must undo. It will be worse than the cave in Mowad. This scroll is of demonic origin, most likely from Obsydia's personal collection. It makes me itch just to touch the thing."

Runa nodded solemnly. "I will be there. I must be there."

"We better get to work," Neelam suggested.

"What should I do?" Runa asked.

"Be patient," Cathal told her gently. "Until then, be ready to help Opaline and Taran. It's going to be a hard and cold night for us all."

Panthara carefully stepped closer to Runa. "Cathal is right. Opaline will need you more than ever, Runa. A daughter's love for her father is often unfathomable and without reason. I understand this fact more than most."

Before Runa could speak, Panthara walked away.

~ * ~

No one slept. Runa and Caliste kept the coffee flowing as the mages worked against time to formulate the reversal ritual. Runa and Mellypip stayed out of the way while mages with centuries of experience worked, despite their eager curiosity. It was near dawn, and those not involved in the careful conjuration of magic anxiously waited.

I hope we are in time, Runa said to Mellypip who was curled up in her lap. *I keep thinking about the tree of bones, how they are dying. What if we are too late? I always wished to know my mother. What if they fail? What if my only chance is gone?*

We must have faith, Mellypip sent back. *Cathal and Neelam understand this dark magic. They are the most ancient of mages. Iona knows about souls and the Otherworld. And Raghnall is the best mystical healer. I do not think this gathering is an accident. I think fate wants to help us. I feel sorry for Balder. He has been guarding the tree of bones for Raghnall. It must be lonely and scary there.*

I think you are beginning to like Balder.

He's not so bad, as long as he doesn't slobber all over me. He was kind when I was sad about Rono

We should do something nice for him, no matter what happens.

Do bears like honey?

Oh yes, I think you could call it drobba for bears.

Iona rushed down the stairs, without her concealing black veils, her face bright with hope. "We are ready. I think we are ready."

"You completed the reversal ritual?" Runa asked.

Iona nodded and embraced Runa. "Yes, at least we hope so. I pray this magic can undo the tree of bones and free them. Thanks to Cathal's translation, it was not as difficult as we feared."

"Demonic tongue tends to be strange and guttural," Neelam said. "This is Bloodstone magic, the darkest brand."

"There is no light in its origin," Iona said. "I sensed that when I too touched the tree of bones, as I am sure you did, Runa. This is different. The souls of Yllia and Rualla, whom the tree of bones holds captive, are the only elements of Light I sensed there. We can only do the ritual—and hope."

"Scary if even a Necromancer is afraid," Mellypip said.

"Aye, it's not very comforting," MacTabbish agreed.

Haunted by the memory of the tree of bones, it filled Runa with dread. *They are dying.* That thought had haunted Runa every day since she found the tree of bones in that cursed forest. "If they cannot survive when they are free of the darkness, I want to kiss them goodbye."

Cathal briefly embraced Runa and grabbed his staff. "At the first sign of danger, such as if Koll shows up to take Xabral back, Neelam and Darcus have my full permission to get you out of there. Xabral is a bargaining tool right now, but it could also draw Koll out into the open where he could be vulnerable."

"I would welcome that," Darcus said. "I will stand by you, Cathal. If Koll shows up to fight, he will have to face all of us."

"May I come?" Panthara asked simply, head held high, holding Azmadu in her arms. His eye patch was crooked, and his black tongue lolled out of his mouth as he panted in little grunts.

"Yes, Panthara, I want you to come," Runa replied.

"Thank you," Panthara whispered.

"Come Panthara." Iona beckoned. "We will go on ahead and prepare the way."

After they left, Gabriel and Namir joined them in the living room. He had washed and changed, though the circles under his eyes were still quite vivid.

"I thought Pointessa banished you to the crystal room," Runa said, throwing on her cloak.

Gabriel took an empty cup and filled it with coffee. "Alas, in all the chaos an important message from Thema has been delayed. That damned crystal needs to be replaced."

"What's the message?" Cathal asked.

"It's from Jiana, and an Ironian fellow named Hinkleburr Crowyn."

"Jiana! Hinkleburr! My friends!" Mellypip cried with excitement.

"What's wrong?" Runa asked when she saw Gabriel's bleak expression.

"Hate to be blunt folks, but more bad news. Koll attacked them in Thema at the royal museum. Queen Sarabia was there to witness it as well."

"More foul mirror work," Neelam grumbled.

"Anyone killed?" Cathal asked bluntly.

"Fortunately, no," Gabriel replied. "Koll seemed focused on taking a relic they believe to be the Scythe of Rygon. Jiana swears Koll just appeared from the corner of the room and took the scythe. That's the short version. I know we're rushed for time. Queen Sarabia is furious. Jiana confirms it was a bloodstone relic and highly magical."

Neelam hobbled toward the door, scowling. "Damn it! The fiend now has the scythe. They probably need it for their own profane ritual."

"What is this scythe?" Runa asked.

"Another hell relic forged in the netherworld," Neelam said. "According to myth it was cooled by Rygon's own breath. It was supposed to reap the souls of warriors on the battlefield. Or punish cowards by taking their souls to the Dark Netherworld. There are many legends around it. It's quite real, but it was supposed to be buried in some tomb."

"I thought the Scythe of Rygon was a myth," Runa said.

Belwyn shook his beak, golden eyes grim. "One that's about to bite us in the ass. If Koll was busy doing Obsydia's bidding, it explains why he hasn't shown up yet, especially now that he has access to Obsydia's mirror. He may not even be aware Xabral is missing."

"That won't last," Cathal said.

Gabriel drank down his coffee in one gulp and refilled it. "Need an extra staff, Cathal? I could use a sweaty, magical battle to take the edge off. I'd also love to get Koll in my sights. Make him pay for what he did to my father and everyone else he has made suffer."

"We can always use your hot temper in a fight," Cathal invited.

"Are you sober?" Belwyn inquired sharply.

"Like a cloistered monk," Gabriel swore. He rubbed Namir's head. "Come on kitty. We have a job that does not involve ale."

"That makes me happy," Namir replied.

Neelam shimmered and shapeshifted into a snow eagle. "I'll see you folks at the tree of bones. Come, Surya." They flew out the open window on snowy wings.

Sirah and Arial returned with a solemn Opaline and Taran. Sirah shapeshifted into white wolf and sprinted out the open door with Arial. Taran was tight-lipped and fled outside without speaking to them. MacTabbish, in a rare burst of speed, quickly chased after his sorcerer. Only Opaline remained, with Grimm at her side.

"Are Sirah and Taran alright?" Runa asked softly. "Are *you* alright?"

Opaline nodded and wiped her eyes. With no need for words, Runa and Opaline embraced each other. Then they quietly left together side by side, with Mellypip in Runa's arms and Grimm close and steadfast.

Xabral little head weaved. "Koll's magic will not be undone by such unworthy and feeble mages! Koll will vanquish all of you into dust! I shall have vengeance!"

"Shut up snake!" Darcus warned.

Xabral hissed and cursed in crude language until Darcus snatched up the jar with his large, calloused hands. "Silence, you nasty snake, else I will take up Dabiro's suggestion and serve you on toast." He shoved Xabral into a leather satchel. "This malicious little snake is going with us for safekeeping."

Belwyn's golden eyes were hard. "Let's hope we don't have to keep him for long,"

Chapter Thirty-Four

Encircled by the wall of thorns, the tree of bones was approachable only though the tunnel Runa mystically carved that first day. She walked through the wintry tunnel quickly, holding Mellypip close, staff in her other hand.

It's so strange, Melly. I don't remember doing any of this.

I'm glad you don't remember, since you were ensorcelled by a strange power. You frightened everyone, including me. I lost you in those terrible moments.

The power of my mother and grandmother summoned me here, not the tree of bones conjured by Koll. They slept for years, waiting. Koll's bloodstone scroll not only imprisoned them, but prevented rescue. His dark spell buried this whole area with thorns. No one knew they were even here.

Until your magic burned through it all, Runa. Their magic cries led you to them, but the method of it scared me. You shattered the bone forest, Runa. I'm going to write your heroic tale.

I just hope it ends with happily ever after.

Runa exited the long-barbed passageway and walked across the parched loam until she came to the base of the tree. She gazed up at the images of her mother and grandmother, their frozen faces the only stark beauty in this bitter place. Their hands were clasped together, their eyes closed, heads held proudly high in tragic pose, refusing to bow in submission, even to death. The tree towered above them; bony branches heavy with black leaves tipped with red thorns. This ominous giant of the grim forest spread over them like a canopy of death.

Mellypip burrowed his little chin into Runa's mass of hair, feeling sadness. She whispered a brief prayer to Araema.

The tree looked old, before bad magic killed it, Mellypip thought.

The tree was ancient before the curse transformed it. Poor thing. Now its bark and leafs are a skeleton of death. How much of the woodland is cursed?

Grandpa Cathal says several acres, but even he is not sure. I better start laying the light crystals. Caliste said it was part of the ritual.

Runa opened the pouch of light crystals and placed them on the bone-crusted earth, her booted feet crunching chips of yellowed bone that were once blades of grass.

Mellypip thoughts of the many forest creatures that might have been snatched in the wake of Koll's evil spell brought a different kind of shiver. Grief for innocent life lost fueled his anger.

Panthara helped sow the light crystals around the wood. Silent and soft of step as she carried her velvet bag of crystals and placed them where Cathal directed. Taran helped her, MacTabbish in his arms, a gentle guide. Azmadu followed Panthara, his blue and green scales contrasting with the blanched landscape of the forest. The crill lizard's little wings quivered with fear and he did not stray from Panthara.

Even fierce crill lizards are afraid here, Mellypip observed.

Runa and Panthara, uneasy sisters, nodded as they passed each other. *Do you think she meant what she said, about wanting our family restored?* Runa asked.

Mellypip did not want to cast his opinion on this sensitive subject. He clutched his staff for wisdom. *Maybe. She hasn't done anything evil since she woke up. That's a good sign. But still, best not mention it to Opaline. She and Panthara tend to bubble and fight when they get too close.*

A soft hand touched Runa's arm. She turned to find Caliste, loving and comforting Aunt Caliste, ready with a strong embrace. Caliste put her arm around her shoulders, bolstering her with fresh strength.

"It's going to be fine," Caliste assured her. "Cathal is the best sorcerer I know."

"If anyone can unravel this wickedness, it's him," Sanura added, her blue eyes watchful in this terrible haven.

"I know Grandpa is powerful," Runa agreed. "This is not just about a spell; this is about the life. He lost them all those years ago. Now he may lose them all over again, even if the ritual is a success. I know this is hard for you too. I dreamed of them all my life, but you grew up with them."

"Losing them broke him," Caliste whispered. "Cathal withdrew and became a shadow, lost to everything and everyone. When Ryen brought you to him, you brought Cathal back to life. You must be that anchor again if need be."

Belwyn descended to the parched earth, though he was clearly uncomfortable on the ground, as he moved back and forth on his talons. "Are all the crystals planted as Cathal instructed?"

"Yes, Belwyn," Runa replied, turning away to drop another crystal, brushing a tear away. Belwyn gazed keenly at her but did not pry.

Iona summoned them away. "Come Runa, we are about to begin

to the ritual. Be ready, child. Though you are young and inexperienced with such a powerful ritual, your blood ties to Yllia and Rualla will be a strong force. If you wish to decline, you may do so."

"No," Runa answered. "I want to help. I am ready." She joined the others, taking her place between Cathal and Caliste.

Opaline gave Runa a quick hug in passing, since she was only witnessing the ritual. She retreated outside the circle with Grimm. The others not participating joined her and watched in silence from outside the circle. Though Panthara was experienced in high rituals, Iona suggested it would be best if she didn't participate.

Darcus took watch at the edge of the grove, sword already in hand and Redstorm at his side, his breath misty in the raw air. Darkleaf watched over Rono. Panthara and Taran stood together, their familiars in their arms, eyes anxious. The familiars stayed close to their mages, though Baldur's enormous bulk took up a great deal of space, protective and watchful, focused on the magic being summoned. Pointessa's lost look was heartbreaking as she watched everyone pair up.

Cathal turned to Gabriel. "I know you're a seasoned sorcerer, but I would ask you be ready for battle."

"That I can do," Gabriel replied.

Cathal tossed the jar containing an angry Xabral to Gabriel, who caught it with his large hand. "If the snake gets too annoying, feel free to cast a silence spell on him," Cathal told him.

"My pleasure," Gabriel replied in his gritty voice. Xabral glared at Gabriel, but the sorcerer's brittle stare unnerved the snake and he curled into tiny ball to brood.

Runa looked at the mystic circle gathering magic—Cathal, Gabriel, Neelam, Caliste, Jadon, Iona, Ulan, Myrsalian, Sirah, Liat, and Raghnall. Solemn, their familiars close, they concentrated. Mellypip sensed the swell of light magic, but even this power did not wash away the darkness.

Each mage held a white crystal as they formed a circle before the tree of bones. Neelam stepped forward to the center of the circle and wrote on the air with sorcerous fingers; the shimmering golden runic symbols remained floating in the air. They were known to Runa as symbols for light and healing. Cathal joined Raghnall and his fingers scribed darker, more powerful symbols that hovered in the air. Iona joined them, her words glowing with a different blue light that mingled with the mystical script. As Raghnall and Cathal wrote glowing magical words, the other mages lifted the light crystals in their hands and cast even more light onto them, so they were as little suns in this den of shadow.

Cathal removed the Bloodstone scroll from his robes and lifted it with both hand, as though making an offering. His voice was powerful as he spoke:

> *Bloodstone Curse, born where Darkness dwells*
> *I command dominion over this spell*
> *Open your leaf of shadows and gloom*
> *Reveal the words that cast flesh and flora into doom*
> *Reveal your secret curse of bone*
> *So your Darkness will be overthrown*

The scroll in his hands rose in the air. It floated there, and the scroll seemed to struggle against the light magic around it. The mystical words lingering in the air wrapped around the scroll, holding it captive. It unrolled to its full length, and every symbol and word of the spell was exposed. Binding the scroll was the first step, and Cathal's powerful sorcery held it captive. Cathal then took his light crystal and sent streams of thin blue light that coiled around the scroll. His voice rang out, "In the name of the Light, I banish this curse, I banish these words, I banish this spell. Release your hold and return to the Netherworld of Darkness."

Runa stepped forward at Cathal's signal. She stood before the ominous floating scroll, her voice clear. "In the name of the Light, I banish this curse, I banish these words, I banish this spell. Release your hold and return to the Netherworld of Darkness." She closed her eyes, and her light, that strange, beautiful light that was a mixture of Drusai and Sorcery, flooded from the crystal in her palm. The brilliant light wound itself around the Bloodstone scroll. The scroll jerked in the air but remained captive.

Runa stepped away for Caliste, who took her place, and with regal grace repeated the same words of the enchantment. When she was done, her light formed its bright knot around the scroll and she returned to the circle.

Jadon stepped forward, his long black hair swept back and deep blue eyes bright. He spoke the spell with a passionate voice. His hands, so strong with bow and sword, glowed now the Drusai light that streamed from his crystal and encircled the floating bloodstone scroll like a ribbon. Then he stepped back.

Each mage took a turn and repeated the chant before the Bloodstone relic that floated in the air and bound the scroll with light. When they finished, they fell silent as the script on the scroll, written in a strange mysterious ink, glowed like red fire. Then all the mages chanted together the spell so carefully created to shatter this curse—

Bloodstone Curse that binds this forest old
Bloodstone Curse that holds two lives in bones so cold
We banish this Darkness and summon the Light
Free the two graceful souls bound where it darkens
Vanquish forever this evil curse, to the Light we hearken

They continued the mystical mantra. Cathal stepped away from the circle and stood before the suspended scroll. He recited the bottom line of the scroll, speaking its strange demon tongue. Runa shivered, remembering those words from the vision she had when she saw the past. She took a deep breath and concentrated on the light crystal in her hand. Then when Cathal finished reading the curse, he commanded aloud in normal speech, "In the name of Light, I banish this curse back to the Dark Realms."

The scroll snapped and sizzled as it battled the bonds of Light strangling the Dark. The demonic letters congealed into lava-like flame and dripped from the ancient parchment to the ground!

Cathal read aloud the next line of the curse, and then repeated the banishment spell, and the ancient script burned and literally peeled off the page, raining the ground with burning ash. Cathal repeated this for each line of the curse, while they continued to repeat the spell in the background, until Cathal eradicated every line of the curse.

Look at the scroll! The paper is blank now! Mellypip cried in her head.

Now barren of writing, the scroll hovered in the air, bound by strands of light conjured from the mages. The bloodstones at the ends drained of their dark light, shattered into fragments of red and black. The paper crumbled and wrinkled as they all continued their chant, their voices rising with power in the terrible grove of death. The paper shuddered as it seared with embers of light, spilling its ashes to the ground. It continued burning until nothing was left of the scroll, not even the rod that held it, for it too dissolved into dusty ash.

The mages ceased their impassioned magical chant—and waited.

Silence followed, broken only by the chill wind. Mellypip and Runa clung to each other, breathless, waiting. Suddenly a force rushed up from the earth! The light crystals flared like bright suns, feeding the parched ground with pure radiance as Light magic did its work. The healing was not smooth and peaceful, for the earth was angry at its long torment and rumbled beneath their feet. The ground heaved up and they were all tossed about. Runa fell into Jadon's arms, and Mellypip got squished between them. Opaline stumbled, but Grimm remained close, howling as only a wolf could. Arial's mournful howl joined Grimm's in the chaos. Then a loud boom deafened them; they all fell silent with fear and hope.

A wash of brilliant light flooded the forest, banishing bleached bones and death. The wall of cruel thorns that guarded the grove dissolved into the earth. The tree of bones transformed from the mangled exposed roots to the tip of the longest skeletal branch. A flood of life surged through the deathly tree, turning it from yellow bone and black leaf, to rich bark and green leaf. In its metamorphosis, the bone statues of Yllia and Rualla transformed too. Bone transformed into flesh and hair again. They woke and cried out in painful voices as they were freed from their prison.

"They're free!" Runa shouted, running toward them.

Cathal and Liat followed, their familiars rushing behind. Cathal caught Yllia, and she moaned with agony as he cradled her in his arms. Liat caught Rualla, who cried out once more, and then fell silent.

"Cathal! Rualla won't wake!" Liat cried, holding her limp body.

Runa fell to her knees next to Liat. Something tugged inside Runa when she touched Liat. Her Drusai powers sparked and unveiled a revelation she was not expecting, nor could she think about now. *He loves her. Liat loves my mother!* Runa gasped to Mellypip through the bonding.

Yllia was not fully conscious but stirred with life. She struggled for breath, and for an instant opened her eyes, and a shaky fingertip touched Cathal's face. "Damn it Cathal, you know I...hate...beards!"

Cathal laughed and cried simultaneously, but this exhaustive phrase sapped her strength and Yllia fell unconscious again.

Runa grabbed her mother's pale hand. "Mother? Please wake up!" Runa begged, touching her face. Then Rualla began to convulse.

"Raghnall!" Cathal cried. "We need you now!"

Raghnall barked orders as he rushed toward them, "Quick! Bring the wagon! Keep them warm!"

The wagon was stationed just outside the wall of thorns which had vanished. Ulan ran and leapt to the wagon and drove it into the grove. Sirah covered the back of the wagon with thick blankets. Cathal and Liat carried Yllia and Rualla away from the tree and gently laid them down in the wagon. Raghnall waved everyone away and sent a wave of soft blue magic over Rualla which formed a nimbus around her and calmed her shaking. "This is only a bandage until I can get them somewhere safe."

Runa dropped her staff to the ground, unaware the carved panther eyes glowed hot, but Mellypip saw.

"Runa, your staff!" Mellypip pointed, frightened of the shimmering eyes.

Rono spread his wings wide in terror. "Evil is coming! Evil is coming!"

"Get them out of here—now," Cathal commanded.

"Demons rising!" Gabriel shouted, pointing at the growing shadows beneath the tree. "Damn, are those goblins?"

Pointessa's quills rose threateningly. "Let's see if they bleed."

"They're using the damned Eye of Shadows!" Neelam shouted.

Neelam and Gabriel fired deadly magic at the hideous creatures crawling from the gnarled roots of the ancient tree. The shadows cast by heavy leaf and branch formed into a portal of darkness that exploded into the newly sunlit woods. Goblins invaded the grove from other points of shadow. They shrieked with pain as Neelam sent spears of magic at them. It crippled them and drove them back. More enemies rushed from the shadows, not only goblins, but human assassins wielding blades.

Cathal confronted the advancing assassins and demons, staff blazing, Belwyn at his side. "Koll sent some friends."

"Let's give them a nice red welcome," Gabriel suggested, marching toward the fray.

CHAPTER THIRTY-FIVE

Mellypip's terrified focus was forced from the glowing eyes on Runa's staff to the horde of goblins emerging from darkness with drooling maws. Runa backed away and scooped Mellypip with one hand and grabbed her staff with the other. "This is bad," Runa cried.

Mellypip tried to morph into his giant wampu size which was his special familiar magic, but nothing happened. Frustrated at his failure to summon his power, he could only stay close to his sorceress.

"Raghnall, Caliste! Get them out of here! Runa, go with them!" Cathal ordered, his staff blasting brilliant white sorcery into all the light crystals they had planted in the wood, flooding the whole area with bright sorcery. "Darcus, Jadon, protect them!"

The crystals flared as Cathal's sorcery transformed them into a shimmering barricade of latticed-shaped cages of hardened light that trapped the invaders. His network of light shields barred most of the enemy from advancing, but Mellypip noticed a few patches unprotected by the crystals, allowing stray goblins and assassins to crawl through to attack.

Belwyn winged over Runa's head. "Get in the wagon now, young lady, before I start pecking!"

Jadon seized Runa by the waist. Mellypip leapt to her shoulder and clung to her hair. Jadon carried her to the back of the wagon and dropped her next to Rualla and Yllia. Mellypip became entangled in Runa's long hair, his staff clutched in one paw.

"I can fight!" Runa protested.

"You can die. I forbid it," Jadon snapped. He quickly kissed her before turning to join Cathal. Jadon glanced over his shoulder at Mellypip with stern blue eyes. "Mellypip, *watch her!*"

Frantically trying to unravel himself from Runa's tangled mass of hair, Mellypip cried, "Yes, sir!"

Runa looked at her mother and grandmother and knew she could not leave them. She took her mother's pale hand and touched her grandmother's cheek. "Drive!" she called. "Hurry!"

"Look after them," Liat shouted as he leapt from the back of the wagon to join Cathal. Pointessa and Dabiro followed him, growling and anxious for battle. The mages formed a line of defense around Cathal.

Caliste climbed up the wagon next to Raghnall and grabbed the reins. "Those crystals were a good idea."

"What do you mean a good idea? I was laying a trap!" Runa exclaimed, covering her mother with another blanket. She touched her mother's hand and winced at its coldness.

"Yes, but we didn't want to worry you," Caliste said. "Cathal knew there would be trouble. We took precautions."

"Raghnall, I will follow, but for now I fight," Baldur roared. "Go now."

"Taran, quick, Rono can carry you!" Opaline cried. She and Grimm leapt onto the wagon next to Caliste. "Take Panthara with you."

Runa glanced up at Opaline with a raised eyebrow.

Opaline shrugged. "What? I can put my personal feelings aside when there's a crisis."

Taran, MacTabbish tucked under one arm, mounted Rono and pulled Panthara up behind him. "Fly boy!" Taran shouted. Rono spread his wings and carried them up to the sky, Azmadu flying close behind them.

Caliste clicked the reins and drove the wagon. Sparkling green magic flowed from Raghnall's hands and dusted the horses, which propelled their speed to a rapid pace. Runa and Opaline grabbed the sides of the wagon. Jadon and Darcus flew above the wagon, their perytons easily keeping pace with the swift horses.

Mellypip clung to Runa's arm, clutching his precious warrior staff as the wagon jostled over rough terrain. "Aren't Cathal and Belwyn coming with us?"

"We can't just leave them behind!" Runa cried, holding her mother's hand, looking back. "They're outnumbered!"

"Oh, they won't be fighting alone. Cathal made certain of that," Caliste replied smoothly.

Mellypip held onto Runa as the wagon sped away. The invasion of goblins and assassins faded from view, though the smell of sorcery and blood did not.

~ * ~

Assassins and goblins hammered against the magical shields with blades and claws. The few odd demons and assassins who were able to crawl through unprotected dark spots savagely charged the mages. Liat, Myrsalian, Neelam, Sirah, Gabriel, and Ulan stood shoulder-to-shoulder with Cathal, staves fiery with magic as they fought them back, easily taking them down before they advanced close enough to attack.

"This may be easy now, but I think it's time to invite our friends to the fray," Neelam suggested.

"Good idea," Cathal agreed. "We know what's coming." Gray light issued from the staff he held aloft and its magic mushroomed into a great cloud which swept the area, stripping away Cathal's invisibility enchantment to reveal an army of Thill soldiers encircling the grove. Clad in crimson royal armor, astride massive black warhorses, King Caladynn Rhule and his son, Prince Ulric, led their force of warriors closer.

"Archers ready!" Captain Vasya shouted as he rode past the line of warriors. Each royal archer took their position, bow in hand, arrow notched. Vasya spurred his warhorse forward, alongside the King and Prince.

"Clear out now!" Cathal warned everyone. The mages hurried toward the band of soldiers waiting beyond the light shields' perimeter.

King Caladynn raised his sword to signal the archers. "Fire!"

The Thill archers loosed a barrage of arrows, flooding the air with feathered death. Trapped by Cathal's network of magic, the assassins and demons fell quickly to the archer's assault.

Belwyn alighted to Cathal's shoulder. "Are you sure he will come?"

Cathal grimaced. "Positive. We'll need more than simple arrows then, but I made plans for that too."

A thunderous roar erupted, shaking the ground violently.

"Be ready!" Cathal shouted. "I think Koll finally decided to join us."

The earth shuddered again and from its shadowy bowels a giant black and red scorpion snake slithered upward. Koll's giant snake shape smashed mercilessly against the cages of light imprisoning the assassins and goblins. Wails of terror echoed in Koll's destructive wake, but soon they joined their dead comrades as Koll's massive bulk crushed them beneath his weight.

"Where is my familiar?" Koll demanded, the sorcerous form as a giant scorpion snake amplifying his voice to godlike resonance. "Where is Xabral?"

"Now!" Belwyn cried, swooping down to Cathal's shoulder.

Cathal extended his staff and beams of white energy flooded around Koll's snake shape, quickly forming a barricade of light encircling the massive snake. The magical cage expanded, matching Koll's vast proportions as he struggled against his bonds. The sorcery strained, but Cathal's magic held strong.

The massive serpent raised its head, baleful yellow eyes glaring down at Cathal. "Where's my familiar?" Koll's heavy-scaled body writhed, struggling against Cathal's containing wall. "Give him to me now!"

The King's archers aimed their bows, ready to fire their own fury against the caged scorpion snake. From within the cage, Koll summoned his magical shielding, deflecting any deadly magic or arrows.

"You think simple tricks will defeat me?" Koll roared.

Gabriel reached into the pouch he wore and held Xabral's jar high. "Is this what you're looking for? Your little worm?"

Koll's head snapped toward Gabriel, eyes burning with unrestrained anger. Gabriel smiled, shaking the jar vigorously. The tiny scorpion snake banged against the glass, shaken to and fro like a salad, but far less appetizing.

"Want your slimy snake, Koll? Catch!" Gabriel tossed the jar into the air, and as it plummeted back to earth, he gave it a hard, swift kick, sending it flying toward Koll.

Gabriel's action distracted Koll momentarily and he did not notice Belwyn carry an arrow to Cathal. Belwyn dropped the arrow and Cathal caught it easily. Quickly, Cathal traded his staff for a simple long bow from Liat. Cathal hefted the long bow, smoothly notching the arrow. He took aim, ignoring Koll's howls of frustration as the jar with Xabral rolled into the newborn grass, bouncing to a stop against a cage of light confining Koll. Cathal loosed the arrow, just as Koll reared back his head with a final desperate roar of anger. It pierced the neck of the massive snake. Though miniscule compared to the giant snake's body, its effect was considerable. Koll shook his massive head from side to side, as though trying to clear his head. His great body weaved, slightly at first, and then terror filled his fierce, yellow eyes.

Cathal's flinty stare locked on Koll. "Sorcerer bane stings—doesn't it?"

His magic vanquished by the sorcerer bane, Koll howled as his giant snake shape began to shrink smaller and smaller; the scales and stinger vanished, hair and skin became visible as his human shape was forcibly restored. He collapsed to his knees, clutching the arrow protruding from his shoulder.

"Too bad your aim wasn't better," Belwyn remarked dryly, gliding down to earth.

"Let's not quibble," Cathal replied.

"Kill Koll!" King Caladynn commanded. "Now!"

Koll's eyes burned with hatred for the warriors swarming toward him. With blades drawn and archers ready, the Thill soldiers hurried in, eager for the blood of this dark sorcerer. Koll, unable to summon his sorcery as long as the sorcerer bane was lodged in his body, could only look at his executioners as he lay wounded. Caladynn's archers shot their arrows at Koll, unleashing a volley of arrows upon the fallen sorcerer.

Suddenly, an explosion knocked everyone, warrior and mages, backward. Scarlet smoke blinded them. The mages thrown by the blast were buffeted helplessly against the currents of a darkness invading the grove. From the smoke and chaos arose a red-skinned demoness with streaming black hair and fiery eyes. She summoned a shield to deflect the bombardment of arrows before they could strike Koll's prostrate body.

"Chimera," Koll called, dragging himself toward her.

Enraged, Cathal willed himself to stand, though every bone in his body screamed with pain. He recognized the demoness from the temple; the cut on his cheek itched with the memory.

The mages banded together and loosed their magic at both Koll and Chimera, a myriad of colors rained upon her. Neither magic nor the King's archers could penetrate her shield. Cathal sprinted toward Chimera and Koll, driven by fury.

"Cathal, come back!" Belwyn warned, flying after him.

The demoness laughed boldly, and just when Cathal was close she summoned a circle of black fire around her which flared outward. Most of the others managed to evade the demon's fire, using magic or the soldier's raising their shields. Cathal, unwilling to retreat, was brushed by the fire before common sense stopped him. He felt a quick tug on his body and realized Belwyn's telekinetic magic pulled him back before he was consumed in the demon's black fire. His rage and pain roared as Chimera's flames burned his hands and face before he dropped to the ground, magically banishing his fire on his person before it did serious damage.

The deep laughter of the demoness pained Cathal more than his scalded flesh.

Are you trying to kill me? Belwyn screamed in his head.

I was trying to kill Koll.

That's the demon from the temple, and you thought to fight her alone? Belwyn shouted. His wings beat frantically; pecking at Cathal's robes, to make certain his sorcerer was no longer on fire.

I know, I know, Cathal snapped. *Anything useful to tell me?*

Captain Vasya hurled a lance, just as Chimera reached for Koll. It impaled the demoness; a wound that would have gutted an ordinary mortal. She straightened and wrenched it free in a single motion, tossing it aside with a hiss of annoyance.

King Caladynn and Prince Ulric charged, spurring their horses forward. A second wall of hellish fire sprang up, forcing back their fierce warhorses who reared in terror, scarcely avoiding the demon's flames.

"Chimera!" Koll moaned. "Save Xabral!"

Chimera rolled her eyes and scooped up the jar which contained Xabral. Chimera ripped the arrow tipped with sorcerer bane from Koll's shoulder. His blood flowed from the open wound, spilling onto the ground. Chimera flung Koll across her shoulder as though he were no heavier than a feather pillow and dropped into the shadows as easily as diving into black water.

"Damn it!" Cathal raged. His hands and face burnt raw, but the real pain he suffered came in Koll's escape.

Belwyn's anger matched his sorcerer's. "I don't know about you, but I'm tired of evil getting the upper hand."

CHAPTER THIRTY-SIX

Darcus and Jadon carried Yllia and Rualla through the Abbey doors. Abbess Odelia personally directed them to a guest room, with two narrow beds placed side by side. Darcus and Jadon carefully laid Yllia and Rualla on the beds. Runa helped Caliste cover them with blankets. Sanura had shapeshifted into her panther form and guarded the door.

"Is the other room prepared?" Raghnall asked as he gave each patient a cursory examination.

Abbess Odelia nodded nervously, slipping her hands into her long sleeves. "Yes, as you specified, Lord Raghnall. We prepped a potion room. It is in the room across the hall. There were a few mystical herbs we didn't have on hand."

Iona set Amun down on the chair and removed her heavy veils for the task ahead. "That's quite alright, Abbess. We knew that and I brought what was needed with me. We are indebted to you and the sisters for your help. Caliste and I will take care of the rest."

Upon seeing Iona's naked face and hair, Odelia bowed respectfully. "Necromancer, you honor me with this trust. If you need anything, please send for me. I will leave you to your healing. Araema's blessings on you all." Odelia departed silently and closed the door.

Raghnall waved Darcus and Jadon away. "You've done your duty gentlemen. Now leave us."

Caliste and Iona immediately began work at the potion station on a long table in the corner.

"You too, Runa," Raghnall added. "If you want to help, just send us pots of tea to keep us alert. Be a good girl and wait outside. I swear if there's any change, I'll summon you. I promise."

Darcus' firm hand guided Runa out the door. "Come, Runa. They have a lot to do. We will only be in the way."

Runa chewed her lower lip with frustration. *Melly, I want to be with them.*

Mellypip clung to her shoulder and stroked her hair with his paw. *I know, I know. But they need quiet to think and brew big magic.*

Opaline and Grimm joined them in the hallway, disheveled and weary. "What's happening?" she asked.

"They just started," Runa whispered. "Right now we know nothing."

Darcus' keen eyes surveyed the long halls of the Abbey. "Jadon, brighten up these halls. The light's too dim."

"Dim? But there is ample light in this abbey," Jadon replied, looking around.

Darcus looked around suspiciously. "The Eye of Shadows Neelam told us about, remember? Our enemies can use that cursed mirror to step anywhere, as long as there is a fragment of darkness or shadow to slip through. Grimm confirmed that too. Use your Drusai ability to fill every nook and cranny of this abbey with light."

Grimm sat on his haunches. "The warrior is right. Obsydia explained its unholy origin and I listened well, though I despised being near such evil. The wicked mirror made my fur stand on end." Grimm folded his ears back and lowered head. "Traveling through the mirror was unpleasant. I never would have passed through it, but I was compelled to follow by the Wizard, Neelam. However, since it brought me here, I am glad of it. Neelam knew how to manipulate its power, but even I sensed his discomfort."

Grimm shivered and Opaline bent down to stroke his shaggy fur. "Don't worry. You will never have to do that again," Opaline promised.

Runa held out her hands and they glowed. "We must cast more light then." A surge of bright white light flooded everywhere, so bright they had to cover their eyes.

Mellypip covered his face with his paws. "Ouch! Too much bright, Runa!"

Darcus squinted painfully and touched her arm to get her attention. "Not so much that we are blinded, girl."

Runa's mouth puckered with embarrassment. "Oh dear, sorry about that." She waved her hands and the brilliance softened.

Opaline rubbed her eyes. "Better. I think your worry is affecting your magic. Speaking of worry, where's Panthara?"

"I think Panthara and Taran are in the stable taking care of Rono," Jadon said.

"Then we will wait together," Opaline decided. "Perhaps we can get some tea and toast in the kitchen. We didn't exactly have time for breakfast this morning."

"I'll wait here," Runa said stubbornly. "I'm not hungry anyway."

"Now I know there's trouble," Opaline said resignedly, sitting next to her.

Time dragged in cruel fashion as Runa paced in silence the narrow hall outside the sickroom, holding a very patient Mellypip. The heady scent of magic brewing tanged the air. Caliste or Iona would walk back and forth across the hall with vials of mystical elixirs, smile in a comforting manner, but were too busy to tell them anything.

After a torturous period of quiet, Runa's emotions bubbled to the surface. She began to pace. After a time, her pacing became rapid. "Maybe we should have taken them to the Sorcerer House? Where's Grandpa? Is he injured or worse? What about our friends fighting those creatures? We have no idea what's going in the woods with those goblins and assassins coming through like vermin. Maybe Koll showed up to take Xabral back, bringing more demons. Grandpa told me about the hellstone Xabral used when Koll escaped before. Who knows what else is at Koll's disposal?"

"Cathal knows what to do. He had King Caladynn waiting with a whole legion under an invisibility cloak," Darcus assured her. "Believe me girl, I wanted to stay and fight it out. That's what I do. But Cathal tasked me with protecting his family and I will do so until my last breath."

Runa threw her arms around him. "Oh, Darcus, you're the bravest man I know." Little spurts of magic, ranging in a myriad of colors, from blue to amber to gray, flickered from her fingertips. The gust of sorcery flared and struck Darcus on the arm, stinging him. Runa jumped back and put her hands to her face, mortified.

"Don't worry, girl," Darcus laughed. "I'm not injured."

Opaline patiently sat on the wooden bench, petting Grimm. "The Abbey was closer and safer. You know that. We had to get them somewhere quickly. The Sorcerer House is a target. This was part of the plan—remember? Stop pacing. You'll wear out your new boots."

"Yes, calm down please," Mellypip begged her. "You just wounded Darcus. You're leaking sorcery. Who knows what that will do?"

"Opaline would know," Darcus laughed. "If I start growing tusks or get shaggier than usual, let me know."

"Embarrassing but true," Opaline agreed. "Darcus, I thought we had an agreement there would be no more troll jokes?"

"But I can't just...sit!" Runa cried. More wisps of sorcery

sparked from her fingertips. "I won't leave them."

"Then we'll stay in this cold corridor instead of a warm kitchen," Opaline agreed. "Maybe the sisters have some knitting we could do, to keep you distracted and prevent your sorcery from dripping."

"You're mocking me now," Runa said.

"Let me have my moment," Opaline said, rising and taking Runa's arm. "I'm the one whose magic is usually out of control. Let's walk out to the garden. Maybe have tea."

"Listen to Opaline. Raghnall needs peace to work and you're not very peaceful now," Darcus warned softly. "What happened to Yllia and Rualla was beyond most mages' powers. He needs all his focus now."

"My mother was shaking so violently. *My mother*. It's so strange saying that. I have a mother now, but for how long? I should be in the sickroom, helping them."

Opaline stopped Runa in mid-pace and took her by the shoulders. "Let's get some fresh air. It might help you relax. I'm nervous too. My mother and grandfather are fighting at Cathal's side. Ulric's there too, fighting alongside his father."

Runa hung her head. "I'm sorry. And you've had so much grief this day. I'm not a good friend. People you love are a risk. Your father just died. Yet, you're so calm."

"It's my princess training. We can always put on a good face in public. Alone is another matter. My father's death was tragic. I'm positive Koll and Levandius assassinated him. I will mourn him, but I know his crown meant more than family. All I can do now is pray for his soul."

Sister Danu walked toward them, carrying blankets. Though humbly robed in plain blue cotton robe and veil, the former princess still retained her regal bearing. "Runa, your Grandfather and the others just arrived. My father is with him."

"Ulric?" Opaline whispered.

"Is well," Danu said with a smile. "My baby brother always relished a good battle."

"What about Koll?" Darcus asked. "Did they kill Koll?"

Danu shook her head. "I cannot say."

When Runa glanced with anguish at the sickroom door, Danu touched Runa's cheek. "The whole Abbey is praying for them, Runa. You are safe here. My father has stationed soldiers to guard the Abbey while they're here. I remember Yllia and Rualla too, from when I was a little girl at my father's court. They are strong women with good hearts, Runa. Just like you. Have faith, my child."

"Let's get some fresh air," Opaline insisted, taking Runa's arm.

"That's a wonderful idea, Opaline," Danu smiled. "I'll send my brother to you soon. In the meantime, I'll see hot food is prepared for everyone. You must all be exhausted."

"Thank you, Danu," Opaline replied with affection.

Sister Danu rapped on the sickroom door once and entered at Raghnall's impatient invitation. Runa glimpsed the pale shapes of Yllia and Rualla lying under a pile of blankets. The door closed. Opaline did not permit Runa to linger at the door and walked her down the hall, their familiars following.

"Go protect them," Darcus said to Jadon. "I'll stand watch here. Just stay close and beware of shadows!"

Outside, the day was bright and the vivid flowers of the garden beautiful.

Sirah and Arial joined them in the garden. Sirah embraced both young women quickly. "How is everyone?" Sirah asked with concern.

"My sorceress is distressed," Mellypip said.

Sirah tenderly touched Runa's cheek. "She has a right to be upset. Dear, I know this is hard for you."

"Where are Grandpa and the others?" Runa asked. "Is he alright? Did anyone get hurt?"

"Cathal and Belwyn will be here soon," Sirah answered. "We're all fine."

"Is Koll dead?" Runa asked bluntly.

"No," Sirah replied. "That part is not fine. We came so close to killing Koll. He was trapped. Cathal shot a sorcerer bane arrow into him. Koll was helpless. Solder and sorcerer alike were about to end his life without mercy, but a demon called Chimera appeared from shadows and blocked weapons and magic from hurting Koll, and then she swept Koll away into darkness and away from justice."

Grimm growled in his throat. "The demoness used the Eye of Shadows. Foul mirror of Hell."

"We must take extra care now, as our enemies have an unfair advantage. No one is to be alone. Understood?" Sirah said firmly.

"Yes, Mother," Opaline murmured.

Combat-sullied with scorched and stained robes, Cathal entered into the garden, Belwyn on his shoulder. Burns marked his hands and face. His weary and angry expression changed into relief when he saw Runa running toward him.

"Grandpa!" They hugged tightly for a second, until his cry of pain caused her to jump back. "Sorry! Did I hurt you? You're so burned!"

"You're crispy," Mellypip said.

Cathal brushed off his ashy clothes. "I look worse than I feel. These robes are done for though. I got soot all over you, Runa."

"That doesn't matter," Runa said.

"What am I? Chopped troll?" Belwyn sniffed.

"Oh, Belwyn, I love you!" Runa said, reaching up and scratching his beak. "Did you get singed?"

"No. I had sense enough to fly clear of the fire. Cathal, however, is getting sluggish in his old age."

Runa nodded glumly. "Koll escaped. Sirah told us."

Cathal frowned again. "Yes. Xabral also escaped in the frenzy, thanks to Chimera. Koll was beaten down, but because of that demon, he eluded capture. I'm sure Koll's been taken to wherever they have Obsydia tucked away."

"Good riddance to Xabral. Damned slithering beast made my feathers itch!" Belwyn snapped.

Cathal stroked Belwyn's beak. "We liberated Yllia and Rualla. That was the most important task this day. Now let's hope we can save their lives."

"Have you seen them?" Runa asked in a tight voice.

Cathal's features tensed with emotion. "Briefly. Raghnall says they're still fighting, but they are fevered and suffering from the debilitating effects of the bloodstone sorcery. This is going to take time. He says you can sit with them for a while. Then young lady, you're to eat a proper meal and get some rest. The sisters are fixing a room for you and Opaline right next to their room, so you will be very close."

Runa examined Cathal's hands. "Those are some bad burns."

"I've had worse," Cathal shrugged.

"Now you're sounding like Neelam," Runa remarked. "He's a bad influence."

"Let's go see Yllia and Rualla first," Cathal coaxed, taking her arm.

Jadon squeezed Runa's hand before she left. Darcus opened the door for them. Opaline and Sirah remained outside. Runa and Mellypip followed Cathal back inside.

Inside the sick chamber, magic spiced the air. Two pale feverish women lay beneath piles of quilts. Iona and Caliste busily worked side by side, their familiars watching over their work. A sorcerous orb of golden light floated free of gravity, providing ample illumination in the room.

Baldur sat between the two beds, meditating between Yllia and Rualla, his giant paws touching their hands.

"Baldur is using his empathy powers to help heal the wounds that are not physical," Cathal whispered.

"He is amazing at making you feel better," Mellypip agreed. "He will surely save them."

"Of course he will," Belwyn said. He swiveled his head around and to Raghnall. "Any changes in their condition?"

"They're still fevered," Raghnall replied, checking Rualla's eyes and heartbeat. "Rualla's seizures have stopped, but she must be watched carefully. She is the weakest. I don't know of anyone who has been through this horror, so my measuring stick is all guesswork, Cathal. If they survive until morning, they may have a chance."

"Your guesswork is the best I know, Raghnall," Cathal said. "If anyone can save my girls, you can."

Cathal guided Runa to a stool Raghnall had vacated to check on Yllia. She sat by her mother and Mellypip carefully leapt to the bedside table and laid his staff down. He crawled to Runa's shoulder and with careful paws he took the cup from Runa's hand and set it on the table. *Melly, they are even more beautiful than the pictures in the locket.*

Indeed, they were, despite their illness and suffering, they were lovely, though fragile in their strange slumber. The long, almost white, blonde hair of her grandmother, Yllia, gleamed in the light. Rualla's dark hair was like Runa's. She touched her mother's soft hair. "What do I do?" Runa asked.

"Just sit with them. Love them." Cathal answered as he sat next to Yllia. "We will take turns talking to them and tell them about our adventures."

Belwyn perched at the foot of Rualla's bed, and his golden eyes settled on Mellypip. "Furball could tell them the stories he's been writing. That might wake them up."

Mellypip nodded vigorously. "Oh yes, I will be the best storyteller in the world for them."

Runa's thoughts flowed into Mellypip's head with emotional release. *Rualla and Caliste are almost the same age. They grew up as sisters.*

For the first time, I can imagine them as young girls, giggling and whispering dreams beneath the blankets at night. My grandmother, she looks so strong, even though she sleeps! She looks younger than I imagined. Queen Sorcha is beautiful, but even she looks older than Yllia, who must be over a thousand years old too, just like Grandpa! Runa reached for her mother's hand beneath the covers and found it, cold and sweaty, but still alive.

Iona brought the vial of blue glass, shimmering with vapors swirling within. Raghnall took the vial and carefully tipped it to Yllia's lips. Tendrils of misty magic swam into her mouth. Cathal took an identical vial of mist from Caliste and repeated the same application for Rualla.

"What kind of magic did you brew?" Runa whispered.

"A strengthening magic, for healing and purification," Raghnall replied. "We must flush any residue of dark magic from their bodies."

"Like what you did for Caliste and Sanura?" Runa asked.

"Similar, but more gentle. They're so weak and the long-term effects of this curse concern me." Raghnall rummaged through his medicine bag and pulled out a jar of pungent ointment. He dipped his fingers in the gooey stuff and reached out for Cathal.

Cathal leaned back, wrinkling his nose. "What in the blazes is that vile stuff for? And why are you attacking me with it?"

"It's for your burns, oh great hero," Belwyn said. "Now be a good boy and let him apply it unless you want your butt pecked."

Raghnall smeared the ointment on Cathal's burned cheeks. "Don't argue with me. Last thing I need is another Neelam. His stitches ripped open and he won't let me sew them up. Brave soldiers and sorcerers! Brandishing battle scars and blood stumps like some bizarre aphrodisiac. Never understood it, myself. Risk infection on your own hourglass! Stop wiggling, Cathal."

"The Wizard has spoken Grandpa," Runa said. She gazed at Yllia and Rualla. "Please live," she prayed over and over.

CHAPTER THIRTY-SEVEN

The priest roughly stitched Koll's wound. Koll could endure the pain. The real agony was the sorcerer bane Cathal fired into his flesh. It drained the sorcery from him. Not even those draining isolated weeks when he was Cathal's captive, bound by sorcerer bane, could compare to that deathly poison which sapped his sorcery. Only when Chimera's strong hand pulled the arrow from his flesh did the bane cease devouring his magic. The priest's needle roughly tugged at his skin.

"Just finish," Koll snapped in a deadly tone.

"Sorry, Lord Koll," the priest apologized. "We're trained in rudimentary medicine, but our lot in life is the glory of sacrifice, not healing."

"I know what you do, Priest! That doesn't excuse your bungling fingers!"

"You're unworthy of Rygon's black mantle," Xabral spat. "We will speak to Zhelon about the poor choices his temple is making for the priesthood."

Chimera strolled into the room. "Yes, there is much to complain about now. You vex me, Sorcerer. You rushed off to save Xabral without telling me."

"I could not leave Xabral to death's fate," Koll replied.

Xabral coiled at Koll's feet, restored to his full nine-foot glory, he was happy but exhausted after his ordeal. "You were magnificent, Koll. A vision of godlike serpentine beauty."

Chimera poured red wine into two smoky goblets. "Cathal was clever this time. He nearly killed you and sent you to the Gate of Souls. Didn't I warn you about that? It's a good thing I was watching."

Another clumsy stitch and Koll impatiently shoved the priest away. "I've had enough of your ineptness, Priest. Leave me."

With shaking fingers the frightened priest cut the thread with a small knife and fled with his bloody needle. Koll's stare maliciously followed his retreat. "Perhaps the next holy day will find you on the sacrificial alter instead of presiding over it." He touched his shoulder, frowning. "I still don't understand how Cathal reversed the curse."

Chimera sipped her wine and handed Koll a cup. "You play with curses, like a baby plays with a rattle. Curses are never as reliable as death. Now, you must restore your strength for the ritual." She fingered his blood-caked hair. "You should purify yourself too."

"Is the ritual complete?" Koll asked eagerly.

"Yes. I scribed the spell on a black vellum scroll. I even used my demon blood as ink. Now we must gather the sacrifices and bring them to Skarros as planned."

"You still plan to do the ritual in Skarros?" Xabral asked. "Wouldn't the temple here in Tiamet be safer? Our enemies know how to reach her temple now."

"No Koll, the ancient knowledge says she must in the same place."

"Who will be taken as sacrifice?" Xabral asked eagerly.

She tickled Xabral's chin, her smile deadly. "It's a surprise."

~ * ~

Grimm enjoyed the cool, brisk air. After so long a time in the harsh desert, Grimm relished the green lands again; the feel of moist green grass soaked his paws and the fragrance of flowers and earth soothed him.

Grimm sat with Opaline in the Abbey's sunlit garden. Her golden hair was bound in a simple bun at the nape of the neck, though the breeze freed wavy tendrils from her hairpins. She patted his head. "Enjoying the afternoon? I just adore this cooler weather." Opaline yawned and closed her eyes, setting her book down.

"Perhaps you should rest," Grimm suggested. "You have not slept."

"At least Runa is finally sleeping."

"The little sorceress watched over members of her pack for a long time."

Opaline's smile was impish and her voice conspiratorial. "Until Cathal's firm order banished her to bed. A cup of hot drobba with a sleeping herb finally did the trick. I just need to unwind a bit. Then I will sleep. I promise." She returned to her reading, a small book of psalms she borrowed from one of the nuns.

Grimm was still hesitant about his future. He spent every moment he could with Opaline. He wished she would not wear the bane to hide her sorcery. Could he have a home at last? Had his fate changed? Perhaps he was not doomed to be alone.

Grimm's musings were interrupted by Mellypip. The little wampu scampered up to them on hasty paws, wide-eyes and panting for breath. "What is it, Mellypip?" Grimm asked when he rushed up to his feet. It was so strange to have a meal as a friend, but Grimm was adjusting. He liked the chubby wampu, who was kind to him.

"Hide me!" Mellypip begged, tugging at Opaline's skirt.

Opaline dropped her book to her lap. "Did you annoy the badger again?"

"Define annoyed," Mellypip replied innocently.

"Where's that hairy rodent!" Dabiro roared, waddling outside with a cranky expression.

Mellypip squeaked and dived beneath Opaline's heavy skirts. "I'm not here…act normal."

Opaline suppressed a giggle and lifted her book to conceal her face when Dabiro walked up to them, sniffing the air suspiciously.

"I smell wampu! Where's the little runt hiding? Come on. Fess up."

Opaline casually turned a page and replied smoothly, "He ran by us just a moment ago. I have no other testimony for his whereabouts."

"Why are you angry at the wampu?" Grimm asked, baffled. He thought the bonds of familiars were friendly.

Dabiro scratched his fat belly. "He stole the last honey bun."

"Ah, a dreadful crime indeed," Opaline said dryly.

"Is that sarcasm dripping from those perfumed lips, Princess?" Dabiro grunted.

Sirah and Arial, who patrolled the Abbey grounds, joined them. Sirah frowned when she saw the badger. "Dabiro, if you hurt little Melly, you'll have to deal with me. Do you *want* that?"

"Well, I wasn't going to eat him," Dabiro replied uneasily. The badger lowered his head and his long claws scratched at the grass. "Just having a bit of fun, you know."

Sirah suppressed a smile. "Good, I would hope you would not eat little Melly. Make yourself useful. Liat is patrolling the Abbey grounds too. Go help your sorcerer."

"Oh, all right!" Dabiro grumbled and ambled off, complaining about spoiled wampus and strenuous duty on an empty stomach.

Sirah rested her staff against the bench and sat down next to her daughter. Arial took her place by Sirah, next to Grimm.

"Hello, Grimm," Arial nodded her head in greeting.

Grimm bowed his head. "Hello, Arial," he repled formally.

Mellypip finally poked his nose out and audibly sniffed several times. He cautiously crawled out from the protection of Opaline's dress. "Is it safe?"

"Yes, Melly," Opaline whispered back. "The big bad badger is gone."

Mellypip crawled up onto the bench and sat next to Opaline. "Thank you."

Sirah grinned and rubbed Mellypip's tummy. "You shouldn't vex Dabiro, you know. His temper can be quite volcanic when denied his treats."

"I'm sorry," Mellypip replied, curled up next to Opaline, picking at his fuzzy toes. "I asked the Abbess for a sweet roll first. I didn't think I needed permission to snack from old grumpy butt. And I am not a rodent."

"Of course not," Opaline agreed.

Sirah leaned in close to Mellypip and whispered. "I think Abbess Odelia saved you a cinnamon bun. Why don't you go to the kitchen before Dabiro returns from guard duty? It will be our secret."

Mellypip's long fluffy tail swished with joy. "Thank you, Sirah!" he jumped down and ran toward to the kitchen. "I'll save half for Runa."

Opaline laughed. "Runa is so lucky to have a familiar like Melly. I hope someday I'll be that fortunate."

"I know, dear. Because of that, we must also think about our new friend, Grimm. He needs a mage."

Opaline ruffled Grimm's fur. "Yes, he must bond with someone. Would you like to be my familiar, Grimm?"

"No," Sirah said quickly. "That is not possible, dear. You're not ready."

Opaline's face was stamped with disappointment. "I know I'm not ready yet, but maybe someday Grimm could be my familiar."

Sirah put her fingers to Opaline's lips to still her pleas. "I'm sorry. You have a long way to go before you will be ready for a familiar or to carve your mage staff."

Opaline looked crushed. Grimm laid his head in Opaline's lap; morose and fearful he would be snatched from her this very moment. Why was fate so cruel and deceptive?

"I will wait for her," Grimm pleaded.

"I'll focus harder at controlling my sorcery," Opaline said. "If Grimm doesn't bond with another mage, we still have a chance someday. I already feel a bond with him."

Sirah stroked her daughter hair. "I just don't think it's fair to make Grimm wait."

"Is it fair to try and pair him with someone he doesn't want? Please, don't send him away."

Sirah brushed a stray curl from Opaline's face. "Don't upset yourself, dear. I will think about it. I know you're both fond of each other. He should have bonded with someone as a cub. Wild familiars are so rare these days, it's an unusual situation. Cheer up, Opaline. Look, there's Ulric. Go greet your sweetheart. We'll talk later."

Opaline put down her book, sadly ruffling Grimm's ears before she walked away. He saw a tear escaped her eye, which she whisked away.

Grimm!

Grimm's flattened his ears in annoyance. He knew that voice. Midnight's shimmering form appeared.

"What do you want now?" Grimm barked at him, unhappy.

You're not done, Midnight warned.

"Done with what?" Grimm demanded.

Fighting evil, Midnight replied, unseen to all but Grimm.

"What's wrong Grimm?" Arial asked, seeing the wolf converse with air.

"Perhaps it's the ghost Rono told us about," Sirah replied uneasily.

Midnight moved alongside Grimm. *The man across the yard is not Prince Ulric…it is not even human. It's Chimera, the demon.*

Grimm dashed across the yard after her. "Opaline, stop! Get away from him."

~ * ~

Mellypip did not want to wake Runa, who was finally asleep, so he took his treasured cinnamon bun to the stables. All the perytons and horses were gone on patrol, but Rono was there.

"Melly, Melly," Rono shouted happily.

Mellypip broke half his bun and gave it to Rono. "I was hoping you would be here. You look tired."

"I patrolled all night with Neelam. He swears a lot, but he was nice to me."

"There are so many soldiers and mages protecting us, I think we will be safe. Won't we, Rono?" The strange look came over Rono's eyes. "Rono, what's wrong?"

Rono gazed down at Mellypip. "Evil is here."

~ * ~

Opaline spun around, perplexed, shading her eyes with her hand. "What's wrong?"

The false Ulric came up behind Opaline and reached out to touch her.

"Opaline get away!" Grimm shouted.

Grimm leapt through the air, panic fueling his power as he attacked the false prince. His assault knocked Opaline down and her confused cry echoed in his ears as Grimm pushed the imposter to the ground. His companions yelled at him to let go, but Grimm refused.

"Please help me! The wolf's gone mad!" The demon was taking advantage of the chaos and sympathy, feigning fear.

"Mad I may be, but I know demon when I smell it." Grimm bit its wrist and black blood poured. The taste sickened him. He lifted his blood-stained muzzle. "See—it's a demon wrapped in human skin. Run Opaline."

"Yes, run!" Sirah screamed. She released a high-pitched warning to summon the others.

A fierce roar escaped false Ulric's mouth and the prince's image vanished in an instant, replaced by Chimera. Opaline turned on her heels and fled, hiking up her skirts.

Chimera leapt to her feet her dark eyes primordial. "Yes, run Opaline, I love to hunt innocence."

Sirah shot beams of orange-hued magic at the demon, but the demoness walked on, oblivious to the hot magic, though her red skin was scorched by the light magic.

The gryphon appeared above, screeching a war cry, Mellypip clinging to his back.

Rono dived at Chimera and gripped her with his talons and flung her against the Abbey's stone wall. She fell to the earth, but rose to her feet unharmed, black eyes glinting.

Grimm attacked Chimera, ravaging the demon with fang and claw. Arial joined his assault, ripping at its foul flesh. Arial and Grimm's fangs tore at Chimera's legs, but she tired of the tussle and seized each wolf by the throat and hurled them across the yard over a hundred feet like they were rag dolls. They struck the wall hard. Arial lay unconscious, but Grimm struggled to stand, desperate to protect Opaline.

Sirah's sorcery flew her to Chimera, blocking her path. Chimera simply flicked her hand and hurled Sirah several feet. Sirah scrambled to rise, but ropes of black weeds sprouted and bound her to the ground.

"Grimm!" Rono cried, landing roughly, his talons tearing up grass, nudging Grimm to his feet. He glanced back at Mellypip. "Find Runa. She's in danger. Go."

"Rono is right," Grimm moaned. "Find your sorceress and protect her. I will protect mine."

Mellypip ran toward the Abbey, glancing back with regret before disappearing inside.

Body wracked with pain Grimm pulled himself to his feet. Chimera's demonic speed propelled her to Opaline's heels before she could get away. The demon caste a dark shield around them. Opaline ripped off her amulet of sorcerer bane; her sorcery of golden light streamed wildly from her hands, and her magic burst against the shield. Grimm noted with satisfaction it raised welts on the demon's skin. Desperate, Grimm gnawed at Chimera's shield, muzzle raw and bloody from the demon's sinister magic. Rono clawed at the barrier, screaming.

Chimera clutched Opaline by the throat as the green grass beneath transformed into a shadowy pool from which gnarled, clawed hands dragged Opaline down into its murky depths. Opaline's frantic screams tormented Grimm as he watched her disappear into the black abyss. Then Chimera followed her down into the abyss, laughing. The cruel shade vanished and the spot hardened to solid green earth again. The weedy ropes that bound Sirah vanished.

Sobbing, Sirah crawled to the patch of earth where demon hands had pulled her daughter into oblivion. Mages and soldiers swarmed the garden, but the damage was done. Grimm clawed frantically at the earth, his howls of grief rivaling the warning bells.

Opaline was gone.

~ * ~

Runa dreamed Opaline was drowning in a dark pool and bolted up in bed. The Abbey bells were ringing. The sorcerer alarm rang harshly in her ears. She squinted against the magical light that brightened the room. She threw off her covers and got up.

"Melly?" she cried, worried. "Opaline?"

The sound of fighting outside alerted her. She looked around for her staff. She must have left it in the kitchen after her hot drobba. She went next door to check on Yllia and Rualla, but the hallway went black. A misty black, its odor sinister, spread along the walls and doors.

"Raghnall!" she cried, afraid to touch the darkness. "Grandpa! Belwyn!"

"They are not here."

Runa spun around. Chimera boldly strode toward her, jets of black vapors seeped from her body like a poison, extinguishing the light as she passed. Runa fled, breathless against the evil pursuing her.

Panthara flung open her door as Runa passed her room, holding Azmadu. "What's happening?"

Runa pointed at the advancing demon. "That's happening!" She grabbed Panthara's hand and they fled the pursuing demoness. The inky mist spread around them, blocking out everything. The sound of familiar voices bolstered her courage. Cathal and Belwyn charged, followed by a roaring Mellypip, who had shapeshifted into his giant wampu size. Darkness sprang up and barred their way.

Denied escape, Runa tried to break through the strange mist with her sorcery. "Do something!" Runa shouted to Panthara, sorcery dribbling from her fingertips.

"I can't!" Panthara cried. "I lost my magic when the wraith touched me in the cave."

Azmadu fiercely attacked Chimera, but she swiftly subdued him, crimson webs cocooning the lizard to the ceiling.

Pitch-black streams emanated from Chimera's fingers, snuffing out all remaining light. A shadow orb imprisoned the two sorceresses. Panthara weakly raked at the mystical veil with her nails, barren of her sorcery, weeping for Azmadu who cried to her from his webby prison. Trapped by the orb, Runa desperately pressed against the shadow prison, the echoes of her family calling to her growing faint. The black orb was small, just big enough to contain Runa and Panthara, but unyielding. A spectral portal opened beneath the orb and Chimera pushed them through its threshold.

Runa and Panthara clung to each other as they fell into the black void.

CHAPTER THIRTY-EIGHT

Images of a red-skinned demoness haunted Runa's unconscious mind. The demon chased her until inky shadows blotted out the haven of light and she fell into a black abyss. Tormented by these nightmares, she woke only to scream at the bug-eyed goblin who pressed its gruesome face up to the iron bars next to her. Runa scooted away from it, but her flight was confined to the meager measure of the tall iron prison cage they were locked in.

"Get away you ugly beast!" Opaline shouted, kicking against the bars.

The goblin snarled and hopped back like a gangly frog; it squatted a few feet from them, clutching its jagged sword in gnarled hands.

Runa summoned her sorcery, which did nothing. She was confused until Opaline pointed to the slim rusty metal band locked around her wrist. Runa saw she wore one too. *Sorcerer bane.* Runa was concerned about Panthara, who mutely stood apart from them.

"How's Panthara?" Runa asked.

"When Panthara finally woke, she just went to her corner to sulk. Panthara isn't wearing a bane band. Why?"

"Panthara has lost her magic," Runa whispered.

"What! When did this happen?" Opaline whispered.

"When a Wraith Guardian touched her in Mowad. That's all I know. I just found out when I was being sucked into a black vortex!"

"Are you hurt?" Opaline asked as she pulled her to her feet.

"We're alive, so let's focus on the positive," Runa whispered.

Opaline shivered, looking around. "I'm finding that difficult."

"Gabriel was right. Goblins are uglier than the pictures in books," Runa remarked, looking at the squatting goblin.

"Goblins are the least of our worries," Opaline whispered. "I've glimpsed strange things creeping in the shadows. I'm not sure what they are, but I don't think I want to know. Grimm told me strange things live in this cursed place. Now I understand why poor Grimm was so morose."

"Where are we?" Runa asked.

"I don't know, but I suspect we're in Skarros, the Wasteland. We're deep underground in the sunken temple palace of Obsydia."

"How do you know?" Runa asked.

"Remember what Grimm told us? This place is exactly as he described. Plus, it just smells wicked."

Baffled, Runa looked down at her white sleeveless shift belted with a matching sash, which all of them wore. "Why are we all garbed in white?"

"I don't know, but I'm not anxious to find out. I'm not even sure how long I was unconscious. I woke up first with a dreadful headache, wearing a drab dress not to my taste. I was worried. You were unconscious for a while."

"Now we're dressed in white and locked up in a cage." Opaline suddenly shuddered, a look of revulsion on her face. "Oh gods, you don't think one of those hideous goblins stripped off our clothes, do you?"

"No, little maidens, I did." Chimera dropped her black velvet hood. She stirred a stone cauldron with gusto.

"Somehow, I'm not comforted," Opaline replied. "What the hell are you anyway?"

Chimera's mouth curled into an iniquitous grin. "The correct question should be—from which *Hell* do I spring? I am demon, a true demon, which is why your sorceries only irritated me. See how your nasty marks have already faded." She opened her cloak, revealing smooth crimson skin garbed in a scant black shift tied with a scarlet sash. She returned to stirring the cauldron of jagged gray stone, glittering with smoky crystals and carved with strange runic symbols Runa could not begin to decipher. Scarlet vapors rose from the weird brew as Chimera swirled the murk with a rod of silver and a rod of ebonite.

The vast chamber was darkly illuminated by blue flame. Marble pillars seemed to soar forever, and the domed ceiling had strange murals of unearthly art. Priests in stark black robes and red-painted faces gathered in groups, whispering ominously. Vicious Rashurkeen assassins guarded the chamber, but their hard eyes glinted with fear. Hideous goblins scampered in the gloom, dragging their ragged swords behind them. Near Chimera's dark cauldron, goblins polished a throne of black marble on a dais with a large bloodstone at its head. Behind it loomed a giant mirror framed with ebonite and glittering with gems.

"That must be the Eye of Shadows," Runa whispered.

Priests and soldiers dragged in prisoners in chains, wielding whips. A larger iron cage on the other side of the chamber was opened as they forced several men, women, and children, into the prison. Runa recognized two people huddled together in the jumble of terrified people.

Selyf the Storyteller and his daughter, Raven.

"Selyf! Raven!" Runa cried out, kneeling down, and reaching her hand through the bars.

"Selyf and Raven are here?" Opaline gasped. "I'm so sorry, Selyf. How did this happen to you?"

Selyf clutched his daughter Raven close. "We were traveling in a caravan bound for the east. We were attacked by Rashurkeen. We're to be sacrificed, because they're bringing Obsydia back to the world." He gazed sadly at the opulent ruined palace of his stories. "I've spent a lifetime spinning the tales of Obsydia the Bloodstone Queen. I had no idea someday I would become her victim."

"You won't be! Please, don't give up hope." Runa noticed blood on Selyf's robes. "Are you badly hurt? Is Raven all right?"

He sighed mournfully. "My pain is minor, though they stole my storytelling staff. I cracked a Rashurkeen head with it before they snatched it away." He shifted with pain. "They punished me for my insolence." He looked down at his daughter and stroked her long black hair with tenderness. "She hasn't spoken since we were taken. If there is a chance for rescue, if something happens to me, no matter what, please save my daughter."

"You will both get out of here," Opaline said quickly.

"Promise me!" Selyf cried.

"We promise," Runa nodded solemnly.

A goblin rushed up to the cage and struck his sword against the cage of terrified prisoners, silencing Selyf as he shielded Raven with his body. The harsh treatment angered Runa and Opaline. Panthara glanced at the scene, but her expression was blank.

Opaline's voice was tinged with anger. "I don't know about you, but I'm getting sick of being dragged into Koll's wicked rituals."

Panthara stirred from her lethargy to look up at the domed ceiling, ornamented with strange, ethereal paintings. "That image of a faceless king crowned in fire must be Ahridum, Eternal of Dark Chaos. Beneath his image is a woman with black hair, writhing in agony. She must be Lilith, Obsydia's mother."

Runa looked up and gasped when the sad image of the woman actually moved!

Panthara continued to gaze. "At bedtime, Koll often read to me as a child. Lilith was taken to a black tower in the middle of the wild sea. No one has ever been able to find this place, as it rises only for an eternal. She was His chosen dark bride. There, Ahridum ravished her. It was only a fragment of Ahridum's essence too, a touch of his breath, since no world can contain a true eternal. Moments after she was ravaged by the Darkness, Lilith perished giving birth to Obsydia. She accepted her fate. In the end, she crumbled to ashes. Koll made her fate sound glorious. How could such terror be joyful? She submitted to her fate and was destroyed because she had faith."

"Your childhood was disturbing," Opaline said dryly.

"She put her faith in the wrong god. I don't intend to go to my doom easily," Runa said.

"This place is full of dangerous evil. How can we escape?" Panthara asked.

"You would know," Opaline muttered under her breath.

Panthara's blue eyes smoldered and she clenched her fists. A tinge of her old imperious tone returned to her voice. "I've had enough of your sly insinuations!"

"I think my insinuations are very direct," Opaline replied.

Panthara narrowed her eyes. "Taran says you are terribly stubborn, you know."

"Really? I'm still trying to decipher what my brother sees in you," Opaline replied tartly.

"You're judgmental and vain," Panthara snapped.

"Fine words coming from the temptress of Mowad."

"Stop it!" Runa insisted. "We're about to be sacrificed and all you can do is bicker!"

"At least she's talking now," Opaline shrugged with a smile.

"I doubt you fired me up for noble reasons," Panthara remarked dryly. "

"Silence!" Chimera commanded.

Koll stepped from the shadows like a phantom, Xabral coiled heavily around his shoulders. "Welcome to Obsydia's throne room," he said.

"Can we leave now?" Opaline asked.

Xabral shook his stinger with menace. "Alas, they don't understand the glory of dying for Obsydia. It's a great honor."

"Then you die for her, scaly," Runa taunted. "I dare you."

"If you were not needed for the ritual, I would sting you! I'll never forget your slights when Cathal's sorcery shrunk me." Xabral rested his heavy head on Koll's shoulder and pouted. "She called me …cute."

"I take it back," Runa said dryly.

Koll stroked Xabral's scales. Runa noticed he wore a ring of bloodstone set in ebonite. It was beautiful and emanated the aroma of dark magic. "Soon, Obsydia will be restored. You three virgins have a sacred role in our ritual. You should be honored."

Opaline raised an eyebrow at Panthara. "You're a virgin?"

Panthara exhaled sharply. "Don't act so surprised."

"Your sorcery is gone, Panthara," Koll smiled. "I know. I've watched you from the Eye of Shadows. A just punishment for betraying me."

The tall mirror glowed and hummed with power. Several Imperial White Dragon guards came through the mirror and formed two lines facing each other, followed by two men dragging a massive troll through its mystical smoky glass, heavily chained and muzzled. They shackled the troll to a pillar near their cage. It seemed to sense Opaline and became agitated. Drool dripped from its long yellow tusks and it madly yanked at its chains.

Then Levandius stepped through the mirror, dressed in rich purple and black satin, the imperial crown on his head. He looked bored as he strolled past his guards, a fur cloak casually resting on his narrow shoulders, which he flung off for a guard to pick up.

Levandius approached their cage, giddy with joy. "Well, little sister, not so proud now, are you? I brought Gorvanus, though he's hard to recognize as a slobbering raging troll because of your cursed magic. After you are properly sacrificed, I intend to feed your rotting corpse to him. What do you think of that?" The troll howled with rage, tugging at its confining chains. "He remembers you. How sweet! Now I am in power."

"How did our father die?" Opaline asked bluntly. "Or do I even need to ask?"

"By poison, of course. Chimera brewed a wonderful poison. I watched Father die of course. It was most satisfying. He suffered quite a lot before the poison stopped his shriveled heart."

"Assassin! Get away from me, traitor!" Opaline said coldly. "Be glad I am bound by sorcerer bane; else you might suffer a fate worse than being a troll."

Levandius frowned, clenching his fists. "I am Emperor now!

How dare you!"

"I dare, you worm!" Opaline spat. "You killed our father. You assassinated him! You're not worthy to speak Father's name—or mine. You're the most fetid lowly parasite to crawl out of a dung heap. You're dead to me! I banish *you* now. I sever all ties with you. I am with my real family now. Go rot in hell, worm!"

Opaline's denouncement clearly stung. Levandius winced and his soft lips quivered as each word struck, but his gloating mask soon returned. "I have powerful new friends. With their help, I will soon rule the world, for Obsydia of course. She's my new goddess."

"Your taste in gods reeks," Opaline replied with icy calm.

When he brushed back his short blond hair, Runa noticed he wore Tarsicius' ruby ring and on the other hand a bloodstone ring set in ebonite, exactly like Koll's. "Nice ring? Is it symbolic of your bond with evil or just pretty?"

Levandius extended his soft, perfumed hand, admiring the ring. "Ah, it is lovely, isn't it? You're not the only one who can do magic now. This ring was enchanted by Obsydia herself a thousand years ago! I need only say the right words and it will open a portal to the mirror, no matter where I am. Most convenient, you know."

"You speak too freely," Chimera warned.

"It's a treasure indeed. Does it come off or is a curse attached to the magical benefits?" Runa inquired.

Levandius smile faded at her last question. "I hope your courage holds when they cut out your hearts for Obsydia's glory."

"I hope she chokes on it," Panthara said sharply. "And leave Opaline alone. Your alliance with Obsydia comes with a heavy price, emperor of fools. Enjoy their gifts of power and honeyed promises now, but remember Koll's lies when they turn the knife on you, pig! Mull that over while you're killing innocents."

Sullen, Levandius walked away, flanked by his personal guard.

"You go too far, Panthara," Koll warned.

"Not far enough! What do I have to lose? I lost my magic. I lost my crown. Even my poor mad mother. I committed wrongs in my past, for you. I'm sorry for my sins, but at least I will not fear for my soul when it travels beyond the Gate of Souls and stands in judgment before Tysis and Uros." Panthara turned her back on Koll. "I regret having been a part of this grief and hatred. I take responsibility for my actions. Koll is my enemy and always has been. I can only ask forgiveness. Koll is the reason each of us have lost a father."

Runa closed her eyes and thought of her father Ashur and the final words Ashur's soul spoke to her in the cave in Mowad before he returned to the Otherworld with Urvuz.

Know that I will always love you.

"Our father was lost to us because of Koll," Runa agreed. "Ashur loved us both. We must never forget that love. We are sisters, all three of us really. Not only through the loss of our fathers, but what is in our hearts. We are sisters, whether it's by spirit or blood.

Opaline lifted her chin. "Yes, we are sisters." Opaline took Runa's hand in her own, and then, hesitantly, grasped Panthara's. "My father is dead, not only because of Levandius' treachery, but by Koll's hand who guided it all."

Their pain and loss forged a new bond between the three young women. Their newborn solidarity stunned Koll.

Chimera's deep voice broke the somber moment. "Stop tormenting the sacrifices! We must begin when the two moons rise!"

"Yes, run and obey your demon, Koll," Panthara taunted.

Koll's black eyes burned with anger. "Silence, Panthara! Though you are needed alive for the ritual itself, afterward, when Obsydia is freed, you will still die as a sacrifice to her glory. How painful depends on you."

"Or what?" Panthara urged, recklessly, as her temper bubbled up without restraint. "What can you possibly do to me now? Come on show me! I hate you, Koll! Your magic is foul and you're weak, you sniveling mongrel of a trickster!"

Koll's fury erupted and his arm shot through between the bars and clutched Panthara's slim throat. He roughly yanked her off her feet and slammed her body against the iron rods. She struggled against his cruel grip. Opaline and Runa tried to free Panthara from his grasp as he choked her.

"Koll! Let her go! We cannot sacrifice a corpse!" Chimera scolded.

Koll released her and stormed off. Panthara stumbled back, coughing. She collapsed to her knees, holding her neck. She was shivering violently.

"When he touched me I felt his darkness. His soul. It's black!"

"I don't understand," Opaline asked.

Panthara shook her head and sobbed, "You don't understand! When he touched me, I felt his soul. I saw his soul. In my mind, and I felt it! I even smelled it! It was horrible! A fetid chasm of black! A death soul black as pitch and cold as obsidian stone!"

"You sensed his soul?" Runa gasped. "Are you sure? That's something—"

"Only Necromancers can do," Panthara whispered. "What did the Wraiths do to me?"

The mirror shimmered, signaling the coming of another though its dark enchantment.

"Behold the coming of the Queen of the World!" Chimera called out. "All bow before her Glory!"

"Obsydia is coming," Runa whispered. "We must have faith the light will win."

"I am ready," Panthara added darkly. "But they will not kill me easily.

"So am I," Opaline said bravely. "I will fight them each step of the way."

As the mirror's dark light glowed, Runa, Opaline, and Panthara joined hands to witness the dark Queen's coming.

Zhelon Thor stepped from the mirror's gloomy portal first. His golden hair flowed loosely, black silk robes trailed behind him as he walked barefoot, swinging an incense burner suspended on a long chain, singing a hymn to the Dark Trinity.

Two muscular men in black loincloths, their bare bodies and shaved heads tattooed with red symbols, carried two long poles carrying a heavy woven litter that contained a large object covered with red silk. The cloth fluttered, exposing flashes of intense light. On the floor they gently set down their burden and backed away with bowed heads. Koll stripped the cloth away to reveal a crystal of such brilliance it forced many in the murky chamber to shield their eyes. Rashurkeen assassins squinted, goblins and troll whined and cowered, and the priests murmured prayers as they knelt, not for the Light, but the dark jewel at its core.

Runa did not turn away or shield her eyes but welcomed it. This was the Light her grandfather conjured a thousand years ago to trap this evil queen. A woman, if she could be named so, opened silver eyes and surveyed her prostrate court. Her pale, exquisite beauty was of Eternal origin. She wore a deep crimson gown with a high-winged collar and her hair was floating shadows which curled around her porcelain cheeks. Blood red lips parted in a sigh. Her bitter beauty stole the breath and chilled the heart with fear. It was without soul or heart. It was Darkness made flesh.

Zhelon Thor proclaimed joyfully, "Behold, Obsydia, the

Bloodstone Queen, Living Goddess of this world. Let all bow and despair before Her Eternal radiance! Today we rejoice, for Obsydia shall walk among us again when Her prison is shattered by the Chosen One, Koll."

Koll pointed at the three sorceresses in their cage. "Bring forth the three virgins born of magic."

A priest quickly unlocked the cage and pulled the three young women out at spear point. They were pushed toward Obsydia, no more than a few feet from the crystal's radiant light, though all three women refused to close their eyes. Runa, Opaline, and Panthara were lined up, shoulder to shoulder. Strong, gloved hands gripped Runa and forced her to her knees. She threw off the offending hand and glared back at the priest.

Runa's heart beat rapidly and her brain whirled with thoughts of flight, even as the cold, sharp blade pressed against her throat.

"Begin the ritual!" Obsydia commanded.

CHAPTER THIRTY-NINE

He lost Runa.

Mellypip was ignored in the chaos. Everyone was busy with some urgent task. Tension was heavy with preparations for a great battle. There was anger too…anger the likes of which Mellypip had never seen. He would never forget Cathal's wrath after Runa was taken. His fury would have shattered stone in its wake.

He lost Runa.

In the aftermath of the abductions, even the gentle nuns suffered fury's mark. Abbess Odelia, the most kindhearted of souls, cursed so vehemently, using words no nun should even be aware of, even Darcus shuddered in her presence. She assured them her temper was not directed at them, but at that foul black-heart Koll and his demon that blasphemed their sacred earth and kidnapped those poor girls!

He lost Runa.

The shock had stunned him at first. Mellypip was left alone in the confusion, sucking his paw, contemplating the events of the catastrophe. Belwyn finally told him to go outside and wait in the garden, like he was a helpless kit. No one talked to him. No one comforted him. Runa was *his* sorceress. If there was a rescue plan, he needed to be included. Mellypip heaved a heavy sigh and clutched his little staff prepared to fight. He was not a baby anymore. He would not cry! Rono stayed with him in the garden, a silent comforting presence. Tears threatened and he brushed them away.

Stop it, he scolded himself. *A warrior mage does not blubber. They do not whine.* He had to be strong now for Runa. And for Opaline and Panthara! They were victims too. Mellypip waited impatiently in the garden, so peaceful now with the setting sun. How could the sky be pretty colors when such horror was happening?

A glimmer of hope flickered when Jadon and Darcus led their perytons across the yard. Mellypip ran over to them, anxious.

"What's happening?" Mellypip asked.

"Cathal said to wait here. That's all I know, Melly," Darcus replied.

Grimm joined them. The black wolf's forlorn expression broke

Mellypip's heart. Grimm had grown attached to Opaline in a very short time, he knew. He was never far from her side. It must be very sad, to be a familiar with no mage. Though Grimm was very angry, his grief was evident.

"How did Rono know the demon was here?" Darcus asked.

"The gryphon can sense evil," Grimm said. "He told me this when we were in Skarros the Wasteland. I have found his senses to be reliable in such matters."

"Do all gryphons have this ability?" Darcus asked Rono.

Rono lifted his head and blinked. "I don't know. I have not known many other gryphons, not since I was a baby gryphon."

Darcus gently stroked Redstorm's scarred, angry face, his hooves anxiously tearing at the grass. Darkleaf just looked devastated.

"Darcus, when do we save Runa and the others?" Mellypip asked.

"Cathal ordered us to gather here and wait," Darcus replied. "That's all I know, Melly. Have faith, little one. You know we'll rescue them."

Gabriel strode in the yard, his clouded leopard, Namir, running at his side. The tall, muscular man crouched down, holding his staff across his knees, and rubbed Mellypip's head. "It'll be all right," Gabriel assured him. "We'll go break some heads and bring our girls home, safe as wishes."

Soon, the rest of their sad magical circle gathered in the garden. Dabiro and Liat, Ulan and Rosepetal, Myrsalian and Felisia. Caliste and Pointessa were staying with Yllia and Rualla, but Sanura was joining the war party. Myrsalian and Taran gently guided Sirah, her eyes swollen and red from weeping, Arial and MacTabbish followed them. It was strange seeing MacTabbish anxious for anything, but the plump orange tabby was quite livid.

"What's with all the damn singing," Dabiro complained.

Gabriel turned his head toward the chapel. "The poor little bluebirds are singing to Araema for help. We'll need all the help we can muster. I would not mind if a god lent a hand for a change. Though I am sick of demons getting in my way."

"When demons tread holy ground, it's unnerving," Namir agreed.

"Abbess Odelia plans a ritual cleansing because of Chimera's trespass," Gabriel muttered. "She's commanded the entire Abbey House be purified after the sullying steps of the foul demon. Frankly, I'm not sure it's possible. I just want Koll's head on a spike, and that she-beast Chimera's too."

"Oh, don't worry, Gabriel. Koll's going to need a burial after this one," Dabiro roared.

"We all want Koll's death, but what is happening is beyond even that sorcerer," Liat said in a low voice.

"I'll just start with the death of my enemies," Darcus said.

Gabriel nodded to Darcus. "Good to have a clear objective. Death to our enemies it is. Got your weapons gathered up?"

Darcus whisked a couple of long, lethal daggers from the inside of his boots. "I do, and I have spares. Anyone need any?"

Gabriel accepted a spare dagger and slid it into his wide leather belt. "Most obliged, friend. A good sharp death is the best thing for an enemy." He checked his longsword strapped to his back in an old leather scabbard and hefted his mage staff in his hand.

"I'll take a blade too, if you can spare it," Jadon said. "Just how many daggers do you carry, Darcus?"

"About twelve or so," Darcus replied casually. "Usually."

Jadon blinked and looked Darcus up and down. "Where? You're a walking arsenal," he finally asked.

Darcus winked and handed him an extra blade. "That's why I'm alive after fighting half my life as a soldier. I find it best to keep them concealed until needed. I'll teach you later. Anyone who can handle a weapon is getting one. Cathal's orders."

"I don't understand what's happening. How do we reach them in time?" a distraught Darkleaf asked. "Not even with our swift wings can we reach Skarros so fast. How does Cathal know they'll be there?"

"Cathal said we go to Skarros," Darcus said. "Then that's where we will go. I make a point of not arguing with powerful sorcerers, especially when they're ticked off. Little Runa will not suffer a terrible fate, nor will Opaline or Panthara. I intend to save our girls from those fiends, and it won't be the last thing I do either. The last thing will be Koll dying painfully by my hand. I don't care how much magic he can summon; death trumps magic any day."

Belwyn flew into the garden and landed on Redstorm's antlers. "Excellent sentiment, Darcus."

"Did I invite you to perch to on my rack?" Redstorm asked, ears twitching.

"Consider it a favor," Belwyn twittered.

"Even if that's where they've been taken, not even our perytons can fly fast enough to get there in time," Jadon said. "We don't have days, or even hours!"

"Leave that to us," Neelam said brusquely. He marched into the center of the group, Surya on his shoulders. He limped a little, and not only had his staff, but the sword with the beautiful sapphire set in the hilt. From his belt hung a velvet tome pouch stuffed with crystals. You could smell the magic like strong perfume. "If anyone has any crystals tomes they want to take, make sure you have them and they are within easy reach. Any additional spells you want charged into your staves, do it now. There's no going back until this is over."

"Where are your extra tomes?" Myrsalian asked Ulan.

Ulan held up Rosepetal. "She's right here. Her most important special ability is that she is a living tome."

Rosepetal hiccupped with pride. "I can carry hundreds of spells and summon them for my Ulan."

Sirah extended her hand. "I need a weapon."

Darcus whipped out a long, lethal dagger that had been concealed in his leather arm bracers and handed it to her. "I would never deny you, Lady.

Myrsalian wrapped a protective arm around Sirah. "We'll save our Opaline."

"We were arguing right before it happened," Sirah said in a dull voice, holding the dagger in her hand. "She wanted Grimm as her familiar. I told her there was no chance since she was so afraid of her magic and untrained yet. Then I sent her off to that…that demon! And it took her!" Her hand closed around the hilt and she tucked it in her belt.

"You thought it was Prince Ulric," Myrsalian said quickly.

"Mother, you couldn't have known," Taran said.

Felisia tried to comfort Sirah. "Don't you fret, my love. We'll get her back. And I'll peck out that demon's eyes too! Mess with my kin, will she! I'll send that stinking demon back to the hell in bloody chunks."

"Your temper is up, I see," Belwyn commented to Felisia.

Felisia's tiny head swiveled around to Belwyn. "Whatever Cathal has brewed up better work, Belwyn! Else I'll be after you next!"

"I would expect nothing less, Lady Felisia," Belwyn said.

Baldur, the giant grizzly, came lumbering out of the Abbey House.

"Baldur!" Mellypip cried, running over to him.

"Take heart, little brother," Baldur said as he walked. "We go to fight. Raghnall is staying here with the sisters to take care of Yllia and Rualla. Cathal is saying goodbye to them now."

"You're in ravishing feline form," MacTabbish complimented Sanura as she passed by. She had shapeshifted into her panther size. Sanura, of course, ignored him.

Jadon's strong hands picked Mellypip up and cradled him in his arms. He wrapped his paws around Jadon's neck and hugged him. "Is it okay for warriors to hug?"

"Of course, Melly," Jadon whispered. "We'll rescue her. Then I will tell her I love her."

Iona joined them, swathed in her concealing black veils, Amun on her shoulder. Quivering in her arms sobbing with intense sorrow was Azmadu.

"I better go help," Mellypip said to Jadon. "Iona has her hands full."

He put Mellypip on the ground and he rushed over to them. He felt sorry for the crill lizard, which was an odd feeling. But Azmadu clearly loved his sorceress, as Mellypip loved his Runa. Panthara and Runa were sisters, and that made her family. So was Azmadu, which was an even weirder fact. Mellypip was not quite sure how he felt about that.

"Azmadu hush now," Iona soothed, holding the small crill lizard, bouncing him gently. His blue-green wings drooped, and his eye-patch was crooked as he bawled his grief.

"I...want...my Panthara!" he wailed.

"We will save Panthara," Iona promised in a soothing tone. "We will not abandon her."

"But no one cares about my Panthara!" Azmadu blubbered. "They hate her."

"No we don't. You know we forgive her." Mellypip hoped that did not sound like a lie. But he had no time for pondering or reflection.

"See! Your fears are not true," Iona said gently. "We all care for Panthara."

"Of course we don't hate her," Taran assured the little crill lizard. "Let me take him for a spell, Iona. When he gets like this he doesn't stop." He took the lizard into his arms and rocked him, patting his back like a baby.

MacTabbish, sitting by Taran's feet, looked up and sighed, "Such a massive flood of tears for only having one eye. Calm yourself, my lizard friend. We will return with your sorceress safe and sound. You wait here, like a good familiar."

Azmadu's weeping ceased almost instantly and he raised his head. "What…do…you mean wait here! No! No! I'm not staying behind. Must rescue my Panthara," he wailed, wiggling in Taran's arms as his misery ballooned into a tantrum.

Belwyn looked down at Mellypip from Redstorm's antlers. "Better watch over Azmadu while were gone," he said. "Be a good boy while we're gone and obey the sisters."

A strange tempest seethed within Mellypip as Belwyn's words sunk in. Stay here? When Runa was stolen and in grave danger! When her *life* was in peril! Koll had taken her! Another tantrum erupted.

Mellypip's tail bushed out and his large round ears perked up. He rapped his staff hard against the ground. "No!" he shouted with such volume everyone else fell silent. "No!"

"Wonderful. Now both babies are upset," MacTabbish moaned.

Belwyn's golden eyes burned with impatience. "No! What do you mean no?"

Mellypip stuck out his furry chest. "I mean no. You can't leave me here. Not when Runa's life is at stake! I'm going with you! I'm going to save my sorceress and you can't stop me!"

Belwyn winged from Redstorm's rack and dropped down to the ground in front of Mellypip. He glowered down at the wampu. "I can stop you and I will! I am your teacher, and I say you stay here where it's safe."

Mellypip inhaled deeply and swatted his staff against the earth again, scattering clods of dirt. "No! I'm not a baby anymore. Runa is my sorceress and we are bonded, forever. I will help rescue her. You can't stop me. No one can."

Belwyn tapped his talons and his ear tufts flattened with extreme annoyance. After an eternity Belwyn sighed. "Then take care, Furball. I will not coddle you on this trip." With that the owl turned away.

Surprise and relief washed over Mellypip. Belwyn was letting him go! How did he win an argument with the intrepid old owl and survive with his hide unpecked?

"I'm coming too!" Azmadu cried. "I can fight! I'm fierce in battle. I'm a dreaded dragon of the desert!"

"A wee little dragon," MacTabbish remarked under his breath.

Mellypip signaled Rono to lower his head, so he could climb up to his back, holding his staff. He looked down at Azmadu, and a weird tug of kinship compelled him. Runa and Panthara were sisters. Azmadu's pathetic face tugged his feelings. They both loved their mages. Koll was their enemy—on that they were equal. "You can ride with me…if you want to, Azmadu," he said.

Azmadu sniffled, and looked up hopefully at Mellypip. He spread his wings and flew up to land on Rono's back behind Mellypip.

"Is everyone through bellyaching?" Neelam shouted.

"Your sensitivity is overwhelming," Surya remarked.

"Where's Cathal? Evil won't wait you know," Neelam said.

"I'm here," Cathal announced, striding up to the group, his dark hair flowing past his shoulders. He had changed into a gray tunic and black trousers with tall boots, a black satchel was across his shoulders. Mellypip could smell the magic from the crystal tomes inside. Along with his mage staff, Cathal had two long dirks protruding from his belt. "Is everyone ready?"

"We're all here," Neelam said.

"Are you sure about this?" Neelam asked in a low voice.

"I'm sure," Cathal said. He raised his staff. "It's the last one, you know."

Neelam nodded and added with an impious grin. "I know. They hate being bothered too."

"I don't care what they want," Cathal remarked gruffly. "They owe us."

"How will we get there in time to save them?" Sirah asked. "What magic do you have that is so powerful?"

"It's not just magic," Cathal assured her. His staff levitated before him and dark blue sorcery rained from his hands over the head of his staff. A blue nimbus circled the noble carving of Belwyn at the top; it glimmered and then the wood shifted and folded back like paper to reveal a secret at its core. As the wood magically released its secret prize, a small stone of shimmering colors fell out into Cathal's open hand. Its brightness was powerful in the garden's twilight. "We have something better than magic. We have a promise."

Cathal hurled the vibrant stone up into the air, where it hovered for a breath, and then flashed with multi-colored lights. A wind had risen with the magic, and then the colors molded into a whirling mysterious tunnel.

Belwyn flew to Cathal's arm and together they entered the iridescent passageway of lights. "Follow me," Cathal called over his shoulder.

Neelam grinned sharply and leapt in after Cathal. "Hold on, everyone. It's going to be a wild ride."

"We save my Panthara now?" Azmadu asked.

"We will save them all." Mellypip twisted around. "Don't make me regret this, Azmadu," he added.

Mellypip took a deep breath and urged Rono to fly into the mysterious tunnel of colorful lights.

He would save Runa.

CHAPTER FORTY

After an eternity of torturously long prayers, Zhelon bowed before Obsydia and handed the incense burner to a waiting priest. He beckoned to Koll. "Come forth, Chosen of Ahridum and Redeemer of Shadows."

Koll unwound Xabral from his shoulders and gently passed him to Chimera's waiting hands. She laid Xabral on a special stool of velvet, where he coiled up to watch. Koll bowed before Zhelon.

"Are you prepared to free the Bloodstone Queen, Obsydia? Do you vow to free Obsydia or lay down your life as a willing sacrifice?"

Koll solemnly raised his arms. "I do, for I have been chosen by the Dark Trinity. I have been chosen by Eternal Darkness to free our rightful Goddess. We shall undo the dreadful Light that binds her. We shall release the Dark. If I fail, I offer my heart to the Dark Trinity in penance."

"Let Darkness Descend," the priests intoned.

The cold marble floor made Runa's knees ache. The knife at her neck was not helpful either. *If only I could get this band off my wrist*, Runa thought. She wondered if she looked as terrified as she felt. She refused to be a willing sacrifice. The ceremony was taking a long time, and for that she was grateful. She glanced to her right. Opaline and Panthara were regal and stoic. Years of royal training had instilled a mask of pride and calm, no matter how they felt. Runa was a bit envious of that, certain terror was stamped on her face for all to see.

The priests circled around the crystal of light, silent and anxious as Koll babbled about his dark goddess. Standing behind the priests, Levandius knelt on a pillow, flanked by his Imperial Knights. She wondered suddenly about Pol and Korun? Where they here too? They could not possibly follow such evil, could they? Or had something happened to them? The troll was chained to one of the pillars, but even he cowered at the ritual of dark and whimpered.

Runa looked left at the towering double doors, over fifty feet high, closed to the world outside—and to escape. The sinister beauty of the doors was mesmerizing. Obsydia's face was embossed on the dark metal, her image surrounded by hundreds of ruby skulls. How did one open such massive doors without a stable of burly warriors, or magic, or a team of mules?

Closer, behind Chimera, Runa saw the scythe of black metal gleaming in the shadowy light. The Scythe of Rygon, held by a nervous priest.

The sound of voices chanting rose. "Let Darkness Descend," echoed in the chamber.

In the din, she risked speaking and whispered to Opaline, "Any ideas?"

Opaline did not turn her head, but continued to gaze straight ahead. "I'm barren of ideas, but Panthara's at least trying her magic. Can't you hear her cursing?"

Indeed, Panthara was trying to summon her sorcery, despite the obsidian dagger pointed at her neck.

Koll walked toward Runa now. Strong hands held her tight as he took a curved blade of obsidian from his robes. A priest grabbed her hair and pulled her head back hard, exposing her throat. The prick of the blade nicked her at the base of the throat, and her blood stained the black blade. She tried to remain silent, tried not to wince, but was not sure of her success. It was all surreal and dreamlike now.

But she was not dead—yet. No, that would come after the release. Appeasing the Light demanded no death be committed within the ritual itself.

Koll walked to the cauldron, holding the bloodstained knife high, and dipped the blade in the mist that simmered. When he extracted it, it was clean again. Rivulets of blood flowed down to the neckline of Runa's shift, the snowy white stained with red now.

Koll repeated the ritual act of drawing blood from Opaline, and then Panthara. He repeated the pilgrimage to the cauldron and dipped the blade into the diabolical potion Chimera so carefully brewed.

Chimera lifted a tall bottle of twisted red glass, painted with weird runes, and spoke in her demon tongue until the vapors roiled and bubbled, and the strange mist streamed into the mouth of the bottle. She carried the bottle to Koll and bowed. He took the potion and raised it high, speaking strange words. The language was not mortal or magical, but had the same harsh, guttural sounds of the scroll Cathal recited from when he vanquished the curse of the tree of bones. He spoke in Demon tongue. The vapors flowed from the long, twisted glass. Red and gray mist coiled around the crystal of light. Obsydia, the hostage of Light, looked on eagerly as the steam spun with sorcerous purpose around the crystal prison of the dark queen.

Runa twisted the sorcerer bane band around her wrist, trying to slip it off. She searched the chamber, counting enemies with swift calculation. "There must be at least hundred priests here."

"And at least fifty guards," Opaline whispered back. "I would rather not think about those goblins."

Runa twisted her bane bracelet, grimacing. "Who knew dark rituals could be so dull?"

"Zhelon Thor loves to pontificate."

Chimera unrolled a scroll of black with scarlet writing. She recited from the scroll in her strange native tongue. The mists swirled around the crystal of light, growing darker and stormier.

Then Koll read from the scroll. It was still harsh, but there was an almost musical rhythm to his conjuring. Finally, he ceased speaking and then dropped the scroll into the cauldron of stone. Darkness eclipsed the chamber for an instant, and a heavy boom followed. Runa's ears popped and her very soul puckered with dread.

Koll then spoke in common tongue. "We have spoken ancient words of power, so Darkness may banish this Light. We beseeched the Shadows to bless to our conjuring song, spoken in your native ancient language, to appease the Dark. We have made offerings to the dreaded Light, with the essence of the three mages who made this cruel enchantment. They were not harmed by our hand. We consecrated their essence with the blood of the magical virgins, untouched and living. We offer this to appease the Light, so it may release our Goddess Queen. The Dark demands her freedom. I summon now the sacred scythe from shadow's ancient kingdom, so I may shatter the cursed Light."

"Let Darkness descend," the crowd murmured.

Zhelon Thor took the scythe from a somber priest and offered it to Koll. Koll held the Scythe of Rygon and closed his eyes.

"When Light is conquered and Obsydia is free, kill the virgins," Zhelon Thor commanded.

Runa shivered, feeling the sharp edge of the blade pointed again at her throat, the priest eager for the evil queen's release so he could murder her.

Everyone was entranced by the powerful magic that hummed in the air; the spectacle of darkness enchanted them. Runa noticed their attention had strayed a little from their task.

Koll walked up to the crystal prison of Obsydia, scythe clutched in his hands. The mists continued to whirl around the Light as he raised the scythe high above his head.

"Let Darkness Descend," the priests chanted.

Runa could hear the shallow rapid breaths of the men around her, absorbed in the mysteries, anxious for evil's liberation. Runa tugged at her bane band, desperate to pry it open.

Koll swung the scythe and struck the crystal once.

An ear-shattering boom followed his blow. Runa thought her bones would shatter from the force she felt as it echoed throughout the chamber.

Excited gasps and mumbled prayers followed Koll's first strike. The crystal was still undamaged. Not even a crack in its jeweled shell.

"Let Darkness Descend," the priests chanted.

Koll swung the scythe a second time, and the force of the blow was louder. Zhelon fell to his knees, crying out his prayers, ecstasy on his face.

"We're out of time," Runa cried.

"Damn it!" Panthara raged, and a flood of scarlet sorcery burst from her fingers, searing the hand of the dark priest who held her.

The act startled the guards, as it did Panthara. They rushed to action to subdue Panthara. The hand on Runa's shoulders loosened and the blade drifted away from her skin in the pandemonium.

Without missing a beat, Opaline moaned and pretended to faint. When the Rashurkeen tried to catch her, she elbowed him hard in the neck and then poked him hard in the eye. He stumbled back, clutching his throat with one hand and his damaged eye with the other.

Runa pointed her thumbs and stabbed upward and back, hoping her aim was true. She felt her thumb stab one of the eyes of her captor and cringed at the feeling.

Opaline grasped the scimitar from his scabbard and pulled it out. She made a vicious swipe at him. But the Rashurkeen was quick and jumped back, evading her blow.

Several guards surrounded them, their scimitars threatening.

"Stop them!" Zhelon cried, fearing the disruption. "But whatever you do, don't kill them until Obsydia is free!"

Chimera scowled and the demoness walked toward them with deadly purpose.

Panthara's magic sparked again. Its blinding flare sprayed from her hands, crippling several guards around her, but her sorcery fizzled quickly. "No! Panthara cried, staring at her hands in disbelief. "Come back!"

Runa ran from her captor, but almost bumped into an irritated Chimera when she turned.

"The little sorceress is naughty," she hissed. Chimera reached down and grabbed Runa by the neck and held her high in the air with one hand.

Panthara's guard punched her hard across the face and she fell to the floor, unconscious.

"Panthara!" Opaline cried, and stabbed the guard in the side, killing him. Another assassin yanked the scimitar from her hands and kicked Opaline in the stomach. She doubled over and fell to the floor.

"Opaline!" Runa cried, struggling against Chimera's brutal hold.

Koll lifted Rygon's scythe for a third blow.

Chimera cried with joy. "Here it comes!"

Before Koll struck the crystal a third time, a rumble in the earth heaved the whole chamber. Chimera was knocked off her feet and in the confusion dropped Runa. Koll stumbled to his knees, holding the scythe as another quake shook the room. The ebonite doors, fifty feet high, burned red. Runa smelled the magic of light invading the temple of shadows, a feeling of hope surge with its heat. Obsydia's image, stamped upon the black doors for a thousand years, softened and melted. Powerful streams of light burst through the swelling metal until the doors buckled.

"No!" Chimera cried. "Hurry, Koll! Strike! Strike now!"

Koll raised the scythe again to strike the third and final blow.

The doors exploded outward! The force of the explosion threw everyone back. Koll was thrown across the chamber and the scythe went flying into the air. Rashurkeen and priests rolled across the floor. The captive prisoners in the cage screamed with terror. Burning braziers were tipped over and a river of flames spread. The force carried Runa across the room and she crashed against a marble pillar. Breathless and shaking, every bone in her body rattled with pain as she groaned. Dazed, she lifted her head and turned. The massive doors were bent and ruined, and one hung dangerously off its hinges.

In the strange vortex of colorful light illuminating the chamber, she gasped to see her Grandfather and Belwyn flying toward her, soaring into the dark chamber on a tunnel of colors.

Cathal was not alone. Warriors and mages charged in with him. Runa knew and loved these familiar faces. But another force fought at Cathal's side. A power Runa had never fathomed to see.

Flying on luminous wings of multi-colored patterns, bright as iridescent moon moths but void of mortal feathering, they dazzled the eye. Their long, muscular bodies and aquiline features molded with ethereal beauty; they swooped down on the enemy like warrior butterflies. Garbed in dark armor, they wielded swords, spears, and arrows. Their long colorful hair, matching the shades of their wings, streamed behind them. They rose from old myth to battle the new darkness.

The Winged Fey.

CHAPTER FORTY-ONE

Cathal stalked through the chamber, cutting down goblins and assassins crossing his path with sorcery and sword. Belwyn sped overhead, keen golden eyes hunting. Cathal's fleeting gaze met Obsydia's hostile stare as he passed; its hate would have shocked any mortal man; but trapped in the crystal of Light, Obsydia's silent threat was barren.

Mellypip and Azmadu soared in, clinging to Rono's back. The gryphon's black wings folded in as he drifted to the ground.

The Winged Fey hovered above Obsydia's crystal with spears and arrows, forcing back the dark priests and assassins. Goblins, hideous faces stamped with demonic origin, scuttled away from their shining presence like roaches. Blue-black flames swelled throughout the chamber from toppled braziers. Bodies of unconscious or dead enemies were scattered in the opulent ruin of Obsydia's temple palace. In the anarchy of battle and the aftermath of the blast, the Eye of Shadows and Obsydia's crystal prison were unscathed and firmly rooted. The bold assault of the sorcerers and the Winged-Fey clashed with the survivors emerging from the rubble and flames.

Runa, shaken from the force of the explosion, pushed herself up. She frantically waved at them. "I'm over here!" She stumbled toward them over fallen bodies in a bloodstained white shift.

Iona stepped from the colorful portal, Amun on her arm. When her black veil with the silver beads fell away and exposed her face, a priest gasped and shielded his eyes, running away, fearful of her Necromancer caste. Iona glanced at his fleeing back, restoring the veil across her face. "Yes run, wicked priest, for even a fool can see your doomed soul."

Runa darted across the chamber toward Cathal. A goblin leapt at her; a knife clenched in its ragged teeth. Cathal's staff blasted a bolt of sorcery that seared the goblin in mid-leap. The hideous goblin screeched with pain, dropped to the ground, and darted back into the chamber's hollows.

Relieved, Cathal held Runa briefly amid the chaos. "Are you hurt? Gods, you're bleeding!"

Trembling and elated, Mellypip jumped to her shoulder, hugging her head. Runa took deep breaths, shaking. "It's just a nick. I'm fine. Panthara and Opaline were with me, but I don't see them now."

Cathal turned to Azmadu and Rono. "Search for Panthara and Opaline."

Azmadu spread his wings and soared, crying for his Panthara. Rono bravely dashed into the fray, skittish in the spreading fires as he searched for them.

"Let's go," Cathal urged, pulling her across the floor.

"No wait!" Runa scanned the room until she spotted the cage of prisoners, which had been blasted across the chamber and was titled on its side. "There's a cage full of prisoners back there. We must save them."

Goblins swarmed across the prison cage, poking at the terrified prisoners with spears and jagged swords. Darcus flew Redstorm overhead, the peryton's sharp antlers striking the goblins off the cage, staining Redstorm's massive rack with black gore. Jadon guided Darkleaf after the shrieking goblins, chasing them away from the prisoners. Cathal's bolts of magic stung the lowly demons stubbornly clinging. They squealed and scuttled away into shadows.

Runa ran toward the cage, twisting at the bane on her wrist. "Damn it. They've locked a band of sorcerer bane on me. I can't do magic until we get the damn thing off." Runa jerked against Cathal's hold when he tried to guide her to the portal. "No! I won't leave without Opaline and Panthara. I just can't!"

"Damned stubborn females," Belwyn barked, beating his wings in the sweltering air.

Cathal nodded quickly, exasperated. "When we get home, we're discussing the virtue of obedience, Runa. Watch for trouble, Belwyn!"

"Like I need to be told," Belwyn grunted.

Neelam marched past Cathal, swift despite his bad leg. "Never argue with a woman, Cathal. The girl can look after herself. I'll hunt for Koll and Chimera. You get those prisoners freed. It's time for some demon hunting." The Wizard disappeared into the fray, Surya flying overhead.

Cathal summoned a fallen spear to his grasp and handed it to Runa. "Here. Don't go wandering without protection. Keep your head down. Now, let's get those people out." They ducked the fighting and flames heated and spread, which Cathal dosed with bolts of cooling blue magic, smothering the fire throughout the chamber.

The prisoners bawled in terror, hands reaching through the bars for rescue. Cathal magically turned the cage on its right side. Jadon opened the iron door with his Drusai magic and helped the survivors out of the cage.

"Ulan, guide these people though the portal," Cathal ordered.

The prisoners were terrified, but they obeyed Cathal as he guided them to Ulan, who waited with a Fey at the entrance. Ulan's deep voice was soothing and gentle. "Don't be afraid. They'll see you to safety. It's all right."

Ulan led the ragged prisoners to the mystical tunnel swirling with colors and two of the mysterious Winged Fey carried the people to freedom. Only Selyf and Raven remained in the cage.

"Selyf, come out," Runa cried. He just lay there moaning, his daughter clinging to him. "I think Selyf's too injured. He needs help."

"Selyf, hold on," Cathal urged, returning. "We'll get you out."

Darcus stepped into the cage. Raven was glassy-eyed and mute in the shadows, holding onto her father. Darcus carefully lifted the man's head.

"Take her," Selyf begged, trying to pass his child to Darcus. Selyf's coat was open, exposing the bloody gash in his side. "I'm dying, warrior. A Rashurkeen stabbed me for resisting. I was foolish."

Mellypip scurried inside the cage. "Selyf, please don't die. We'll save you. You have more stories to tell. Raven needs you." He gently touched Raven's face, but she did not respond. "Remember me? I'm Melly." Raven mutely buried her face in Selyf's shoulder.

Runa dropped to her knees and put her head in her hands. "Selyf said he was wounded, but I didn't know how badly." Cathal nodded solemnly and gripped her shoulder.

"I'll bind your wound and carry you out," Darcus said, trying to move him.

Selyf shook his head. "I cannot leave this world without knowing my Raven will be safe. Take my daughter. I give her to you. You're a Ranger, a human who serves Raven Wing. My Raven is half human and half Ilyrran. It is fate, warrior. She's your daughter now. Do not abandon her as her mother did. Accept her! Call her daughter."

"Yes, I accept her," Darcus said not fighting the tears. "I will call her daughter. Now let me help you."

The life from Selyf's eyes faded and his head went limp in his arms.

"Come to me, girl." Darcus gently detached her from her father's dead arms. "You're safe now. No one will hurt you again. I will protect you." Raven wrapped her arms around his neck, tears streaming down her face.

Mellypip sadly left the cage and leapt into Runa's arms, grieving not only for his death, but for the broken-hearted child.

"Please take Selyf out of here," Darcus asked Ulan as he cradled Raven. "I won't have the last memory of her father be being entombed in this hell. We will take him home and bury him properly. No one is left behind on my watch."

Ulan nodded sadly and gently put Rosepetal in the pocket of his robes. He pulled out Selyf's body and carried him over his broad shoulders. "We need a bit of cover, Rosepetal. The mystical umbrella spell, I think."

Rosepetal's quills shimmered in his deep pockets and an orb of protection burst, covering not only Ulan and Liat, but all the other refugees, with an umbrella of magic that protected them as Ulan guided them to the portal of colorful lights and stepped in.

"Take Raven to the Fey's passage, Darcus," Cathal said gently. "You have a new duty, Ranger."

Raven clung to Darcus, shivering and silent. Darcus stroked her hair and looked helplessly at the child in his arms and followed the Fey into the tunnel.

Runa wiped away a tear. "You should find Koll and his demon that did this. Neelam will never let you live it down if he finds them first." She dared to glance at the crystal and its captive. "What about Obsydia?"

"She is for the Winged-Fey. They'll decide where to hide her. Now let's find those girls." He paused. "Then, I will kill Koll," he added angrily.

They searched the rubble for Opaline and Panthara. Evading the assaults of the goblins and soldiers, Runa clutched the staff, hungry to use magic but denied because of the bane. Sirah and Myrsalian helped hunt. Their familiars pushed back assaults. Felisia's tiny beak dripped red from aerial attacks. Arial remained near Sirah's side; her muzzle bloodstained from defending her sorceress. Liat and Dabiro fought off enemies. The badger was in his glory, jumping on the backs of assassins and clawing them to bits. Rono sniffed for Panthara, staying close, snapping at bold goblins that strayed too close.

"Opaline and Panthara must be close," Runa said, breathless, looking around. "We were next to each when you burst in."

Mad priests with red-painted faces and torn black robes attacked, swinging obsidian daggers and short swords. Cathal turned to face them, pushing Runa toward Sirah

Taran and MacTabbish joined Cathal's fight, striking both goblins and humans, MacTabbish's plump furry body sprouted orange wings and flew above Taran, searching. The chubby cat was briefly distracted when an assassin nearly speared Sanura, he dove then ripped and scratched at his face until the man reeled and fled.

"You can fly?" Sanura remarked to MacTabbish as he buzzed over her head.

"Impressed?" MacTabbish called back, as he flew back to help Taran hunt.

Cathal sliced down a few, and then summoned a shield that protected them while they searched for the sorceresses.

Grimm cried out above the din. "I found her! She's over here!" Opaline, her forehead bleeding from a nasty scrape, crawled over the fallen body of a goblin, grasping Grimm's back for support. Opaline's flaxen hair was wild and her white gown was torn and bloody, but she was alive! Sirah and Myrsalian joined them, simultaneously hugging Opaline.

Shaken, Opaline pointed to some wreckage as Runa helped her up. "Panthara's unconscious over there under some dead bodies. I've hurt my ankle. I'm sorry, but I can't walk." Opaline grimaced, leaning on Runa's shoulder. Sirah and Taran rolled the bodies off Panthara, who moaned and blinked, and suddenly pushed them away in terror, panicked in her half-conscious state.

"Panthara, wake up! It's Taran," he cried, grabbing her wrists.

Panthara stopped struggling and her fear transformed to joy when she saw Taran kneeling over her. She smiled and embraced Taran. Azmadu flew down into Panthara's arms. Iona rushed to her side and Panthara leaned against her, sobbing.

"Go to safety now," Sirah urged them. "We'll follow soon."

"I'll see them to the portal," Cathal said.

"I'll carry Opaline," Rono offered.

Runa took Opaline's hand, helping her to mount the gryphon. Gorvanus the troll burst up from the rubble, shrieking and drool dripping from his long, yellowed tusks. The force unhinged a stone that struck Cathal on the head, knocking him out. Runa knelt by Cathal, shielding him as best she could. Freed of his chains, the troll grabbed Opaline and dragged her away. Grimm attacked the troll, jaws firmly clamped onto his furry leg.

Sirah, frustrated, cast a shield over Cathal and Runa for protection. She used magic on the troll, but he was oddly resistant to her assaults. "I can't fire any sorcery that'll subdue the thing without hurting Opaline. Not even sleep can subdue an enraged troll!"

Rono's talons clawed at the troll, attempting to drive a wedge between his friends and the troll. The monster grabbed Rono's beak, forcing him to the ground and twisting his head back, still clutching Opaline with one furry paw.

Runa was terrified the creature would snap Rono's neck. Grimm edged himself between the troll and Rono, forcing the monster to release his hold on Rono and Opaline. Sirah and Runa rushed to help a dazed Rono and Opaline. Belwyn and Felisia buzzed above the troll's hulking body, biting and clawing.

Grimm jumped on the troll's back, biting savagely into the back of his neck. The troll screeched and spun around, throwing the black wolf to the ground. Sirah rushed toward Opaline and pulled her away.

"No," Opaline cried. "I won't leave Grimm!" She reached down and grabbed a chunk of broken marble and hurled it at the troll's head, taking its focus from Grimm.

"Hey Troll! Gorvanus, you ugly troll!" Opaline shouted, and hurled another piece of rubble at the monster. "Leave him alone."

The troll's red eyes blazed with hatred and he charged. Gabriel jumped in and pulled Opaline away from the danger and threw up a shield, barring the troll from touching her. Grimm tried to rise, but the troll saw him move and fell upon the wounded wolf. Locked in battle, troll and wolf ripped fur and flesh. Rono charged into the fray to defend his friend, biting a huge chunk of fur from the troll's hind quarters.

Assassins charged Sirah and Myrsalian from behind. Sirah pushed Runa down as she sensed their approach. She stabbed an assassin with the dagger Darcus gifted her, plunging it into his neck; with the other hand a stream of sorcery swirled, roping the other attackers with orange bindings.

An arrow struck Rono from above, wounding him in the neck. He collapsed and Runa tried to shield him from a wiry goblin who, his gangly legs wrapped tight around a pillar from above, was shooting arrows down.

Namir jumped into the air to shield them with his body. The beautiful cloudy pattern of his fur transformed to a silvery sheen and the arrows bounded off Namir's magical armor as though he were made of metal. Gabriel's sorcery struck the goblin with a fatal blast, and it fell to the floor.

Gabriel grabbed Opaline by the shoulders. "I'll save the wolf. You stay here. Don't move!"

Opaline tugged at the bane band locked on her arm. "It's killing Grimm! Get this collar off my wrist. Remove it! Now!" Opaline's resolute stare forced Gabriel to carefully work his fingers around the metal ring and pull, trying to snap it at the lock.

"Hurry!" she cried.

"Patience! I'm trying to break the metal, not your pretty wrist," Gabriel grumbled through his teeth.

"Then break it!" Opaline demanded. "Bones heal. Only I can stop this!"

Gabriel grimaced and his strong hands snapped the metal lock and removed it. Opaline cried out in pain. He tossed the cursed bane aside. Opaline grabbed his arm with her good hand and climbed up, hobbling on her good leg. The troll's deadly claws ripped at Grimm's side and throat. The wolf's howl silenced as he fell limp in the troll's clutches. Opaline's sorcery burst out in shades of deep lavender. Opaline extended her hands, aiming at the troll, and screamed out, "Be human! Gorvanus be human! I command Gorvanus be restored to being human."

Smoky waves of Opaline's sorcery entwined the enraged troll. He dropped the wounded Grimm and dumbly looked around, as though confused, until he realized sorcery entangled him rooting him to the spot. The troll bayed as her magic glimmered and lashed around his hulking body in a flare of lavender light.

Opaline limped over to Grimm and knelt before his ravaged body. The wolf was bleeding profusely from several long gashes in his side and from his neck. Grimm's breath still struggled with life.

"He's still alive!" Opaline wept, cradling his head in her lap, trying to stop his running wounds with her hands.

Sirah removed the shields protecting Runa and Cathal. Cathal turned over and groaned. "Is he alright?"

"I think so," Runa said. "Help me get him on his feet."

"Cathal's had worse," Belwyn remarked, landing next to Cathal.

"I heard that," Cathal grumbled.

Gabriel sheathed his sword and lifted the wounded wolf in his arms with ease. "Don't fret. I've got the puppy. You go on, Princess.

Rono, come with us, boy. We'll get you healed. Watch our backs, Namir."

"I always do," Namir replied.

Gabriel and Namir passed through the portal; Grimm cradled in his arms.

The magic that bound the troll burst, throwing the troll across the floor where he landed hard. A painful whine escaped the throat as his shaggy, gray black fur flamed with light and he howled, as only a monster could howl. Then the troll's horns and tusks shattered. Claws vanished. His sorcerous metamorphosis transformed smelly troll fur into human skin. Naked and slick with sweat, his human body ripped from battle, Gorvanus whimpered. The face was no longer that of a troll, but was that of a familiar human monster who had murdered for gold and status.

Gorvanus.

Gorvanus pushed himself up on his elbows and howled, at first a faint sound of troll, and then fully human. Gorvanus gawped in fear, until his eyes locked on Opaline. "You! You did this to me!"

CHAPTER FORTY-TWO

Gorvanus stumbled after Opaline, blood still seeping from his many wounds. The sorceresses backed away from him.

"Stay back, Gorvanus," Sirah ordered, shielding Opaline.

"I'm going to kill all of you!" Gorvanus threatened, but when he extended his arm, no magic issued. He stared open-mouthed at his hands, barren of magic, shaking with rage. "No! No! No! No! Where's my sorcery, you bitch!" Gorvanus screamed, stamping his feet. "I'll kill you the mortal way, you troublesome witches! I demand your death!" Gorvanus screamed, blundering toward them. Remnants of his troll curse, patches of gray black fur, still sprouted on his legs. "I demand death!" Gorvanus repeated over and over. He stumbled over a dead goblin and smiled as he took its sword. He waved it above his head, a naked madman in the center of a war zone. "I will not be denied! Vengeance will be mine! I demand death! I demand death for—"

Suddenly, Gorvanus' ranting was silenced. His eyes glazed over and his mouth gushed blood when a jagged blade pierced his chest from the back. He collapsed face down to the floor, a sword protruding from his back.

Levandius stood over Gorvanus' corpse. "I grant you death, you idiot." His malicious stare turned on Opaline and Sirah. "I preferred him as a troll. He was more useful. Your deaths are coming too. Beware, sorcerers, for your time has come to an end in this world. Obsydia will see to that. Magic will be purged from the world. I will destroy all of you. Soon all of you will perish." Levandius laughed as though he enjoyed a great joke.

Sirah's anger and sorcery flared, shielding her daughter. Levandius paled and fled for the mirror, the ring of bloodstone on his hand shimmered and the mirror's magical glass turned smoky. Sirah tried to follow, but the strong grip of Opaline and Myrsalian held her back as Levandius leapt into the Eye of Shadows and disappeared.

"No, not now," Myrsalian pleaded. "We will deal with him later."

Sirah's light softened and she took a deep breath. "You're right. Enough of this madness. We must flee. We must help Rono through the portal. He's been badly injured."

"I will help our friend," Baldur offered.

"I can make it," Rono said weakly.

"We'll guard them through," Dabiro roared. The badger was in his glory. His muzzle was smeared with both goblin and human blood, proudly walking at Liat's side, who was just as bloodstained and disheveled.

"Come quickly, Sirah, Opaline, Myrsalian," Cathal called, leading them through the colorful lights, their familiars with them after Baldur helped Rono. Liat and Dabiro followed them.

"Now you go, Runa." But the mystical doorway to safety would not carry Runa. She frowned and touched the band locked on her wrist.

"Move it, Runa," Belwyn urged.

Panicked, she looked at Cathal. "The sorcerer bane won't let me."

"One of the Fey will carry you then," Cathal said.

A blast of dark magic knocked Belwyn across the room, grey and white feathers scattering as he spun in the air. Cathal was thrown back, skidding across the marble floor until he hit a pile of dead bodies. Mellypip squeaked in terror as he was roughly torn from Runa's grip and flung across the room. He slid across the chaos and finally skidded to a stop.

Koll materialized over Runa in a haze of red mist. She tried to scramble away but he seized her by the hair and shoved her against a pillar. She jabbed at him with her broken spear, but he wrenched it from her hand and his sorcery transformed it to smoke in his grip. Koll struck her with his fist so hard he knocked her across the floor, where she slid to the base of the crystal. She lay there, dazed and bleeding. She glanced up, shivering at Obsydia's cold smile. Koll straddled on top of her and pressed a long dagger to her throat.

"Stop him!" Cathal begged the Winged Fey who guarded Obsydia's crystal.

Belwyn recovered from Koll's blow and dove toward them with talons exposed. "Let her go!"

Mellypip rushed toward his sorceress, but Koll summoned a smoky shield around them, barring interference from anyone. He scratched against its sorcery, looking into Runa's frightened eyes. Belwyn spewed so many curse words Mellypip thought the air would curdle.

"Runa!" Cathal shouted from across the chamber and flared

with silver light. He soared across the burning cavernous chamber, banging on Koll's shield. "Let her go! Fight me! She's just a child."

Koll's black eye glinted. "Evil does not play fair, Cathal, and neither do I. What will you do to me if I don't? I have faced death. I am chosen to serve the Dark. I don't fear you. You cannot bargain for her, not even with your life."

"Free her and fight me!" Cathal screamed.

Koll loomed over Runa, smiling coldly. "Poor little Runa. Can't do magic while wearing the bane; I know the agony and frustration of losing the magic. Still, I can cast it around us, as long as it's not on you. This is disappointing, as I wanted to kill you with magic, but this dagger will suffice. I'll kill her, Cathal, but you have one chance to save her. Let the third strike come and I may spare her."

"The third strike from the scythe will free the dark queen," a Fey warned. "We cannot permit that."

Cathal's gaze pleaded with the lead Fey, his blue and black wings beating above the crystal. "Dareem, you can vanquish Koll and save Runa."

"We do not interfere in a mortal matter," Dareem replied. "That is not our role."

"Winged Bastards!" Neelam shouted. "Save the girl."

"What will it be, Cathal? The third blow or Runa's death?" Koll needled.

As they argued, Zhelon Thor staggered from the shadows toward Obsydia's crystal, dragging a scythe of gleaming black metal behind him. Zhelon Thor's face was bruised and his elegant silk robes were torn. He looked deranged as he lifted the scythe.

"Stop the priest," another Fey cried, seeing him raise the scythe.

"Yes. Please. Stop him. Runa will die if you do," Koll promised.

Cathal's voice choked. "Runa!"

Koll pressed the dagger to her neck. "Choose, Cathal. Obsydia or Runa? What does your good intention guide?"

Panic sent Mellypip's internal magic surging and his special ability manifested. Without warning he shapeshifted into a giant wampu shape. He roared as he expanded to a size that rivaled Baldur. He thrust himself at the barrier separating him from Runa, but Koll's sorcerous shield would not let him pass.

"Strike Zhelon!" Koll commanded. "Free our Queen."

With a cry of zeal, Zhelon raised the scythe. Dareem descended with blue and black wings and hurled a spear, piercing Zhelon's body.

He dropped the scythe and crumbled to his knees. His agonized wail was brief as he fell backward to the floor. Zhelon Thor, the Priest King of Urgonclaw, was dead. Cathal cried out in anguish.

"You bloody idiots!" Belwyn shouted.

Koll's face twisted and the dagger at Runa's throat strayed a few inches when he witnessed Zhelon's failure. Then rage overtook him, and he raised the dagger over his head. "No rescue for you."

"No!" Cathal boomed and dropped both staff and sword. He sprinted toward Runa as Koll raised the dagger and released a torrential blast of dark gray magic so powerful it charged the atmosphere with magical currents. This sorcery surged not just from his hands, but his whole body illuminated with sorcery that lit the whole chamber for heartbeat.

"Duck, Furball!" Belwyn shouted.

The giant wampu crouched down at Belwyn's warning.

Cathal's jet of sorcery not only vanquished Koll's shield in the blink of an eye, but his torrent of gray nebulous shimmer vaporized the weapon clutched in Koll's hand an instant before it plummeted into Runa's neck. Runa cried out, but she was protected from any magical harm because of the sorcerer bane. Her face paled as the comet of Cathal's sorcery spread from the dagger and the hand that held it, all the way up Koll's entire arm. Koll's anguished screams resonated as his arm vanished in a flare of sorcery. He rolled off Runa, clutching the shoulder where his arm had once been.

Cathal grabbed Runa and carried her away. Mellypip jumped over to them, his enormous girth almost knocking them down.

"Damn you!" Cathal shouted at the Fey. "You almost cost Runa her life!"

"Is your granddaughter's life more important than the soul of your world?" Dareem replied grimly.

Chimera burst from the shadows in a wave of scarlet smoke. "Foolish mortals! Useless imbecile Fey! I shall free her!"

The Winged Fey charged the demon, shooting arrows and spears at her. Chimera was impervious to these mortal injuries. Black barbs whipped from Chimera's hands, entangling the bodies of mortal and Fey with numinous webs that rendered them helpless. Only Runa was immune from the barrage of demon magic because of the bane. Runa desperately pulled away the webs cocooning Cathal and Belwyn.

Chimera snatched the scythe from the pool of Zhelon's Thor's blood. With demonic speed and strength, she struck the Scythe of Rygon against the crystal. The reverberation of Chimera's blow shook the entire chamber. The sound was deafening. Chimera fell to her knees with joy. "Let Darkness descend!"

The Winged Fey flew backward as the crystal's Light flared with a final glow before it dimmed. Cracks seamed around the crystal, so carefully enchanted a thousand years ago. The fractures along the crystal burned and smoked, the fissures spreading from the chiseled cut of Rygon's Scythe, like the black embers of burnt paper. Obsydia's laughter echoed as her prison ruptured.

Cathal struggled to sit up and shouted. "Everyone Get down!"

Runa knelt by Cathal and Belwyn's helpless bodies and covered her head. Mellypip, though covered in webs, tried to protect them by shielding them with his huge furry body, whimpering a little with fear, his staff looking more like a toothpick in his massive paw.

A terrible flare of shadow erupted as the crystal exploded into a thousand fragments. A scream, so thunderous it vibrated the soul, issued from Obsydia's red lips after she burst from her crystal prison. Obsydia's howl, the torment of a thousand years of Light's torture, forced even Chimera to cower. The few dark followers still living prostrated in terror and covered their ears.

Obsydia was free!

CHAPTER FORTY-THREE

The crystal's radiant Light vanished with its shattering. Escape vanished too, for the Fey's colorful portal was destroyed in the tide of immortal fury unleashed by Obsydia's deliverance from her captivity. Darkness shrouded all, even the blue-black temple flames expired with Obsydia's liberation. Obsydia continued her devastating shriek. Runa and Mellypip trembled in the dark cavity. Koll moaned as he weakly crawled toward Obsydia. Xabral, who had been hiding in the ruins, slithered toward his wounded sorcerer and curled next to him, hissing and shaking his stinger.

We must help the others, Runa cried through the bonding, wincing in the theater of Obsydia's screaming, covered with fragments of crystal dust.

I'm all sticky, Mellypip cried painfully, covering his large ears against Obsydia's cries. He clumsily struggled against the webbing.

Belwyn winced at the agonizing pitch. "Where are the Fey?"

Runa pointed to the ceiling. "Trapped up there! Chimera's bound them to the ceiling with black webs.

Cathal's sorcery burned though his bindings. Runa found a stray a knife and cursed vehemently as she impatiently cut through the webs tangling Belwyn. Cathal grabbed his staff and jumped to his feet, Belwyn taking wing above, wispy webs clinging to his feathers. Runa sliced through Mellypip's webbing and tucked the blade in her sash. Mellypip and Runa cringed at Obsydia's howl of agony which continued unabated.

Jadon's magic seared through his bindings. His sword glowed after he cast light his sword to cut the darkness, his face ashen in the supernatural storm, searching for Runa. Jadon and Runa found each other by the glimmer and embraced in the terror and gloom, a giant Mellypip looming protectively over them.

The shadowy chamber brightened suddenly as Surya the snow eagle flew overhead, a beacon of light.

"Thank you, Surya," Mellypip whispered.

The Fey's magic blazed and soughed through the dark bonds and dissolved the dark webs into smoke. Enraged, they circled Obsydia with spears and swords, their light added to Surya's mystical light, breaking the stark blackness of Obsydia's release.

Then Obsydia's screams finally ceased. The priests who survived bowed to Obsydia, quivering in terror, but they were too terrified of the Fey to fight back. Cathal charged Obsydia, his sorcery hurling the few Rashurkeen who blocked him overhead where they crashed into walls. Running on mystical rage, Cathal gleamed with unbridled power.

Chimera wielded Rygon's mystical scythe, blocking Cathal's offensive with speed. The eerie humming sound the scythe made in the air sheared at the nerves.

Neelam broke through Chimera's webs and rolled across the floor to retrieve his fallen staff and sword. He raced to help Cathal, but Chimera kicked Neelam back so hard he soared through the air and crashed into a pillar.

Obsydia's lamentation finally spent, the dark immortal crumbled to her knees. Her crimson satin gown spread out upon the black marble, and her arms supported her as she struggled to lift her head. Zhelon Thor's blood stained her white hands as it drained from his body into a scarlet pool around her. The long captivity of Light left a feeble mark on the dark queen. Obsydia lifted her head, framed by shadow hair and high-winged collar of blood-red satin, surveying her enemies with contempt. But even a frail immortal is a deadly force. She stood in blood on the dais, a queen of shadowy and terrible radiance. The Fey assaulted her, but she summoned virulent storm clouds which formed a ring around her. The mystical storm battered the Winged Fey across the chamber. When each tried to trespass her sphere, a stormy chaos erupted, pushing them back. The effects of the dark magic, born of Eternal rather than mortal origin, sapped even the Winged Fey's strength. Their struggle rocked the temple.

Obsydia's infirmity from Light's misery did not subdue her rage when she saw her enemies. Her eyes focused on the wizard first. "Neelam, you foolish little Dwarf," Obsydia whispered. "You die first!"

Black vapors streamed from Obsydia's body; her mystical currents lashed around Neelam's neck, choking him. She clenched her fist and yanked Neelam up into the air and then slammed him to the floor. He gagged as he struggled with Obsydia's wraithlike noose. Jadon and Runa tried to cut through the black noose strangling him. Obsydia waved a hand and both Runa and Jadon were thrown across the chamber.

Obsydia began to reel in the black ethereal rope, dragging Neelam across the floor. "Yes, come closer, little Wizard. The better to see you die."

Cathal's sorcerous beam shattered the stranglehold that choked Neelam. Surya flew down to Neelam's side and Neelam gasped for breath as Cathal hauled him to his feet.

Neelam rubbed his neck and summoned his staff. "Not dead yet, hell-bitch!"

"Do you have a death wish?" Cathal muttered.

Obsydia turned her burning stare on Cathal. "You're the wellspring of my misery. This ritual was your creation. Borel may have guided you, but your vision created this hell that kept me captive! Death will be too easy for you."

The floor violently lurched and heaved and a rumble in the earth shook the whole temple. Darkness and Light came in waves, and the essence was strangling. Runa stumbled as the floor swelled up again. Jadon caught her and held her in his arms. When Runa glanced up at the domed ceiling, she saw the dark patch bloom with Obsydia's image at Ahridum's side.

"What's happening?" Runa's voice trembled.

"The temple is rising!" Jadon gasped, pulling her to her feet.

The large wampu squeaked with fear and Runa hugged him. "Be brave Melly."

Dareem, the Fey with blue and black wings swept by Cathal. "We must capture her before she revives fully. She cannot escape!"

"Whose fault is that?" Cathal accused.

"Take the scythe!" Neelam shouted. "It's enchanted with Rygon's powers! That may hold enough power to kill her!"

Dareem nodded at Neelam's words and charged, attempting to grasp the scythe. The Fey's explosions of light seared against the ring of darkness. The blinding storm charged air with Light and Dark, but Obsydia's forces of shadow expelled Dareem and his circle of Fey from her ring of power, but the drain was noticeable as she stumbled from her proud posture.

Koll lay at Obsydia's feet suffering, clutching the stump of his arm, lying in a pool of Zhelon's blood. His arm did not bleed, but glimmered with the residue of Cathal's sorcery. Xabral coiled on top of him, shaking his stinger with threat. Chimera kicked Zhelon's dead body away and swung the scythe through the air.

Belwyn buzzed over Chimera's head. The owl's telekinetic magic swept the scythe from Chimera's hands, and his powers carried it across the chamber toward Cathal. Chimera snarled her frustration. Cathal reached out and Belwyn dropped it into his hands.

Runa frantically tugged at the bane. "Melly, break off the collar."

"But I could hurt you," Mellypip cried.

"I trust you. Your paws are almost like human hands. If you can just get a firm hold and peel it back, it might snap the lock. Gabriel did it for Opaline."

"I think he broke her wrist too," Mellypip countered.

"Just do it. If she can take it, so can I."

Mellypip was terrified of hurting Runa. He cautiously pulled the metal ring out as Runa instructed. He was amazingly strong at this large size, but was careful, since her wrist was so slim and delicate. Mellypip's fleeting thought of reaching the cookie jar at this great size almost made him giggle. The lock finally broke, and the bane bracelet fell to the floor. Runa's hands glowed with magic, illuminating the area with her light.

Cathal and Chimera fought across the chamber floor, locked in combat. A harsh swipe sliced across Chimera's middle, and the demoness doubled over. Cathal lunged to strike her down, but Obsydia's dark vapors entangled him.

"Bitch is cheating," Neelam shouted, stalking Obsydia. "Do your job, Fey!"

Shadows whipped around Cathal's throat. He turned blue, dropping the scythe. Neelam rushed to Cathal, falling on his knees and frantically tried to sever the dark magic that choked him. The scythe lay gleaming on the floor. Chimera's eyes flamed and jumped for it.

"Kill Cathal!" Obsydia commanded.

Frantic, Runa's unleashed sorcery summoned the fallen scythe to her hands. "Leave my grandfather alone!" She swallowed her fear, holding the dark weapon with shaking hands, facing an angry demon and liberated wicked immortal.

"Damn it, Runa! Drop it" Belwyn cried from the air.

"Bravery has a price, little witch," Chimera laughed. "Such soft hands and such a dark weapon. It was forged in Hell. It must burn you to even touch it, being that you are so pure."

"I'm not that pure," Runa shot back. Chimera circled Runa, like a snake circles its prey, enjoying Runa's growing panic.

Cathal was losing his own battle and fell limp. The blade and wizardry of Neelam did not cut Obsydia's stranglehold like the last time. A Fey female dropped to Cathal's side, folding her green and yellow wings in. She held her hand over Cathal and beams of light flowed over him.

Chimera continued her dark dance and seized a spear. It was bloodstained and she licked the tip. "Human blood. Tasty. Sorceress blood must be even better." She spun the spear round and round in her hands.

Runa's heart beat like a hummingbird. Chimera charged with lightning speed at Runa, who blocked her assault. Runa turned and swung the scythe at Chimera, who evaded her strike with ease. Darcus' combat tutelage served Runa well as she forced the demon back, but she was stalling, knowing she could not win in this foolish attempt. But it was more than that. The blade felt *wrong* in her hands. She could actually sense its origins in the Netherworld.

Don't use the scythe Runa, Mellypip called to her through the bonding. *Use your light magic. Scythe is nasty magic. Throw it to Neelam. He used to bad magic.*

Obsydia's cruel gaze fell upon Runa and the sensation bore into Runa's concentration. Chimera jumped for the scythe, but Runa followed her instinct to use her sorcery. Striking Chimera with beams of powerful light so she recoiled for an instant. In that brief sanctuary of time when Chimera was stunned, Runa rushed to her grandfather's side. She shook him, tears soaking her face.

The Fey vanquished the diabolism choking Cathal, but he stopped breathing. Neelam slapped him harshly across the face and pounded his chest to revive him, but his pose was of stubborn death.

"Damn it! Wake up boy!" Neelam yelled and struck his chest hard with a force of wizardry that burst with green light.

Cathal's eyes snapped opened and he inhaled deeply into his lungs. He sat up, swiftly stroked Runa's cheek and leapt to his feet. He snatched the scythe from Runa and marched toward Chimera. Chimera straightened and leapt at Cathal, but his sorcery glowed around him like a blue-grey nimbus and his focus god-like. The strength of Cathal's love and protection for his family fueled both heart and magic. He forced Chimera back with a single wave of his hand.

Chimera rolled across the floor. With a wicked grin, she leapt into the air across the chamber, not for Cathal, but for Runa. She grabbed Runa by the neck. "Give me Rygon's gift, Sorcerer. Give it to me or I will snap Runa's tiny neck."

Runa's hands burst with magical energy, stinging the demon, causing black welts to swell, but Chimera did not relinquish her prisoner. Runa still had the knife tucked into her sash. Runa grabbed the knife and blindly stabbed behind her. The blade speared Chimera's eye, forcing her to release Runa and stagger back. Mellypip roared and blocked Chimera from approaching Runa when she leapt to her feet in a rage, black blood pouring from her eye socket. Chimera picked the giant wampu up and heaved him across the room. The demon fell upon Runa, throwing her to the floor. Jadon jumped the demon, pulling her off Runa. They rolled and fought across the floor. Chimera savagely bit into Jadon's neck, ripping flesh. Jadon cried out and his hands glowed with light and gripped her shoulders, singeing her until she backed away.

Runa pulled Jadon from harm's way. Blood seeped from his wound and his body spasmed. "No Runa!" Jadon gasped, pushing her away. "Stay back. I am fouled by darkness. I'm losing my light."

Fury consumed Chimera and with a howl she charged Cathal, sparks of red flaming from her fingers, her sharp teeth exposed. When she leapt for him, Cathal sliced off Chimera's head with the scythe in a single blow. Chimera's head landed with a heavy thud and rolled to Obsydia's feet. The demon's body collapsed, but no blood gushed from her severed neck. Her Netherworld origins flashed with dark flames and then dissolved into smoke and ashes.

Cathal's flinty stare met Obsydia. "Let all demons perish so, as you will perish now, Obsydia!"

Weakened, Obsydia's stormy circle of shadow had faded. Cathal swung the scythe, striking back the black powers brewing from her hands, and struck Obsydia's neck with the scythe. But Obsydia did not perish. The blade did not even touch her flesh, as though an invisible shield protected her. Her pale immortal flesh was impervious to the sharp blade. Obsydia's smile curled her blood-red lips as she ripped the scythe from his hand and threw Cathal across the chamber so hard he slid several feet across the floor.

Obsydia held the scythe lightly in her hand, as though it were weightless. "Do you think me a simple demon? Do you think my Eternal brother, Rygon, would have gifted me with a weapon that could have harmed me?"

Weakened by her violent labors, Obsydia's circle of storm faded as the Fey beat down its virulent barrier. Her powers drained after centuries of Light's damage, she retreated to the Eye of Shadows that loomed behind her and dragged Koll to the mirror behind her. The tall mirror glowed with power as she heaved Koll through the smoky shadows first. Xabral slithered after him. Obsydia, dragging the scythe with her, stepped through the magic mirror and vanished. The prostrate priests wailed at her desertion.

"She's escaping!" Neelam cried.

"Get us out of here," Cathal shouted to the Fey. "Everyone, gather together. Now! Summon the portal!"

"No!" Neelam shouted, as he rushed toward the mirror. "She can't escape!"

But the mirror blackened and the glittering ebonite frame blazed. Then a thunderous sound, a roar of power, expanded from the Eye of Shadows.

"She's destroying the mirror!" Cathal cried. "Stay back!'

The smoky glass cracked and shattered, exploding fragments across the room. Neelam hit the floor and cast a wall of protection. The broken mirror shattered and shards of smoky glass hit the barrier before it could harm anyone. Then the mirror collapsed, like a sculpture of fragile sand.

Jadon screamed with pain, writhing as wisps of black mist protruded from his body like cruel moths. In his spasms of agony, Darkleaf rushed to his side, but could only look on, helpless at his suffering. Runa helped him mount Darkleaf. Runa jumped up behind him, holding Jadon upright in her arms.

Cathal staggered over and pulled Neelam to his feet and pulled him toward the group. In the ravaged temple, the Fey circled around the survivors. Colorful lights exploded before their eyes. In a dazzling wrench of time, they were carried through a tunnel of lights.

Then the portal opened in the garden of the Abbey, and they tumbled to the ground in heaps of fear and exhaustion.

The Fey around them, nine in number, stood in the garden of night, bright spirits of myth with somber faces. The nuns rushed out and knelt before them.

"Do not bow before us," Dareem commanded. "We are not gods."

Abbess Odelia shivered at his harsh words and turned away and wept. Sister Danu protectively put her arm around her but did not shrink from the Winged Fey.

Darcus, still holding Raven, extended his sword. "Show respect when you address the sisters, Fey."

Runa dismounted a shaky Darkleaf. "I need help! Jadon's wounded. The demon bit him. Something is happening to him."

Cathal turned from the Fey to help her guide Jadon off Darkleaf's back. Raghnall and Caliste rushed out to meet them. They saw Jadon lying on the ground and knelt by Runa.

"Let's get him inside fast," Raghnall ordered. "What happened?" Jadon cried out when touched Neelam touched him.

"Hell happened," Neelam replied with weary grief. "We failed."

"Did the other captives make it back here through the portal safely?" Cathal asked.

"Safe and sound," Raghnall confirmed. "The sisters are helping the refugees and the wounded."

"It would have been kinder to kill him," the Fey remarked when he looked down at Jadon. "Perhaps you should do so now."

Cathal marched over to the Fey leader and punched him in the face with his fist. The nuns and sorcerers gasped at his bold action.

Dareem did not even flinch. "You always were too emotional, Cathal. The centuries have not tempered you."

"You almost got my granddaughter killed!" Cathal shouted.

"We do not bargain with demons or their minions," Dareem declared. "Obsydia is loosed upon the world again. That is the grief of your world now. Our magic no longer holds the dark queen captive."

"But it is your world too," Cathal argued sharply. "The fact you refuse to live in it is your own problem. Your oblivious attitude enabled this tragedy."

Dareem spoke gloomily, "We watch this world, Sorcerer. That is our fate. This age is dying. A new war of Light and Dark will rise from its death. This time the fate of the world will be permanent, whether Light or Dark wins."

"Stop jabbering like a mad prophet," Neelam snapped.

Dareem turned his back on Neelam. "We leave you now, mortals, and return to our own realm." The other Fey stepped into their bright portal and disappeared.

Caliste gently touched Cathal's arm. "Cathal, I'm sorry, but Yllia is awake."

Cathal's joy was brief when Runa's sobs brought him to her side. Redstorm hovered by Darkleaf, weeping over his ranger.

"This was not a good day," Darcus said grimly, holding Raven in his arms as he knelt by Jadon. "Damn, what did Chimera do to him?

He's changing."

"Don't look, Runa," Cathal begged her, trying to push her away.

Runa would not turn away but held him and cried.

CHAPTER FORTY-FOUR

Riva overstuffed his bag with haste. The long canvas bag soon bulged with crystals, wands, scrolls, and books, and was too heavy to lift. "Maybe I could shrink some of the relics?"

Buzzy sighed mournfully, hanging upside down from his favorite potted tree. "Leave it, Riva. You cannot cram the entire contents of the sorcery chamber into your travel bag. Did you even pack your undergarments? We should leave all this behind. Don't even put wards on the house. Just go. Tiamet is no longer safe. Cathal told us to leave quickly when he contacted us on the calling crystal today. His warning was very succinct—get out. Bad things are happening."

Riva scratched his head, pacing around the room. "I know! I know! We need to leave. There's just so much magic I hate to abandon. When I designed magical security for this house, it was to keep out the occasional thief or curiosity seeker, not a horde of dark priests or assassins. I never thought we would be outlaws in our own country because I'm a sorcerer."

"We had no idea what was coming. Koll is the least of our problems now."

The sloth slowly crawled down to the floor. "Cathal advised us to go to either north to Ironia or east to Thill. Flip a coin and grab your cloak. It's chilly."

"I never liked Levandius. He was a spoiled imp without talent or nobility, but I never thought even he would serve the Dark. On top of that, with Obsydia freed from her prison, we'll have more problems than how to lock out intruders."

Riva nervously emptied the bag and tried to make decisions, oblivious to the repeated knocks downstairs at the front door until Buzzy's slow, irritated voice finally penetrated Riva's thoughts.

Riva, someone is at the door downstairs. RIVA!

Finally, Riva's head snapped up. "What? Who is it?"

How would I know? I'm a familiar not a seer. See who is at the door but be silent.

Riva cautiously ran down the stairs, Buzzy slowly following. Dizziness and an aching head made him pause on the steps. He gripped the banister with one hand and rubbed his temple with the other.

You didn't eat today, did you? Buzzy accusation rang in his head. *What time is it?*

Almost Midnight. You've been running about frantically since morning with only a pot of black coffee in your stomach. Not exactly brain fuel.

The banging on the door became louder and more frantic. Riva stepped up his pace, hands covering his ears, willing the headache to vanish. The banging was torturous now, as Riva rushed to the front door. He looked through the glass peephole first and paused.

Who is it? Buzzy asked, pushing his way toward the door.

Soldiers! Imperial Dragon Knights!

Were doomed. How many?

Two, but then, there could be more lurking about. It's dark out there, you know.

Bang, bang, bang.

"All right! All right! Bloody hell, I'm coming!" Riva shouted. "I'm opening the door on good faith but be warned—I am a sorcerer with deadly powers."

Buzzy scratched his head. "It would more intimidating if your voice hadn't gone all squeaky."

"Please let us in," a desperate voice begged.

Riva stepped back and extended his hand, summoning his staff. When it flew into his grip, he waved at the door, and it swung open. Two Imperial Knights, faces masked somewhat by the plumed helmets, stood ominously before Riva.

"What do you want?" Riva demanded.

One of the knights took off his helmet. A young man with a flushed face, black hair and tortured hazel eyes, looked at Riva. "Please sir, my name is Korun. My mate here is Pol. Darcus was our former commander." The other knight removed his impressive war helmet, a blond, blue-eyed youth with the same tortured expression.

"I don't know you," Riva replied suspiciously.

"But I do," Buzzy said. "Let them in, Riva."

Riva stood aside, and the two men entered the Sorcerer House. Riva closed the door, but was still uneasy, as were the two young men who stared at their boots.

Buzzy lifted a heavy, three-toed paw and greeted them. "Hello boys."

"Hello Mr. Buzzy," Pol said, brushing his blond hair out of his eyes. "Sorry to be so dramatic, but we had to come."

"We didn't know if anyone would be here," Korun said. "But it's important we found someone. If Buzzy is your familiar sir, then you must be Riva. Are you alone here?"

"Why?" Riva asked suspiciously.

Buzzy brushed at Riva's leg to be picked up. Riva lifted him up, and the sloth's gangly arms wrapped around his sorcerer. Buzzy spoke is his most rushed fashion, though to others unfamiliar with him, it would be considered leisurely. "Riva, these two young men are Pol and Korun. They served under Darcus. They are good boys. Emperor Tarsicius promoted them to Imperial Dragon Knights after we saved his life."

"Darcus was offered a knight position as well, but he declined. Which was wiser than we realized at the time," Korun nodded in a choked voice. "We were so proud and happy at first. Then the Emperor died, things went bad fast. You know about the old Emperor?"

Riva blinked, rubbing his temples. "About Tarsicius?" He's dead, though you wouldn't know it by the paltry announcements and hurried funeral."

Pol's voice was angry. "There wasn't even a proclamation sent to the other kingdoms either. It isn't right, you know? He was our Emperor. They've treated his passing like some low cutthroat thief that's been hanged. No respect. Makes one suspicious about rushing such somber business along."

"It's not fitting," Korun agreed hotly. "The old Emperor was a harsh man, but he treated his knights good and fair."

Pol's voice became more and more incensed. "There wasn't even a procession through the city as is custom, no royal casket draped with the Imperial White Dragon standard, pulled by a team of magnificent warhorses, no requiem mass, not even in Rygon's Temple. The old Emperor honored the war god above all others, even Rhone and Araema. It was almost secret and…dirty, the way they went about burying the old man. The people suspect things too, and all sorts of whispering and rumors are rampant now. Rotten business, it was."

Riva took a deep breath, nodding in agreement. "I agree. The funeral was a speedy affair with no pomp or fire. Very shady if you ask me. But why are you here now? Certainly not to lament your previous employer."

"We're here to warn you," Korun said. "The truth is what's really happening is a lot scarier than folks suspect."

"What do you mean?" Buzzy asked.

"The new decree," Pol said. "You must warn all the sorcerers living in the Ivory Kingdoms. Trouble is coming."

Riva tapped his foot nervously. "I know Levandius is banning mages in his borders."

Korun shook his head. "It's more than exile. First off, Emperor Levandius was working with Koll the Sorcerer. Now this ancient queen, Obsydia, has been released. Levandius says we must worship her and reject the other gods."

"We know that bit of putrid news," Riva shivered.

"Emperor Levandius has ordered all Sorcerer Houses in the Ivory Kingdoms be burned to the ground," Korun said. "And any mages caught within his borders will be arrested and summarily executed."

"That we didn't know," Buzzy said.

Riva sucked in his breath. "I wasn't expecting that, not even from Levandius." Riva held his sloth protectively as he paced, stroking his head. "I knew about the exile, but this is vile."

Korun was not finished. He dropped his elegant, plumed helmet to the floor, as though releasing a terrible burden. "Levandius says there's to be a new holy war for this Obsydia. He plans to take over other kingdoms and install the dark faith everywhere and build new temples to worship her."

Buzzy frowned, scratching his head. "It always amazes me when men use the word *holy* when committing acts of war and atrocity. They must think the word *holy* absolves them of their sins."

"Rationalization is a great flaw in my species," Riva said.

Korun shuffled nervously. "Levandius just decreed human sacrifices will be legal now in the Ivory Kingdoms. Before it was just a symbolic ceremony for Rygon, the god of war. Now they're gonna kill people and call it faith! It's evil."

"How did you boys get this vast mountain of information?" Riva asked, suspicions returning.

"Emperor Levandius thinks we are wooden dolls with weapons. He just barks orders and ignores us unless he wants something," Pol shrugged. "He doesn't think we have a thought in our heads. But we do. We still had Princess Opaline's old maps to the secret passages in the palace. So we did some spying. A lot of wicked is brewing in the palace. We don't want any part of it."

Korun gritted his teeth with anger. "We thought we were going to serve with honor. But it's all gone evil, sir. Darcus taught us different. We can't just assassinate folk or watch as people are sacrificed on altars."

"Has anyone defied Levandius?" Riva asked.

"Members of the Imperial Council," Pol said. "Some of them spoke up too, challenged Levandius on his new policies. Levandius called them traitors. Most of them were executed without even a trial, but some are missing. It's bad sir. Mr. Buzzy, you remember the old noble, the Imperial Warden of the Ivory Kingdoms."

"Lord Rhudon," Buzzy nodded slowly. "I remember him at the Abbey. I remember Lord Rhudon was kind to Princess Opaline before they departed from the Abbey, after her ungrateful father banished her for being a sorceress. He was a noble sort and gently kissed her hand and called her Princess. The Emperor did not even say goodbye to her, but Lord Rhudon did."

"Yeah, that's him!" Pol said. "Well, he's not Imperial Warden anymore. The old warhorse refused to even recognize Levandius as Emperor. He sent Levandius a message saying he did not coddle traitors or put crowns on their greasy heads!" Pol looked down at his boots. "That's when Levandius sent us to kill Lord Rhudon."

"But we couldn't do it," Korun said. "We warned him. We sent word back to the palace saying Lord Rhudon and his family fled their villa. That may be treason, but it was the right thing to do."

"It was a plausible lie," Riva nodded.

"And the reason you still have your heads," Buzzy added.

"We never had to lie about our duties under Darcus," Korun lamented. "I should have known it would be bad when they sent us to escort Prince Levandius back to Tiamet. That's when I ran into Darcus at Rygon's Temple in Kra'zum. Darcus warned me he was there for good reason and to back off. When Darcus says back off, you do! So I let him go. It was against my duties, but I let him go. Then there was an explosion. Darcus and Cathal, and some other mages escaped on a flying carpet. It was something to see! I glimpsed them flying just before they disappeared from sight. Levandius was livid. Now he wants all mages dead."

"You risked your lives to come here, boys," Riva remarked.

"It's what Darcus would do," Korun replied.

"They are banning all the other faiths too, so the churches and holy houses are being shut down or burned. After we warned you, we were going to leave the city. Darcus has a sister who's an Abbess.

Her name is Eshra. She took care of little Runa when she was hurt. We need to warn her and the sisters. So we best be going now."

"I wholeheartedly agree," Riva nodded, pacing nervously. "We must help the defenseless. I'll go with you."

"You will?" Pol asked, face showing a glimmer of hope.

"Of course," Riva said. "A sorcerer can be quite handy, and I would hate to see innocence suffer, and a lot of suffering is coming. Now I just need to finish packing."

The sound of horses and voices outside stilled them to silence. Riva, Buzzy clinging to him, ran to the window and peered out. Pol and Korun looked over his shoulder, swords drawn. The hefty hooves of the warhorses and shouts tripped the magical wards scattered around the Sorcerer House. The flower wards buzzed loudly and spit pollen uselessly at the dangerous men brandishing torches and swords.

"There must be a two hundred Imperial Dragon Knights advancing on us," Buzzy said. "Perhaps they heard you were a powerful sorcerer with deadly powers."

Riva's eyes narrowed at the sloth. "Funny. There's a lot of torches and swords coming our way. Got any escape ideas?"

Pol pointed his sword behind him. "We sneak out the back and don't die."

"No argument here," Buzzy agreed.

CHAPTER FORTY-FIVE

Grimm lay in the bed Opaline made just for him. An old quilt the sisters donated, soft with age and smelling of lavender, cushioned his sleep now. His wounds healed, Opaline was ever watchful, sitting on the floor next to him, stroking his head. Sorcerer bane did not bind her now. He sensed her magic, and in return Opaline achieved a calm control over her unruly powers she had never felt before.

Panthara entered quietly, bringing a tray of tea and scones. Taran brought fresh water for Grimm. Taran was always by Panthara's side. She wore the black robes of a Necromancer now. Though her familiar was not the traditional white raven, Azmadu followed her with dignity.

Opaline and Panthara exchanged genuine smiles. The childish grudges and scars faded. In the face of rising darkness, their former fears and emotions vanished as this new bond formed, allowing the hope of complete forgiveness to exist. Taran and Panthara left quietly their bond of love quiet but strong.

Opaline and Grimm enjoyed the buttered scones. Sirah and Myrsalian entered with their familiars to visit.

"You should be in bed," Sirah admonished.

"I'm fine, Mother," Opaline said dismissively. "Have some scones. They are delicious."

Arial walked over to Grimm, sitting next to him. Felisia perched on the bedpost, preening her fawn and cream feathers.

"How are you feeling?" Felisia asked Grimm.

"Better now," Grimm replied. "My stitches itch."

"I will make sure you do not scratch them," Arial said.

"And how's your ankle and wrist?" Sirah asked.

Opaline lifted her robes and showed them her slim ankle. "The swelling is gone, and I can hobble without falling over. Ulric and I walked the entire length of the hallway this morning. My wrist needs time to mend, but don't tell Gabriel he broke it. Just say it's a bad sprain. When are we going back to the Sorcerer House?"

"The day after tomorrow," Sirah replied.

"Good," Myrsalian said. "The sisters are kind, but I miss home and my library. When you're fully recuperated, we'll have a lot of work to do, now that you are ready to truly study and become a sorceress. I was going to look for a young mage who could bond with Grimm, but Sirah tells me he does not want to do that."

"I am meant for Opaline," Grimm said.

"He doesn't want anyone else!" Opaline said.

Midnight appeared before Grimm, a silvery nimbus around the black wolf's spirit. Grimm felt out of sorts. He knew the others could not see Midnight. Rono accepted this oddity, but he knew it made the others feel strange.

"Why are you here now?" Grimm asked.

"To say goodbye," Midnight answered. "You were brave and will make a fine familiar, worthy of the clan of Darkrunner."

"Are you still talking to ghosts?" Arial inquired. "Perhaps we should summon Iona. She might help us see the spirit he talks too."

Myrsalian crouched down and stroked Grimm's head. "I heard about that. Things have been so turbulent I haven't had the chance to get to know Grimm. They say you speak to your sire's ghost? Strange, but all things are possible in this world I guess. You're a handsome wolf. My father had a wolf familiar too, a black one, just like you. What did you say your clan name was?"

Grimm looked up at Myrsalian. "Darkrunner."

A look of sadness overcame Myrsalian and he turned away.

"Tell Myrsalian his father is at peace, and Midnight Darkrunner will now join him on the Otherside," Midnight said.

Grimm repeated what Midnight said, and Myrsalian choked back a sob.

"What is it?" Sirah asked with concern, taking his arm.

"After my father was killed in the Sorcerer War, his familiar vanished. We were never sure if he had been killed or returned to the wild. His name was Midnight…Midnight Darkrunner."

"Farewell, Grimm Darkrunner," Midnight said as he faded. "I told you I would guide you to your destiny."

Then Midnight was gone.

A strange sorrow lingered in Grimm at his father's parting. He laid his head in Opaline's lap, and with all the strength he could summon, sent his thoughts to her. *Opaline, if I am home, then my destiny must be to bond with you as your familiar, else fate would be too cruel.*

Opaline gasped, a smile lighting her face. "Mother! Grandfather! I just heard Grimm's thoughts. We're bonded. Oh, Grimm! Oh, you are truly home now, Grimm! You shall never wander again."

Arial's ears perked up. "I think we have a great deal of magical discipline to teach these two."

"Yes, we do," Sirah said with a smile. "Grimm has a lot to learn about his new family, and his new sorceress."

~ * ~

Darcus put Raven to bed, tucking her in with warm blankets and placed a small light crystal on the side table.

"This light will not extinguish, and will keep the shadows away," Darcus promised. She nodded, but still did not speak. Darcus kissed her brow and departed. He left the door open a crack because closed doors upset the child, and he was careful to make her feel safe.

"Raven is such a lovely child," Sister Danu remarked, meeting him in the hall. "But she has suffered such a great loss and has seen things no one, child or adult, should experience."

"I fear darkness will mark her forever," Darcus said softly.

"But you saved her, Ranger Darcus."

"She still refuses to speak. I don't know what to do."

"She trusts you," Danu said. "That is enough for now. Will you take her home with you to Ilyrra?"

Darcus looked flustered for a moment. "I am to return, though with the coming troubles, Ryen has designated me as a contact with King Caladynn. I'm not married nor do I know the first thing about raising a daughter. How will I look after her?"

"You are doing well enough. I know all the sisters have adopted her in their hearts, but Raven needs you." Danu tucked her hands in her sleeves. "According to Ilyrran law, she is legally and spiritually your daughter. Ilyrrans also understand your duties as a ranger. They will make sure she is cared for when you are away."

"I must admit; I have grown attached also. Speaking of looking after, may I ask you and the sisters to look after her for a short time," Darcus said. "I have a task to do before we return to Ilyrra."

"You're concerned for your sister, Eshra. The Ivory Kingdoms have become a dangerous place, and I fear for our fellow sisters in the west. Take care, Darcus."

"Thank you," Darcus nodded. "I must find her and bring her back. Then I'll return for Raven." He looked back at Raven, and whispered, "How can I protect her? She has already suffered so much."

"I can only pray for the light to hold," Sister Danu whispered.

"But you, warrior, will fight for it."

~ * ~

Runa paced the Abbey garden at sunset. "They have been in there for so long."

"I don't know," Mellypip sighed. He watched her pace back and forth. He looked at his staff, thinking of the day Jadon gave it to him and the lovely carving of Runa's face at the top. He was glad to be small again. It took a full day to return to his normal size after that terrible battle in Obsydia's temple. It was so odd being big.

"Healing magic can take time. Grandpa Cathal told us to be patient."

"Jadon is suffering because of me. That demon's bite was meant for me." Runa's face screwed up, the way it did when she did not want anyone to see her cry. She rubbed off the hateful tears with the back of her hand. It broke Mellypip's heart.

"Perhaps Raghnall will be successful this time," Mellypip said.

"I'm afraid Raghnall may not have the power to lift this wicked diabolism," Runa whispered. "Jadon won't see or speak to me. He stays locked in his room."

Mellypip tried to bolster his sorceress, but even he felt disheartened. "Raghnall's healing magic is strong. Plus, Neelam knows a lot about dark magic and demons. Together they'll think of something."

Iona approached them. "Runa, Jadon is asking for you."

Runa rushed up the stairs to Jadon's room. Mellypip ran after her, his heart beating fast with hope. Cathal and Neelam met her at Jadon's door. Their somber faces told her another spell had failed. Runa swallowed and turning the doorknob, she entered the room. Jadon stood with his back to the door, looking out the window at the rising moons. He wore a hooded black cloak and refused to look at her. Runa reached out to him; a gloved hand raised to forbid her touch.

"I'm sorry, Runa," Cathal said gently. "It didn't work. We need more time."

"I've sent word to Jadon's father and the new Drusane," Neelam said. "We'll gather all the great mages of all three castes. Please, be patient."

"I'm an outcast now, not only among my people, but the world," Jadon said bleakly.

"Then stay here with us," Runa pleaded. "We will find a way to cure you. It's like an infection, a very strange infection, but we will find a cure."

"There is no cure for me but death!" Jadon cried, spinning around. He pushed back the concealing hood and exposed the curse of Chimera's bite. "Nothing can erase this demon's contamination. I'll die like this, marked by her evil bite. You should fear me, not love me."

Jadon's blue eyes, those beautiful storm-blue eyes, were gone. Replaced now by blood-red pupils fixed within eyes, black as night. Eyes that glittered brightly in the waning light of sunfall. His skin too, had been transformed. Now a deep mottled red shade that gleamed like polished leather. His ears, upswept and elegantly pointed, a mark of the Ilyrran race, were twice as long and a deep crimson shade. A pair of stubby horns sprouted from his forehead just below the hairline. His long black hair was no longer silky, but wild and coarse, while the eyebrows grew longer and thicker and his teeth developed two fangs.

"You're still my Jadon," Runa wept. "I don't care what you look like. You're not a demon, a beast or a monster. You're my Jadon."

"I'm not afraid of you either," Mellypip added.

Jadon looked down at Mellypip. "You should be afraid of me. I'm a horrible monster now."

"You are my friend, Ranger Jadon," Mellypip replied simply.

"Then you are a fool!" Jadon screamed.

"You still have your soul," Iona said, entering the room. "Though the shell of a demon has replaced your outer being, inside you are still Jadon. A Necromancer can never be deceived when it comes to the soul. A good soul still lives in this cruel husk."

"And that's why you're still walking boy," Neelam remarked. "Otherwise, I would have cut off your head before we fled the temple."

"Neelam!" Runa gasped, turning to the stout wizard. "How could you say that?"

"I've done it before, to those I loved more than him, because Obsydia turned them into demon slaves. Jadon's been bitten by a demon, not a dark goddess bitch. Granted, the creature was pure demon, but there may be hope."

Jadon turned away from them, lifting his gaze to the rising moons. "Just go. Leave me alone."

Cathal gently took Runa's hand and drew her out of the room.

"Let's give the boy some time."

Runa felt time was the enemy. She and Mellypip watched over her mother that night until Cathal ordered her to bed. Her usual vibrant appetite vanished. Not even Mellypip was hungry. Runa slept uneasily, tossing and turning until the cool sunrise. When Runa and Mellypip woke they both had a feeling something was amiss. This fear was confirmed when Runa opened her door and found a note on the threshold upon a folded napkin, tired with a green ribbon. Runa ripped open the letter.

> *Dearest Runa,*
>
> *I am an abomination. There is no sanctuary for me in this world. I will resist the darkness, but I cannot trust myself in this cursed body. I leave you now because I must, because I love you. Take care of my Darkleaf. He will need a friend now. He loves maple crisps and apples. I ask you to say my farewell to my father, Ryen. Tell Mellypip I treasured our friendship and the secrets he kept safe for me. I have nothing else to offer you but a token of what might have been.*
>
> *Goodbye,*
> *Jadon*

Inside the linen was the beautiful wooden ring Jadon carved for her secretly with love. Runa gazed upon the wooden ring with the delicate rose at its center. She wept, holding it close, as Mellypip burrowed into her arms, hoping to give her comfort in her grief.

CHAPTER FORTY-SIX

Caliste stoked the fireplace against the chill. Sanura lay stretched out in front of the small hearth. The autumn chill had brought an early frost, but their magic kept the room warm.

Yllia was awake and lively, though still weak from her long suffering. But everyone was concerned for Rualla. Even after her fever broke, she still remained bound by slumber. No magic or healing potion would rouse from her dark spell of sleep. Raghnall sat in a corner, researching potions, trying to create a magical draft that would stir Rualla from her sleep.

Mellypip sat on Rualla's bed, reading her one of the fairy tales he had scribed. Baldur sat nearby, hoping his empath magic would help heal Rualla's pain. Mellypip read his tale to Rualla, and Belwyn perched on the footboard, his magic turning the page, so Mellypip's words would not falter as he read aloud— *"Once upon a time, there was a Princess with long chestnut hair; so long it covered the length of the magical tower from the tip of the magical tree to the root. She was enchanted by sleep and could not wake until a Prince would come—"*

Cathal whispered to Runa, "It's so sweet he's reading her his tales. I wonder where Melly got the inspiration about the long hair. I recall a certain wayward spell by Opaline made yours grow the length of a tower too."

Runa looked out the window, the sky darkening with night. "Melly's written all of the stories too, though Belwyn says he needs to work on his spelling."

"And the magical deer spread his wings and flew high, carrying the prince as high as the moons."

Yllia beckoned Runa to come closer. "Come closer Runa, let me look at you." Her grandmother was still weak, but her deep voice was commanding and brooked no rebuff or excuses.

Runa went to her grandmother's bedside and Yllia squeezed her hand. "You're so like my Rualla when she was your age. I bet you are stubborn too."

"Only a little," Runa whispered.

"Or a lot," Belwyn added.

Yllia shook her head. "I never thought to see you again. I never dreamed my hope would be granted. I am sorry for poor Striker. He was a wonderful familiar. It breaks my heart he died, but Cathal showed me your staff. His eyes are imprinted on it below Mellypip's likeness. Striker's spirit must have waited, knowing you would come.

Mellypip waved his little paws as he read. "*And the Prince fought the wicked goblins with a magical sword.*"

Liat and Dabiro appeared in the doorway. Runa saw his heartbreak. Rualla was indeed like the sleeping Princess Mellypip spun in his tale, bound by unknown sorceries that could not be dispelled. How could she save her? Maybe she needed all the possible love, and Liat had suffered in silence for years. She could not deny his love for her mother.

Mellypip's voice continued. "*The Princess was protected by magical owls guarding the tower against the wicked Sorceress—*"

Runa beckoned him inside. "Please stay, Liat. You should be with my mother, if you truly love her. You should be with the one you love."

Liat looked at Runa with such gratitude; it brought tears to her eyes. He walked to Rualla's bedside and knelt, caressing her hand. Dabiro slunk in behind Liat, grunting, and jumped on the bed next to Belwyn. He curled up at Rualla's feet.

"That was kind," Cathal said softly.

"There has been enough sorrow. Oh, why won't she wake?" Runa asked.

"We don't know, Runa," Yllia answered. "There is so much we don't understand. This curse of bones was bloodstone magic. My poor Rualla was so heartbroken after Ashur. If only we could reach her somehow, maybe she would open her eyes."

Cathal put his arm around Runa and she leaned into him. "Maybe she's lost her hope, so we must keep strong for her. Cling to hope, no matter how threadbare it is. I know you are worried about your mother, and poor Jadon. I've been shattered by loss more than once in my life. Not only when I thought Yllia and Rualla were lost to me forever, but long ago, when I was about your age, I gave myself over to despair after my teacher, Borel the Sorcerer, was killed by Obsydia. It doesn't help or heal. So hold onto hope. I stand here today because darkness can be defeated. I will not let you give up."

Runa nodded, trying to feel that warmth, that possibility, as Mellypip's voice spun his fairy tale for her mother.

"*And the Prince bravely entered the tower. He saw the beautiful Princess and with his kiss—"*

"I feel so lost, Grandpa. How can you be so certain about the future, after all that has happened?"

Cathal cupped his hand under her chin and tilted her face up. "We are the keepers of magic in this world. That makes all things possible."

CHAPTER FORTY-SEVEN

The mirror carried Obsydia and Koll to the shores of the Isini Sea. The black tower soared above the violent sea and a moat of storm clouds thundered to welcome her home. This was the place of her birth, where Ahridum had seeded her mother, Lilith. A boat of red glass steered by the hooded guardians carried them back to Obsydia's black tower. There they carried Koll to a great bed where he lay, weak from Cathal's sorcerous attack, despite days of rest.

Obsydia stroked his brow. "You will heal, beloved servant. Your sacrifice will be remembered. Soon, we will rise."

Koll did not stir, but lay upon the silken bed, Xabral coiled at his side. "What now, my bloodstone queen?" he whispered.

"We wait. The Bloodstone Era is my past. It is dust in my eyes. My new age shall be called Obsidian, much like the name my blessed Eternal father, Ahridum, consecrated me with."

"Why won't Koll heal?" Xabral asked.

"Cathal's sorcery has left its mark, but we will restore and heal Koll," Obsydia said. "Even I, an immortal, must take time to build strength again. I suffered centuries of Light. Its pure radiance speared my heart too long and left me frail. I must bathe in the Darkness of my Father's house. I will seduce new worshippers to my fold and build armies of demons and men to assure our victory." She gazed down upon Koll, "I've asked the Hooded Guardians to fashion a new arm of ebonite and velvet for you. The Netherworld will forge it with power. My beloved Father will send handmaidens to wait upon us."

"I will have my revenge," Koll whispered. "Cathal—"

"Hush, my dark servant. They will suffer destruction by our hand," Obsydia assured him.

Obsydia gracefully stepped outside onto the balcony of the tower, silver eyes ghostly in the gathering gloom. The sea winds blew back her shadow hair as she lifted her face. "No one shall imprison me again. This world will once again serve only me. Light will fall. Blood shall cleanse the temples. Kingdoms will tremble. The Obsidian Era will rise and only Darkness will remain when I am done with this world."

ABOUT THE AUTHOR

Verna McKinnon always loved science fiction and fantasy. She believes in the power of heroines and they feature in all her tales. She is the author of the novels, *The Bardess of Rhulon, The Bastard Sorceress,* and *The Familiar's Tale* series, *Gate of Souls* & *Tree of Bones*. She has published many short stories over the years through various print anthologies, magazines, and webzines including *Aberrant Dreams, Mystic Signals, Scribal Tales Webzine, Bards & Sages Quarterly,* and *Forest of Dreams*. Many of her short stories are available on her website at *vernamckinnon.com.*

Follow her on Facebook & Instagram for updates on her work and life. She writes obsessively and drinks too much coffee. Verna lives in Seattle, Washington with her husband, author Rick Hipps, and too many books.

More Books by Verna McKinnon from WolfSinger Publications

Gate of Souls – Book One: A Familiar's Tale

Familiars.
Magical animal companions of sorcerers.
Keepers of spells and secrets.
Most important, devoted friends for life.

When one such familiar, Mellypip, bonds with the young sorceress Runa, he shares in the wonders of magic. Together, Mellypip and Runa train under the tutelage of Runa's grandfather, Cathal, and his cantankerous mountain owl familiar, Belwyn. But secrets and spells do not make for good sorcery. Old friends begin to vanish even as enemies from Cathal's past return, threatening to reveal the truth of Runa's parents; a truth from which Cathal must protect his granddaughter at any cost. When Cathal is kidnapped, Runa and Mellypip rush against time to save their family and friends from dark sorcery that will not only destroy them, but shatter the Gate of Souls and release demonic creatures of The Otherworld into the mortal realms.

More Books from
WolfSinger Publications

The Seven Exalted Orders – Deby Fredericks

Arkanost has Seven Exalted Orders. No more, no less. When a magus goes renegade in a far-off province, the Mage Lords demand that something be done.

Ryamon is bitter and frustrated. He longs to be a Fire magus; as a Stone magus, he's miserable. If he can bring the rogue back, he has a chance—his last chance—to fulfill his dream.

It's a great plan—until he actually meets Valdira.

Tails from the Front Lines 2: The Thin Blue Line
– edited by Carol Hightshoe

Come meet some of the four-legged members of Law Enforcement who also serve and protect.

Here our authors will introduce you to the brave K9 officers who serve alongside their human partners. They are their eyes, ears, noses and sometimes when necessary they are their shield, protecting others.

Proceeds from this anthology will be donated to the El Paso County (Colorado) Sheriff's Office K9 program in memory of K9 Jinx who was killed in the line of duty on April 11, 2022.

Ring of Fire – edited by Dana Bell

Enter the Ring of Fire, as unpredictable as the land masses shaking a city and volcanoes erupting covering the landscape. Could there be other reasons for these events? Or could these rings be more than a geological location.

They may be dragons playing tricks
or magic portals opened to mysterious realms
or sacrificing the best work of a lifetime.
Perhaps a rescue during a forest fire
or an attempt to raise the dead
or even while attending a high school reunion.

Journeys are taken to far off lands, another world, and through caves, each with their own unique twist.

Each tale presents a new idea on what the Ring of Fire could be. It is more than what many have been led to believe. Pull up a chair and warm yourself by our fires—just don't let yourself get burned.

Coyote – Charles Combee

While camping in a remote canyon in Utah Jim accidently sees an ancient rite taking place with a coyote like creature presiding over it. Now this creature wants Jim dead.

Audrey and her family go hiking in Utah and are attacked by this creature. Audrey is the only survivor, but she is pulled into a strange world of darkness and glass. She is 'rescued' by Jim, but is still linked to the creature, whose hold on her will end in her death unless Jim can find a way to break that link.

In his dreams, or are they ancient memories, Jim begins to learn more about Coyote as well as the magics that previously bound him. But those dreams end without teaching him the full magics. Can he find a way to free Audrey and stop Coyote from once again terrorizing humankind?

Believing is Seeing – Joanna Michal Hoyt

What we believe shapes what we see. Sometimes the stories we tell free us. Sometimes they trap us.

Some people see things their neighbors can't or won't see. Are they inspired? Delusional? Who decides?

As the faithful people of her village cry out for their god's help in disaster, a young peasant woman faces the terrifying possibility that she may be that god.

A time-traveling Jewish refugee visits 21st-century churches and confronts almost unrecognizable versions of himself.

Three troubled people make the dangerous visit to The Library where the maddening stories lodged inside them can be removed—on certain demanding conditions.

Having been warned away from the vacant lot which is said to house a portal to Hell, the new girl in town naturally goes to investigate.

Early in the grid collapse—or apocalypse?—a Christian lesbian farm couple paint "WELCOME" on their barn and await visitors.

An old man in the Terran diaspora enlists in a crusade to save humanity and belatedly wonders if he's on the wrong side.

Step inside these stories and see what you believe—but don't believe everything you see.

Out of the Darkness – edited by Carol Hightshoe

Mental Health issues have long been stigmatized, with those facing them pushed into the shadows, often unable to deal with the darkness they find themselves trapped in.

In this collection, stories explore many types of darkness—Suicidal Ideation, Death from Suicide, Survivor's Guilt, PTSD, Chronic Pain, Chronic Illness, Depression, Death of a Loved One, Secrets, Bullying, and other forms of darkness are explored. Some related to mental health issues and some not, but all of them offer very human perspectives. As in real life, some stories have happy endings and sadly others don't.

We offer these stories of darkness without judgement, but with hope and compassion. Some roads should never have to be traveled—but we understand that for many they are being traveled alone.

Proceeds from sales of Out of the Darkness will be donated to the American Foundation for Suicide Prevention—or more information on AFSP please visit their website at: afsp.org.

Never Cheat a Witch – edited by Carol Hightshoe

Magical curses. Arcane revenge. Being transformed into a frog. Things evil witches do to mere mortals who cross their path. But, what if there is more to the story…

Deals made with a witch are magically binding and can bring dire consequences to those who even think about breaking them.

Whether they are seeking revenge for wrongs done to them, helping others or simply trying to live their lives—it is NEVER wise to try and cheat a witch.

Open your spell book and join our authors as they relate tales of witches and mortals. From classic fantasy witches to modern day witches and even the legendary Baba Yaga. Good and Evil as well as every shade of gray in between.

And, yes—there is a prince who is turned into a frog.

Blood Bride – Belle Blukat

Dr. Bertram Hoel had ignored all women he'd met until being introduced to Cira Landon at his first Science Fiction convention. Knowing he should ignore the attraction, he still takes the dangerous step to begin a relationship, aware that by doing so he is placing her life in peril.

Cira Landon wrote tales of vampire lovers unaware the handsome scientist she'd just met actually was one. Drawn to him, she finds her life threatened by an old enemy who would do anything to exact his revenge, including kidnapping her and selling her on the black market for rare blood types.

With no other options, Dr. Hoel is forced to appeal to the Elders for assistance, hoping rescue does not come too late for Cira and knowing if she is found, there is but one ancient tradition that may save her life.

Return of the Black Witch – M.R. Williamson

One should not expect to slap the hand of an old crone and expect to walk away without at least a limp. The old witch Ethrel Ibenus is up to her tricks again and this time they've turned deadly. But where did her spirit go after Professor Martin shot her with his wee pistol?

Now, all are looking for the crone's familiar, Seleene. But the big timber wolf cannot be found. The search for the spirit of Ibenus now begins in earnest. Will Entwhistle and her Dwarves be able to help? Perhaps the Green Witch Pereen will be able to use a crystal derived from one of the Witch's own spells will do the trick. Fearing failure, Entwhistle improvises a plan 'C', the use of a mythical creature once thought to be long dead.

Time Capsules – edited by Carol Hightshoe

Time Capsules—history and mystery—a gift or a message from the past to the future.

Messages that can easily be misunderstood.

What were the reasons for passing along a pair of pink, fuzzy handcuffs?

A glass vial containing a perfect dandelion puff?

A Japanese Katana?

A red and blue scarf?

A wooden spoon?

What magic do these items contain? What stories do they tell?

From the past to the future. Mysteries and meanings abound within these pages, as well as reminders of the things people find precious. What will you find?

US/THEM – edited by Carol Hightshoe

US/THEM – THEM/US

Fear of the Other breeds hatred of the Other

They aren't like us—so they must be bad…inferior… dangerous…

Humans are by nature social animals, but we tend to bond with other humans with whom we have something in common: beliefs, experiences, likes and dislikes, etc.

With the expansion of humans across the planet, it seems that, even as our numbers grow, we find ways to whittle our groups into ever narrower, specialized, and exclusive blocks. We target the Other for the most minor differences and interpret everything from THEM as an insult or an attack.

Within these pages you will witness hatred, intolerance and fanaticism as well as love, understanding and acceptance. Most of all, I, and the authors, hope you discover stories that will cause you to pause and think before condemning someone as being THEM and not US.

Crunchy with Ketchup – edited by Carol Hightshoe

It has been said that one should never meddle in the affairs of dragons—for you are crunchy and taste good with ketchup.

Come enter the dragon's lair.

Take your chances with other would-be heroes and heroines who decide to face off against one of the biggest, baddest predators ever.

Witness a dragon civil war.

Hear the true story of the Battle of New Orleans.

Find out what it's like in the belly of a dragon.

Discover why cats can spell disaster when stealing a dragon's egg.

Meet a group of dragon riders who protect us from nuclear devastation.

Follow legends of modern dragons, only to find something very unexpected.

And more…

So enter in **BUT** tread carefully—remember you are crunchy and taste good with ketchup.

Crunchy with Chocolate – edited by Carol Hightshoe

It has been said that one should never meddle in the affairs of dragons—for you are crunchy and taste good with chocolate.

Come enter the dragon's lair and roll the dice. Within these pages you will still meet some of the biggest, baddest predators ever—but if you are lucky, you will also discover some that have a sweeter side.

Meet a dragon with a soft spot for hard luck cases and another who is a hopeless romantic.

Enjoy a musical battle between a dragon and the specter of one of the greatest guitarists to ever play.

Meet a dragon in trouble with other magical creatures because he enjoys hanging out with human children.

Join a mother and daughter and their teams of dragons on a dangerous cross-country race.

Reconnect with an imaginary friend—who is not so imaginary and escape the isolation of the pandemic.

And more…

So enter in **BUT** tread carefully—remember you are crunchy and taste good with chocolate.

Time Out – Jamie Mason

After the war, Chris's family fled to Earth. Chris grew up believing he was human. But his parents' unique cruelties soon awaken him to the truth: he and his family are Chronox, alien beings capable of time travel, now hidden among humans.

Dissatisfied with refugee life, Chris's father decides to break the Chronox pact and use time travel to gain dominion over their human hosts. Chris resists, sabotaging his father's efforts to create a working time machine for the military. In punishment, Chris is placed in the ultimate "time out" by being flung back and imprisoned within the pre-digital past of the 1960s. There he experiences a glimmer of acceptance among Laura, Theodore and Yogi Joe, whose friendship inspires him to awaken his repressed Chronox powers and return to the future to set things right.

The battlelines are drawn. On one side, Chris. On the other, an implacable alliance between time-traveling aliens and the U.S. military. A frightened, shattered boy who has never known love must begin a desperate race through time to stop a global genocide.

Bast's Chosen Ones and Other Stories – Dana Bell

Long ago in the land of the flooding Nile and sweeping sands, Bast created warriors called the Chosen Ones. They are her warriors. To them has been given the responsibility of protecting cats, whether on Earth or other worlds. Not always an easy task since often an ancient evil lurks, ready to pounce.

Not all felines walk in the goddess's domain. Some live in the far reaches of space, battling beside their humans or walk in lands long thought legend. Others tell their own version of human stories, walk as envoys of the creator, or appear as ghosts.

These cats walk where others dare not and do not prefer the comfort of cuddly lap warmers. Rather, they wish adventure, in present day, the past, or the far future.

And more – check out our books at
www.wolfsingerpubs.com

www.ingramcontent.com/pod-product-compliance
Lightning Source LLC
Chambersburg PA
CBHW061522050726
47503CB00015B/2372